THE ORPHEUS PROJECT

THE ORPHEUS PROJECT

Valerie Sinason

First published in 2022 by
Sphinx Books
London

British Library Cataloguing in Publication Data

A C.I.P. for this book is available from the British Library

ISBN-13: 978-1-91257-371-4

Typeset by Medlar Publishing Solutions Pvt Ltd, India

www.aeonbooks.co.uk/sphinx

With thanks to all the courageous children, men and women with dissociative identity disorder (DID) who have helped to educate me, and the dedicated people who have recognised their existence and reality. With particular thanks to those with "installed" DID who had no choice in their other states of mind. This book is peopled from my imagination, but similar situations exist.

Particular thanks to my daughter Marsha for her reading and editing help and David Leevers, Adah Sachs, Susan Gasson, and Sarah Menguc for their helpful editing points.

ACKNOWLEDGEMENTS

This book is dedicated to all those known and unknown heroes and heroines who carry the toxic waste of our century: those who have dissociation as a sane response to a mad reality; those whose dissociation was installed and forced by torture; those who bore witness and recognised the truth in these narratives despite discrediting and denial.

With thanks to my daughter, my loving and first eagle-eyed Editor, my husband, David Leevers who said, "well, you are retired now, so write your mind control novel!". To Brett Kahr, Jeni Couzyn, Susan Gasson, Sarah Menguc and Adah Sachs for their careful reading and suggestions. Thanks to the courageous and caring Sphinx publishers: Oliver Rathbone, Alice Rathbone, Tania Pepper for giving me a voice and Martin Pettit for honing that voice in the hope others could be heard through it.

This book is peopled from my imagination but informed by reality. It is full of trauma triggers, so survivors please read with care and support.

"It is very easy lovely daddy. Bad man Ian Anderson did sex things to me. So did Danny Delta in Vegas. Master grabbed my brains. Hurt them inside. Lady mummy can't listen. She and her friend want me "to shush shush." Ian is big man and I am Down's Syndrome. Bang!"

**Lady Rose Redcliffe, December 24th 2012,
Harvest House Unit, St Joseph's Hospital**

"Mattie Harrison, age 12 (to hereafter be referred to as Child M), was removed from her home after a neighbour phoned the police. Child M was bleeding from a pentagram carved on her back. There were also signs of anal and vaginal bruising and welt marks across her body. She was severely underweight. The child did not speak or engage in any way. Both her parents were taken into police custody. It is not clear if they are biological parents or from a transatlantic adoption. Sargent Clover Davids said the injuries were amongst the worst she had seen on a child."

**Dr Elouise Redine from the St Joseph's Trauma Unit (SJTU) and
Dr Charmaine Landesman from the Lord Glendale Equipa Unit
(LGEU) were both in attendance, December 24th 2012**

"I have spoken to our colleagues on both sides of the pond and they are insistent, Deputy Prime Minister. If your colleagues don't like the word 'bloodline' and find it too biblical, say 'genetic' or 'science' instead. We don't care what word you use so long as your post continues to our mutual advantage. Is that understood? But to further Orpheus, we need the bloodline."

Major D, December 24th 2012, USA

CHAPTER 1

Monday, December 24th 2012, Christmas Eve, 4:40pm, The St Joseph's Trauma Unit (SJTU), London

Surrounded by neat piles of Christmas cards, envelopes, and boxes of chocolate, Deirdre Hislop put down the phone slowly and took a deep breath. Her heart was still beating too fast. The urgency of the voice she had heard on the phone carried on reverberating around the room. Peter Redcliffe...Sir Peter Redcliffe, the Minister for Health and local MP. Such a familiar voice from television and radio. How could it be?

"...the strictest confidentiality...data protection...security of the country."

The large room was silent. Filing cabinets, paper chains, posters from the Samaritans and Rape Crisis, two empty tables, computers and phones, all lifeless and mute. The rest of the admin and therapy staff of St Joseph's Trauma Unit were away on holiday, except the Director, Dr Stuart, and her, of course. If it hadn't been for that phone call, it would have stayed like that for another week.

She was also supposed to be on leave but preferred to work rather than spend Christmas alone. Her tidy two-bedroom townhouse needed no further attention. Her plants could wait for her and so could the dust. Her house would wait for her in its immaculate intactness, her glossy kitchen cupboards filled with unused spices for the visitors she never had. The SJTU and Dr Stuart were her home, despite the lack of a proper office and the dilapidated state of the building.

Deirdre controlled her breathing, in and out, as the words from the phone call burrowed into her head. There had been a relaxation session to help staff deal with stress, and the breathing exercises were finally coming in useful.

Poor Lady Rose, if it was true. A young woman with Down's Syndrome now dealing with abuse too. And the abuse was alleged to be by the Deputy Prime Minister … and a rockstar! This was like Cyril Smith and Jimmy Savile all over again. It somehow felt different when the alleged abuser was famous … or indeed the alleged victim. There was no reason that abuse shouldn't affect the upper classes and aristocracy. Her poor old friend, Digby, the second son of a second son. What traumas there were there. To say nothing of boarding school and all the abuse that went with it. Half the Houses of Parliament had probably gone through that.

Sir Peter had wanted to speak to Dr Stuart directly, but Deirdre knew he would not divert from a phone call with a patient for any such emergency. She offered to ring back the moment Dr Stuart was free, but Sir Peter could not wait, and burst out the message for Deirdre to relay. Dr Stuart would find the most ethical way forward. Clutching her notepad, she rose from her chair with excitement and fear. Her heartbeat was beginning to race again. Her clunky brown shoes clicked on the wooden floor as she made her way down the corridor to the Director's office. No need to walk quietly with all the patients away. She took another deep breath. It was all she could do to provide her usual discreet but authoritative knock on Dr Stuart's door.

"Enter Deirdre," came the distinctive welcoming voice with its strong Scottish accent. There was no extra sensory perception here. He knew she was the only other person in the building.

Dr Gawain Stuart faced her, seated as usual at his desk overflowing with files and bits of medical equipment.

A great bear of a man with Mandela-like shirts and batik trousers, Dr Gawain Stuart had the gift of making everyone he spoke to, whether staff or patient, feel he had all the time in the world, whatever his schedule. With a mass of curly auburn hair and beard, he looked like the philosopher-group-analyst he was. Unlike his close friends, many of whom had either retired at the first chance they got, fallen to heart attacks, or returned to more lucrative private practice, Dr Stuart had stayed, working in some of the worst remaining psychiatric institutions and prisons in the country. A decision which had expanded both his emotional resources ... and his waistline.

"Have a seat!" he beckoned warmly, standing up and brushing off biscuit crumbs from his shirt. "That's my Christmas emergency call over."

"Well, here is another one," Deirdre said, trying to maintain her usual upright posture on the soft leather chair facing his desk, but she sank into it, feeling her body melt, falling lower and lower into the waxy nest.

She somehow managed to state the facts, her voice calmly disembodied from her rapid heartbeat.

"Sir Peter Redcliffe, the Minister for Health, phoned to speak to you personally, but as you were on another call, even though I said I would ring back the moment you were free, he clearly could not wait and decided to go through me. His daughter, Lady Rose, who has Down's Syndrome, has lived for three years in the nearby long-stay Harvest Unit, but when she reaches 21 in just a week, on January 5th she would be moving into the newly-created Lady Rose Independence Unit with three other residents. She had not been the same since a Halloween concert in Vegas. She has shown abnormal behaviour and volatile changes in mood in the run-up to Christmas, her birthday, and the new unit. She kept repeating that the Deputy Prime Minister, Ian Anderson, a family friend, had assaulted her, as well as rockstar Danny Delta at his concert in Vegas.

"Sir Peter wanted Dr Stuart to assess her immediately under the most stringent security precautions. He said the country's security could be affected if what Lady Rose had said was proven to have happened. He wanted a copy of the data protection policy and information governance emailed immediately and wanted an assessment done by Dr Stuart while everyone was away."

Deirdre managed to relay all the information. She had even impressed herself by reminding Dr Stuart that while he had a line management role with the occupational therapists based at Harvest House, and their own Dr Aziz had a session planned for the new unit, it was the Lord Glendale Centre who held the safeguarding and line management for the Day and Night Managers. The Lord Glendale, the new bastion of power on their otherwise shabby hospital site. It was swallowing up all the facilities.

Refreshments would be needed for the meeting. Everyone would be in shock.

3

CHAPTER 2

Monday, December 24th 2012, Christmas Eve, 5pm, Brixton

Consultant Psychotherapist Dr Elouise Redine was sitting on her king-size bed in a green Balinese kaftan. Her back was supported by plumped-up dark-blue satin pillows. She was surrounded by Girls Aloud, *Star Wars*, and *Superman* wrapping paper, representing the tastes of her two sons and one daughter. There was sticky tape, scissors, and three large piles of unwrapped presents carefully counted out and divided. The pile of wrapped presents was visibly smaller. Her television was blasting Christmas songs loud enough to drown out her sobs, the shouts of two of her three children fighting and Dan's good-humoured but tired voice.

What an impossible interview for her to have done on such a day. But a psychiatric staff rota was a rota, and Christmas was only another day, if not a harder day for those with mental health problems. To top it all, Little Mattie Harrison had been taken into care. Poor little Mattie … Child M … that tiny worn face … frozen and alert. That injured little body. It was hard enough to hear adult survivors speak of past trauma in childhood, but to see the reality of a small child and the hugeness of an adult in comparison, or adults, who poured all their cruelty and disturbance into such a tiny container. She couldn't do it again. Those dead eyes …

"Mum," shouted Latoya, her 10-year-old daughter, just outside the door. "Denzel messed up my hair bobble. Can you fix it?"

"Nice try, Latoya love, but the door is locked, and I am doing top-secret work for Santa!" she shouted, stifling her sobs.

"Oh, mum," giggled Latoya, "it's not fair. What if I say it was Tyrone?"

Tyrone, 13, the quietest and oldest of the three children, was likely to be curled up with a book. He was a year older than Mattie.

Elouise smiled just for a moment... but then reached for her glass of wine. Dr Stuart had warned her not to work with abused children the same age as her own. To say nothing of Dan's worries. She wouldn't do it again.

But as if Dan could talk: he worked in a category A prison with the same kind of people as Mattie's parents... parents who saw their children as raw meat. They sickened her, these toxic Fred and Rosemary's. Yes, yes... they had also been damaged in their childhoods. But think of all the survivors who did not pass it on.

What they had done to Mattie was evil. It reminded her of Child A, Adam, a ritually abused child with a dissociative identity disorder she had assessed a couple of years back. The child had been so traumatised that he needed to break into different parts, sharing out and hiding the unbearable memory parcels of torture and betrayal. Nothing in her past training had prepared her for that, and without Dr Stuart at the SJTU and Dr Kestle in America she would never have managed.

At that moment, her iPhone buzzed. Deirdre. Why? She had already sent a Christmas Festival Good Wishes email. But no... it was an email to the whole senior staff group.

> Dear colleague,
> Many apologies for disrupting your Christmas planning. There is to be an Extraordinary Christmas Eve Meeting of great confidentiality. Dr Stuart has asked me to contact you as your presence is urgently required in person at 7pm. One hour only.

What did that mean? It wasn't Deirdre's usual language. A thief or hijacker? No... it was not asking or hinting at that kind of help. But it was clearly urgent. And confidential. The meeting obviously couldn't be done over Skype or Zoom.

Galvanised, she started wrapping with more urgency. In one hour she would have to leave poor Dan to put the children to bed.

She would be back for the joint Christmas Eve activities, and the rest of the wrapping. Dan could be Father Christmas tonight. Mother Christmas had done enough today. She would start on the cooking. And whatever the emergency was, it would distract her from Mattie's face. Oh, that little face, those dead eyes.

CHAPTER 3

Monday, December 24th 2012, Christmas Eve, 6pm, The SJTU

D r Stuart went into Deirdre's cubicle in the corner of the empty open-plan administration room. In order to phone Sir Peter back. They had considered, rightly or wrongly, that one of the general office phones might be less liable to a security breach than the Director's dedicated line. There had been a previous sophisticated hacking attempt.

Deirdre had also made a quick trip to the one local supermarket still open and bought a serving platter of cheese, which she now placed on Dr Stuart's large coffee table. Fresh bread already cut into slices, a tub of butter, grapes, melon, mince pies, and Christmas cake completed the picture. She only had the tea and coffee to prepare, and everything would be ready. Just in case. The staff, unlike her, would mostly be going back to family celebrations, and there was a risk of unwanted food, but there was a unit history of providing nourishment at difficult times. Even if it was only for Dr Stuart and her.

Deirdre's mind wandered to her team. Poor Elouise: she had three children under 13, all keen on Christmas—or rather on presents. Jon might be out on a date. Undertaking a 4–6 year psychoanalytic training on top of a full-time National Health Service job was gruelling, and at least he might have a break now since it was a Christmas break from his analytic training term as well as his job. She hoped so but doubted it. And Abdul always had such a responsible and generous attitude to staff crises that she knew he would always come unless his family were ill. But three pings. All were coming. What an amazing team! Her activity served to distract her from the frightening feelings stirred up by the reasons for the meeting.

At 7pm loud and friendly Christmas greetings could be heard in the entrance hall while coats and hats were removed. All were there with analytic punctuality: Jon wiping his steamy gold-rimmed glasses with a tissue, Elouise warmly hugging everyone and holding out a spare jumbo tub of popcorn, and Abdul offering a platter of vegetarian pakoras courtesy of his wife, Mina.

Deirdre looked at them affectionately. What troopers they were! It was Christmas Eve, and they were brought back from whatever break they were having with no complaints. Only Jon, to her knowledge, was a singleton like her, but he was at least two decades younger.

She brought them into Dr Stuart's warm book-lined room. The therapy rooms were too small for such a meeting, and the open-plan office lacked a sense of privacy and contemplation. They had lost their much-loved staff room in the move to this larger though rather uncared for premises.

Elouise looked aghast at the mince pies on the table as Deirdre had feared.

"I really don't appreciate it if this is some mad surprise Christmas party. That is beyond the call of duty when I have more presents to wrap and a neglected husband." The lushness of the food brought back his tiny, malnourished body—Mattie.

Abdul beamed gently at her while adding his platter of pakoras to the spread.

"That is not what Ms Hislop and Dr Stuart would do. What I guess we see here is our hardworking Operations Director making sure we do not go hungry during a serious crisis."

Deirdre nodded appreciatively, and Elouise swiftly apologised. "Sorry Deirdre! I am too quick on the draw again! I've already had a hell of an assessment this morning." By way of apology, she put a mince pie and a pakora on her paper plate and sat on the large sofa.

Jon looked round anxiously. "It's not one of my patients threatening suicide is it?" asked Jon. "You were covering for two of mine."

"As if I could ever forget, sweetie!" smiled Elouise. "Definitely not!"

"A kid," she said slowly, looking intently at Deirdre. "A twelve-year-old with the deadest eyes you ever saw. And a little body you would have thought had come from a famine or a concentration camp."

"So sorry, Elouise. We do see the worst of the world here," said Abdul. "And today preparing for Christmas with your children, anyone's defences would all be down."

He moved to the sofa next to her and reached out to take her hand.

"How do you manage, Abdul?" asked Elouise. "Your Alisa and Alesha are a similar age."

Deirdre listened intently while pouring the tea. She knew everybody's requirements: green tea for Abdul, chamomile for Dr Stuart, ginger tea for Elouise, and black coffee for her and Jon.

"Everyone I love most lives under my roof...I am very grateful. And I was not on Christmas cover!"

Jon sat down on the edge of the sofa and breathed a deep sigh of relief. His plate was filled with bread and cheese. Deirdre smiled approvingly at him. He needed to put some weight on.

"I couldn't work with abused children," he said, "It would upset me too much or make me angry. I don't know how you managed Child M, Elouise. Dissociative Identity disorder feels hard enough for me to consider when working with adults, let alone the reality of what a child has gone through."

"Is Dr Stuart alright?" he added nervously.

"He is in a *hospital*," grinned Elouise, her good humour momentarily restored. "The best place to not be unwell. And no, I don't know how I managed that work, and I don't feel ready to face it again. Without Dr Kestle and our Dr Stuart, I wouldn't have survived."

A warm booming "Hello!" entered the room, filling and enlivening the space. "Thank you, thank you, please sit. This is most unusual on such a day, but I did not feel it right to proceed without discussion with my excellent team."

They sat nervously.

At that moment, as they all looked at Dr Stuart, the loud entrance hall bell rang out, followed by a key turning in the lock. As if in slow motion, they could hear Jonas the caretaker's voice. They looked at each other in surprise—he was supposed to be on leave.

"This way, Governor," he said in a cheery voice. "They must be in Doc Stuart's room."

The SJTU team sat transfixed as there was a firm knock on the door.

9

"Enter," called Dr Stuart.

Jonas opened the door widely, smiled at everyone, and waved. "Happy Christmas all! No homes to go to? Elf and safety called me out of my family Christmas. They should have got Mo. Nighty night now. See you soon."

Behind him stood a tall, severe-looking man in his 50s with close-cropped silver hair and piercing grey eyes wearing an elegant evening suit.

"Dr Stuart? Happy Christmas. Not the way I wanted to introduce myself and, as you can see, I have a dinner engagement shortly. I am Professor Frank, Chris Frank, from the Lord Glendale Foundation and Centre. I have the unfortunate task of stating that your unit is formally closed for Christmas, and you do not appear to have any permission to be here—until Monday 31st December when a skeleton staff will be back.

Your caretaker had to be interrupted from his family leave as a result of your action. I appreciate there were different rules when you were simply linked to St Joseph's, but it is different now, and, with all due respect, you will have received all the new information regarding out-of-hours use of Trust facilities."

A heavy silence descended on the group.

"And this—this food," He pointed to the serving plates on the coffee table.

"Cleaners are also on leave until next week, and there cannot be food remains left on the premises. It infringes..."

"Health and safety?" asked Elouise standing up to her full height, only an inch shorter than Dr Stuart. "And what about the health and safety of patients in crisis."

Professor Frank turned his cold glance onto her. "Miss...?"

"Doctor!" Gawain emphasised. "The eminent Dr Elouise Redine, she is a real doctor with a PhD like you, as well as being a psychiatrist."

"Well, Dr Redine," said Professor Frank icily, "you will know all safeguarding issues should be reported to the safeguarding lead in my unit, if it concerns an outpatient you work with, and the St Joseph's Lead, who is based in the Foundation Centre, if it concerns an inpatient. There is 24-hour cover thanks to there still being residential units and a hospital on-site. It concerns me even more if you are inappropriately here without informing those who report to me."

"Professor Frank," said Dr Abdul Aziz gently, rising from the sofa, "You will not remember me. I chaired your very interesting paper on memory five years ago in India."

The tone changed immediately. "What a diplomat!" thought Deirdre approvingly.

"I do indeed. It was in Delhi, wasn't it, Dr Aziz?" said Professor Frank, holding his hand out to Abdul.

"Creep," thought Elouise.

"Yes, Professor. I am still an Honorary Consultant at the school there, and we are planning a major conference on the topic in the next year. I was hoping you might consider coming back."

"Won't you sit down, Professor Frank," said Gawain, understanding the change in the atmosphere as always.

Everyone sat again with Professor Frank perched on the very edge of a wing chair nearest the door. He would clearly not be staying long.

Gawain cleared his throat. "I deeply regret the trouble I have caused with my excessive zeal and take full responsibility for it." He added, "I shall apologise to Jonas and to your staff. Please understand it was our desire to be fully up to speed on the changing governance issues that have caused this meeting, and we would be very grateful if, just this once, you allow us an hour to complete our task. Otherwise, our families and friends are going to be furious with me that I have called out my senior team for no purpose at all."

Professor Frank's face relaxed. "I do apologise, Professor," said Deirdre in her smooth formal tone. "I am Deirdre Hislop, Operations Director here, and I must state my responsibility too for this unofficial meeting."

Professor Frank frowned at her. "Ah! Ms Hislop. I would have expected you to know the rules better than that."

"I do apologise," she added, "and I assure you that by next week I will be properly up to date."

Professor Frank stood up and looked with disinterest at Jon and Elouise.

"Goodnight, Dr Aziz. A pleasure to see you outside of the Delhi Royal National Hospital, and I am very glad we have someone of your calibre here. I do not need further introductions. Goodnight gentlemen. Everyone must be out by 9pm."

"Goodnight, *gentlemen*," screamed Elouise when she heard the front door close.

"He remembered my surname; I didn't even have to say it," said Abdul.

Abdul and Gawain smiled at each other. "You know, you have improved on everything I ever taught you," laughed Gawain.

"What a dangerous bastard," shouted Elouise. "He wrote that paper attacking survivor memories. He is one of those 'false memory' academics. Wonder what happened in his history to make him so vicious."

And then they sat down, filling their plates and mugs while waiting for Gawain to tell them what had happened.

CHAPTER 4

Monday, December 24th 2012, Christmas Eve, 7pm, Westminster Square

The Redcliffe residence

Sir Peter and Lady Lily were in the study. His favourite room. The thick oak doors ensured their loyal housekeeper, Maria, could not hear their conversation, and Rose was watching a Disney film—again—in the snug with Mona, a reliable and longstanding constituency aide who also worked for them as an occasional carer.

The gracious windows looked out onto a Westminster Square lit up with Christmas lights decoratively wound around the trees and elegant lampposts. On his green leather desk in front of the windows, pride of place was given to four silver-framed photographs—one was his wife with the Queen and Prince Philip, and another of his wife with Lord Glendale, Ian Anderson, and his mother, Lady Marjorie. Beside these stood a photograph of Rose with the Queen and Prince Philip, and finally, a portrait of him as a young father with Rose on his lap, holding his hand. A family tragedy in a handful of photographs.

Lady Lily, a former model, was a society beauty with her soft blonde feathery hair framing a heart-shaped face and the most stunning deep blue eyes. And there was Rose—like a distorted photo of her mother. Same beautiful eyes and hair but the unmistakable signs of Down's Syndrome. Lady Lily had never recovered. Her husband understood that. He also understood that Lily could not bear the distorted image of herself. Even Rose's grandmothers: Lily's mother, Lady Priscilla, and his own, Lady Marjorie (both formidable political figures in their own right), had advised putting Rose in a home at birth, as they were worried it might spoil his political chances.

Peter had fallen in love with his tiny daughter from the moment he saw her. The force of his love surprised Lily as well as himself, and she agreed Rose could stay with them. She had locked herself in her room for a day, muffling cries of sadness and rage, and when she opened the door to his entreaties, fully made up and icily calm, there were conditions attached. She insisted there had to be 24-hour in-house help from the start, a day nanny and a night nanny. He also had to agree that from the age of 14 she would go into a residential facility.

After he agreed, almost immediately, she also made it clear that Rose was their first and last child, and she would not put her body through that experience again, and Peter had agreed—in the way he had almost always agreed with her ever since. Somewhere he knew a part of Lily had been destroyed forever. Somewhere he knew a part of him had also been destroyed through Lily's actions. Poor Rosie—the fruit of their love—was a slow-acting poison. In some way, they both found his increasing senior political profile a useful distraction.

Rose's formidable grandmothers reluctantly accepted her when they saw how the public warmed to Peter as a result of her disability. Indeed, all disability services benefited from the link and Peter's appointment as Minister of Health was an extremely popular one, albeit largely fuelled by the politically astute Lily.

On reaching 18, Lady Rose became a resident at St Joseph's University NHS Hospital, instead of a private facility, thereby sparking national debates on dependency and independence issues: community placement or hospital. Somehow, the earlier concerns about institutionalised treatment at Harvest House lessened in the knowledge that the Minister of Health's daughter was there. Surely, he wouldn't let her be there if it wasn't safe? There were still news stories and articles on the internet about Lady Rose being relentlessly bullied in the state primary school she had attended and the sexual abuse she endured at the hands of a minicab driver at 14 while at secondary school.

With millions of pounds poured into the Anglo-American Lord Glendale Foundation and Centre, thanks to their close friend Lord

Glendale, Lady Lily had pointed emphatically to the further constituency capital that could be gained from Rose being placed there at 18. Rose's secondary school life was over. The Lady Rose Redcliffe Independence Unit, situated in a block just to the right of Harvest House, was especially endowed to provide independence training and would be opened on her birthday on January 5th—if all was finished—with Lady Rose as its first resident.

It was a win–win situation until the last few weeks. The long-stay wards—situated in Harvest House—alongside the new individual rooms—were appalling. Even restricting her visits to a private room, with a perfumed handkerchief held to her nose, Lady Lily found that the smell of urine pervaded her clothes, and every hair on her head. She scrubbed herself ferociously after each visit, wanting to clean her daughter out of herself. Rose kept wanting to hug and cling on, calling her "mother." She could not bear her. She could not bear to be called "mother" or to hear those words "Lady Rose" used towards her. She could not tolerate being approached by disability organisations, the warm smiles from other politicians or aristocrats with such children, or the sympathy from her friends.

The familiar eyes she would have loved in a daughter, a proper daughter staring from that face. At least the Lady Rose Redcliffe Independence Unit was new and clean, and the more senior people from the Lord Glendale Foundation would staff it—not those dangerous fools from the SJTU with their emphasis on long-term care. She could talk to the Glendale and them to her. She could talk to Lord Glendale himself tonight. He had been a close family friend of her parents in her childhood and remained a loyal friend of her mother and Lily herself, after her parents' marriage broke up.

Lily's father, Lord Wellbrook, had been severely clinically depressed at different stages of his life, and in his early 50s he began a private psychoanalysis. She had to admit that going for therapy five times a week helped to lift the depression, but he had become restless and dissatisfied. He finally left Lady Priscilla. Initially it was for a woman 20 years younger than him, and now he was married to a woman 30 years younger: Imogen, an inoffensive compliant art gallery assistant who was younger than her, although no one would know by the way she looked. Poor Imogen, with her plain face, dressed like a much older woman. And the blessed baby Toby. Imogen didn't look like a person who had friends, but she had a surprising number around her—"toadies"—who liked the title. To her surprise there were friends of Ian and Oliver who had newly befriended her and were even Toby's Godparents.

Lily had always blamed her father's long-term psychotherapy treatment for her parents' breakup and was virulently against such treatment. And now he was the proud father of—had spawned—a baby boy. An heir. A first son: Toby. The son he had always wanted for his centuries-old bloodline. A son without a handicap. A normal child. He could be heard on TV programmes spouting about issues that concerned him "as a new father." Her mother and her were both wiped out of family history. Like Lady Rose, they were both black marks on the family tree that went back several hundred years.

Imogen dutifully sent her birthday and Christmas cards with an expensive present attached, but not her father. Having a daughter of his wife's age embarrassed him. He was the young father of a baby … a baby *boy*, she corrected herself. A healthy baby boy.

But she was fighting back. Political colleagues, of whatever party, knew the way to get to Peter was through her, his wife. Known as a formidable woman, as well as a beauty, she was proud to have the Deputy Prime Minister, his partner, and a smattering of MPs, actors, and researchers from the Lord Glendale coming for dinner that evening, Christmas Eve, and most without children or with grownup children. Very few political hostesses gained the visitors she did. This party had been planned through parliamentary secretaries months ago. And now this … mess!

How did Rose even use such language when she had a mental age of 10? Television? Listening to crude inadequately trained staff? Her so-called "friends!"? Linking her genetically flawed body with a good friend like Ian Anderson! And Ian was gay anyway.

She hated the innuendos in gossip columns about older men with underage male companions. Such rubbish stuck or left a smear. It added to the sickening waves of homophobia that couldn't separate gayness from paedophilia. It made her sick to consider it. And Ian would eventually be PM, she had no doubt. The PM was old and could retire or be retired at any point. And then it would be Ian's time. The country was almost ready for it.

Ian was also a fine sculptor, something only his friends knew about. In the House of Commons, he was mocked for having gone to grammar school and not coming from a titled background like hers. Well, he had

16

her support. And there was no conflict of interest for her. She and Ian knew that Peter would never be a Prime Minister. Even his current post was largely due to her—and Rose—and he would be far happier as just a constituency MP.

Ian's partner, Stefan Solag, was a brilliant photographer, one of whose brooding landscapes graced their drawing room. He had been with Ian for a decade already, and they were going to marry. Ian didn't like female bodies. How could Rose disgrace her like this? All their life plans to be further destroyed by this aberration of her flesh. As if giving birth to her wasn't hard enough.

That was not how she dealt with matters. She had a far softer strategic approach.

"Are you sure you want to take this further, darling?" asked Lady Lily, twisting her wineglass with suppressed energy. "Ian has been such a good friend to us and has always involved Rose in any disability policy."

"But you heard her, the same as me," he emphasised.

"She has never spoken like that before without good reason. This is why abused children are not listened to, why young carers don't get help, why the physical health of adults abused in childhood is so affected—she clearly stated that Ian..."

"You are not giving a party political broadcast now, Peter," interrupted Lily coldly. "This is me you are talking to."

"Then listen to your bloody daughter!" he shouted in an unusual burst of anger and despair, "was one rape and years of bullying, not enough?"

He was completely unlike his usual calm self and reaching for a whisky glass.

Lily rose slowly. "I am not listening to your rudeness on Christmas Eve. If you want to quote research, look at the Lord Glendale Foundation's work. Look at the thousands wasted on false charges, the Independent Inquiry, colleagues whose lives have been ruined by false accusations. Professor Frank, who is coming tonight, has made it his special study."

Peter reached for her hand. "I'm sorry, love. I grossly over-reacted. I just love our daughter."

"I know you do." Lily curled back next to him on the green chesterfield, her long, blue Alessandra Rich dress gracefully spread out.

Her tone softened. "I know there was the bullying and then the rape. That was all true. I know there is the stigma. I know I could not love

17

her as a baby deserves to be loved." There! She had dealt with it. Any admission of her maternal failure thawed him.

He moved his hand to stroke her soft blonde hair—artfully cut to frame her face.

"Bad boy—I've just had it done for this evening," she smiled, her cold eyes melting.

"Later?"

"If you are good."

"Cancel the SJTU meeting?" he asked.

"Of course. Let's get Professor Frank to assess her and find a therapist for Rose—that way, we can monitor it. Rushing in could be dangerous for her mental state. These things have to be done carefully. And he will have something suitable for her—not what my father had."

Peter recognised her mood and knew there was no point in arguing. He finally poured himself a whisky.

"Careful now. We have our visitors in one hour." Lady Lily shaped her pink lips into a large kiss. "Phone now and say you'll send Rose back for Christmas lunch tomorrow so she can have it with her friends. They'll be fewer calories there than here, and she has put on weight."

She uncoiled from the sofa, blowing a kiss. "Right now, darling!" she whispered theatrically. The iron fist in the velvet glove. "I understand how worried you were, but NEVER, *NEVER* phone an unknown secretary in a shabby unit without speaking to me first."

Leaving the room, she quietly made her way down the elegant corridor to her own study, grateful not to be called by that so-called daughter or her so-called carer. Having to smile and look appreciative and loving all day and night was exhausting. What an idiot Peter was! All this time and work to get him into this position—largely her own work and Lord Glendale's—and now he was ready to throw it all away.

Inside her bright room, filled with the fragrance of lilies, she lifted an extension phone out of a box under her bed and plugged it into the socket behind her filing cabinet. She lifted it quietly, waiting for the small sound that would be made on connection, but Peter had obeyed her meticulously and carried on talking to that ludicrous Gawain figure—the psychiatrist in charge of the trauma unit. What a name! All she could think of was that medieval story, Sir Gawain and the Green Knight. Dr Gawain Stuart was just not up to it. He was not like Dr Simon Green of the Equipa Unit standing up so bravely for trans people. Ah yes... the

Greens were invited for New Year's Eve. But would Gawain hand over the assessment to Glendale?

She carefully put the phone receiver down, unplugged it, and put it back in its box. Then she picked up her own phone. Picking out the memorised number with her long, manicured fingernails, she smiled as it was answered on the first ring.

"Darling? All sorted. She will be back at Harvest House tomorrow at 1pm. See you later."

She walked down the wide hallway to the kitchen. An aroma of spices came through the panelled door. Her cook was nearly ready. The sound of *Follow the Yellow Brick Road* came from the snug.

CHAPTER 5

Tuesday, December 25th 2012, Christmas Day, 9am, Harvest House

S t Joseph's University Hospital had a beautiful view. On that crisp Christmas morning, as Sarah Ransome parked her car in St Joseph Street, rather than just outside the unit, she could see all the way up to the sculpted iron gates at the first security entrance of the newly named Lord Glendale Centre.

Lord Buxton Castellane had built the stately mansion at the top of the trimmed lawns in 1749. He had purchased the land after his first visit to Italy and France with Lady Marie, a honeymoon which was both a celebration of entering parliament and the state of matrimony in the same year. Sarah had read and re-read all the information in the local history guide prior to moving from Leeds. But there was no sign of the Castellanes outside of the guidebook. Lord Glendale had taken over.

Never mind. Coming to St Joseph's University Hospital for the Clinical and Day Manager post gave her a brand-new start. A whistleblower at the Leeds Elmview Sunshine Home for adults with severe disabilities (lovely names they chose!), she had never felt relaxed again there, despite being validated for her carefully charted observations and offered a promotion and pay rise. And then, of course, Steve had suddenly left her. Just left. After 20 years.

She carried two bags of presents—small bars of chocolate and tiny Christmas ornaments as well as craft cards for them to make Christmas cards. She had no knowledge of what the staff might have provided. It mattered that she acknowledged it was Christmas Day. At Elmview, most residents never received any cards or presents apart from what the staff gave them. They had no family; no loved ones. That was why her plans had been for residents to make cards for each other.

Looking up the sweeping drive with its symmetrical row of trees and the later added ornate lampposts, she could almost imagine Buxton and Marie as Lord and Lady of the Manor. But that fantasy was soon dispelled by her knowledge that the white smoke billowing from over the top of the complex came from a crematorium which adjoined the cemetery. It was right by the Lady Rose Redcliffe Independence Unit, which she would be managing in a week, as well as the St Joseph's University Hospital Long-Stay unit—Harvest House—which is where she was heading to now.

"From a stately home to a State Home," the guidebook had cryptically written. There weren't even signs pointing to St Joseph's cemetery or the crematorium at the back of the estate. A familiar burst of anger swept through her. Only old people's homes and residential homes for the intellectually disabled had ensuite cemeteries. Johan de Groeuf had written that. And the cemeteries were always at the back. For the residents, even death wasn't a way out.

And then there were the new signs: "Lord Glendale New Hope Trust," "Lord Glendale Neuroscience Research Lab," "Lord Glendale Equipa Centre." They were all in the New Hope Trust green and yellow colours with the logo of a budding leaf. Her anger turned into a wry sense of humour. Why did these places have such "sunny" names Harvest House, Hope; how about a National Illness Service instead of a National Health Service?

Hearing her name called distracted Sarah from her train of thought. It was the porter in the security portacabin by the first iron gates, a tall gangly man in his 50s with a broad grin on his face.

"Morning Miss, car conked out or putting in some legwork?" he asked.

She looked at him, confused.

"There is unofficial parking right by the C's to spare you the walk. You are going to the C's I assume?"

"C's?"

"Crematorium and cemetery and everything round there. People for the C's disappear here faster than in a whodunit. It is a big relief when someone new is starting. It's the Lord Whatsit that gets all the posh new people. You wait! In another year Back-Enders won't be allowed access here!"

Sarah took a deep breath as she looked up the hill ahead.

"Better take in a big breath of fresh air!" exclaimed the porter. "It's not what you'll get inside those doors, if you will excuse my forwardness."

Sarah was taken aback by his crude familiarity but recognised the truth of the statement. It was too soon to be making enemies. What was it about her that allowed him to speak in this way? He would not be talking to "posh" people like this.

After ten minutes of a steep incline, she approached the circular drive in front of the main mansion. She stopped and took a deep breath. She was unfit. Too many glasses of wine since Steve had left.

A magnificent sign and gilded map sparkled in the cold winter sun. There was the coat of arms of Lord Glendale, and there was the "You are here" sign and those ubiquitous green and yellow symbols. But there was no picture of St Joseph's University Harvest House Long-Stay Unit, or the crematorium or cemetery. The C's were invisible.

A security guard in a smart new uniform approached her. "This is restricted entry only, Madam. Do you have a security pass?"

"And a Happy Christmas to you," said Sarah, showing her photo identification.

"Ah—thank you Mrs Ransome. This entrance is not for you. You want the back end," he said dismissively.

"The C stream," she laughed. Thank goodness they didn't appear to grade children quite so brutally now as in her childhood where the A stream were the bright, wanted children and the C stream were the unwanted, clumsy ones …

22

CHAPTER 6

Tuesday, December 25th 2012, Christmas Day, 12:30pm, St Joseph's Hospital

"Happy Christmas! You two get remission for good behaviour? It must be nice being occupational therapists. Getting out early and not having school dinners—now that is what I call a bloody good deal," laughed Mo, the tall security guard standing in for Jonas, the caretaker, as Faith, the older OT, and her junior, Maureen, briskly walked past.

"Sorry Mo, Happy Christmas!" called Maureen. "I didn't notice you."

"Charming!" retorted Mo. "Been one of those days?"

"Yes," replied Faith curtly, without stopping to turn her head, "We don't often need to go out for lunch! But *it is* Christmas, and I booked our table a month ago! Who knows, we might have a staff lunch on-site next year and one that is not just butchered turkeys."

"If the Glendale hasn't swallowed us up," Maureen added wryly.

"Ladies who lunch," bowed Mo, "…or is it more a Christmas tipple at the Stag and Hound than being out to lunch?"

"No, that's where you go, Mo, and a bit too often for your wife's liking," laughed Maureen, running her fingers through her hair. "We are off to Jenny's for a vegetable lasagne."

"Oh dear! I stand corrected. I better get back in my dog kennel. Happy Christmas."

"How did you know his wife's views?" asked Faith admiringly, as the younger woman laughingly caught up with her. "I find him so intrusive; I never know what to say—but how you spoke to him really shut him down."

"His wife Carmen used to clean in the Drug Dependency Unit. She was really reliable, quiet, and hardworking. I wish she was cleaning Harvest House instead of Edna."

"Hmm," replied Faith. "Anyone would be better than Edna. Is Carmen the woman with short brown hair and the studs all over her face?"

"Yes, that's her. Her face all covered with those piercings. She's a very dedicated worker. I know Mo seems intrusive, but he and Jonas do their job really well. They really know who goes in and out: in all senses of those words!"

Faith laughed. "You mean Lew Masters' love life … or should we say lowlife? Thinking of him, I could almost go to the Stag and Hounds—I haven't felt so exhausted for months."

"Me too. I don't know what it is. Lew is no worse than always. His sexism always gets me. Maybe it is the impact of Christmas on our clients. I brought in all those art ideas for Christmas, and they were just freaking out. Sinita and Tim, did you see them?"

"What about Dykes and John? I've never known them to look so terrified."

"Yes. It has been such a long period of uncertainty for clients … and for us. I used to find it hard being spread out over LD services and drug dependency, but in this economic climate it makes me feel a bit safer."

"Safer? This whole site is such a mess! Supervision in here, line management in there! Social services in one place, health service another, and the Glendale is gobbling up everything that's left!"

"Yes. Feels a bit like an East European map with all the constant border changes; we could wake up with a new green and yellow flag over our heads tomorrow. But poor clients! If we feel confused, what about them? All those interviews for a Day Manager—to say nothing of Miss Princeton just mysteriously running off, that really unsettled them, and even with Sarah starting this morning it will take a lot of time."

"If she isn't frightened off," said Maureen.

24

They turned down Peacock Street, where Jenny's restaurant shone welcomingly.

"You know," said Faith sadly, "Dykes actually said to me, 'no one wanted this job did they, Miss Faith? They don't like being near us defectives.'"

"That's awful," responded Maureen. "And such language for him to use too. He has been in the system so long, and I don't even think he has a learning disability."

"I know...I have thought the same about him and John," Faith replied. "Thank goodness Sarah Ransome took the job. The first decent person for ages."

"Yes, I really took to her. She is genuine and her heart is in the right place. She had a hard time where she was before. It must have taken a lot of courage to be a whistleblower. I googled her. I'll forward it if you like. Do you think we should have invited her to come with us?"

"You are a mine of information!" smiled Faith. "But plenty of time for that. As for Sarah, she has got Lady Rose, poor thing, coming back for Christmas lunch and we will be there to help her later, so better she gets to know everyone else now."

"Okay, that doesn't sound very nice sending Rose back for Christmas lunch when she goes to them so rarely, and is always so happy to go there. I don't think her mother has ever coped with having a child with a disability. She never visits. It seems like that makes no difference if you are rich or poor."

Faith sighed. "Poor Rose. It is so much more painful at Christmas. It upsets me more than it used to. Hardly anyone gets visited now, and some don't even get a card outside the one from us. Only Sinita's mother. Ah well. Perhaps it is just as well Lady Lily is not coming. I don't feel like trying to sound enthusiastic over work anyway. Not with dinosaur staff like Lew and Edna about. So now for something completely different and away from work."

She opened the door of the cosy restaurant, and a wall of heat greeted her together with *Jingle Bells* blaring from a loudspeaker. The woman, who approached them warmly, wished them a Happy Christmas and pointed to a comfortable corner table.

"Happy Christmas! You two are from the hospital, aren't you? It is terrible with all those units closing. Everything is just posh now with those Lord Thingy Foundations. Do you know Mary Anders? She is a niece of mine. She was placed in the Rehab Unit for 18 months. There still isn't a community placement for her."

For a moment, Maureen and Faith froze. It was Maureen who managed to say, "Sorry, we don't know about that unit," while Faith robotically followed her to the table.

The two women sat stiffly until the waitress disappeared. Then Maureen broke into peals of laughter, followed by Faith.

"Out to lunch," chuckled Maureen.

CHAPTER 7

Tuesday, December 25th 2012, Christmas Day, 6pm, Harvest House

Time to leave. Sarah wrinkled her nose with discomfort. Only now was she aware of the smell of urine that she had been breathing in all day. She lifted her wrist to her nose to see if her breakfast dab of perfume had lasted.

"Poison! what a name for a perfume!" she remembered Steve saying that years ago. The air she had breathed all day, the smell of unwashed clothes, urine stains, and faecal smears combined in an intolerable way.

"You should charge them for a 'Poison' allowance instead of a clothing allowance," Steve had joked at Elmview.

Harvest House. H Unit. With the return to the community of the most able residents, and the creation of the Lady Rose Redcliffe Independence Unit, which would take the second most functioning group, staff and residents alike called it "H" or, with only a mildly humorous tone, *Cell Block H*, the title of an old television programme about a female prison that many of them watched re-runs of.

Lew Masters, the Charge Nurse on night duty, apparently always referred to staff and residents alike as *Prisoners on Cell Block H*, and, as much as she disliked him on sight, Sarah recognised the truth of that comment. He had come in earlier to meet her and go through the handover. It had been a negative experience, probably for both parties.

Sarah nervously put on her brown suede coat, looking around to see if any "residents" had noticed she was leaving. She had only been there one day and already found herself overcome with guilt. There was a three-hour shift after she left and before Lew Masters usually arrived held by a Senior Nurse, Brenda something, and a health care assistant with an on-call from the Glendale Centre. The long-stay wards had their own separate nursing cover at night that did not involve her. It was a messy structure, and maybe she would be able to change it.

Very few residents had been visited by their families. In fact, in the long-stay ward, two elderly mothers were the only visitors. Others, like Lady Rose, were returned hastily before Christmas lunch, like unwrapped presents, under the excuse of "they like to be with their friends for Christmas, bless them, they are more comfortable with."

The faded walls were covered up rather garishly with Christmas decorations—and some primitive artwork—an attempt by Faith, or was it Maureen, to cheer the place up. At least there were two good people to work with. There was also one empathic Nurse, Brenda, from an agency, who did a patchwork of afternoon and evening cover, but the others looked as dour as the environment.

Tim stood rocking rhythmically at the end of the long corridor—his thin shoulders tensed; beside him was his friend John Finch.

"You go now, Mrs Ransome?" asked John Finch.

"You go now?" repeated Dykes. Dykes was his surname, but because his first name was John, just like his best friend, he went by his surname.

John and Dykes were two mildly disabled men in their late 40s who dedicated themselves to the staff. Although they wore identically shabby bad fitting blue jeans and faded white t-shirts, their physical appearance was very different. John was a big powerful man with blue eyes and blond hair. Dykes was of a much smaller frame with dark eyes and a mop of black hair.

"Yes, John and Dykes, it is time for me to leave. But I will be back in the morning," answered Sarah.

The two men made Sarah feel protected while reminding her of the painful survival techniques of "trusties," inmates who could be trusted by staff. John and Dykes had been in institutions all their lives and had paid for their privileged position as trusties with staff by acting as unpaid assistants.

"Will monsters come tonight?" Dykes asked, unusually timidly.

"Oh no, Dykes, are you frightened?" Sarah sympathetically put her hand on his shoulder. He flinched, and she quickly removed it.

"Me not scared. Me not scared. Me not scared," he repeated.

"John, not let monsters get Dykes, John big," said his friend proudly, punching his large right fist into his opened left palm. Dykes moved closer to him. Sarah could tell both men were deeply worried about the night ahead.

"You are big, John, and good at protecting people. Nothing will happen tonight any different than any other night," Sarah assured.

Oh dear, she had done it again. How could she know what could happen to anyone at any time? She must not say that again.

"Well, nothing different or bad should happen tonight, and that is why there are people on duty and alarm bells to ring."

"Me not scared," Dykes continued.

"Night, day gone!" shouted Sinita, a 36-year-old Spanish woman with epilepsy. "Night night. Night night."

She was in a pink nylon nightie with childish short puffy sleeves and nursery motifs. She carried "Serby," a grubby teddy bear.

Sarah looked worriedly at her. There were fresh cuts and bite marks on both of Sinita's arms. "It's time for me to go, Sinita, but it's not night-time yet."

"Day gone! Night, night!" Sinita continued to repeat. "Sleep tight. Don't let the bedbugs bite. Santa Claus is coming to town!"

With a raucous laugh, she walked along the corridor, pushing Tim momentarily out of his rocking. Tim stood still for one brief frozen moment to gather himself from this interruption before resuming his rock. Sarah walked hesitantly up to him—not too close though, after her error of judgement with Dykes.

"Goodbye, Tim. I will see you tomorrow morning—Boxing Day."

He continued rocking and did not look round at her.

Tightening the brown suede belt around her coat, she turned to leave and strode purposefully towards the door.

"Stay!" screamed Rose, appearing from out of nowhere. Barring the door of H Unit with her short fat body, she held onto Sarah for dear life, almost knocking her over. "Don't go! Stay!"

"It's alright Lady Rose," said Sarah breathlessly, trying to extricate herself from Rose's frantic arms.

"You will see me again tomorrow. You will see me every day except at the weekend. And you will be moving into your own unit. It must be

29

hard to believe with Miss Princeton leaving as she did. I did not meet her. Maybe you miss her?"

"Princeton gone. Left me. Stay!" sobbed Rose. But her arms and voice suddenly lost their grip.

"Anderson stick willie in the bottom. Stupid Rose. Dirty Rose." Her right hand suddenly took on a life of its own and began hitting her pale, plump face viciously and repetitively.

"Now stop that," said Sarah sternly, removing Rose's right hand from her reddened face with both her hands. She helped her onto a chair by the door and reluctantly sat beside her, struck by the anguish in her beautiful blue eyes. She was already 15 minutes past her finishing time.

"Coat off!" Rose pleaded, tugging at Sarah's brown suede coat ineffectually.

"No," said Sarah gently. "I'm sorry if Christmas has frightened you, and maybe it was strange to be with your parents and then be back here for lunch. But right now it is time for me to go home."

"What you eat, Sarah?"

"Spaghetti Bolognese tonight," she grinned at Rose. "That's if I get home in time. You don't want me to be late, do you?"

"No!" said Rose. A shiver passed over her, and then she relaxed. A slow grin appeared on her face.

"Man should cook himself!" she said.

"Rose!" said Sarah, in a mock teasing voice. No need to provide the truth here.

They both laughed. Sarah opened her bag and took out a tissue. Gently she wiped Rose's blue eyes.

"Not a baby," said Rose sadly.

"No. You're not," said Sarah. "But you are sad, and we grownups cry when we are sad. But I must go home now."

"Yes," said Rose quietly. "Come back tonight?"

"No. Not tonight. I will come back in the morning," explained Sarah softly.

There was a pause.

Sarah wondered why Rose was so worried tonight? Why were they all so worried? Did Christmas remind them of abandonment from home or abandonment at home? They didn't seem to particularly care about Miss Princeton. Perhaps, for Rose, coming from her wealthy home to this environment must be hard. Thank goodness the new unit was nearly ready.

"The new agency assistant, Tracey, will be here tonight. Is that why you seem so worried? Another new person? But your usual Nurse is here."

Brenda Harris, a tired but gentle looking woman, approached, with her face transformed by the warmth of her large smile.

"Tracey is a nice young woman, I have heard," said Brenda, "and people say she will be just right for this job. She comes on tonight at 8pm, when Mr Masters usually comes in. But I am here now. You can go, Mrs Ransome. Oh, Rose, that worries you. I know Tracey wasn't scheduled to start work until tomorrow, but we have asked her to start one day early because Sonia has called in sick."

Sarah straightened her coat and ran her fingers through her hair. The "ordinary" outside world was calling, and it really was time for her to go. "Rose, I really must go now, but I will first leave a note for Nurse Brenda here to give to Tracey, so she knows how you are feeling tonight, okay?"

Rose looked down at the floor and timidly responded. "Yes. Good Rose here. Don't worry."

"Very good," replied Sarah, "I will see you in the morning Rose; you have a pleasant evening, okay?"

She went back inside the office and wrote a quick note to Tracey, which she then passed to the Nurse as Rose walked back to the day room.

Then she left, guiltily glad to close the door of H Unit behind her. The memory of Rose's scream and tight hold began to fade as Sarah walked into the cool night air. Tomorrow she would park on the muddy space outside Harvest House, but today she would enjoy the longer walk.

She stretched her arms out, releasing her coat from the shape Rose had constricted it into. The very fabric of her clothes took a deep breath and expelled the creases, lines, stains, and smells of unit H.

It was beginning to grow dark; the St Joseph's Hospital estate looked gloomy in the dusk. The only welcoming light came through the stained glass windows of the small church near the cemetery.

"But there can't be much life there," mused Sarah—although she had been told some of the residents had been made very welcome by the priest, Father O'Neal, who apparently did his best to give it a multi-faith focus.

Up to the top and around the plateau and then down the hill, past the next security guard at the glittering Lord Glendale Centre, down and out into the welcoming noise and light of ordinary life. The fish and chip shops, restaurants, and Asian grocery stores, all with their Christmas glow, greeted her like a vision of paradise.

CHAPTER 8

Tuesday, December 25th 2012, Christmas Day, 6pm, St Joseph's Hospital

"Bed. Nobody there now. Dirty Rose. Stupid Rose. Go and wash."
A creak of the hospital bed.

Rose's feet padding across the floor in her dirty fluffy slippers.
"One step, two step, tickle you under there. Ha. Quiet. Bad girl. Shut your mouth. Go to the door, Rose. Nobody there now. Sarah gone. Tracey coming. Mr Masters. Shut your mouth, Rose. Go to hell. Bad man not there. Bad man. Ian Anderson. Willie on bum. Bad man, Danny Delta. One step, two step … Creak. The Master there. Master. Oh no. His hands grab brains through head and pop them. Bang, bang, bang. Sarah. Want Sarah. Day gone. Dead Rose. Day Gone. Little Rose wants mummy."

The sound of her mutterings could be heard along all the corridors of H Unit. And all the inmates, without words, or sounds, shuddered.

CHAPTER 9

Tuesday, December 25th 2012, Christmas Day, 6pm, Harvest House

Tracey O'Bridey reached for a cigarette but changed her mind, sticking some chewing gum in her mouth instead. The "No Smoking" sign in the office attached to the sleepover room was almost obliterated by layers of grease and dust, but she was in a hospital now.

"As if anyone would fucking notice," she cynically commented. After all, it was not a proper hospital. It was only looking after mental people, and they didn't care how many GCSEs she had passed. It was more like being a babysitter. Nevertheless, she didn't smoke. She had stopped. Even though she still carried one with her.

The place was dead. In fact, it was worse than dead. Mingling with the haunting stench of urine were the muffled thuds and bumps of night-time ghosts.

"Head-bangers—I suppose I should go and see them," she suggested to herself. "But on the other hand, why bother? These retards, not that they can help it, always do things like that."

If she went up to sort it out, she might never get back again, and there was still time to call her other friends on agency night duty, as well as read her horoscope.

"Just my luck, stuck here at Christmas instead of at a rave."

On the other hand, it kept her away from the noisy squat she had lived in, the cold streets, and everything else she ran from to try and escape her past. Staying with Reg, just for a month, had given her an address for college and allowed her to get some dead-end work. Worth his faded smell, farts, and thin wet lips.

She put her legs up on the crowded desk scowling at a ladder in her black tights. She took out a bottle of nail varnish from her bag and painted over the ladder. Then she reached forward for the phone. Just then, there was a soft knock on the door. Before she could even say, "Come in," the door opened, and a man walked in. He was in his fifties, short and muscly, powerfully set with a bald head and open denim shirt.

"Medallion man," Tracey giggled to herself, looking with curiosity at the brass pendant he wore.

In his left hand, he suddenly flourished a clown mask with mistletoe on the top and peered through it at her. He lowered it and laughed.

"You're the new agency one, aren't you? O'Bridey?" he said, leering suggestively at her long legs on the table, as her hands guilty retreated from the telephone.

Tracey wanted to move her legs from the table and her hands from the telephone but froze.

"And anyway," she thought to herself, "why should I move? He's in luck. My legs are good to look at."

"Don't mind me. I'm all for you broke young'uns getting a few phone calls done. If it's for a party, count me in—just call me. Call me!" he emphasised, miming being on the phone.

He moved nearer, smelling of alcohol and cigarettes.

Oh, how she wanted a cigarette!

"I'm Lew Masters; you'll know who I am."

Tracey lifted her legs down from the table, pulling her skirt down. Lew Masters was acting Head of the Night Shift, and she was answerable to him.

Lew Masters grinned. "Skirts go up or down," he paused, "according to the fashion. I like it when they go up...or down," he added suggestively.

Tracey laughed. She was on home ground here. A younger upgraded Reg.

"Like a cigarette?" he asked, holding out a pack and a lighter. "Some rules are meant to be broken," he added, watching her eye the hospital "No Smoking" sign nervously.

"And this isn't a proper hospital—more of a zoo, and I am the boss here."

Tracey gave up. "Well," she said brightly, "that solves that fight with my conscience."

She took the cigarette but held her body back as he offered a light. Something about his smell and manner both disgusted and excited her.

"Jiminy Cricket," he pronounced, "from the film Pinocchio? Round 1 against your conscience. One down and seven to go."

"Seven?" she queried.

"Seven. It's my lucky number. So, how come a pretty young lady like you is agency working in a dump like this?"

Tracey inhaled deeply and watched the smoke come out. "Money! Why else would I come in a day earlier than I was hired to, especially on Christmas Day?"

"So, it's the filthy Christmas lucre?" he nodded sympathetically.

"Well, there's plenty of filth here, so we need the lucre."

"The noises," she added emphatically.

"The noises?" he emphasised mockingly. "Do you mean the inmates' charming practices of banging their heads on the furniture?"

Tracey giggled. "I wasn't going to put it like that. I thought you'd…"

"Sack you? Wouldn't mind. Being in the sack is one of my best places." His right hand settled on her left shoulder like a heavy bird.

She wasn't that easy! He'd have to do better than that. She gracefully extracted herself. "Well…I better go check on things. Mrs Ransome has left me this note about a patient going to the Independence Unit named…Lady Rose?"

"Oh, you mean Rose—some lady," he retorted dismissively. He looked enquiringly at her. "Let me see the note," he demanded.

Tracey nervously handed it over while repeating what it said.

"I can read, girl!" Masters barked. "This should have come to me. I will handle this. You get on with your phone calls or whatever you do—leave the zoo to me."

Reaching out and giving her shoulder a final squeeze, he left the room, picking up the clown mask with a flourish. Tracey sat still on her chair. There was a warmth on her shoulder where his hand had been that she resented. It was spreading over her body like a creeping stain.

"Filthy creep," she muttered as she drew on the cigarette nervously. She put her legs back on the table and reached for the telephone. Her bag contained a small bottle of whisky. She had everything she needed. Everything. Even though she couldn't go to Trish's Christmas party, she could still ring her.

"Fancy a geezer like Masters coming onto her like that! And younger and cleaner than Reg...or the other guys she usually attracted," she thought, and her manic chuckle filled the room, providing a barrier between her and the thuds and cries of H wing.

It was midnight now, and the ghouls cried and mumbled along the dark corridors of H Unit. The smell of urine was unescapable, and as the night progressed the scents and sounds increased. In the smoke-filled office, Tracey drank to relieve her own personal hell. Music from her Walkman, Kesha, "Die Young," blotted out all the cries.

CHAPTER 10

Wednesday, December 26th 2012, Boxing Day, 8am, Balham

Sarah Ransome's residence

It was 8am when Sarah awoke to the alarm, and she stretched lazily. Her right foot reached out to touch Steve. "Happy Boxing Day," she whispered. He was not there. His side of the bed was empty. He was gone and would never be there.

Two silent tears rolled down her face. Her right hand went to her ring finger. Empty. She had removed it. She wanted to throw it away but somehow had not been able to, so she had hidden it somewhere, and now she did not know where. She quietly slipped out of bed. Reaching for the fluffy white towelling robe, she tiptoed into the bathroom: force of habit still directing her movements, as she was acutely aware that she now performed in an empty auditorium. She did not need a dressing gown; she did not have to tiptoe. She could play Adele and sing along at full volume.

One day, she promised herself, she would relish this. The new shower, with its range of silver knobs, offered choices from rainforest to sea to storm, and the pretty row of shampoo bottles and shower gels she had bought were no consolation yet. How she had tried to pretend her flat was a luxury hotel, and not a home. She cried along with Adele, a perfumed rain falling over her.

Out of the shower and again safely wrapped in her fluffy towel, she boiled water for an egg and put a slice of brown bread in the brand-new toaster. Steve had left her, and she had left the flat they had shared—just left it, along with everything and everyone.

"Wake up now!" she exhorted herself. "New job, new flat, new Boxing Day." She switched on the television and sang along with *Jingle Bells*. Her toast and egg disappeared almost without her noticing herself eating. Clothes appeared on her, and then she was out, ready to fight on Boxing Day.

Rose—Lady Rose Redcliffe—was now in her mind, taking over from thoughts about Steve. Indeed, she hardly noticed the drive to the hospital.

"Good morning, Mrs Ransome," a throaty young voice called out as she parked on the muddy grounds. Mrs? She wasn't anymore. Not really. Sarah looked up from locking her car door to see Tracey waving as she bounded eagerly towards her motorbike. What a voice of cigarettes and alcohol from a girl barely out of her teenage years.

"Good morning, Tracey. How was your first day ... or night, I should say? We are both new girls here, I guess." Her sharp eyes noted the laddered tights and inappropriate work clothes, but she had a soft spot for girls like Tracey. She guessed where Tracey had come from and the things she still had to face.

"It went rather well, thank you," Tracey answered formally.

Sarah walked towards her and asked, "And how was Lady Rose?"

"Well—when I showed Mr Masters your note, he told me he would see to her," Tracey nervously replied. "Was that alright?"

"Of course. Did you introduce yourself to her or any of the patients?" Sarah asked.

"No, Mr Masters wanted me to stay in the office and tend to the phone. I did a bit of a clean-up but wasn't sure what to do with some of the paperwork; there was no computer. I can type," she proudly added.

"I see," said Sarah. "We have an extra new computer coming in today that should help organise things better. But I would like you to introduce yourself to all the patients, so they aren't worried if they see you there in the night. It will be good to have someone other than the Agency Nurse to be there. I think it is Sonia Goldstone on duty tonight—or is that tomorrow—but the agency will ring if you are needed. I will speak to Mr Masters about that. Enjoy your day but get some sleep too."

"Thank you, and you too," Tracey returned with a slightly embarrassed expression as she climbed onto her motorbike with difficulty.

"Not the easiest clothes for a motorbike," ventured Sarah sympathetically. As the motorbike moved off, Sarah took a deep breath before turning to Harvest House.

Caught between institutionalisation and redevelopment, St Joseph's University Hospital's H wing had low morale that showed itself through the peeling walls and smell of urine. Many of the staff had lost all hope and were as stressed as the clients. The sleepover duty office was at one end of the H shape and stunk of smoke despite the no-smoking policy; the smell of alcohol also sometimes wrestled for dominance. And it wasn't just the disturbing run of uncommitted agency nurses or healthcare assistants. If Sarah thought about it, there was also one man she particularly objected to. Lew Masters, her night-time counterpart. When she first met him and said, "Good morning, Mr Masters!" he had replied, "Just call me Lew. Or, if you prefer, Master. Mrs Ransome? Do I hold you to ransom, or is there another name?" She did not have any sensible reply available—what had happened to her? A feminist with years of management experience, and yet something in him had disabled her. She just stared frostily back at him, wishing her white blouse with its high collar and tight rows of buttons were even more buttoned up. He was not professional. He was beyond sexist. There was something perverse and bullying about him. The files were not updated, and when he did write it was minimal and not of any value. Complaints had apparently not worked in the past either. She would check the supervision and line management policies but with ten disabled patients shortly due to be rehoused, four going to the Lady Rose, and a long-stay ward that no one wanted to work in, sexism was hardly going to come high on the list. Unless Lady Rose's security was concerned.

As she entered the security code on the peeling door of unit H, a feeling of despair entered her. She took a deep breath of the cold outside air as if to protect her lungs against the rotten atmosphere. As the door closed behind her, a tide of shambling figures swept her up in its midst with the fallen Christmas decorations crumpled around them. She could do this, and she would.

40

In the large dayroom, a television was already blaring. It was blaring in the TV room too. Men and women sat rocking or walking up and down aimlessly. The Nurse on duty was sitting reading a magazine. She gave her a wave.

"Morning Mrs Ransome," called Sinita, who came up to her first in ill-fitting elasticised trousers and a patterned blouse. Sinita flinched when Sarah took her by the arm to steer her out of the way of the other residents.

"Does your arm hurt, Sinita? I'll look at it in a minute. I just have to go to the office first. Morning everyone. Morning Edna."

Edna was the sour-faced cleaner/nursing assistant who, Sarah noticed, seemed to spend all her time spreading ever-larger circles of dirty water. She would have to speak to Lew about her. Lew. She did not like saying "Lew" or "Mr Masters."

What was it about him that was so unpleasant?

Outside her office, she could see Tim standing outside the sleepover room at the end of the corridor, his face even more frozen, if that were possible, than the night before. He was in a dirty pullover and jeans, and a speck of toothpaste stood out on his thin face. She walked towards him.

"Morning Tim," said Sarah, cursing the fake brightness in her tone. "One day here and I'm sounding like Joyce Grenfell," she muttered to herself.

Suddenly Sinita charged at Tim, knocking him against the wall and drawing blood from his pale face.

"Sinita!" shouted Sarah.

Sinita scratched her own face and darted away while Sarah led Tim into the night staff room, which doubled as the first aid room. The office was small, smoky, and untidy. Sarah wrinkled her nose in disgust. She walked to the window and suppressed a curse when the heel of her shoe stuck to a large piece of chewing gum. O'Bridey, no doubt! She pulled uselessly and then took her shoe off and opened the stiff window. Cold air came in and ruffled the papers scattered across the top of the heavily scarred desk. She would clean it herself if she couldn't force Edna. Where was the first aid box?

"Let's have a look at you Tim," Sarah said as she helped him to a corner chair.

Tim sat down robotically. His blue eyes stared through her. Holding his head up to examine the small trickle of blood on his left cheek and above his left eyebrow, she sadly noted how even a sudden attack could not stir him into a normal response.

"Sinita really hurt you! I don't understand what happened, but perhaps you are lucky you don't carry on like the rest of us would if our faces were scratched. I will write a note about it in the incident book." There was not even a flicker in his eyes. Looking round at the untidy filing cabinets and shelves, she found a small wall cabinet with the faded Red Cross on it.

"Let's find some cream and a plaster. There should be something here." As she opened the door and reached for a box of plasters, she gave a small cry. A large black spider sat malevolently inside the box. She dropped the box onto the floor and the spider scurried away. Tim did not respond to her cry or to the loud sound of the box falling. But at the sight of the spider, his face suddenly went white, and he started rocking violently. Dribble began to fall from the side of his mouth.

"Why Tim, I am sorry. I was frightened of the spider and now I have frightened you," said Sarah. She put an arm around Tim's thin tensed shoulders to comfort him. But in a sudden violent movement he threw her arm off and rocked up and down even more desperately. Sarah stood very still and took several deep breaths.

"Perhaps Tim is doing to my arm what I have done to the spider," Sarah thought.

"Tim, I am sorry I frightened you when I dropped the box. The spider gave me a shock."

Tim suddenly froze.

"Are you frightened of spiders too, Tim?" To her shock, Tim turned his head and looked into her eyes. "Why! He is scared to death!" she thought.

"Oh, Tim—you really are frightened. It is okay. Let me put some cream on those scratches and a plaster. Then you will feel better." Dressing his wounds, she realised she was spared the sight of his anguished eyes.

"That's better," she said. Smoothing on the plaster, talking to herself more than him, she added. "Let us take you back to the dayroom, and I will go and see what Sinita is up to."

But Tim remained frozen in the chair. Sarah could not make him move. "Are you scared of seeing the spider?" asked Sarah. There was a flicker of movement in Tim's eyes. "That spider will be scared of us," said Sarah emphatically. "It has been dropped from a big height and got

42

my scream too." She giggled, cheered up by her own performance. But Tim remained frozen.

There was a sudden series of cheery knocks on the door. "Come in," she called, quite glad of a diversion. It was Lew Masters. Sarah felt a sudden tensing of Tim's left shoulder. Through his thin frame, she could sense the speed of his heartbeat.

"Hello, hello, hello," he leered in a mock policeman style. "What have we here? Is he giving you any trouble Mrs Ransome? Anything I can do to help?"

Sarah felt her own body tense. The man's insolent intrusive stare went right through her. "No thank you, Mr Masters. There was just a minor incident between Sinita and Tim. Was there any problem with Sinita in the night?"

"Sinita?" he asked, savouring the name. "No—slept like a little lamb. Just like a little lamb, isn't she Tim, my boy." Tim began to rock, an incoherent sound tearing out his lips. "Sad, isn't it, Mrs Ransome. You do your best, but they don't get any better."

"I'd like to see your evening notes please Mr Masters. It would help me if they were here in the morning," said Sarah in the most formal voice she could manage.

"Evening notes, eh?" smiled Lew Masters, his right hand playing with his medallion. "Some music...discords..." He laughed heartily. "Now they will be coming to set up that new computer today—maybe then we could have proper notes. But this place will still be in the dark ages. Evening notes...Mm...Well, there was shit from Lady Rose...sheets...pyjamas, and more shit from Sinita...and shit and vomit from John and Maurice, and piss, shit, and vomit from—Oh, look Tim—on the window-ledge. Just look at the size of that spider!"

Tim turned deathly pale, seeing the spider that frightened him and Sarah moments ago. He began to rock side to side, biting at his clenched fist. Sarah was speechless with rage. She watched, unable to say or do anything, while Lew Masters moved in to capture the spider.

"I am so sorry Tim," Lew Masters sarcastically spoke, approaching him with the spider in his hand. "I didn't know this little creature of God would frighten you so. Here, let me just get rid of it for you." Masters threw the spider to the floor and forcefully stepped on it. "See Tim, this is one spider that will never frighten you again."

"That is enough Mr Masters. If you could leave us now," stammered Sarah, holding her authority around her like a tattered jumper.

43

Sarah noticed that her tone seemed to ease Tim's tension as she knelt beside him. Masters grinned.

"So sad to say goodbye! But I need my beauty sleep now, don't I Tim? Stayed up especially late to see the new queen, the new boss Mrs Ransome. Come on Tim. Say it for me. Sleep tight, and don't let the spiders bite."

Tim jerked his head frantically from side to side.

"I think they are biting already," laughed Lew, kicking the lifeless spider out the door and slamming it behind him.

There was a profound silence. Tim sat up and resumed his frozen expression, rocking rhythmically. Sarah went to the window and poked her head out. Masters made her sick. He was a sadistic brute. He reeked of all the worst attitudes of old-style institutionalised staff, and she had to face him every day in her new post…until she could restore some order and standards.

"Er…" Hearing a sound struggling from Tim's mouth Sarah turned round guiltily. If Lew Masters was hard enough for her to face, what was it like for the vulnerable residents?

"Are you trying to say something Tim?" she asked. But Tim's face returned to its usual frozen mask. Taking his stiff hand, she led him out of the office. The pervading smells immediately dampened her relief at moving into the larger space.

CHAPTER 11

Wednesday, December 26th 2012, Boxing Day, 9am, Harvest House

Maureen locked her bicycle to the rusty metal bar outside Harvest House and took off her waterproof mac.

"Got wet, did you?" insinuated a leering voice. Lew Masters was fastening his black motorbike helmet. He was here late. She usually arrived after he had already left.

"Piss off, drip!" shouted Maureen.

"Tut tut, bad language," mocked Lew, revving his motorbike.

She watched in a rage as he drove off, the exhaust spurting out of his speeding bike. "The old fart!"

Faith Walker stepped out of her blue Ford Escort at the same time. "Did he bother you, Maureen?" she asked.

"He always bothers me, and gets me reacting in a very unprofessional way."

"I am sure he does," said Faith. "He could go to a Halloween party as the devil and not need to dress up, the old goat!" she added, and the two women, laughing nervously, entered their security numbers.

"I think I feel the need for another lunch coming on!" said Maureen.

"Yes. Something tells me today is going to be bad. And we are not on the Boxing Day lunch shift."

Usually, the entrance hall was crowded. The night shift was not a competent one, and residents usually rushed to greet the trusted day staff the moment they arrived. Faith and Maureen looked around in surprise. Tim stood like a statue, plasters on his cheek and above his eyebrow. Mary and Steve walked up and down like clockwork toys. Maurice was rocking and retching, vomit sticking to his old T-shirt.

"What's happened?" asked Faith.

There was no reply. At the right-hand corner of the hall, near the office, Edna was on her hands and knees cleaning.

"What's happened, Edna?" she called, walking towards her, followed by a nervous Maureen.

Edna looked up aggressively.

"What's that?" asked Maureen. Next to Edna's bucket was the crushed spider Lew Master had killed. "Ergh! That's huge!"

"Yes," grinned Edna.

"What's been going on here today?" asked Faith.

"What are you asking me for? I am only the cleaner. And no amount of cleaning will clean this lot up. Should be done away with if you ask me!"

"Edna!" came the shocked voice of Sarah walking into the entrance hall. The unusual outrage in her voice startled all the women.

"I will not have attitudes like that expressed in this place. Our residents have gone through enough without hearing things like that in their own home."

"Their own home? It is the council's home and the sooner they know that the better." Delicately wrapping the crushed spider in a tissue, she lifted herself insolently and slowly walked away.

Sarah stood frozen for a moment. Edna and Lew Masters both needed to be reported. And she had only just started and after going through what she had at Elmview Sunshine Home. What had she done? All the trauma of uprooting only to find this. What was the Aristotle quote: "no matter how many seas you cross, you always take yourself." Sarah the whistleblower was here, and there would be no time off for her—crude attitudes to the disabled existed everywhere.

"Are you okay, Sarah? Thanks for saying that. I would have said it if you hadn't." Faith touched her right arm sympathetically.

"Her and Lew Masters are so alike—piss-artists the two of them, excuse my language—neither of them should be in a place like this," said Maureen.

Sarah nodded seriously. "But isn't that awful? Two in such a tiny staff group? Oh dear, that's the first thing anyone has said this morning that I agree with."

The three women burst out laughing.

"I am sorry," said Sarah. "That's me laughing because I am so shocked. I didn't think London, let alone a university hospital, could allow such behaviour."

"It's everywhere, but what is going on here?" asked Faith. "I was expecting some disturbances because you are new, and Christmas is always a bit of a stir-up-but…"

"Oh—it seems that last night was difficult—although Mr Masters does not keep proper records. I saw Sinita attack Tim—his face was bleeding. Sinita herself looks terrified—I don't know everyone's name yet—but they all seemed frightened to me this morning. I don't know if Christmas scared them. And I haven't found Rose yet. Maureen, do you think you could look for Rose and bring her to my office? Faith, I believe you have half an hour before your first patient. Could we discuss things now?"

"Sure," said Faith, "I will bring us some coffee. How do you like it?"

"Strong and black!" emphasised Sarah.

"You are in for a treat," laughed Maureen as she left them. "Faith is the only person with decent coffee."

"I just bought a new coffee maker and everyone, including the patients, is tantalised by the smell."

"Is it a filter type?" asked Sarah.

"Nespresso! Even better. I will be right back. Meet you in the office?"

"That is fine; I will have things ready, including my taste buds, for some good coffee."

"Faith! Sarah! Quick! I've found Rose!" shouted Maureen. "She is down here in the laundry room behind the dryer. She's all covered with faeces and blood, rolled up in a ball."

CHAPTER 12

Wednesday, December 26th 2012, 11am, Westminster

Rt Hon Ian Anderson: a phone call to Lew Masters

His fingers on his left hand, with the ornate signet ring, tapped impatiently on the marble table while the right hand held the phone. His jowly face went pink with anger.

"Answer, you stupid bastard," said Ian. He had rung with the seven requisite rings twice now. He put the phone down heavily and redialled. This time it was answered on the seventh ring.

"Boss?" came a sleepy voice.

"Listen, you idiot. You answer on the first ring! Understand?! I don't care if you are witnessing the resurrection or have had no sleep for a week. You made a mess with your fun and games last night."

"But…"

"Shut your mouth when I'm speaking. We don't usually employ gorillas." The distaste dripped icily.

Masters was unusually silent.

"You have left a mess. In fact, several messes. We now have several complaints leading to you."

"Those stupid cows! Faith and Miser–"

"And potentially two new ones."

"Oh, there won't be a *trace* from one," Masters said lasciviously.

"Keep your cock to yourself, Masters. We will have to decide what to do about you. Your little fiefdom has served its purpose, but now it is proving a mess. Shirt, tie, and apologies immediately might just turn things around quickly and get rid of that female monster of yours too."

"It goes both ways…"

"Shut it, gorilla."

The call was terminated.

CHAPTER 13

Wednesday, December 26th 2012, Boxing Day, 3pm, Harvest House

Lew Masters fingered his pendant nervously. He was exhausted too. Rubbing his finger over its ornate shape, he then lifted his white shirt collar over it and did up the small white buttons. Then came a dark-blue tie. He didn't feel comfortable: this was not how he liked to dress in a loony bin like this. Why did *he* have to dress up if a fucking psychiatrist like Dr bloody Stuart could wear his ethnic pyjamas? But the Society had spoken. Things were changing. The Master of his lowlife coven had somehow encountered Anderson. A pillar of the "Society" and a politician to boot. How he did this was unclear. They saw a joint beneficial possibility with him as a pawn for them both.

Anderson was a real bastard. Not like his boss. Not like him. He had heard things about what Anderson liked doing. Mad pervy poofter things … gay was one thing, but this bastard was pervy and dangerous with it. His Master wasn't like that, and nor was he. He did what he had to do and no more. He didn't even know if the Society had the same beliefs as him. Or indeed if his Master did. Those stupid therapists who said it made no difference if the "perpetrators" believed what they were doing or were doing it to scare the victims; it was only what the victim felt that counted.

Well, it did make a difference. And he knew it. Because he believed. And that was why they needed him.

Gorilla! He knew the lengths he was going to keep it the way "they" wanted. Anderson had no idea. What the hell was his Master up to being sucked in to a nothing like this, despite his position? Wasting his gifts. He knew what Lady Rose had, why the bastard had wanted her, one of the 13 secret bloodlines that happened to include aristocracy. Anderson thought he could find a speedy passage to paradise and power... a speedy back passage more like. He just wanted to do it to anyone, and didn't understand what couldn't be done with someone with a mental disability. The programming couldn't hold. It was too much. Just a few well-chosen ritual triggers were needed.

His Master had "inherited" the coven when the last one died. It was a pretty rundown, seedy one, to be honest. Suited him and his lousy neighbourhood, and it found him and accepted him when he was still shaken raw from Afghanistan. He was exempt from coven Christmas duties because what he was doing at Harvest House was seen as more important, but he knew which women he would have seen in the parkland spaces used for the night-time rituals some of the women were already "split" and used to being multiple from their broken childhoods. They did it themselves. Like magic. One minute a drunk, thick dad was giving it to ten-year-old Donna and a minute later there was a 12-year-old Don. Simple. It wasn't like the top-level stuff with their white coats and charts and family trees of created personalities and seven levels of heaven and hell. The Master didn't know that; he had no idea how to install DID like the higher-level groups did. He was just grateful the children and adults didn't cry at ceremonies because they could switch to other states. They were all garbage really, his home, his coven, and his job. Somehow he could always see his own Godhead through all this, in whatever gutter he was placed.

It had not been easy with Edna. A couple of twenties were needed, and a bottle of whisky as a sweetener. She wouldn't buy him putting them into the same category either, the old-style staff that were having to change.

"Don't give me that crap, Lew. Zipping my mouth is a darn sight easier than zipping your flies. And my mouth has been pretty zipped anyway over what you leave lying around, to say nothing of spiders either!"

51

However, angrily and resentfully, she agreed to attend to the ugly staff sleepover room. She knew she wouldn't get another job that was so flexible.

Then he sought out Ransome with her prissy clothes and political fucking correctness. She was in the television lounge talking to the retards. They all started like that, but a few months later she would change. They all did. And look what happened to prudish Princeton; she couldn't even take one touch of her shoulder before running.

"Mrs Ransome," he called, savouring her shudder of surprise at seeing him in his off-duty time. "I have come to apologise."

She stared at him, not making it any easier. "I think we have all been overworked with Christmas and the plans for the Lady Rose, and I regret I had not properly instructed our cleaning operative, Edna, to have the sleepover room ready. She is working on it now. I am also aware that because of uncertainty about Christmas shifts I have been working in my off-duty clothes. This will now be corrected. Please let me know if there is anything I can do to make your task easier." There. He had fucking done it. Had he done it in time?

She gazed back at him with an unreadable flustered expression. "Why thank you, Mr Masters! That will really help staff morale. It must be difficult with tasks divided between two units."

He nodded politely and left. He even managed to walk past Faith and Misery without grimacing. They better not be hanging him out to dry. He knew their game, and his Master's. He was ex-army, ex-Afghanistan. He served something higher, which made him stronger than all of them.

CHAPTER 14

Wednesday, December 26th 2012, Boxing Day, 5pm, Harvest House

Tracey O'Bridey was removing her helmet when Mrs Ransome rushed up to her. "Tracey, can we meet in your office please. Maureen is in mine. I'll have coffee ready."

Tracey shivered. She recognised the urgency in Mrs Ransome's voice and instantly felt to blame. What had Mr Masters said? Would she get the sack? Had they found out about all the personal phone calls she had made? Had she left any cigarette ends? Did they know what she had done?

The entrance was silent, and the small staff sleepover room and the office were transformed. The smell of smoke had somehow evaporated into the cold air. The windows were open, and the white metal gleamed now all the accumulated grease had been scrubbed off. A computer sat on the polished desk. There were even flowers in a vase.

"How did you do it?" she asked incredulously, surprise overcoming her fear.

Mrs Ransome handed her a mug of coffee and pointed to an office chair. "This room has been well below the standard expected of a staff room. And somehow our cleaning operative kept missing it. However, Mr Masters kindly spoke to Edna in his own time and the room will be cleaned properly now." Smiling gently at Tracey, she added "It is of course a no-smoking room, as are all hospital and Trust rooms."

Tracey waited to be handed her notice. Why was Mrs Ransome stretching it out like this? "I'm sorry, Miss; I did smoke," she said nervously.

"Of course you did, Tracey. Everyone smoked there. The room stank of smoke, but you have only just started; this is not just from you, it has clearly been used as some wretched hideout rather than a professional space dedicated to looking after vulnerable people. But that is not why I needed to talk to you."

Tracey took a deep breath. "I understand if you want me to go. I did smoke, and I did follow what Mr Masters said instead of talking to the … um … people." There! She had bravely faced it. She would get sloshed tonight and then start again.

"Tracey. No one is asking you to leave. The opposite. We want to train you to work here happily, so we don't lose you."

Tracey burst into tears, wiping her heavy mascara and eyeliner across her face.

"I am still here then! I have a job!" An unexpected relief shivered through her.

"It's something I need your help with. Something frightened Lady Rose Redcliffe, one of our youngest residents, on the evening of Christmas Day, and she has not recovered."

CHAPTER 15

Thursday, December 27th 2012, 5pm, Highgate

Dr Stuart's residence

"Wine is in the fridge, darling," called Moira.

"Nibbles on the table. Are you sure you're OK?" Gawain's voice boomed down the stairs from his first-floor study.

"Thanks love. Down in a minute."

"You don't have to on my account. I am off to rehearsals now. Hope it goes well. But answer the phone at 10pm. It could be James and Martine. I have my travel case and passport with me in case. When you go to bed, check if I am back!"

Moira had moved from Scottish dancing to teaching Scottish dancing in her late fifties after James, their only child, had moved to Quebec. While studying for his French and History MA at Edinburgh University, he had met Martine, his future wife, who was French Canadian. She had persuaded him to take a teaching job in her hometown, and he had become fascinated with the "French connection" between the old world and the new world.

What was going to be just a few years overseas studying and working had changed. Martine was over eight months pregnant and Moira was ready to fly at any moment, even if Gawain had to continue with patients. Her bag was already packed.

A warm chuckle was Gawain's response as Moira closed the front door. Only when he heard her car leave the drive, did the smile leave his face. He had been researching on the internet. It did not take long to move from clear fact to the powerful regressive pull of social media, disinformation, conspiracy theories, and half-truths.

> There were hundreds of entries about Ian Anderson. Danny Delta. Lord Oliver Glendale and his younger brother Harold Fitz-Hugh West, The Washington School Scandal, St Joseph's Hospital. Lady Rose Redcliffe. Lady Lily Radcliffe. Professor Chris Frank. Equipa. 13 Bloodlines, Ritual abuse accusations, Mind Control, installed dissociative parts, Illuminati, programmed retractors.

Putting the printed-out paper into a new folder marked "Ethical Assessment," he walked slowly downstairs. He was not yet sure how much he would discuss with his staff. Deirdre was his right-hand woman, but she was not a clinician and some of the potential issues could disturb her too much. Jon Levine was a fine clinician, but the extra analytic training he was doing would make him risk-averse and fearful. Elouise would understand all the ramifications and had previously managed a case involving ritualistic abuse and dissociative identity disorder. Adam. They had needed to enlist a transatlantic consultation from Dr Judith Kestle as it was so complex. However, Elouise couldn't leave her family tonight and needed to be protected too. That last case had devastated her, and she needed a space. Abdul was thoughtful and responsible: he might be in the best situation right now to take this on. But in the end, it was all of their responsibility.

The doorbell rang at 6pm, and Deirdre, Abdul, Jon, and Elouise walked in.

"I couldn't miss this," said Elouise, unwinding her huge multicoloured scarf and smiling at Gawain's surprise. "But I will owe Dan big time."

Gawain ushered them into the open-plan lounge-dining room. Reliable as always, Moira had left cakes and savouries on the pine table interspersed with carrots and cucumber and yoghurt dips. Vegetarian for Abdul and kosher for Jon. As always, she remembered everything.

Deirdre nodded approvingly. "You will thank Moira, won't you, Dr Stuart," she said. The others nodded. Moira's "nibbles" were famous. Especially given she was rarely there to receive their praise. A beautiful feisty woman, she carried herself like the dancer she was and, apart from Deirdre, Gawain's staff mainly saw her from her Christmas concerts. But the "nibbles" acted like an ongoing family communication.

Once seated with drinks poured, they fell silent, turning their heads to Gawain. He produced his file and started the discussion. "Okay—let's cut to the chase. We have a problem. It was hard enough on Christmas Eve, but now it has gotten much harder. A senior politician from our own constituency rings the unit somehow knowing that Deirdre and I will be at the SJTU on Christmas Eve.

He tells Deirdre that his daughter has made allegations about a senior politician, Ian Anderson, and a famous singer, as well as others. She has a disability but has the capacity to tell the truth. She spoke correctly about bullying in primary school at 10 and rape by a minicab driver at 14. She has never made such allegations as these before.

He wants an assessment carried out immediately with no one else being informed. His daughter is currently a patient at H where Abdul has sessions. I have some line management for the rather good OTs, Faith and Maureen, that Abdul supervises. Next week she will be a patient at the unit that her family have endowed, which is also practically next door to us, and where Abdul will be the consultant psychiatrist.

However, as Professor Frank so kindly informed us, thanks to Elouise confronting him at our *illegal* meeting, safeguarding issues from H are not under our jurisdiction but belong to the Lord Glendale Foundation. The actual Lord Oliver Glendale is a close friend of Ian Anderson, and Sir Peter and Lady Lily Redcliffe and Lady Lily's mother. He has also personally funded Professor Frank's memory research lab and the LGBT unit, Equipa.

Lord Glendale's brother, Harold Fitz-Hugh West, has been accused of the abuse of children at the children's home in Washington that he founded. On the internet, there are hints of ritual abuse. This case was ethically complex enough already.

Now it is worse. Our senior MP, The Minister of Health no less, has rung to say he over-reacted. He would like his message deleted and for there to be no record of his call. He had failed to consider the impact on his daughter of leaving Harvest House after three years to move into the unit named after her. He and his wife wanted her to be given some robust treatment and would discuss this with Professor Frank.

He had personally intervened to help create the new post that Dr Aziz was about to take, and it was possible the SJTU could be expanded with larger premises off-site."

He stopped. There was a shocked silence.

CHAPTER 16

Thursday, December 27th 2012, 6pm, Harvest House

Sarah did not like working beyond her allotted hours. She knew how easy it was to slip into working longer and longer hours—especially with the hole Steve had left in her heart. However, after the surprising change of behaviour from Lew Masters and the equally surprising burst of extra cleaning from Edna, she had the energy to try and make sense of poor Rose's behaviour and all the issues it raised. This was her new beginning. She did not wish to take it home with her. Like Elmview. Like Steve.

Tracey had worked hard to make up for the first-night delinquencies, and it was not hard to see that Lew Masters had pressured her to stay in her room and not be involved. Sarah had read the rather patchy CV, which yelled failed potential and a lack of stability—a classic mark for abusive older men. She had plans for Tracey. She felt she could reach her just in time. So many vulnerable young people were turning to health-care or nursing. She had never thought before that she was a wounded healer, an abandoned healer.

She considered it important to review her own contact with Rose's family. There was concern about adult capacity and confidentiality in the disability field and when family should be contacted. It was of course all the more difficult in these circumstances with Lady Rose's family endowing the new Independence Unit.

Despite the clear failures of the unit's notes and filing, Faith and Maureen had been able to show her, through their well-kept OT notes, that the brand-new Lord Glendale Foundation and Centre held the safeguarding role. Ringing the number, she was shocked to be asked to provide clinical details on the phone without any introduction. On making clear she would not divulge client confidentiality without a direct named person, she was transferred to Professor Chris Frank.

It was hard being a Day Manager as well as a Unit Manager with no clear chain of command; day staff, night staff, and supervision and line management were all in different places. To say nothing of starting on Christmas Day after the surprise disappearance of the former manager—Ms Princeton. And what was her first name? No one seemed to remember her. But then-this was why she had been given the job. Why else would a middle-aged Northern woman, fresh from a scapegoating triumph and a marital breakup, gain a London job at a university hospital?

Professor Frank had congratulated her on all she had achieved in just two days, and, to her surprise and embarrassment, she had told him everything, including her doubts about Lew Masters and Edna, and their surprising turnaround. She felt she was blabbing to him, like being a needy student again, wanting validation. But somehow he had not taken it that way.

She had taken careful notes from Tracey and Masters, and had spoken to Faith and Maureen, as well as the two nurses. And finally, she had spoken to Rose herself. Poor Rose had a jumble of words. She was still incoherent but comfortable. A stream of names and words rushed out of her mouth, but Sarah was not concerned with that. She went for stabilisation. Rose had been washed and dressed, wrapped in warm blankets and settled down with her favourite music. Faith and Maureen were not happy that Rose wanted to listen to Disney songs and musicals—"Follow the yellow brick road" was her latest obsession. However, Sarah did not think a crisis was the right time to focus on ideas of what was age-appropriate.

Professor Frank said she had done the right thing. Despite it being slightly unusual, he was a close family friend of Sir Peter and Lady Lily. That was why they had endowed the unit. They had told him she had been extremely disturbed over the last few days. Indeed, Sir Peter had initially wanted an emergency assessment from Dr Stuart at the SJTU. However, given the powerful feelings about the new unit in Rose's name and the change of staff, Sir Peter had approached Professor Frank instead, and Professor Frank would liaise with Sarah about providing the supportive work.

At the end of the conversation, Professor Frank suggested Sarah use a number or letter when speaking of the names mentioned by Lady Rose. As her parents were key figures in the public eye and their friends were similarly well known, great care had to be taken over confidentiality.

Sarah agreed absolutely. Too quick an assumption in this field could lead to many dangers. Her closest friend Penny had caused several problems at Elmview by believing literally everything the patients said. Enough bad things happened to people there with disabilities without following every false lead.

However, with time to reflect, she felt she should own her authority as a manager. She would inform the parents that Lady Rose had been unsettled but was now relaxed. Indeed, she would send an email saying just that, and that she had contacted Professor Frank for advice, and he would liaise with them. Should Professor Frank and the parents stop being friends, something different would be needed.

CHAPTER 17

Thursday, December 27th 2012, 9pm, Westminster

The Rt Hon Ian Anderson, Lord Glendale, and HRH Prince Carl-Zygmunt were drinking whiskies in a discreet velvet-draped room. A nervous uniformed waitress knocked on the door, "Your Highness, my Lord, and … er … gentlemen—may I ask if anything else is needed."

Ian's large jowly face and pink complexion, beloved by caricaturists, broke into a steely smirk—he was the only one without a proper title. He had to settle for Right Honourable Member. He gestured imperiously for her to remove two empty bottles.

"Gentlemen!" As the waitress approached, he thrust a large hand viciously under her short skirt and pinched hard. She uttered a shocked gasp and ran from the room, crying while the other two men raised their eyebrows and looked worriedly at each other.

"Is Halloween not enough for you, Ian?" asked Lord Glendale.

"Rose was a fucking mistake, and no Master came out. The programming failed," said Ian pompously. "Masters messed it more with his thick level spiders."

The others ignored that.

"So how is your Dishonourable Member?" asked Lord Glendale heavily.

"Yes. She is Peter and Lily's daughter," added Prince Carl-Zygmunt.

"And it does not work properly on people with disabilities," he added.

"You misunderstand me," said Ian coldly. "Rose was a fucking mistake from the start. A blot on the bloodline. Peter's mess. And no pleasure to anyone anyway, unlike that waitress or the waiter before her."

"Genetics are still a key issue—even though it should not have been her," emphasised Lord Glendale. "That is why Toby matters."

"Is it tidied up?" asked Prince Carl-Zygmunt emphatically.

"The waiter, this waitress, or Rose?" smirked Ian.

"Rose," said Lord Glendale.

"But that has had to be my call. I've had our little pocket puppet, Professor Frank, dealing with it. He hasn't got a clue, dear man. But with his particular attitude to the fallibility of abuse memories, he and his team are useful distractions."

"And if she needs treatment or blabs to the press or her staff?" asked CZ.

"Well, Lady Lily is onside so Frank and Co and Stuart can fight it out. It is a win–win. If she needs long-term treatment with Stuart, they have to keep confidentiality, and nothing will be said. If she blabs or someone listens, it is a disabled woman with a mental health problem. If it is short-term treatment provided through Frank, he might blame the H for reinforcing her delusions. That could hasten us selling off the long-stay unit. Equipa needs more room. They have been a good return on my investment—the Greens. We can always bring in Fiona, who writes for *The Mercury*, as a last resort. Do you remember? She can always do the juicy story of a poor aristocratic disabled young person destroyed by therapy or hospital treatment. Those little anti-Satanic abuse papers will like that too."

Prince Carl-Zygmunt thoughtfully fingered his ring. "They have been very useful to us, those memory researchers."

Ian nodded, and a smirk crossed his jowly face. "And the dross?" he asked.

"Our lowlife Luciferian narcissist?" chuckled Glendale, relieved to change the subject.

"Yes. I do like that touch—Lew for Lucifer, and fancies himself as a Master," said Ian with an amused expression on his face, made unreal by the chilling menace in his voice.

"I warned him to tidy up." He smashed his fist on the table, shocking the other two men.

"He is useful," emphasised Prince Carl-Zygmunt, stroking his tidy beard. "He seems to have tidied himself up a bit. Might last longer. He did some good basic work, keeping subjects at a certain level of trauma so that their simple splits would become solid. He has done better than many of the Americans. But disability units are not a suitable base in the way they were and nor are the subjects."

"He's a gorilla," reproved Ian. "And I know what to do with gorillas." Prince Carl-Zygmunt and Glendale looked at each other worriedly.

"Easy," smiled Glendale, touching his ring emphatically.

"With Frank strutting around his small stage, we have a perfect research setting, and Equipa is loved by victim groups everywhere. We will be so popular."

He turned his smile to Ian. "But we expect you to be PM, Ian. We need you to equalise with our transatlantic interests."

A smile crossed Ian's face, and his large fist uncurled.

"Prime Minister, Ian," repeated Prince Carl-Zygmunt, "Not a number 2 anymore."

"So no messes, Ian," emphasised Glendale. "Keep it zipped. Stick with Stefan. You need to take a break."

"A break? A break? Keep it zipped!" shouted Ian. "It is your brother you should be talking to—Fitz-Hugh West—look at all the problems he creates!"

"Gentlemen," remonstrated Prince Carl-Zygmunt. "Stop! We can't have this when we are so close! A Centre of Excellence with impeccable credentials in the middle of a rundown hospital. Feeder units. Just think! A borderline personality disorder unit, eating disorders, perhaps an adolescent unit, and then a residential children's home and Equipa. Then Orpheus and all who sail on her have a chance and all our scientific and military devotees."

A collective sigh filled the room.

"To the Society of Orpheus," said Glendale raising his glass.

"The Society," echoed Ian.

"When I said 'a break,' I mean to our colleagues in my hometown," said Glendale.

"Washington?" asked Ian, eyes lighting up. The facilities and luxury provided there far surpassed his UK situation. And there were no native HRHs or Lords there. Rt Honourable took you a lot further in all directions.

"Yes," he agreed, "and your brother, shall I see him? I have very fond memories of him."

"Of course. You might be able to help him." Carl-Zygmunt thought for a moment. "I need to go there too. To see Sandra. Just checking her out. You know. Someone made for me. It has been a hard time."

"A girl in a million," smiled Glendale.

"More than a million dollars in research fees so far," agreed Carl-Zygmunt, "and worth every cent."

"And Lee?"

"No. He is for Major D; Zed would not allow it."

"Well, gentlemen," said Anderson, rising up heavily from his seat, "since Zed/Zee/Last-letter-in-the-alphabet-man doesn't deign to talk to me, and I don't have a million dollars to invest, I have business to attend to out there. I assume you will settle everything for me. Good-night gentlemen." He savoured the word of insult on his lips and walked out swiftly.

"Is he safe?" asked Carl-Zygmunt nervously. "Lily loves him, but he is volatile and dangerous to everyone else."

"She will keep him calm," soothed Glendale. "Unfortunately, and Zed agrees, we still need him."

"Unlike the country," laughed Carl-Zygmunt.

A cloud of whisky and cigars rose from their polished table.

CHAPTER 18

Thursday, December 27th 2012, 9:30pm, Highgate

Dr Stuart's residence

They had all gone. Empty Plates, cups, and glasses covered the table. Moira would be pleased. Only a few lone carrots and cherry tomatoes.

He turned the light out and closed the door.

He walked slowly up the stairs gripping the wooden bannisters. He felt tired. It was not just the ongoing ethical problems this case would evoke; it was also the sense there were strings being pulled from higher up.

Sitting on the chair in front of his desk, he turned his computer on, opened the window, and reached in his pocket for his cigarettes. The world was layered with cruelty. What always amazed him with the trauma in each society was that every country was not at war all the time. And not just the humans: all species. Where was the help these internet apparitions needed? Let alone the flesh and blood ones on his own hospital site. What time would Moira be back? Had she taken her case? He did not think he could wait up.

The telephone rang, interrupting his thoughts. The telephone! His son! Where was it? There it sat, as usual, next to the computer.

His son! He picked it up breathlessly.

"Dad!"

"Jamie."

"Dad!"

He had never heard his son's voice so loud and joyous. "This is to inform you that you are a granddad. My son. My son! Your grandson! James Martin Stuart weighing 9lb 1oz has just been born. Mother and babe are all fine. In case you don't know, mum said to tell you she is already on a plane."

"Oh, my son!"

CHAPTER 19

Thursday, December 27th 2012, 10pm, The Lord Glendale Centre

rofessor Chris Frank sat on his black leather chair, looking over his polished desk to the thick dark-blue pile carpet and on to the floor-to-ceiling windows. The room was everything and anything he had ever wanted. And not just the room. As well as the ensuite bathroom leading off to the left of his office—there was the communicating door to his secretary's office. The best photocopiers, telephone systems, and scanners. With a flick of a switch, he could expand the size of his office when needed, and just as simply reduce it back.

He had hit the jackpot this time. So what it wasn't Oxbridge: it was possibly even better. There had never been such a flow of funding, and with no strings attached. He had the freedom to invite all the greats, talks, projects, and collaborations.

Collaborations! This could be the end of the difficult links he had had to endure with most of his erstwhile colleagues. The subject of memory was threatening to all at the best of times. With memories of abuse bringing in the possibility of police involvement, it was even more important it was treated with care. To be wrongly accused was to be abused.

This subject was too important to be contaminated by some of the allegedly innocent families who had originally made up the core of many international False Memory Societies. Such families, privately accused of sexual abuse by their grownup children, made the accusations public and demanded press sympathy. Sometimes deservedly so, but all too often not.

However, they were all equally unscientific. Survivor groups, parent groups, and some therapists. Some believed everyone and everything—sometimes correctly—while he knew that some of the families who quoted him adoringly were not innocent. He did not want the purity of his work damaged by either of them.

The field had only just started recovering from Ralph Underwager's "indiscretion" in 1993 when, as one of the founders of the False Memory Society, he gave an interview with the Dutch paedophile magazine, *Paedika*. He was reported as saying that having sex with children could be seen as "part of God's will." The other co-founders of the FMSF, were Pamela and Peter Freyd, whose adult daughter spoke privately of childhood sexual abuse. The American media gave the parents almost unquestioning support until their daughter, distinguished psychology Professor Jennifer Freyd, felt obliged to speak out to limit the damage that her parents and their organisation were doing to abuse survivors.

Reluctantly, Professor Frank was aware that he admired her research and her delicate way of handling her parents. He would like his research to be of a quality that would impress her, a proper researcher. Not have his academic reputation tarnished by his unchosen links with the deniers of familial abuse, or those who used unethical means. He was outraged by the Loftus "Lost in the Mall" experiment and could not believe psychological societies allowed such ethical breaches. He did not want the Glendale to become a home for the new wannabe, or old wannabe, anti-abuse people with low-level PhDs.

His pure aim was to show the dangerous fallibility of all memory—trauma memory too. This would aid courts, police, and true victims. There was no room for questionable professional behaviour or theories in this field. The damage of both being wrongly accused or not being accused was too great.

Thank goodness Mrs Ransome had followed protocol and come to him. He would keep an eye on her. A sensible woman. Poor Lady Lily. A child like Rose coming from such a beautiful mother was a tragedy. Rose could bring some dangerous publicity to the Foundation and affect her father's political future. He had rung Lord Glendale to let him know he was containing it. He could not face Glendale taking his millions elsewhere.

But he was protecting himself too. With no restrictions on his role, he was seeking for St Joseph's University Hospital to earn half of its income from private patients, charities, and commercial activities. With the "step change" in private patient activity and restrictions lifted on Trusts' private work, the number of private patient units had doubled. The LGBT Equipa Unit had trebled in donations.

Professor Frank was not sentimental about the NHS or private practice. But he considered that NHS patients would benefit, as the surplus would be reinvested. Securing the hospital also secured the staff and his research.

Dear mother—how could he have hurt her? What pain had he caused? And to his sister and her family. All lost to him. He would always do right by his mother—even if she was no longer here to know it. How could he have done it? He had ruined all those years of her life, and still had a giant black hole of memory from 7 to 14. He had spent his life trying to understand that. And he would continue to, so long as he had breath.

CHAPTER 20

Thursday, December 27th 2012, 10pm, Fleet Street

Mark Dyer from *The Chronicle* could not understand it. Why would a classy political couple, rolling in money, put their Down's daughter in a shit-hole like Harvest House? It didn't make sense. The impact of institutionalisation on children and adults with intellectual disabilities was well known—even for a rag like his—and Harvest House was known to be one. Why would the family endow a private unit in her name in the same place three years later? It didn't make sense.

His friend Fiona from *The Mercury* had the same view. But she couldn't do one of her "your money is being wasted on ..." pieces when the family were spending their own money on the new unit. And she couldn't do a "why is private money needed" piece berating the NHS when Glendale was making up for it. He grinned as he drank the last sip of his craft beer. It all made sense now. No political backlash, whatever the action! This was Dodo time—"all shall win, and all shall have prizes!" He crumpled up the press invite to the Lady Rose Redcliffe Independence Unit launch and threw it into the bin. No story there.

CHAPTER 21

Thursday, December 27th 2012, 11pm, Harvest House

L ew Masters crushed a wineglass in his right hand, slowly and carefully, watching a small trail of blood make its way down his hand. He had never been so disrespected. His superiors would be informed.

His Master would be told. And if he did not like the response, he would take his own action. He had been in the coven long enough to know their punishments and treatment of traitors. They wouldn't dare try it on him.

He listened to the rage inside himself. Zip up indeed! The sacrament of his arousal transformed into some low-level jinx. So, they thought their Society was the pinnacle of power, did they? Well, they were in for a surprise. They were underestimating him—all of them. He might look like a lowlife but inside, deep inside, he was a God.

If Harvest could not provide the crops he required, he could go elsewhere. Easy. Just a few weeks more to alter the reference and he would be off. An NHS reference was the most beneficial for their purposes in the UK. It was not Ransome's fault. She was only doing her job and had totally bought his Damascene conversion. He could even like her, soft fool that she was. She could have got rid of Trace and him on the spot. She was not the enemy.

There was a tentative knock on the door. A smile crept across his face.

"Thought you might like a cuppa, Mr Masters," said Tracey nervously, half opening the door.

He grinned again at the sight of her in a slightly longer leather skirt. Like him, she was dressing more suitably to please Ransome. He and Trace—both survivors—knew when it was worth complying! He carefully wrapped the broken glass into a tissue and threw it into a bin.

"What a generous soul you are," he smiled sarcastically. "All the way from the kitchen when my electric kettle just sits idle here."

Tracey blushed, cursing her pale skin. She knew he could see it. What was wrong with her sucking up to old bastards like him who made fun of her? New Year's Resolution: no more wrinkles; wankers all of them!

"I was just making myself one and thought you might be tired and fancy one, but Sod's law I'll just sling it or have it myself." She turned to leave. That was more like it.

"You are right. I am tired, and I do fancy one," he said relenting, a twinkle in his eye. "I am glad it is you on duty tonight and not Goldstone. Wearing a shirt and tie exhausts me."

She grinned back, freed from her humiliation. "I always welcome more filthy lucre."

"I prefer wearing nothing," he added with his old defiance.

Tracey giggled. Now she was on home territory again. She hadn't been wrong. He fancied her rotten underneath it all.

"I'm lucky. Mrs Ransome has said my clothes are difficult for getting on and off my bike, but she hasn't asked me to dress differently yet. She got a real shock seeing me in this. But she is a classy woman. She didn't say anything."

"Stay how you are," said Lew emphatically, surprising himself by his vehemence.

"All quiet on the Western Front?" he added, needing a distraction.

"All except the famous four! John and Dykes are asleep but snoring like engines, Sinita is just rocking Serby, and Rose is screaming and whimpering in her sleep. I tried talking to her like Mrs Ransome said, but it didn't make any difference. It seemed like she didn't know I was there."

"Ah. Let's try the magic touch. Watch and learn." Taking a further swig of tea, he clutched a tissue in his hand. Tracey stood uncertainly by the door; her body was flushed with excitement. Lew smiled. "Lead on

73

McDuff," he said, placing his left hand on her soft shoulder. She moved slowly, shamed by the heat that was spreading.

The corridor outside the office/sleepover room now smelt of lavender, albeit with a lower bouquet of urine. Edna had really pulled her finger out, and it made H block easier to endure. Ahead was the large day room, dining room, kitchen, TV room, laundry room, OT office, and Sarah's office. But turning left at the next corridor was the way to the sleeping areas.

The walls were peeling and in need of decoration, but slowly photographs and artwork had been placed there by Faith and Maureen.

Originally there were 50 patients in four single-sex wards with single-sex bathing facilities and shared dayroom activities. There were now only 30 patients left, a ten-bed male ward and ten-bed female ward, both staffed with a nursing shift, and ten more capable residents in single or double rooms. Three of the most able within that group would shortly be joining Rose in the Lady Rose Independence Unit, and there were still doubts over the placement of the remaining residents. Indeed, the whole unit was under threat.

Although in need of almost total refurbishment, the unit was large and could be far more profitable for the Trust. Some of the old staff offices had already been turned into individual or couples' ensuite rooms.

At the end of the crossover corridor was the rest of the H shape. To the right were the "night" corridors with their glass windows for peering in, and to the left were the small number of ensuite rooms with Dykes and Jon's room, Sinita's room, Tim's room, and then Lady Rose's at the end. Snores and cries unravelled into the corridors and Tracey shivered.

Masters gripped her right shoulder tightly and steered her past. "You'll get used to it," he whispered.

She shuddered, and it was not just because of Masters. She knew she wouldn't get used to this. It was worse than her squat. It was worse than when she'd slept on the streets. Fucking wounded animals. They should be put down. It was not bearable. Hot tears started forming behind her eyes.

And, as if the corridor had ears, the cries and whimpers got louder.

They were outside Rose's room. "Day gone," came a scream, "Day Gone!"

Masters removed his hand. "Now," he said sternly, "I want you to knock on the door. Three knocks. Call 'Rosie' three times; helps her come out of a flashback."

"Flashback?" asked Tracey.

"Are you listening Tracey?" he asked, whispering furiously "Three knocks and call 'Rosie' three times." He held her right wrist tightly.

The young woman's pallor increased. He released her wrist and softened his tone. "When someone has gone through a trauma, it can come back and take over their mind, so they think they are still there."

"Oh! Like her not realising I am in the room. I never realised. I think my brother got that from Afghanistan," said Tracey, wide-eyed. "How do you stop it? He can't get a job because of it."

"Poor bastard," said Lew, suddenly taken over by the thought. "I was there too. But you can't do anything. Vietnam vets still have them four decades later. All you can do is learn to live with them."

"You get them too?" asked Tracey.

A shriek came from the room, a welcome distraction for Lew. He signalled Tracey towards the door with his head; she knocked three times and loudly called "Rosie ... Rosie ... Rosie."

Silence.

Masters nodded at Tracey as she tentatively opened the door. Lady Rose Redcliffe lay utterly still, the light from the corridor framing her terrified face. "It's me: Tracey. I am just here with Mr Masters."

Rose remained silent.

"Talk, talk, talk, you can do it, Rose," said Masters, walking gently into the room. "Rose, Rose, Rose."

Tracey turned the light on. The room still disturbed her. She had not met anyone so "posh" before and had expected the room to have smart china or ornaments or jewellery. But no, as she had said to Mrs Ransome earlier, whatever designer clothes her mother swanned around in, Rose was dressed in cheap rubbish.

Rose had nothing, absolutely nothing, in her bare room that could have shown she came from a wealthy family. "Good Rose," said Rose looking at Lew Masters. "Screaming Rose stopped."

"Good Rose," affirmed Lew. He turned to Tracey: "See kid: three knocks and say her name three times, and she will be as right as she can be."

"Thank you, Mr Masters," she said.

"Hear that, Rose?" he asked.

"Hear Master," replied Rose.

"Sleep now."

"Good girl," said Masters.

75

"Night, night."

Tracey closed the door and took a deep breath. "Now what?"

"And now we are free," he grinned.

But as they turned down the hall, an unrecognisable, deep, and low male voice could be heard. It was hostile; forcing through the tiny gaps in the doorframe and corridor, threatening to engulf the whole hallway.

"Day Gone, disgusting mongol girl. Close this time. Don't want to have to hurt you."

Without a pause or thought, Tracey rushed back into Rose's room with Masters close behind. Turning the light on, ready to face an intruder, Tracey found herself facing Lady Rose. But was it Lady Rose? Sitting upright, an angry man was staring at her. He had Rose's deep blue eyes and golden hair, but his expression was out of a horror film.

"Rose, Rose, Rose," called Masters. The angry face looked confused. Then upset.

"Sorry Tracey. Sorry Master. Day Gone. I go to sleep now."

Lew nodded, pulled Tracey out while she stood staring at Rose and gently closed the door.

CHAPTER 22

Friday, December 28th 2012, 10pm

Major D: a confidential telephone call
to Rt Hon Ian Anderson

The American voice on the phone was harsh and used to obedience.

Ian suppressed his outrage.

"This is your work phone, Deputy Prime Minister, so I am formally ringing you, and I am therefore giving you your usual official courtesy."

There was a sadistic emphasis on the word "deputy."

"I have spoken to our colleagues on both sides of the pond and they are insistent. If your colleagues don't like the word "bloodline" and find it too biblical, say "genetic." If they can't cope with the truth of eugenics, say "science" instead. We don't care what word you use so long as your post continues to our mutual advantage. It matters for science and the military."

"The work needs to continue," said Ian. "You know I back it, but I cannot *officially* back all of it. You should know that better than most and should have used my other number. I have to be careful in my position or we all lose out. These are sensitive areas."

"Your position is the least of our worries, Deputy," emphasised the voice.

"Genes are genes. War is war. For this, in the tasks allocated to you, only Lily is the exception. We have others focusing on Imogen and Toby and the other bloodlines. We have time to wait for him: maybe years."

"I know you want bloodline to be part of the protocol, but it could seriously impact all other planning. I was told I had done that inadvertently."

"Only you have caused a problem," said the voice coldly. "You and Danny. Even Bloodliners draw the line at Rose. This is far bigger than Glendale and myself, Deputy Prime Minister, as I would have thought you might realise by now. It will be our choice. It is military and scientific."

"The mess outside of my own could be considerable—and we have different views on that—but you clearly don't give a damn," retorted Ian.

"The mess without it would lead to dangers you cannot imagine Mr Deputy. 'There are more things in heaven and earth, Horatio, than are dreamt of in your philosophy'. Goodnight, Deputy Prime Minister."

Ian slammed the phone down with such force that his new nervous young private secretary heard it through the thick oak-panelled walls and trembled. He had heard rumours of why his predecessor had left. There were limits to what he would accept in order to get on.

CHAPTER 23

Friday, 28th December 2012, 9am, Harvest House

Dr Aziz wiped his shoes carefully on the doormat after Maureen and Faith opened the door of Harvest House for him. There was a smell of polish, disinfectant, and fresh air. A new broom had arrived!

"Dr Aziz! What wonderful timing!" said Faith.

"We didn't think you were back until next week," added Maureen excitedly.

"So, this is the famous Dr Aziz," smiled a smartly dressed personable woman coming out of the day room.

"What a kind welcome, ladies," smiled Abdul.

"Happy Christmas! And you must be Mrs Ransome," he added, looking at her appreciatively.

"I can't believe the progress you have made already. More in two days than Ms Princeton managed in as many months."

"Yes. There has been a lot to do. And we were in the middle of a serious emergency review. Would you be willing to join us in a slightly larger group than usual doctor? I hope this is not a breach. I have left a message for Professor Frank at the Lord Glendale who might call back while you are here but as supervisor for ..."

"It is quite all right Mrs Ransome. I am able to assist you within my brief, and I am delighted it is such an opportune moment. New staff, new unit about to open: Christmas and feelings of loss and abandonment! What could be the problem?"

Faith and Maureen broke into relieved laughter, and Sarah took a sigh of relief.

She led the way to her office with Abdul praising the Christmas decorations.

"Even a painting from Tim," he approved, pointing to the picture of a large black spider with glitter all over it.

"Please also meet…"

"I'm Lew Masters, Dr Aziz, night manager," said a short powerful-looking man. "And this is my new assistant, Ms O'Bridey."

A traumatised young woman with a tear-stained face, Tracey was sitting at the large old table with a chipped mug clasped between her hands. Abdul noticed the bitten fingernails and the terrified expression.

"May I sit down here?" he asked.

"Sorry. Tea or coffee, Dr Aziz?"

"No need. Please, tell me what's happened?"

The remaining staff sat around the table.

"Mr Masters, could you explain?"

The sombre-looking man clenched his right fist. "The Lady Rose Redcliffe Unit, which opens in just under two weeks, is taking Lady Rose."

"It's OK, Mr Masters. Thank you for being willing to provide the details, but I know the background. Please take us to the crisis."

"On night duty last night, there were concerning screams and behaviours coming from Lady Rose's room so, as written in the incident book, Ms O'Bridey and I went to investigate."

Sarah nodded appreciatively and handed Dr Aziz the night notes. He scanned it speedily and looked at Ms O'Bridey. "What concerned you most?" he asked.

Tracey looked at him intently. "Have you ever seen *The Omen*?" she asked, Lew Masters stiffening beside her.

"I have."

"Well, she just changed! There she was all crying and upset poor thing, until Mr Masters calmed her down. And then there was this disgusting awful male presence—like a devil—with this awful expression and words! I thought Rose had been killed, and there was an intruder there who had killed her. His look. His ugly voice. And then Mr Masters calmed 'it' down, and Rose was normal again."

She burst into tears, and Lew put a hand gently on her arm.

"How very concerning," said Dr Aziz. "And yet Mr Masters knew how to calm her."

"That's when I was so grateful to have an experienced night manager," said Sarah looking warmly at Masters. She had really underestimated him.

"She has been disturbed for the last few months," added Maureen, looking at Faith for support. "Really volatile. Since their Vegas trip. I don't think it helped that her family did not spend much time with her since then. She experiences such gaps as abandonment. I have been taking her out more to try and empower her for the opening of the new unit—looking at furniture and colours. Her family have not done any of that."

"You didn't see her or hear her!" shouted Tracey. "If you had, you'd be amazed her parents saw her at all. I've been around. I've been in a children's home. I've been homeless. I have seen fucking anything. But nothing like this."

Sarah's mobile rang. "It's Professor Frank," she said nervously.

"Do put me onto him," said Dr Aziz calmly.

"Hello Professor Frank. Yes. A crisis concerning RR. I have Dr Aziz here—yes…"

She walked around the table to pass the phone.

"Good morning, Professor Frank. Yes. That is correct. How would you like us to proceed? Yes … Yes … I do understand. A joint assessment or review? Here or the Lord Glendale? We will be setting a precedent I suppose. And I will be involved with the new unit too. That would be excellent. Thank you. A generous use of your resources. What time? Yes. I can do that. That is very kind of you, sir. I would be honoured. 11.30am it is. I will indeed. To Mr Masters and Ms O'Bridey too. Thank you, Professor Frank."

They all looked up expectantly. He scanned their faces while filtering his own processes. Masters was watching with a curiously cynical expression.

"Well, I am to convey Professor Frank's appreciation to Mrs Ransome, Mr Masters, and Ms O'Bridey. He is sorry he was not available when called but was in a meeting where he could not be disturbed. He has suggested a thorough specialist review of Lady Rose."

81

"At the Glendale," said Masters bitterly.

"Yes."

"Why that tone, Lew?" asked Maureen curiously, finding herself interested in his views for the first time.

"We have a specialist here, Dr Aziz," said Masters angrily. "He's good enough for us and the Lady Rose Unit, so why does it need them? Just because he is friends with her mother."

There was silence.

Faith and Maureen looked at each other.

Dr Aziz smiled reassuringly. "That is possible Mr Masters. This is indeed a difficult situation. We have the daughter of the Minister of Health about to be moved to a new unit paid for by her family. And her family are close friends with Lord Glendale, who founded and, more relevantly, funded the Glendale Centre and Foundation. And Lord Glendale personally appointed Professor Frank as Chief Executive Officer."

There was a sigh of relief that the context had been openly discussed. It was what Faith and Maureen always said about Dr Aziz. He had no agenda and was always open and courteous.

Masters lowered his head, surprised at his own words and the response to them.

Sarah nodded her head slowly.

"Thank you, Dr Aziz. I emailed Lady Lily about the last incident, but there was no reply. Our normal practice with a further assessment would be to let the family know unless the resident did not want that to happen.

I would see this as a responsible part of the last communication. You have already told them and Professor Frank that her behaviour has been different in the last few months. Now you have told me. This is the professional response. You can send a brief formal note that the Glendale and Harvest House have arranged a specialist assessment, and you will inform them of the results. Professor Frank and I will discuss the letter to the family."

"Yes," said Lew Masters, "because with all the publicity for the new unit any delay in opening it or any setback in Lady Rose's treatment and behaviour will cause a storm somewhere."

Sarah gazed at him in shock. "I never thought about that."

Faith and Maureen were silent. Sarah Ransome looked at the floor. She did not know what to say.

"Mr Masters. That is a correct and helpful point. The media have their job, and we have ours. And ours is to help Lady Rose and make sense of what is happening. I know you and Ms O'Bridey have had a long hard night. Please get some sleep. Mrs Ransome and Mr Masters— you will, I am sure, have some ideas as to how to relax Ms O'Bridey, so she is not traumatised. I need to cancel some meetings at the SJTU and will be back."

He stood up to leave. To his surprise, Mr Masters followed him out.

"Just a query, doctor: how did Frank know Trace and I were on duty last night? It was going to be Sonia Goldstone until the last moment." Lew turned back to Sarah's office, leaving a momentarily bemused Dr Aziz. With a pleasant thought in his mind, he felt for his pendant and smiled. He would show who the gorillas were.

CHAPTER 24

Friday, December 28th 2012, 10am, The SJTU

Outside H unit, Dr Aziz stood still for a moment breathing in the cold morning air. He could see how difficult the path ahead would be and the complications his new post would cause. The only way to manage was to be scrupulous and open. That was all anyone could do.

Mrs Ransome was a breath of fresh air and he could see she would turn that place around. With support from such stalwarts as Faith and Maureen, it would not be *Cell Block H* anymore. What a waste! Isn't this what always happened? A place deteriorated so a new one was created, but it just at the point of change when the old one turned round. "Time is no healer, the patient is already dead," said T.S. Eliot. By the time some things were put right, it was too late. So long as he could ensure good basic staff for the Lady Rose. It would be so good if Sarah could be joined by Faith and Maureen for a solid block of sessions; that was the plan, but it was impossible to predict.

Now he came to his thought of Lew Masters. He had learned from Faith and Maureen of the impact of the man's sexist behaviour and bullying. Yet, he had shown such political insight; people were rarely black and white. There was always something else there. He found himself back at the SJTU with Deirdre almost at the door, ready to pounce.

"He's waiting for you," she smiled, the warmth on her face incongruous in the circumstances.

Abdul walked to Gawain's office, reflecting on the key issues. A knock on the door revealed an unusual sight. Gawain himself opened the door with the most joyous expression on his face. There was champagne on his table.

"Abdul. I am a grandfather. My Jamie's had a baby." The two men hugged. "Moira is already there. I will go tonight."

The two men moved to the sofas. So that was why the loyal Deirdre looked so happy!

"It puts everything into perspective, doesn't it," said Abdul gently.

"Yes. I want to make the world safer for him. Tackling corruption on this site is doing something for the world."

There was a companionable pause. "It makes me feel for poor Lady Rose. Here is Jamie, welcomed and loved by all his family, and he would have been whatever disability he might have had. Lady Rose was not loved by her mother, and her mother must be suffering. So where are we, Abdul?"

Another gentle pause.

"I went to Harvest House at 9am and was invited by the excellent new Clinic and Day Manager, Sarah Ransome, to join them in a review as a night assistant had been traumatised hearing aggressive male speech come from Lady Rose's mouth. Whatever personal reasons led Ms Princeton to go so quickly and unexpectedly, there has been a gift to us. Mrs Ransome had appropriately notified Professor Frank, who rang while I was there and is offering a review at the Lord Glendale at 11.30am. I accepted this as I think collaboration is important here. The problem is more likely to come over determining appropriate treatment."

The two men exchanged sharp glances.

"Is the SCID-D an appropriate diagnostic test for mild intellectual disability?" asked Gawain.

Abdul looked at him intently. "You think she is dissociative?"

"I would have thought that is one possibility if she spoke like a male in a different state of mind," said Gawain reflectively.

"Or the imitative capacity some adults with Down's Syndrome have?" queried Abdul.

"Or any chance of a possession disorder?"

"Or a transitional schizophrenia?"

85

The two men smiled. "Like the old days Abdul."

"Yes, Gawain. I think the key issue is to keep an open mind over everything. Then the explosion will happen after. The description of a male personality taking over will not be easy to explain politically."

"We can be sure of that, my boy."

"So we can, grandfather."

The two men hugged.

"Take care Gawain; you and Moira deserve the pleasure of this."

"And you Abdul. I cannot think of anyone more suited than you to tread this difficult path. Poor Lady Rose—as if money and title has brought her happiness."

CHAPTER 25

Friday, December 28th 2012, USA

Major D's office

Johnny Cash was playing quietly in the background. Danny Boy. His own Danny and the Danny in the song merged poignantly. It always got to him while he sipped his skinny latte.

Oh, Danny Boy, the pipes, the pipes are calling.
From glen to glen and down the mountainside.
The summer's gone, and all the roses falling.
It's you. It's you, must go, and I must bide.
But come ye back when summer's in the meadow.
Or when the valley's hushed, and white with snow.
I'll be here in sunshine or in shadow
Oh Danny Boy, oh Danny Boy, I love you so.
But if you come, and all the flowers are dying,
And I am dead, as dead I well may be.
You'll come and find the place where I am lying.

He turned it off, quickly wiping away a tear as there was a discreet knock on the mahogany door. No one would expect such a display of emotion from him, a decorated veteran of the worst wars humans could provide.

His private secretary brought in a printed-out email.

"Damn it." His muscular arm and fist thumped on the table. The West House Children's Home again. WAM: The Washington Association on Child Maltreatment was holding a major conference with international speakers on organised and ritual abuse in the new year, and a reporter had lazily repeated the same old shit.

> Accusations of organised abuse had surfaced concerning the West House Children's home founded by local philanthropist Harold Fitz-Hugh West in the late 1990s. However, these were not upheld. Harold Fitz-Hugh West is the younger brother of Lord Glendale, a British peer. Both brothers see themselves as Anglo-Americans with Lord Glendale spending part of each year in Washington with his brother. Their mother, the late Lady Olivia Glendale, is buried in Arlington National Cemetery.

Someone had better attend the conference. Just in case. No. That would be too time-consuming. Someone could alert one of those false memory groups or factions, or get a retractor involved! Retractors were particularly useful. They were often hysterical women who found a benefit in it, usually financial, or were out for revenge, blaming their treatment team for wounds incurred elsewhere.

He chuckled. They didn't have to do anything for that result to happen. He could even feel sorry for some of those therapists and psychiatrists. Or, and this was his area, they were multiples where one part or personality in them knew the truth and another didn't. This was the area he cared about: that Orpheus and the Society cared about. Deliberately created and installed dissociation. Specially made people. The main personality, Sandra, together with Sandra 2, her tireless supporter and backup, could be counted on to ruthlessly destroy any testimony from alleged victims, deal with the media and, with only a small brain topping up and tweaking, with electric shock usually, had gained huge financial damages against her former hospital and therapists and a huge social platform. He would get her to look at the SJTU in preparation. Just a little seed of doubt in the media should work.

He would have social media checked too. Small fry. Usually, complaints or risk of litigation shut them up. But at a time like this there could be no mistakes. She was media gold, better than his so-called "brothers."

She was worth all the millions they had invested in creating her. Indeed, Orpheus himself had said she was the last prototype in his "Immortality Installation" work and then they were ready to go. There was no need for all the hundreds of parts and inner universes for this work. It could be stripped down to its basics. A part made for you, a replica of yourself or a loved one, capable of outliving the original. Immortality.

It didn't matter that Orpheus had partly failed with Lara and Leandra as personalities, as they continued to disclose details of abuse despite all the punishment. In the end, it was irrelevant what the child or Leandra said. All were finely titrated to allow Sandra and her backup Sandra 2 dominance.

The Orpheus Project was too delicate at this stage for total success. There were weak London and USA links in the chain. Carl-Zygmunt or perhaps Glendale too had not adequately restrained Anderson, who was second class and a sadist to boot. But right now it was also Glendale's background which was a problem. His brother, Harold, should either be aggressively defended or thrown to the wolves. Poor Oliver, he didn't deserve a brother like that. And Danny Boy?

D for Danny and Delta and his own letter too. Why did he need Danny? His poor honourable wife was secluded on their pristine estate, her childlessness dealt with by dogs and horses. She didn't deserve this either, although she was a stoic sensible woman like many of the army wives. She knew how the breakdowns of his men had affected him. He would need to talk to Zed. It was indeed the end of the alphabet for him. And Lee, his secret, his financial and emotional investment, was hidden deep in Sandra. Was he safe enough?

Major D had no religious beliefs as such—not that anyone had to. But he felt himself as a semi-failed/semi-successful God, creating people out of people. He could not save the lives of all his soldiers, but he could do something. Eve was created out of Adam's rib—a single creation. He and the Society of Orpheus could create hundreds from just one body. Let the Luciferians and Gnostics, Jews, Christians, Satanists, and whatever add their own personal or tribal mumbo jumbo at the lower levels. He and Z were military scientists. And, as such, he had been allowed to install Lee, far behind Sandra's amnesic wall; no need for the huge lineages of internal family trees and seven hells and seven heavens and colours and numbers and languages. Orpheus was about installed immortality as well as Manchurian candidates. The fewer the personalities, the better. There was greater control and easier tweaking.

CHAPTER 26

Friday, December 28th 2012, 11:30am, The Lord Glendale Centre

The rain had already muddied the unofficial parking area, a wasteland in front of the SJTU that extended along the right to Harvest House, but Dr Aziz felt like a walk, so he set out across the treacherous terrain. The few minutes between the SJTU and Harvest House allowed him time for some reflection and, as he was going to be entering the Lord Glendale for the first time, he needed it. He cleared his throat and straightened his tie.

Ascending St Joseph's Rise, he looked up at the back of the Glendale, dominating the view as it did. He hadn't been inside since Lord Glendale had taken over. What would that be like: being alive and having a building with your name? In his area of work, this happened after people had died—not in their lifetime. Was he being unfair? He preferred it to be like that—recognition and a pleasure and honour to be continuing the work. But he did not know people like Lord Glendale and their motivation.

As he turned the corner, a smart uniformed man approached him. "Coming to the Glendale, sir?" asked the man.

"Yes," said Dr Aziz continuing to walk.

The man walked just a few inches behind him. "Name, sir?"

"Dr Aziz here to see Professor Frank. Is this your usual welcome, or is it for security?" He asked lightly while trying to fend off the heavy feeling descending on him.

"Both, Dr Aziz," said the man. "We have many high-security visitors."

Walking up the wide marble stairs together, Abdul paused deliberately for a moment to turn and look at the view down the hill and admire the immaculate lawn and sweeping drive. He was not going to be rushed.

"This way, Dr Aziz."

So here he was entering the Lord Glendale Centre for the first time.

Another uniformed man came forward to take over from the first and open the large glass doors. "Dr Aziz! Welcome to the Lord Glendale," said the man.

Abdul looked to the left and right of the man. The vast aristocratic entrance lobby with its magnificent high ceilings was a cross between an airport terminal, a private dental clinic, a military installation, and a five-star hotel. And this was the home of Professor Frank's Diagnostic and Research Centre as well as Equipa, the new treatment and research unit to take over the previous LGBT Centre. The idea amused him.

"Thank you."

"Please take your case and coat through security screening on the right there, or you can wait here while I check you in."

Abdul struggled not to look shocked. The Forensic Unit was used not for knife checks but for screening senior staff?

"That's all right—I will take it."

"Just to your right, sir."

Like an airport, there were ten or so small queues on the right, each waiting to be processed through security. But there was no excited buzz of conversation like there would be at a hospital or a university. The men and women he could see looked extremely serious, and there was no conversation between them.

There were bright blue seating modules interspersed with matching coffee tables on the left. There were coffee machines, tea machines, and water dispensers.

He had not seen anything like it.

It was hard to recall his visits here as a Senior Registrar. There had been a wood-panelled staff lounge, toilets, a waiting room, and admin.

There was a noise of people, staff, and patients. How would Lady Rose manage coming here?

Staff, like the two men he had previously met, stood to attention in dark-blue uniforms and captains' caps.

Moving slowly to the nearest queue, he tried to catch the eye of the middle-aged woman in front of him. She had placed a handbag and several heavy foolscap files onto the tray.

"Dr Aziz," he said gently.

"No, that's not me," she said nervously, looking around and meeting the eye of the nearest uniformed man. Just as he was about to correct her, the man approached.

"With apologies, sir. We have to ensure a code of confidentiality because of the nature of some of the work here."

Dr Aziz looked at his watch. 11.25am. It felt weeks since he had stood in Gawain's cosy room.

"Please place your jacket and case on the tray, sir," said the formal assistant.

A brisk attractive woman in a straight, dark-blue skirt and uniform jacket and high heels whisked the woman, who had been in front of him, away through further glass security doors. A blue motif and a green leaf were visible on her jacket.

He watched in amazement. Air France had Christian Lacroix designs and Virgin Atlantic had Vivien Westwood. What was this?

Professor Frank suddenly appeared at his side while he picked up his scanned case and jacket. "Dr Aziz. Good to see you. I thought I would meet you here as it is initially rather overwhelming."

Abdul smiled gratefully. "Thank you, Professor Frank. I was not sure what country I was in. I used to be a Senior Registrar here."

Professor Frank nodded. "Just your guest badge now and a sign-in."

Abdul realised the sign-in form was a single piece of paper to avoid breaching confidentiality. "So, they have to put the names together?"

"It is already on the computer."

Once this was completed, Professor Frank smiled. "Now I can take you to my unit."

They walked towards large glass doors that opened automatically when approached. As soon as he walked in through them, the glass doors on the other side opened. And suddenly a world of carpet greeted him. Dark-blue, thick, and velvety pile; there were almost acres of it.

He had never seen so much. A handful of people were walking across it in different directions. Some were talking to each other, but he could not hear any sound. Was this some new technology for aural privacy? There were huge plasma screens on the old grand wood-panelled walls with directions to rooms and times. But they were numbers and not names. Through the floor-to-ceiling windows could be seen a tasteful Japanese garden with water features in view. It had the illusion of being outside but it was internal; the wall surrounding them was the original inside wall. There was no real outside.

Abdul repeated to himself like a mantra—be true, do the best you can—be professional—as he followed Professor Frank in and out of several large glass doors that he thought were rooms but were lifts and into what he thought was a lift, which was a room.

He had heard that the outside of the Centre (the magnificent old house originally built by Lord Buxton Castellane) was an exoskeleton in which everything inside was transformed. But this was an Escher painting in actuality. He had no idea what floor he was on or what direction he faced.

The room looked small upon entrance: dark-blue velvety carpet, a chrome desk, and four comfy armchairs in the same dark-blue colour. Professor Frank gestured for him to sit, while picking up a remote and clicking it, causing an apparent wall to rise up into the ceiling and doubling the size of the room. Dr Aziz breathed a sigh of relief seeing a familiar assessment scene with a doll's house and children's toys on shelves, as well as games and jars of toy animals. Psychiatrists who worked with children and adults often had the best facilities for people with severe or profound intellectual disabilities: those who needed to express themselves physically.

Another click and the room expanded on the other side, or appeared to, as suddenly there was a view of a Japanese garden outside the room. He realised it was impossible to tell what floor he was on with the "outside view" on the same level as the inside.

Another click produced lights and the heading "assessment."

A sharp-faced woman in the ubiquitous uniform of either blue or green smiled formally. "What would you like to drink, Dr Aziz?" She turned to Professor Frank. "Your usual hot chocolate, Professor?" Professor Frank patted his flat stomach ruefully.

"This is my daily indulgence, Dr Aziz."

"I will have the same then, sir," smiled Abdul.

The woman left the room. Dr Aziz did not know how to refer to her. She was like an air stewardess, but without the courtesy he experienced on British Airways.

"Excuse the question, Professor Frank, but what is it like working in this environment? How do clients find it? The nature of the receptionists?"

"Like you, Dr Aziz, I am committed to my work and where I do it is less important to me than the fact of it being housed and who will provide me with the tools I need."

"You said that in Delhi, Professor Frank, five years ago, and I believe it encouraged me to come to the UK."

The uniformed assistant returned with two hot chocolates and a plate of muffins, and warm chocolate cookies. "Enjoy," she said with a small smile.

"Thank you," said Abdul.

Professor Frank nodded appreciatively as she left, and the smile remained on his face as he looked at Dr Aziz. "You gave me a good platform for my work on memory, Dr Aziz, away from the unscientific heat of the issue here, and in the USA."

"India is an old country, Professor Frank—perhaps that allows for a broader view of these things! In six months an update is being planned. You will be receiving a letter."

"Is Professor Sharma going to be involved?"

"Yes. My mentor."

"Then I will be delighted; date dependent." He put his mug down.

"And now, before Lady Rose joins us, I have a range of options for a differential diagnosis." A click on his remote.

CHAPTER 27

Friday, December 28th 2012, USA

CNN reported it first, and the world's media followed. Danny Delta had been found dead in his dressing room shortly before a major sell-out Vegas concert. Over 110 million certified unit sales. His Christmas album *You Come Back* was already platinum and every announcement of his death included a track.

Hysterical grieving fans brought photos and flowers, transforming the area outside his exclusive mansion in the golden triangle of Connecticut. The album cover of Danny's face with his right eye framed between his hands like the pyramid above the dollar bill went viral.

```
"Danny Dollar rises again!"

                    "No comeback for the comeback kid"

"Golden voice lives again"

                              "Danny Druggo"

"Danny Draggo, LGBT hero"

                    "Golden voice and dark rumours"
```

"Delta of dollars"

        "Abuse victim speaks out"

"Dirty dollars"

        "Cashing in on the dead"

The internet was swamped with conspiracies.

        "Danny Dollar Illuminati victim"

"Delta was a programmed assassin for the CIA"

        "Danny and I were abused in mind control ring"

"What do Madonna, Britney, and Danny Delta have in
common?"

        "Who did Danny's last album cover?"

"British Deputy Prime Minister's lover photographed
Delta's album"

        "Why does the dollar have a pyramid on it?"

"Danny Delta, the President of the United States, the
British Deputy Prime Minister, the Glendale brothers…

        "Say O for Orpheus"

CHAPTER 28

Friday, December 28th 2012, 10:30am

Lord Glendale: a phone call to HRH Prince Carl-Zygmunt

"Ian is in Washington?"
"Yes."
"Better not visit Harold."
"Agreed."

CHAPTER 29

Friday, December 28th 2012, 11:30am, Westminster Square

The Redcliffe residence

Lady Lily looked at the email, which was also copied in to her husband and to Professor Frank. "Oh, very careful," she mocked, "only sent to everyone! Why not send it to Sir Gawain? Why not Uncle Tom Cobley and all making sure the parents are involved when this fucking mother does not want to know anything."

"Did you call, my lady?" asked Maria knocking on the half-open door.

"No Maria. I was just cursing. As you know."

"Anything I can do? A cup of tea?"

"No. Tea can't help with a problem like Rose."

"The assessment?"

"No point holding it back! You hear everything anyway."

"If it affects you, my lady, I always try and listen."

"I know. Thank you, Maria."

Lady Lily gave a wan smile and paced up and down in her silk kimono. "I'm sorry. I just want this to end. Twenty-one years and it never ends. Now the assessment. Another assessment. My whole life with her has been an assessment. Chris is there doing it too—so we will hear quickly. But that doesn't stop it from happening. I just don't want to have to think about it anymore ... I am fed up with everything."

As Maria walked in towards her, Lady Lily burst into tears. This uncharacteristic response did not shock Maria as it may have anyone else. Maria knew how to respond in these moments: she led Lady Lily over to the blue velvet sofa and held her softly in her embrace.

"It has been an awful year for you, my lady. Your father and his new baby, so disloyal, so besotted. Sir Peter and his job taking up your energy. All your political dinners to help him, your mother and mother-in-law, and that's all before we get to Lady Rose. What relaxation have you had? Not enough. Who looks after you?" The women leant towards each other, their heads lightly touching.

CHAPTER 30

Friday, December 28th 2012, 11:45am, The Lord Glendale Centre

The assistant returned. "Lady Rose Redcliffe has arrived," she announced with crisp efficiency.

She was like a radio announcer, thought Dr Aziz.

"She is with a family friend, Mona Lasky, who has accompanied her from Harvest House, and we also have Ms Tracey O'Bridey, who was on duty when the last incident occurred."

"Thank you," said Professor Frank. "We will speak to Lady Rose first. If you bring her and Ms Lasky in, and ask Ms O'Bridey to wait, please."

Dr Aziz leant forward. "Ms O'Bridey works on night duty."

"Ah. Her sleep, Dr Aziz. I see what you mean. Let us see her first."

The assistant left the room and Professor Frank pointed his remote, closing half the space. A bewildered Tracey entered and was ushered onto an armchair.

"A drink, Ms O'Bridey?"

"Bloody hell! I need a whisky coming through this building. Excuse my language."

Dr Aziz hid a smile.

"Seriously though. This place is like some Sci-Fi horror film."

"Tea or coffee, Madam?" asked the assistant.

"Coffee—black and strong—and I am Miss, not Madam or Ms or Trace."

The assistant nodded with no change of expression and left.

Professor Frank impassively turned his attention to Tracey. "Thank you for coming, Miss O'Bridey. We know you need to get home to sleep after a very heavy night duty, and we would be grateful to hear your recollections. Please say anything that you remember, however minor it appears to you, as it could be extremely helpful. It would allow us to understand better if we do not have to write down what you say but record it. Here is a permission slip."

She looked worriedly at both Dr Aziz and Professor Frank. "I won't get into trouble for my language?"

"I give you my word," said Professor Frank.

"You are helping us," assured Dr Aziz.

With great concentration, Tracey wrote her signature. The assistant, returning with coffee and biscuits, collected the signed form from Tracey. Professor Frank turned the recording on. "This is Professor Frank and Dr Aziz with Ms Tracey O'Bridey at 12pm on Friday 28th December; the interview is taking place in my office at the Lord Glendale Centre. Ms O'Bridey has given her permission for this recording."

"Well," began Tracey, "Mrs Ransome wanted to make sure I had checked on Rosie."

"You mean Lady Rose Redcliffe?" checked Frank.

"Well, there aren't two of them," laughed Tracey. There was a small pause before she realised his meaning. "Oh, I see what you mean. Her last name. She is the only Rose/Rosie in the unit." She smiled infectiously. "It's because I did *Under Milk Wood* at school and there's 'knock three times and ask for Rosie.'"

Both men looked confused.

"It was Mr Masters: he said she would calm down if I knocked three times on the door and said her name three times. You see there were terrible moans and everything coming from her door. Mr Masters said it was a flashback, and then I realised that was what my brother got from when he was in Afghanistan—he thinks he is there and goes mad for a bit and then he realises he is safe. Too much for me to live with. And Mr Masters said if I did that—knocked three times and said her name three times—she would calm down, and I did it, and she did— calm down. And she repeated what he said. And he asked if she had heard me properly and was out of it and she said 'hear Master,' and I thought that was funny because his name is Masters, not Master, and it sounded like she was calling him her Master, and we all thought she was fine and left the room and then there were horrible noises like she was being murdered by a wild animal, and I rushed in and—this sounds mad—it wasn't her—Lady Rose—it was like there was a demon in her bed, and I thought he must have killed her. But Mr Masters calmed "it" down and she returned. Like a horror film. Like a devil. Never seen anything like it. When Alf—my brother—is back in the war in one of those flashbacks, it is still him. He looks the same, however scared shitless he is. But she wasn't herself. It wasn't her. I wanted a priest. I think she is possessed. Not bonkers. I can recognise that. My uncle on my dad's side—Albert—had schizophrenia, but he didn't change like this. I am frightened. I am frightened of seeing her tonight."

She suddenly stopped her flow of words and burst into tears.

Professor Frank froze in his chair.

Dr Aziz pulled his chair next to her and held his hand out. She seized it and burst into louder tears while he put an arm around her. "Tracey, you have done well. It was a horrid sight. Really frightening and Professor Frank and I will sort it out."

Her crying subsided and he gently removed his arm. "I think it will help you if you can go back to H after a good sleep, but I will tell Mr Masters you can stay in the staffroom. Would you agree, Professor Frank, that it is better for Tracey to go back to work so as not to develop a phobia about it?"

He took care to look Professor Frank in the face, to include him.

Professor Frank nodded briskly. "I agree with Dr Aziz, Tracey. My assistant will call a cab to take you home." He recovered his equanimity. "You have done really well and have been extremely helpful. We will tell Mrs Ransome."

Tracey sat up energetically. What resilience she had! "Thank you. Thank you," she said, wiping her eyes vigorously. Smiling, she followed the assistant out.

Dr Aziz and Professor Frank both took a deep breath.

"Healthcare should be a graduate profession," said Professor Frank seriously.

"It is a sign of how little we care about mental health that we give the least educated the most onerous hours and duties," said Dr Aziz gently.

"But many of the most educated would have felt like Tracey even if they didn't express it the same way," he added.

"You are saying in your polite way that I am a snob?" asked Professor Frank with a genuine smile. "I think my post here allows me to stand up for excellence for the first time in my clinical life."

Dr Aziz compared the brisk air-stewardesses against the warmth of Deirdre, Sarah, or even Tracey. Additionally, after all the research on the importance of consistency in clinical settings, whether psychological or medical, why was it a different person each time? How was it that the most esteemed academic researchers seemed to ignore attachment research?

"It is a big responsibility, Professor, as well as a pleasure," he replied.

"I am glad you realised, Aziz," he smiled.

Abdul noted the public school way of addressing him by surname as a sign of favour and nodded.

"Dr Aziz," said Professor Frank formally, "before we invite Lady Rose in, I need to check out a few things with my assistant, and I am sure you could do with ten minutes for any calls or notes. The guest computer is there with your name already on it and the password 'Harvest.' Pick up the phone and dial 3, and you will have an outside line."

Abdul smiled to himself. The moment of intimacy had gone. A suspicion entered his mind. Would his notes be copied? Would his call be monitored? Following that chain of thought, he stood up and walked towards the glass wall through which he could view the Japanese garden. The "windows" opened, and he was out in cooler air. Looking up, he could see what looked like a piece of high ceiling open to the outside air. What a convoluted place it was.

He watched water pouring out of a carved stone dragon's mouth and making rivulets on the surrounding rocks and elegant plants. A little bridge crossed a long pond filled with lilies. He bent closer. Yes, they were real. The deepest part of the pond showed flashes of gold. Surely not! But yes, graceful koi moved through the quiet waters. He stood watching the flashes of gold.

"Aha! It is good, is it not!" said Professor Frank, causing him to jump. "So, you like our garden!" smiled Professor Frank.

"It is beautiful. I hope it is alright. I just walked to the wall."

"It is part of the perfection that is intended, Aziz. Sensory motor screens that anticipate actions, nature itself aiding optimum thought, encouragement to move from a sedentary position."

103

"I wish Harvest had such facilities," said Abdul bluntly. He quickly corrected his indiscretion. "I assume the project's success is being evaluated for application elsewhere."

"Indeed. I have had the luxury of seeing the architects for Google, Invention Design Gallery, and Nokia. They flew me to all those places. It has been unforgettable. The impact of architecture on the working environment has not been adequately studied."

For a moment, his face was transformed, and Abdul saw the schoolboy longing underneath the cold exterior.

"Well, I will not forget this trip," said Abdul warmly.

A different assistant came in. Same clothes but with a different face. He could not keep up. Where was the perfection in this? Where was the understanding of the need for a secure attachment figure? If he felt such a loss, what about the patients?

"Lady Rose Redcliffe with Ms Mona Lasky." With a click of the remote and the warm assessment space opened. Dr Aziz was getting the sense of this.

But to his surprise in walked Lady Rose, alone.

"Chris," called Lady Rose excitedly. "Chris! Good friend!"

Of course! He was a family friend.

"Rose," called Frank with a warmth Abdul had not seen in him before.

Abdul looked closely at the young woman, eliciting this unusual warmth. He had never seen Rose before.

CHAPTER 31

Friday, December 28th 2012, 1pm, The Lord Glendale Centre

Lady Rose had short-cropped golden hair, which was cut in a way which Abdul was sure his wife would call an elfin cut. What stood out were her sparkling deep blue eyes. He felt she was significantly overweight and dressed rather inappropriately, in clothes that would suit a middle-aged woman rather than a 21-year-old. It was a tragically familiar sight. Was it due to her mother? Frumpish dressing in women with a learning disability was, in his experience, due to the protective longing of mothers. They wanted to protect their daughters from sexual rejection and pain, yet unknowingly made it worse.

"You give me hot chocolate, Chris?" she asked.

"Of course," he replied and nodded at the assistant, who swiftly left. A Stepford Wives type of assistant thought Abdul; that was what Chris and his staff reminded him of.

"You got toys and dolls house out again, Chris. Rose is grown up. Good Rose, Good Lady!"

"Again?" Abdul thought.

"You are a Good Rose," said Chris warmly.

An assistant returned with a mug of chocolate and Rose sipped it with gusto.

"Told Mona to wait. Rose grown up," said Rose. "She come back when Rose finished."

Abdul listened carefully. He could hear her class-based sense of authority in how she had told Mona to wait. Professor Frank then introduced her to him, and he said "Pleased to meet you, Lady Rose."

"Not Master?" she asked.

"Master? Do you mean Mr Lew Masters?" he asked.

Rose shuddered. "Good Rose," she said. "Stay quiet. Bang, bang, bang." Her voice started to get louder.

"It's alright, Rose," said Professor Frank softly. He turned to Aziz. "I think mentioning his name could have brought back the traumatic memory."

"Possibly," said Abdul diplomatically.

He was reminded of Tracey's evidence of "Hear Master" and the meaning of the word, let alone the apparent repetition of her name three times like a hypnotic injunction, but there was not enough evidence to broach it with Frank. It would have been so good to speak to Gawain right now.

"It is not alright, Chris," said Rose loudly. "Good Rose gone. Day gone. What this shit?" she asked, pointing to her hot chocolate. "Shit drink."

Chris Frank, surprised, turned to look at Abdul when there was a loud crash as Lady Rose threw the mug with its remaining chocolate at the wall.

"Rose back. Good Rose. Don't be cross, Chris. Don't want the Master hurting me. Bang, bang on my brain. Take my brains out."

For a moment, Prof Frank was speechless.

"You are a Good Rose," said Abdul, "and the Master won't hurt you."

Rose took a deep sigh of relief and then her face contorted. "Stupid mongol girl. Stupid Chris. Master can do what he wants. I am Master. Day gone. Shut up Frank. Ian Anderson put willie in Rose bottom. With Danny Delta. America. Vegas. So fucking what! But Master says no more brain bangs here."

Professor Frank said, "Poor Lily." He pressed a button, and the last assistant returned and mopped up the mess very swiftly and quietly. Professor Frank held his head in his hands.

Abdul did not know the best way to proceed. Professor Frank was behaving like the family friend he was and not the professional. This was a serious conflict of interest. "Sir," he said gently. "You have had a

106

friendship shock. Would you like me to proceed—or with a colleague of yours!" he added diplomatically.

To Rose he said gently, "I apologise. We made a mistake. No more brain bangs."

As Professor Frank removed his hands from his head, Rose's affect altered. The angry masculine expression disappeared, and the "smiling" appeasing face of Down's Syndrome reappeared. That never failed to concern him. The emotional experience of looking different caused that apologetic appeasing smile and with it, he considered, split-off anger.

"Good Rose back. Master gone. Sorry Chris. Sorry new man Aziz. Good Rose here."

"Well done, Good Rose," said Abdul.

To his surprise, Professor Frank stood up suddenly and walked out of the room.

"Sorry, Rose—Aziz—please carry on," he barked. He walked out of the room or rather disappeared behind a changing wall or window. This was like some Harry Potter experience. Indeed, the walls were rather like the different states of Rose's mind.

Or indeed Chris Frank's.

He could not cancel the meeting and leave Lady Rose with a double rejection and nor did he feel comfortable carrying out formal tests on his own when the political consequences could be so dangerous.

"Why you sad new man? Has Master got you in trouble?"

Abdul was shocked at her emotional intelligence. Whatever limits there were on her educational capacity, she was emotionally in touch. Poor Rose, perhaps she had to be so aware for survival. People with learning disabilities had a radar for being unwanted and rejected.

"You are a very clever person, Lady Rose. You are right. I did feel a little bit in trouble but not because of you. It is because ..."

"You think Professor is big man and you are little, but he is friend: Chris. He will come back. Glendale bigger than him and bad man Ian Anderson and Danny Delta, but Chris is my friend. Nice man. Danny bad but can't help it. He does what he is told. Bad Danny. Good Danny. Eats funny sweets."

Abdul was feeling more and more concerned. There was no overt psychosis in her language, and she was very clear on hierarchy. Yes, she had dysregulated moments, but that was minor. This was going to be a political nightmare for the new unit. Was it possible as a reality? He could not even go there.

CHAPTER 32

Friday, December 28th 2012, 1:15pm, The Lord Glendale Centre

"Lily," said Chris urgently, when she picked up the phone.

"Oh, my poor Lily. It is worse than I expected. No wonder you have had such problems."

"You are frightening me, Chris. What is it?"

"What you said. She is talking about Ian Anderson, electric shocks, Danny Delta."

"We know that," said Lily curtly.

"The only question," she continued, is what we do with it. The opening is in a week, and if she talks like this to the press ... God knows what it will do to Ian and Peter."

"You amaze me, Lily. If only you were Prime Minister ..."

Lily's voice softened. "You are an old softy, Chris. Who would believe it! Now. Where is she now?"

"With Dr Aziz. He is an honourable man."

"Well, get back, or he will be reporting a conflict of interest."

"You have missed your vocation, Lily. Will you tell Peter or Glendale?"

"They are not bothered. Peter had to be calmed. But this was already expected. What we need to plan for is what diagnosis is given and what treatment occurs as well as the press interest next week. Now go back.

Right now. Aziz does some short treatments, but he also works at the SJTU, and we know what happens there."

"I do. I will. I will contact you later."

"Only if there is anything different to report," said Lady Lily authoritatively.

"Yes, Lily."

"So cool and beautiful," he thought, "but so cold if you did not really know her."

Sir Peter did not know how lucky he was.

CHAPTER 33

Friday, December 28th 2012, 1:30pm, The Lord Glendale Centre

"How old are you, Rose? May I call you Rose, or Lady Rose?"
The deep blue eyes sparkled at him.
"And you? Aziz—Dr Aziz?"
They both laughed.

"My name is Dr Abdul Aziz, and you can call me Abdul or Dr Aziz."
She giggled. "Abdul."

"Okay, you have decided, and so I am Abdul, and you are Rose. Where do you live, Rose?"

A cloud covered those blue eyes. "Mummy doesn't want her living with her. Wants her in Cell Block H. That is a telly programme, but the name of where we live."

He carefully noted the way she spoke of herself in the third person. Was this a transitional dissociative position as a defence against rejection from her mother?

"How do you feel about that Rose: not living with mummy and living in Cell Block H?"

A beautiful smile crossed her face; she would have been so beautiful. No, correction: she was so beautiful. "I am grown up, Abdul, so don't live with mummy, even though daddy would like me to. More grown up next week when I am 21, so new home with nicer furniture."

My God! What a diplomat. She really was a politician's daughter. Look how she dealt with his careful question about her mother. Keep going, Abdul; he was enjoying himself. Although Frank could be listening behind a wall. Anyone could.

"New furniture?" he asked.

"Yes. New bed and bedspread and wallpaper and carpet and beautiful soft new towels."

Frank silently slipped back into the room while she enumerated, smilingly, what would be in her new room.

"Hello friend Chris. Telling new doctor man called Abdul about new room. Did you call mummy?"

Abdul watched as Frank blushed, an unexpected sight in such a man.

"Well yes, Rose, I had promised I would," he replied jerkily.

Abdul was impressed by his truthfulness and transparency,

"I have had a really enjoyable conversation with Lady Rose—who wishes me to call her Rose."

"And Rose may call you Abdul?"

"Yes. Rose and I agreed to speak in first names."

Aziz turned to face Frank directly. "It is lovely to hear how Rose welcomes her move to the new unit," he said pointedly.

Professor Frank understood the message. "Thank you, Dr Aziz. Thank you, Rose; I apologise that I needed to leave before. There was a lot for me to think about."

"Of course," said Dr Aziz warmly. "She is a family friend too. Perhaps we should do the testing on Monday."

"She has already been here quite a while. I did not feel it appropriate to go ahead without you present, but I could see she is regulated again. Whatever our final diagnosis, perhaps we can agree that whatever volatile state she can engage in, she is able to regulate herself."

Professor Frank nodded formally. "I am in your debt, Dr Aziz. What time is convenient for you?"

"Same time Monday?"

"Definitely."

Professor Frank turned to Rose, who had been studying their faces carefully.

"You have been very patient, Rose."

"Good Rose," she smiled. "Chris is friend. Mummy will be pleased with Rose."

"Yes, Rose. Everyone is pleased with you," said Abdul.

"Can we meet again Monday, December 31st, at the same time?" asked Professor Frank.

"At 11.30am," emphasised Abdul.

"Call Mona," said Lady Rose. "We go now." She stood up with dignity in her frumpy clothes.

"Yes, Lady Rose," said Professor Frank pressing the button for his assistant.

CHAPTER 34

Saturday, December 29th 2012, USA

Major D's residence

Danny Delta's last song echoed around the large beach-facing room: an estuary where the ocean meets the river. How he had loved it.

It is never too late,
To illuminate.

What a fool! How could he do it? Why didn't someone in the Society stop him? Or did someone higher up intervene? Too much of the white stuff? A lack of balance in the system? Too many giveaways in the song? To lose it so close. Oh, Danny Boy and the harp sound...

CHAPTER 35

Saturday, December 29th 2012

Lana Lorson's internet blog

Internet sites are buzzing over the possible meaning of Danny Delta's last song. Conspiracy theorists point to the alleged secret society known as the Illuminati, suggesting that Danny could have come from one of the 13 bloodlines.

Adam Weishaupt (1748–1830) was the founder of the Bavarian Illuminati, which was a secular secret society, a product of the enlightenment. It was founded on May 1st, 1776, with the aim of fighting superstition and religious influence in public. Charles Theodore outlawed the Illuminati—along with Freemasonry and other secret societies—with the help of the Roman Catholic Church.

Many groups have claimed to be descendants of the original "enlightened ones," but this has not been formally validated. More recently, the term has been linked by conspiracy theorists as being part of the alleged New World Order, a combination of powerful figures from banking, the arts, politics, and the aristocracy. The 13 bloodlines go way back in history before the Bavarian Illuminati.

Harp music in Danny Delta's last album is said to link to the contro-
versial HAARP project. The lyrics in Danny Delta's last song are said to
explain the cause of his death. Survivors say he was an Illuminati slave
speaking out about the HAARP project and the deliberate creation of mul-
tiple personalities. Did Danny Delta take an overdose, or was he mur-
dered? Friends say he was at the height of his powers and not depressed.

This is not new.

A Master of Lyrics

Friends and musicians worldwide applauded the lyrics and music of Danny
Delta's last song, When You Come Back.

When you come back
When you come back
Where the water meets itself
Where my hands frame the eye
Where the stars go to die
Speak the truth and never lie
Broken into myriad pieces
Each separate part
A life releases
In this celestial
Helter skelter
Am I Omega am I Delta?
Fight the heavy hand of fate

It is never too late,
To illuminate.

CNN News

In a year noticeable for the loss of major music celebrities, Danny Delta's
death at the age of only 45 on Friday, December 28th, has caused huge
reverberations around the world. He was found dead in his dressing room
shortly before a major sell-out concert in Las Vegas. It is not yet confirmed
whether he suffered a major heart attack or problems from a drug overdose.
Family and friends say there were no signs of the depression that dogged

his 30s and led to periods of rehab for drug abuse. His younger brother, the reclusive writer-singer Byron Santos could not be contacted.

Message in a Bottle: Cassandra's blog

We know what happens to truth-tellers and seers and the level of societal denial that leads to shooting the messenger. You won't listen, or you won't hear, but this is from me on 28th December 2012.

Danny Delta's last album cover is pure Illuminati, and the covered eye was the work of famous photographer Stefan Solag who has been having an affair with UK Deputy Prime Minister Ian Anderson. Ian Anderson is close friends with Lord Glendale, whose brother Harold Fitz-Hugh West was implicated in accusations of child abuse in the Washington Children's Home he endowed. Lord Glendale, a billionaire philanthropist, has given millions to a formerly rundown hospital, St Joseph's, to make it first of all a university hospital and now, with the "all -singing all -dancing" Lord Glendale Centre and Foundation, the most funded research centre in the UK. Pride of place has been given to Academic Director Professor Christopher Frank, who specialises in false memory in abuse accusations and the LGBT Research unit—the Equipa Centre. Is there a connection?

Danny Delta is also a friend of Lord Glendale, who attended all his concerts when in the USA. I have attached photographs of Glendale, Ian Anderson, and Danny Delta from last year. Proximity does not mean anything more than just that—but worth considering when linked with everything else.

I will be back.

Laconic Lawyer: anti-conspiracy theory blog

Here we go again. All the conspiracy theory UFO abductees are at it again—and the MK-Ultra, Monarch, and Ickean serpents.

Poor Danny Delta! Anything else people want to accuse him of now he is dead? It will be abuse allegations, I predict, with the fortune he will leave behind. What about Dr Green and Mengele –and all the Illuminati crowds?

CHAPTER 36

Saturday, December 29th 2012, 9pm, Brixton

Elouise and Dan were settling down for a late meal. Her choice. His cooking. The children were all asleep. Typical moment for the phone to go.

"Don't answer," said Dan. "The kids are all asleep and it will wait." He smiled at her worried expression. "Okay, someone else is in danger! You are not going to relax until you have answered."

With a smile, she moved towards the phone when the ringing stopped. She stopped, confused, and then came the ping of a received message. "It's from Pam," she said. Pam was an old friend who managed a Rape Crisis Unit. "She has attached something from the internet that she thought might be of interest." She scanned the message quickly and then passed it to Dan.

Message in a Bottle

We know what happens to truth-tellers and seers and the level of societal denial that leads to shooting the messenger.

You won't listen, or you won't hear, but this is from me on 28th Dec.

Danny Delta's last album cover is pure Illuminati, and the covered eye was the work of famous photographer Fernando who has been having an affair with UK Deputy Prime Minister Anderson. Ian Anderson is close friends with Lord Glendale, whose brother, Harold Fitz-Hugh West, was implicated in accusations of child abuse in the Washington Children's Home he endowed. Lord Glendale has given millions to a formerly run-down hospital St Joseph's, to make it first of all a university hospital, and now with all the all-singing, all-dancing Lord Glendale Centre and Foundation, the most funded research centre in the UK. Pride of place has been given to Academic Director Professor Christopher Frank, who specialises in false memory in abuse accusations. Is there a connection?

The email went onto another page.

His smile slowly faded. "Usual conspiracy mixture of disinformation, some worrying potential facts and rubbish."

"That's the problem with this work," agreed Elouise. "Reminds me of that awful ritualistic abuse case I had."

"As if I could ever forget. And your first DID one too," said Dan with a worried frown. "And that was before I saw one too."

"Yes," smiled Elouise, "You cost the SJTU money because you weren't au fait with it yet! I needed Dr Kestle in the States for that one. Awful. This does have similarities. I'll text it to Jon, Gawain, and Abdul. Poor Abdul will have assessed someone at the Glendale today."

"Before or after supper?" asked Dan, raising an eyebrow. She hugged him and sent the texts.

"There we are, I'm ready for my personal chef to serve me." She sat at the table where Dan had placed candles and a small vase of flowers.

Mattie, she thought. *Little Mattie...and Little A...a shrine for a murdered childhood.*

And then a cry could be heard coming from Denzel's bedroom. And then the phone rang again.

CHAPTER 37

Saturday, December 29th 2012, 8pm GMT, Quebec

Moira was cooking her special lamb and leek pie with honeyed parsnips, ready for the evening meal. She had already made her Scottish shortbread. Gawain could not remember how he had got there. It had been a six-hour evening flight, and Quebec time was five hours earlier than the UK...He had no idea...he always felt like he suffered existential confusion rather than jet lag. Moira assured him he had told her he slept on the plane.

His mind was full of baby Jamie, who had slept in his arms just hours ago. A bonny wee chappie with auburn tufts and grey-blue eyes, he was fast asleep in a tartan Babygro in a carved pine crib at the foot of his parents' bed. Snuggled on the bed were Martine and James curled up asleep, also in matching tartan pyjamas. The smell of newborn babies wafted through the warm repainted house. Everything was clean and bright.

Gawain and Moira were in the large open-plan kitchen and family room. All wood and tartan. How beautiful a family room was when it was a family you wanted to be with. Gawain found himself drifting off.

"We are too old for this travelling; rather, I am," said Gawain.

"No, we're not!" said Moira emphatically.

Giving him a hug, she steered him to a wooden rocking chair plumped up with pillows and a rug. It sat alongside a wooden hanging chair that she had reserved for herself! She had enjoyed one like that in the 1960s—but made of wicker.

"Now you sleep...," she said, kissing his forehead and tucking the rug around him. She put his mobile on the coffee table beside him. She knew better than to take it further away. Her joy kept her awake, she thought. She was a grandma! Jamie's grandma!

With the pie in the oven and the biscuits cooling, she could have a little nap of her own. Tiptoeing past her snoring husband, she lifted herself elegantly into the wooden hanging chair. Like being a baby, she thought, in a warm wooden womb.

For a while, the whole Stuart household was peacefully asleep. Three generations of breath.

A ping on his mobile woke Gawain up first. Elouise...she would not have bothered him without it being something serious.

"Sorry to interrupt. A friend from Rape Crisis sent me something from the internet. I have attached it in an email. It makes those complications you mentioned extremely real."

"Don't think I can't hear what you are doing, Grandpa," sang Moira gaily from her cocoon. Stretching languidly, she slid out of the chair, stroking his head on her way back to the kitchen. "It is your bread and butter, just as this is mine. You might as well answer it before the little Jamie wakes up."

She giggled. How he loved her.

The email attachment was problematic. Some of it was clearly factual. A significant group of powerful people knew each other and met. Being friends or acquaintances did not incriminate someone. Yet Sir Peter had been so clear, adamant about his daughter's ability to distinguish truth from fantasy. Before his wife and close colleagues had urged him to rethink what happened next, he himself, as a man of influence close to those named people, even friends with them, could still consider Rose's testimony was correct. He was a good Minister of Health. He was a good and loving father. This was going to be complex. Poor Rose. And Abdul was put in the middle of it all. He would not tell Elouise yet that he had read Cassandra's blogs before and found them disturbing. But she needed support.

He texted Elouise back. It did not matter what time zone the UK was in. He had given up working such things out. It would be on silent

120

if she was sleeping, and if it wasn't, she shouldn't have texted him then! They were later, weren't they? "Many thanks-lots for us to consider. Confidentiality is extremely important. Will text Abdul. Will think whether to phone or email."

He could not resist a final internet search. *Sandra Harrison, Cassandra, Presidential slaves . . .*

Poor Cassandra, he mused. The prophetess of Greek legend could see the truth, and this Cassandra sounded as if she had gone through hell, but that did not make her perception of the world necessarily the truth. Such pain is everywhere. Extreme abuse is so ignored and disavowed, especially when it involves bizarre beliefs. And running through all of this appeared to be an issue of dissociation . . . and dissociation of an extreme kind, the installed kind.

And then from the lungs of the youngest Stuart came a cry more powerful than any alarm. It summoned four smiling adults within seconds. "He's awake. Our Jamie's awake," smiled Gawain.

CHAPTER 38

Saturday, 29th December 2012, 8.30pm, Highgate

Dr Aziz's residence

Abdul received the text from Elouise just after his family dinner. His children were asleep, and his tired parents were snoozing in their armchairs, watching the news. Mina was clearing up in the kitchen.

The surreal experience of having to focus on Lady Rose while he was in the midst of his own peaceful family was dislocating him. Old phantoms from India in terms of Hindu and Muslim riots were in danger of appearing; was it dislocation or was it his unconscious leading him to what needed to be returned to? Everything was spinning in his head. He sought the image of the golden koi passing through the tranquil waters to calm himself, as he walked into his study.

"It was really hard for you today," said Mina bringing him a cup of coffee.

"Thank you, my love," he said, toasting her with the cup. "I am sorry. I have not been much of anything this evening."

"No," she said. "Your head and heart are full. Can you speak about it?"

Mina was a physiotherapist who understood the connections between body and mind. "Not yet. I am trying to keep it out of the house. But thank you. It may come to that."

"Call me if you want to talk," she said, leaving the room.

This was what a home was. When people went into another room, it did not mean rejection or separation. You carried your object constancy and attachment with you. The Glendale was not a home. It was a military base, an airport, and a security-centred unit, but without any emotional security. To have so much funding and staffing but no consistent or friendly staff. The staff were all competent but not emotionally engaged. And Chris Frank was a mess, an honourable but disturbed mess. It was not ethical for him to be involved in this way. He was in thrall to Lady Lily. An affair? He did not think so. But there was something powerful afoot.

And Lady Rose! What beautiful understanding she had. He did not consider this could be possession or schizophrenia or psychosis, or a gender dysphoria, although he wished it was. He considered it could obviously be a dissociative disorder. This would mean that the poor attachment between Rose and her mother made her more vulnerable to abuse, which was already proven: bullying in primary school and a rape by a minicab driver. How sad it was that the period where young parents were most vulnerable could lay down the attachment patterns of their child for the future. A disorganised attachment was a prerequisite for dissociative identity disorder.

Could Lew Masters be an abuser too? Why did he knock three times and call her name? Some crude hypnotic injunction maybe? But why and for whom, and was it connected? Could there be two interconnected abuse rings?

The key clarity of the disclosure involved Ian Anderson and Danny Delta. If they were not involved, the path would be so much easier, but her clinical needs and rights came first. He would speak to Dr Stuart first and then go to safeguarding and the Medical Director at the Glendale, who was of course Professor Chris Frank. And that had to be changed first. He would suggest an independent on-site expert like Professor Hamilton. The decision made him feel lighter and he returned to the lounge. He was not the police or social services. He knew what his task was.

CHAPTER 39

Saturday, December 29th 2012, 8pm, Manchester

Jon received the message with a worried sigh. He was in Manchester staying in his mother's flat; he was just at the point where he wondered why he wasn't staying in a hotel instead. Especially at a time when his analyst was on his regular two-week Christmas break and there was no one to share his worries with.

As his mum was always keen to emphasise, his room, which was also the guest room, had all the comfort of a hotel room. There was a television, desk, Wi-Fi, ensuite wet room, and a large fluffy towel. There was also, as she joked, a 24-hour chef and receptionist: herself.

However, that was part of the problem. Since his father's death ten years ago, his bereft mother, Sylvie, had tried to narrow her considerable focus onto her only child. She had been on a mission to have him married. More importantly, she wanted him married with a child and not spending his time and money on this so-called training.

He had not found a way, despite his daily psychoanalysis, to check her loving but intrusive harassment. He knew it came from fear. There was her fear of his health, the hours he worked, the expense of his training, the single-mindedness. And he knew where her fear came from—her own experience of losing her husband to overwork and, further back, her mother's experience of the camps.

"Work?" she asked, hearing the ping of his iPad. He nodded. Why hadn't he put it on silent? But pretending was no use. It just led to her mantra on the nice girls she could find for him. And pretending was not right. Instead, he got the other mantra.

"Work killed your father. It followed him everywhere."

She repeated this in a way he found unbearable. Her husband, his loving but ineffectual father, Maurice, had been a hardworking furniture salesman doomed to failure. Unerringly finding a boss as familiar and exploitative as his father had eroded his time and health. Sylvie could do nothing to alter this—even when she successfully became manager of a local women's dress shop. This brought in regular money and a smile to her face, but it did not ease the anxiety or feeling of failure that followed Maurice like a personal rain cloud. But neither when he was alive, nor since his death, could Sylvie bear her bright son's understanding, when applied to Maurice.

Living and training in London had at least allowed him some respite from that. His personal analysis gave him the space to understand himself and his family more.

He read Elouise's communication with concern. After what Gawain had said, this situation looked dangerously close to the SJTU. If Lady Rose received therapy at their unit, then there would be serious confidentiality problems. To have a Minister of Health look at reports was complex enough to consider, let alone the fact that Sir Peter and his wife, Lady Lily, were known to be in favour of CBT, a short-term treatment. While he was aware of problems that could be managed more effectively by robust short-term work, and the Glendale Centre would have the cream of such practitioners, he did not rate it highest for people who had gone through trauma. Long-term talking treatment was more expensive and therefore unpopular at a time of inadequate National Health Service funding. But for Lady Rose, unless the assessment revealed something different, it would be found necessary. Specialist Supervision would be essential.

That was all hard enough without these social media implications. If "Cassandra" was right, the link to Lady Rose would or could eventually become apparent, and the SJTU would have a lot to deal with, including some potentially difficult publicity. His supervisor at the Institute of Psychoanalysis would not like that. Thank goodness he was not a disability therapist. He would speak to Elouise.

"You want a coffee and biscuit?" asked Sylvie. He sighed. There she was, trying to bribe him away from work again as well as apologise. "Just the coffee thanks mum—I have a couple of work calls to make." There. He had said it. She turned away with a shrug of her shoulders but no words, and he felt a satisfied glow. Turning back to his phone, he dialled Elouise's number.

CHAPTER 40

Saturday, December 29th 2012, Over the Atlantic

The flight had been extremely uncomfortable despite the full-length bed and attentive stewardess. She would have been a pleasing minor diversion if he had not been so preoccupied with other matters. She was announcing his title every moment she could as if the possession of those three letters in her pretty pouting mouth, HRH, His Royal Highness, was a powerful fetish. Prince Carl-Zygmunt was in no doubt about the value of a title in their work. Even from a minor irrelevant principality like Neuplatzstan. It didn't even exist now. Wiped out and pulled apart, it had long lost its history. However, the title saved him, and brought him to the attention of people like Orpheus, who were happy to include him. His money helped as well.

It was not just the turbulence that had affected him but the potential fallout for Orpheus. Glendale's brother was a possible significant complication and, perhaps even more so, Danny Delta. Gorillas and Borgias—the Society had thrived on them. Ian was both. On the other hand, he and Glendale wanted cooler heads and a bigger capacity to have the final aims in mind. Why did he have to deal with a pompous psychopath like Anderson? Ian's personal habits left a lot to be desired and leaked through the hugely generous allowance for bodily needs accepted and encouraged by the Society in the name of science. In fact, he found Ian's sadism unpalatable despite its familiarity. Rose. Buggering her up. What had possessed the Society to allow him to use Rose like that? Who had given him permission? As if her installed inside Master could be stable or ever be stabilised with a disability like hers!

Masters and his low-level pseudo-Luciferian ilk were only pawns that has been brought in. Even Ian, who did not have that bloodline, was a chess piece to be manoeuvred. They were Flat Earthers against the genius of Orpheus. Yet he needed them: the Society needed them ... for now. The bloodline had many surprises. It was not just aristocrats, although the Redcliffe history helped. Things happened over hundreds of years. Kings and Queens were exiled and killed. The royal bloodline could hide for centuries and end up in a local waitress. New beliefs and sub-beliefs were added. Even Crowleyites, like Lew Masters. Crowley said a sacrifice could be made of someone with a learning disability as well as of someone beautiful, but Rose should not have been used like this.

Sandra would help him think. No one relaxed him like her. As Orpheus said, she had been made for him, a reward for his title and investment. He had paid to be chosen as the suitable love interest for an installed sex slave and strategic thinker. A prototype for the immortality project. Wasn't this the genius of Orpheus? Wasn't this illuminating? Wasn't this economy? Sandra for him and Lee for Major D. Absolute fidelity from each within one body's sexuality: such economy! One assassin instead of a whole army. *E pluribus unum*. Wasn't that what Z had told them, the motto of the United States appearing on the Great Seal.

CHAPTER 41

Saturday, December 29th 2012, USA

Danny Delta's last song was coming through her small bedroom speakers.

Sandra Harrison stretched out her arms on her black satin sheets, enjoying their whiteness as a contrast. Long blonde hair artfully curled around her heart-shaped face. She was everybody's sweetheart. This was her reward for being her.

"Good Sandra," she could hear a voice say.

Her parents kept praising her, and so did her friends. Why? It seemed she could do no wrong. Ever since she had shown that her shit of a hospital and that arsehole therapist had cheated her, and stuck grotesque pornography about her poor parents in her mind, she had been rolling in it. She could not remember going to the hospital or much before it. She had been prom queen. She remembered that. She knew she had felt terrible before. All that was in the past; her mother said "don't look back." That's what they all seemed to say. Terrible things happened to people who looked back. That was the story of Orpheus and Eurydice, wasn't it?

The compensation money hit the jackpot, and it was all hers, along with the press. She had volumes of photos at her sex-kitten best with her arms around her parents. What's more, her parents couldn't seem to praise her enough. Instead of being angry, they just showered her with gifts and money. Now she had her own flat now and a proper job.

Prince Carl-Zygmunt of Neuplatzstan and his friends gave her a hundred thousand dollars a year to help other people like her fight their horrible hospitals and therapists. Therapists! The-rapists more like! She would do it for free; the money was just a bonus. Bastards, entering her mind and messing with it. Bang, bang, bang. This was her mission, her war. She was all set to launch her new organisation, Sandra's Searches, to investigate all this obscene pornographic rubbish.

Prince Carl-Zygmunt had said she had been made for him and had been made for him. The first man outside of her father to admire her mind. He had trusted her with secrets, and not just ordinary ones. He and Major D said she was helping her country. Major D was pining for Danny and Lee: a poofter, said her secret sharp voice despite all his muscles and military decorations.

Danny was a fool; a sharper voice inside her pronounced, "soldiers had to die." Get over it! She liked it when she heard that voice, that sound inside her. It was like putting her elegant foot on the accelerator. She knew she was stronger, cleverer, when she felt that.

Danny must have done something wrong. "When you come back?" You don't come back. You walk forward and you keep walking forward. You can't look back. A lone tear rolled down her cheek. The word "Lara" appeared in her head. She hated when that happened, and it gave her a headache. Mother said Lara was a girl she knew a long time ago who was taken in and betrayed by her therapist and hospital and broke her parents' hearts. She did not want to waste time on someone like that. Lara could fucking go back where she came from, because Sandra was going forward. Going forward. The word "Leandra" broke through and made her nauseous. She would tell mummy. Mummy knew.

A flick of a switch to change the music—her favourite Disney song: "Someday my prince will come…" poured through the wet room, and she smiled and twirled like a child as she soaped herself. "Good girl. Good girl. Good Sandra," someone said in her thoughts.

There were seven rings on her phone.

CHAPTER 42

Sunday, 30th December 2012, 2pm, Balham

Sarah Ransome's residence

The day had started well. The Sunday papers had come through her letterbox thanks to the delivery boy at her local newsagents. He was actually a delivery man: a pensioner keen to be active and earn a bit of money. Having a mug of coffee and her egg and toast in bed while watching television was still new and exciting. Steve didn't like the television in the bedroom as it interrupted his reading. She smiled. It was a rare plus against the loss of him.

The papers and television took her to lunchtime, and then the pangs began. What a week in any job! She had moved, and to an area where she had no friends. She felt Faith and Maureen had good potential as work friends, and maybe that would spread into her private life, but that would take time. She was aware of a maternal feeling for Tracey. She had an instinctive aversion to Lew Masters, but even he had improved somehow.

Where should she go for lunch? Should she go out for a walk? She was alone. There was no one to tell her what to do. Her mother, bless her, was dead. Her closest friends, Penny and Frances, had been against the move, and she didn't want to hear the sympathy or "I told you so." Hot tears came welled in her eyes.

Poor Lady Rose. Whatever had happened to her? The way she had clung to her on her first day, and yet such a different state she had returned in with that charming woman, Ms Lasky. She must telephone her. Thank goodness she had Dr Aziz and Professor Frank to discuss Rose with. Supervision in her last workplace had been appalling, given by a Nurse Line Manager with no psychodynamic understanding. Yet there was more assessment needed and it sounded very concerning.

Tracey had returned from visiting the Glendale Centre in an exhausted but excited state. Sarah had insisted Tracey go and rest properly, putting Goldstone on the shift instead. Dr Aziz had briefly informed her of Tracey's comments about her poor brother suffering flashbacks from Afghanistan. Such pain reminded her of her loss of Steve.

When You Come Back suddenly broke through her reverie. Danny Delta's death being the subject of the television programme. Suddenly she was crying again. The yearning in the song brought it all back. She still couldn't accept the loss of Steve. She hadn't left a forwarding address, but he knew her email. She unfriended him on Facebook and blocked him. But she wasn't going to change her mobile or her email. If he wanted to find her, he could, but he wouldn't. Such a teenage moment of defiance, blocking him on Facebook: trying to control what she could not. When he looked at her now, a glow in his eyes had just gone; that light had been extinguished and could never return. She had to face she really had lost him forever.

She had met Steve while doing a Master's degree in social work at university. He was lecturing in economics at the local poly and had given a public talk on economic inequalities in the health system. It was a few years later they met up again. He was like her, an only child, an orphan, really. Now it was all gone, for 20 years. She was Rip Van Winkle. All the lectures, the shared outings, trips to Ikea, saving for new carpets, for a holiday, telly, car. All gone, all meaningless.

He had been so moved when she spoke of her first management work: inspiring change and hope in long-stay homes for the disabled. "They are used to people looking at them with fake smiles and dead eyes," she said, and that was how he had ended up looking at her.

Why couldn't she just let it go? It had been six months already. Why couldn't she take back all she had invested in him?

Danny Delta! What a voice he had! Another of those lost souls who glittered in public while falling apart privately. How lucky she was that her fall did not affect her work.

Lunchtime. A table for one? Here she was, 47 years old, and reborn into orphanhood and singledom.

Tomorrow would be New Year's Eve. She and Steve had always taken it seriously, writing all their wishes and resolutions. They also went to New Year's Eve parties, Penny's especially, or even held the occasional one themselves. There had been champagne and tiny canapés, and Auld Lang Syne, after listening to the chimes of midnight.

She would never have imagined working at Christmas, at New Year, but now it was holding her together.

CHAPTER 43

Monday, December 31st 2012, 11:30am, The Lord Glendale Centre

It was 11.30am at the Lord Glendale on a grey bleak day, and Dr Aziz knew what to expect. After giving his name to the uniformed security personnel, he joined the silent, serious queue to have his case checked. Professor Frank again came to meet him. With serious nods at each other, they walked across the sea of dark-blue carpet, through the lifts and glass security gates, and into the office that he now recognised. One of the Stepford wives instantly appeared to check their drink requirements, and Professor Frank asked for two hot chocolates reminding her that Lady Rose would also probably like one on arrival but to check. Abdul had only chosen hot chocolate to join in the first time and preferred green tea. But he would leave it for today.

"I am sorry about last time," said Professor Frank curtly. "Thank you for holding the fort. I think a full psychological and psychiatric assessment is required."

"Let's hope today is easier for everyone," said Dr Aziz gently,

"Let us begin," said Professor Frank, "could you provide me with your working definition of intellectual disability?"

Dr Aziz was taken aback. This was the behaviour of a consultant psychiatrist taking a junior doctor on a ward round, not an eminent psychiatrist and psychologist speaking to a consultant disability psychiatrist! A pause for a deep breath, and he continued.

"I think, Professor Frank, as you will know from your psychology framework, that it involves a significant impairment of intellectual functioning, significant impairment of adaptive behaviour (social functioning), with both impairments arising before adulthood. We no longer use IQ in a simplistic way but take a far more holistic view of disability. Someone might, for example, have excellent social adaptation while having a significant intellectual impairment. However, I think we can agree that Lady Rose has an intellectual disability, even if the full extent is not certain. The excellent occupational therapists at Harvest House had previously referred her to psychology at St Joseph's Hospital on her arrival, and Lady Rose has been comprehensively tested for both her IQ (which is mild-moderate) and her self-care skills. She has not previously been considered to have a linked area of mental illness-dementia, long-term effects of brain damage, physical or medical conditions, which cause confusion, drowsiness or loss of consciousness, delirium or concussion, symptoms of alcohol or drug use."

"Thank you, Dr Aziz," said Frank formally while nodding at Laura, who brought in biscuits and drinks. He seemed to be back in his stride. "I am aware that while dementia is more common in people with Down's Syndrome, other problems such as depression or schizophrenia could be hard to recognise. There is also the issue of her capacity."

Dr Aziz took a deep breath. There had been no mention of trauma yet or of safeguarding. This was extremely worrying. "An intellectual disability is never the only aspect of why individuals are able to make decisions for themselves. To lack the capacity to make a specific decision, they also need to fulfil the second part of the two-stage test, which requires that they are not able: (a) to understand the information relevant to the decision; (b) to retain that information; (c) to use or weigh that information as part of the process of making the decision; or (d) to communicate [the] decision (whether by talking, using sign language, or any other means)."

Dr Aziz found himself repeating basic psychiatric definitions as if teaching. If Professor Frank needed him to be formal and academic, that is what he would be.

"Two reputable psychologists from St Joseph's University psychology department undertook a capacity test when Lady Rose entered

Harvest House. I note from her file that in considering the way her score varied between what used to be called mild and the top end of moderate, the psychologist needed a very careful clinical evaluation of whether there was significant impairment of functioning. A key difference between psychology and psychiatry, Professor Frank, is that a test taken when the patient is exhausted or traumatised, if indeed it is ethically appropriate to do such a thing, is not necessarily valid in its results. As a psychiatrist, I was extremely concerned about the possibilities of PTSD, amongst other issues, but I was reassured by the way she showed a resilient change of mood."

He paused. "Apart from self-injury, which is low with Down's Syndrome, dementia is the biggest cause of concern, and some of the signs can be incontinence, visual-auditory effects, depression, memory loss, disorientation, and hallucinations or delusions."

Frank breathed a sigh of relief. Aziz was a knowledgeable and sensible man. He did not rush in to safeguarding issues.

"Shall we see her now?"

"Yes," affirmed Abdul.

A click and the assistant appeared. "Lady Rose is here, Professor Frank and Dr Aziz. She has chosen to come into the assessment with you on her own."

CHAPTER 44

Monday, December 31st 2012, 11:30am, The Lord Glendale Centre

Sitting in the glossy waiting room with her favourite Nurse, Brenda, Lady Rose was sitting quietly and comfortably. She had been particularly pleased Brenda's hours had been extended from the daily 5–8 pm shift to two full days. The Nurse was flicking through a fashion magazine, and Rose looked at her own plain elasticised dress.

"Nice dresses here, Rosie; you could buy one like that. Bet your mum has lots of lovely dresses."

"Yes," said Rose. "Mum has lovely dresses. Beautiful woman, says dad."

"She is beautiful and has lovely dresses," repeated the Nurse.

Rose stayed silent. She held out her hands, showing her pink nail varnish. "Look Brenda. Nice nail varnish."

"Beautiful nail varnish," echoed Brenda. "This place is really strange for me, Rose, really smart. All this blue carpet. You've been here before, Rose. I've never seen it before."

"Rose came here first!" said Rose with delight.

"You did!"

"See you later, Bren," she giggled as Laura beckoned her, and she walked through a self-opening glass door and into Professor Frank's office.

"Hello friend Chris! Hello Abdul! Good Lady Rose here."

Both men welcomed her, and she walked confidently to a blue arm-chair. "No phone call to mummy now, friend Chris."

That rare blush again covered Chris Frank's usually impassive face. "No. This is just us today, Lady Rose," he affirmed.

"Do you mind if I have the tape recorder on Rose—then I don't have to keep writing!"

"Sign paper?"

Professor Frank looked confused. "The consent form, Rose, for you to give permission—is that what you mean?" asked Aziz.

"Yes. Good Lady Rose sign," Maureen said.

Nervously, Professor Frank walked to a glossy cabinet to provide a consent form. "Can you read it, Rose?" asked Abdul. He could feel the stress in Professor Frank. Rose was not only showing capacity, but she had also understood the rules of the assessment even better than him! This did not lend itself to an incapacity diagnosis to keep her silent before the grand opening.

"I give perm … permission for …" She put the paper down. "Friend Chris and new man to record me," she finished triumphantly. She looked critically at them. "Maureen has nice pictures for showing con-sent instead of words. At HH. I will bring next time," she added.

"Thank you, Rose. They are a very good idea." Professor Frank looked at Rose. The deep blue of her eyes set in a slightly flattened face with a short neck always hurt him; it reminded him of Lily, but look how clever she was.

"Rose, do you mind me asking questions?"

"No, friend Chris. This is interview like mummy and daddy's, Good Lady Rose."

"Thank you," said Professor Frank. "Interview with Lady Rose at 12pm on Monday 31st December. Professor Frank and Dr Aziz in attendance."

"Rose, do you know why everyone is worried about you?"

"Yes."

Dr Aziz and Professor Frank stared at her.

"Bad Rose cried because bad man Ian Anderson put willy in bum, just like bad man Danny Delta in Vegas." She smiled comfortably, no concern showing on her face.

"Beautiful lady mum and dad took Bad Rose to Vegas for concert and party. Then big, big house, and Ian says stay with Ian."

Frank put his head in his hands.

"Sorry, friend Chris. Master won't hurt you. Only Bad Rose. Not Good Rose or Lady Rose."

Aziz and Frank looked at each other. It was the mention of "Master" that alerted both of them. "Master" had been the word that led to her outburst on Friday. She was just so comfortable, capable, and, yes, autistic, dissociative, cut off from any sign of emotional pain, but there was no tremor in her voice or sign of a raised heartbeat. What was the difference between Friday and today?

"You were upset and angry on Friday, Rose; you threw your drink," said Aziz gently.

"No," said Rose firmly.

"Who did then?" asked Frank

"Master."

"Master?" asked Frank

"Yes. Inside Master. He gets cross when Bad Rose talks. But not cross with Good Rose or Lady Rose."

"Could inside Master get confused about what Danny Delta did? Or Ian Anderson?" asked Frank tentatively.

Lady Rose got up from her chair with great authority. "Interview over, friend Chris and new friend Abdul. Don't be frightened. Bad man Ian Anderson won't hurt you. You can phone mummy now, Chris." She then moved out of the room, waiting for the glass doors to open with great grace—like a queen. Exactly like her mother, thought Professor Frank.

Aziz and Frank looked at each other, rather shell-shocked. Frank said, "Interview terminated by Lady Rose at 12:15pm on Monday 31st December. Present: Professor Frank and Dr Aziz." He turned it off and removed the tape. Picking up the signed consent form and placing it with the tape he signed for his secretary. "A transcript of this to be sent to myself and Dr Aziz by secure internal post."

Dr Aziz looked intently at Professor Frank. "And your safeguarding policy?"

Professor Frank looked flustered. "She is clearly regulated again and perhaps those mentions are delusions linked to schizophrenia or early Alzheimer's."

Dr Aziz nodded slowly and thoughtfully. "Schizophrenia is very rare for people with Down's Syndrome, although still possible. This inside Master could be part of a psychotic delusion controlling her. Her affect was not delusional in terms of early-onset Alzheimer's. I think we have no alternative but to follow normal policy."

"And?" asked Frank.

"We have no choice but to report her allegations to local safeguarding and for them to decide on action regarding the disclosure."

"Disclosure?"

"Professor Frank, this is very painful for both of us. And especially so for you as a family friend with a conflict of interest. I regret to formally say you cannot be the safeguarding lead for Lady Rose, so you will need to tell me who it is at the Lord Glendale or I will provide someone from St Joseph's. We have an excellent Vulnerable Victim Coordinator in the local police force."

Professor Frank sat frozen. What would she say? The beautiful Lily? How she would hate him, adding to her problems like this when she had put such gifts his way—like his mother.

Dr Aziz seemed to have a link to the deepest part of him.

"Sir, Professor Frank, I did not sleep well last night. I do not know Lady Lily, but this situation is beyond the usual and worrying for all of us. We must be very careful regarding confidentiality. The new unit is due to open in one week, and I suggest we have one further joint meeting before that while I keep tabs on the Harvest House staff. If you feel able to supervise Mrs Ransome, that will help too—she is a very sensible woman. We need a prudent safety net around this case."

His words said gently but formally helped to galvanise Professor Frank. Who would have thought there was such a hole inside him? "Thank you, Aziz. We will speak later," he managed, but he remained seated.

"Yes," Aziz found he was longing for a sight of the koi, but he had to leave. Gawain would be back. He really needed to speak to him.

CHAPTER 45

Monday, December 31st 2012, New Year's Eve, 12:30pm, The Lord Glendale Centre

Professor Frank had not moved. Indeed, Laura returned with the printed transcript to find him in the same position.

"Your printed transcript Professor Frank and I will have one delivered securely to Dr Aziz."

"Thank you, Laura. Cancel all my meetings today. This requires time."

She nodded and left just as his mobile started ringing. Lady Lily! It was Lily. It was rare for her to call him.

"And?" came her firm seductive voice.

"She was really calm."

"And?"

"She said Ian and Danny Delta had both anally raped her."

"She's still saying that?" said Lady Lily wearily.

"Yes." He paused uncomfortably.

"Did you go to Vegas with her?" he asked nervously.

"What's the relevance of that? You know we did. With Ian. It was about three months ago, on October 31st, a Halloween gig. We had tickets for Danny's penultimate gig and went to an after-concert party with her. A lot happened around the pool. She saw a lot. Ian kindly took her to look around the house so I could swim in peace. She is phobic about water."

"So, minus the abuse, what she said was true!" said Chris with a shocked voice.

"So what?" said Lily coolly. "You, of all people, know how memory deceives and traps."

"Yes. But first we have to go through safeguarding procedures. She has made clear disclosures in front of witnesses, and they may be delusional, but they have to be respected." Professor Frank was slowly retrieving the fragments of his professional self. "Her behaviour changed three months ago when she was taken to Vegas and saw Ian and Danny Delta," he said formally.

"Chris. You sound like Sherlock Holmes. You are as bad as Peter when he gets on his National Health Service soapbox. We all know that, but if it makes you feel better he had the same feeling as you initially. I didn't go to all this trouble just for another media flare-up just as her unit opens. Sort it out, darling. You can see me when you have," she added in a theatrical whisper.

It was no good saying it would not come to that. Police questions led to actions.

Lily put the phone down on him and the world became silent.

CHAPTER 46

Monday, December 31st 2012, New Year's Eve, 12:30pm, The SJTU

Deirdre Hislop had taken down the remaining Christmas decorations from the unit. Like an empty fairground, they seemed melancholy when past their time. The wrapping paper that could not be folded and reused had also been put in the dustbins. She could not trust Edna to do it properly. If only they had Carmen, Mo's wife, a sensible woman.

She liked this last week of relative quiet with most staff still away: a time to answer letters, draw up timetables, and file things away before the phone started ringing again. Christmas never suited her. With no siblings, no parents, and, to face it properly, no real friends, the SJTU was home to her. "I am the last of my line," she had said in a rare moment of intimacy during her job interview with Dr Stuart.

"Just think—for me to be here on this planet an ancestor of mine has lived in every period of history. And it all ends with me. End of the line. So, I want to do something for a unit that is the end of the line for people who have suffered. Then I will have earned my right to be alive."

She could not remember what Dr Stuart had said, but he and the panel had warmed to her from that moment, and her courage had been rewarded by the post. She loved it, all the staff, the patients, and Dr Stuart. Every day she gave thanks for it. No previous job had recognised her, understood her heart, and needed her, her efficiency, her loyalty, and her love.

Indeed, her will, which she had drawn up on her 60th birthday several months ago, left all her money to the SJTU as an unrestricted fund. If the Lord Glendale Centre gobbled up the unit, the modest amount was to be divided between the senior management team with £50 for Carmen, her favourite cleaner. If they did not sell it and turn it into a golf course, she would be buried in the cemetery on the St Joseph's site, if they did not sell that and turn it into a golf course! Anything was possible with the health service now—and with the Glendale. It could consume up anything.

A rare chuckle came from her mouth, remembering one of Elouise's quips. The Lord Glendale Centre suffered from bulimia.

There were only 25 clinical letters and some delayed Christmas cards from former patients and other units on the site. They had introduced a speedy first-class internal delivery system on-site to try and make up for such external delays. Majeera, a trafficked woman, was now living in safety in Liverpool and had found love with an elderly Afghan refugee. Moments like these were the equivalent of treasured family photographs.

She kept them—not just in the formal files — but in a very special space in her memory. The memory of these special moments would be her retirement gold.

A cream embossed envelope with the crest of the Lord Glendale Foundation caught her attention. It had been hand-delivered. Knowing Dr Aziz would be involved with the assessment of Lady Rose at that very moment, Deirdre perched on her swivel chair to read it.

To her surprise the letter did not concern Lady Rose. It was addressed to the Director, though not by name, and was a referral from a Dr Simon Green, Director of the Lord Glendale Equipa Unit, asking them to come to his Centre. They were going up in the world! Two invitations to the royal palace in one week, or were they summonses?

As a means of providing a collaborative piece of work, the SJTU was invited to take part in a shared diagnostic assessment and case discussion over whether surgery was the right next step for a 12-year-old, Mattie Harrison who, since the age of 6, had experienced himself as a boy in a female body. He had been known as Mattie for years, but there were concerns about the next step.

144

Deirdre swivelled on her chair. Was this the child who had haunted Elouise? Would such a traumatised child be well enough for such a process, or was she becoming paranoid? Deirdre walked to the kettle. She needed a cup of tea. The impact of the Lady Rose incident had clearly affected her. Just a month ago she would have been delighted to imagine these moments of cooperation. Indeed, it had been her initial reaction. But now it was there, she doubted it.

The Equipa Unit was the newly named Research and Treatment Centre that now incorporated the original St Joseph's Gender Dysphoria Unit. Deirdre had attended a previous meeting hosted by Dr Stuart and Lucy Albright for the original unit and had followed it through these changes. Once the Glendale had gobbled up the LGBT unit, she had lost contact, and she did not think Lucy was still there.

Where did they get their money? It was an endless source of fascination for the ever-decreasing St Joseph's campus; she stopped herself thinking about such things—she had work to do. And she wanted everything up to date before Dr Stuart popped in, if he could. She hoped he wouldn't. How could he fly across the world to see his first grandchild just for a few days?

CHAPTER 47

Monday, December 31st 2012, New Year's Eve, 12:30pm, Harvest House

Brenda Harris and Lady Rose walked down the hill to Harvest House.

"Good walking for us, Rose. We need exercise after all the Christmas food."

Rose smiled at her. "What you eat, Bren?"

"Turkey and roast potatoes, too many potatoes and too much Christmas cake!" Brenda turned towards her. "What was nicest about Christmas for you, Rose?"

"Watch telly in the snug with Mona! Daddy said, 'quiet with Oz, so mummy doesn't hear'," she giggled delightedly. She flushed. "Lady mother looked beautiful and gave good Lady Rose lovely necklace."

"That is lovely," said Brenda, as they entered Harvest House.

The entrance was empty, as they were all at art in the dayroom.

"Let's tell Sarah you are here."

Rose walked confidently ahead and knocked on Sarah's door. "Good Lady Rose here, Sarah?"

"Come on in," said Sarah warmly, opening her door and ushering them in. "You have been to the Glendale twice and I have never seen it."

Rose giggled happily as she sat down. "Good Rose and good Lady Rose gone twice. Go again too. You can go now, Bren," she added imperiously.

Brenda and Sarah smiled at each other.

"Okay, Lady Rose, see you later."

"Thanks, Brenda," added Sarah.

"Would you like a drink, Rose?"

"No thank you, Sarah. I had hot chocolate with friend Chris and new man Aziz."

"How was it today?" asked Sarah, hoping she sounded as neutral as possible.

"Don't be frightened, Sarah—Good Rose, good Lady Rose. Mummy will be cross with you, but doesn't matter. Beautiful Lady mother. Told everyone Ian Anderson put willie in my bum in Vegas. Bad man. At Vegas concert with bad man Danny Delta. Others don't matter. Don't say more, Rose. Where are police? Rose has to tell police. Like before."

Sarah took a deep breath. Rose had every right to have her disclosures properly attended to. "You are right, Rose. Do I have your permission to speak to Professor Frank and Dr Aziz?"

"Mummy won't want Lady Rose speak to police. Professor Frank scared mummy will be sad. Daddy scared mummy will be sad."

Sarah found herself unable to stay with the awfulness of this emotional intelligence. "I will speak to them, Rose. And now—do you want to go to the art class. They have got sandwiches there for lunch."

"Maybe you won't speak to them. Maybe you will. Don't be frightened. Good Rose go now."

As she left the room, Sinita suddenly appeared dressed in a new elasticated dress that Sarah had found for her. Before Sinita could speak, Rose took her arm in a friendly way.

"Come to art with kind Lady Rose. Thanks for Serby Bear, kind Sinita."

Sinita gave a loud cry of pleasure, and together they marched down the corridor arm in arm.

Sarah sat still. Please no. Not after Elmview. She didn't have the energy to do this again. Thank heavens for Professor Frank and Dr Aziz. She was not the safeguarding lead.

CHAPTER 48

Monday, December 31st 2012, New Year's Eve, 12:30pm, The Lord Glendale Centre

Keira Denny was in her element. Life at the Lord Glendale Centre was so good she did not want to leave, even to go out for lunch. There was going to be a small in-house restaurant, but that had not been built yet, so she brought in her own sandwiches every day. As PR in-house consultant for the Lord Glendale Foundation and Centre, she had her own large office, with its own toilet and bathroom—unheard of anywhere else! She also had a personal assistant and a secretary. Not bad for a 28-year-old who did a journalism degree at a local poly and an online social media course.

It was almost accidental that she became involved in PR. Due to her father's role in a union, Keira had attended trade union meetings from her early childhood, inevitably leading her to write about the inequalities in the health service in her university newspaper (which was technically still a polytechnic at the time), then her local paper, and then a national.

Len, an ex-boyfriend, used to work for a Prisoner's Rights charity. They had a tiny office, and nearly all their work was pro bono. They made a huge difference to their clients' lives and, more importantly, their clients' families. The charity was nearly closed when a scavenger-level national paper attacked the local prison, which was trying to improve the life of its inmates.

Her parents had approved of her move into PR and her job at St Joseph's University Hospital. It had been a rundown hospital still dealing with the impact of long-term institutionalisation on its disability, psychosis, and forensic work, but then it became a university hospital, and suddenly there were students and Professors and a sense of hope. Thank goodness she was already there when Lord Glendale stepped in with his millions, making the hospital site the most extravagantly funded in the UK. As it was, her parents were not happy with her new advancement considering the philanthropists she was mixing with were the real "hoi polloi"—the "fat cats." But her younger sister Nikita (named after Khrushchev, of course), who was ten years younger, loved asking about such matters.

Her first task had been to publicise the new internal design of the multi-million-pound centre. Locals moved by the tale of Lord Buxton Castellane, and his wife Marie needed a way to make sense of the less public Glendale Centre with its high security. Architecture and technology lectures in the ultra-modern lecture theatres, before the researchers had moved in, slowly allowed for local acceptance. People used to enjoy walking up the hill to look at the aristocratic former stately home and pop into the hospital canteen. That had needed a lot of thinking about. After discussions with Lord Glendale, he put money into a new children's playground on a still derelict site just a mile away. The Lord Glendale Play Area. She wondered if Orson Welles might have had a similar character! She would always remember the credits after his films:

Play by Orson Welles,
Starring Orson Welles,
And produced by Orson Welles.

Then came neuroscience, and then came Professor Frank's memory unit. What a strange man. He had a good memory, for sure, but with such rigid attention to detail and such an unsmiling manner, she could have imagined him running a unit for people with Asperger's. Then came the Equipa Unit, which really excited her and which she could discuss endlessly with her mother and sister, although it made her father uncomfortable.

"It's a bit wasted on me, lass. We are all human beings, all deserving of respect and whose business is it what you are so long as you treat others decently."

At the launch, she produced a star-studded group of celebrities, singers, actors, and musicians. All non-binary. All the papers were full of it and the TV channels. Lord Glendale had sent a personal thank you note.

And now, even though it was still the Christmas holidays, sorry Midwinter, for all those who did not have a Christian belief, she had the launch of the Lady Rose Redcliffe Independence Unit the following week: Saturday 5th January. A good day for a launch and just in time to get into all the Sunday papers the following day. This was an exciting story that she thought she could tell her family about because it was a curious story of an aristocrat going downmarket and then sharing her luck with everyone to lift them up with her.

Lady Rose Redcliffe had Down's Syndrome and was the daughter of the Minister for Health, Sir Peter Redcliffe and his stunning wife Lady Lily Redcliffe. Rose was their only daughter. They lived near the hospital and Sir Peter had been a good constituency MP for years, always concerned about health, especially after his daughter's birth. She faced the problems many people with disabilities faced. Money did not buy you immunity. She was bullied in primary school and raped by a minicab driver in her early teens while at secondary school.

Her father had managed to be partially sympathetic, "Okay, the rich do suffer and money can't buy you health or love, but it makes the downtimes a lot easier." On the other hand, her mother, Eileen, said "You are being cruel, Charlie. Rose has not been wanted. She was sent off to school and then to college, with 24-hour help, so her mother didn't have to look at her. It is like that cousin of the Queen's—the one who lived in a hospital all her life. There's no progress here."

Nikita seemed to agree with that—but then she was still living at home!

Harvest House was a cesspit. Real old school. Some of those poor men and women were put there years ago because they were "difficult" or had a baby out of wedlock or were just "slow" and had just been left there. What appalling lives they had led. Just seeing old-style dormitories had made her feel sick. There were a few ensuite rooms for the slightly more capable, but they too felt like ghosts from another era. And Lady Rose had been put there by her family at 18. What did that mean? Sharing the same facilities as less fortunate people? But that was not totally true because other hospitals and units and disability living centres had progressed so much.

In the long-stay ward, there were still people without teeth because staff in the past had not bothered to find out what was the cause of their discomfort. There was no attempt to understand the communication of their residents. They just whipped all their teeth out.

And Lady Rose would be watching television with them in the large, shared dayroom. But here came the part that did feel good. An old warehouse for hospital provisions had been rebuilt into a stylish house that was a cross between a private home and a residential unit. Each resident would have a large room with an ensuite bathroom, television, and their own colour choice of carpet and wallpaper. There would be four. And downstairs would be a communal television room, dining room, and kitchen. The idea was that staying there would help the four people chosen to slowly become more independent until they could find a home in their local community. Lady Rose, of course, was one of the four people.

What would it be like living in a house that was named after you? Well—Lord Glendale did it, and so did Donald Trump! And what about all the businesses called by peoples' own names, or even their names "& Son"—very rarely "& Daughter."

The launch was important but also very delicate. Sir Peter and Lady Lily were not only important in terms of their political role, they were also benefactors of this fund. They were also entrusting their daughter to this new environment as a sign of confidence. The hardest issue for her was to consider Lady Rose as a self-advocate, speaking about the meaning of the unit to her and for her. Could she go directly to her or should she get permission from Sir Peter and Lady Lily? If Lady Rose was pleased with the idea of her unit, then that would be the most heart-warming moment of all, but would it be too delicate for her? And then again, she might be pleased, but her parents might not be. Would it be a freak show? And what did independence mean when you had an intellectual disability? Was the name of the unit hopeful and exciting, an acknowledgement of reality or a burden?

She would get one of her assistants, Debbie, to make an urgent appointment with Lord Glendale while the other interviewed the staff that would be moving across there and see who would be the most newsworthy.

CHAPTER 49

Monday, December 31st 2012, New Year's Eve, 12:30pm, The SJTU

D r Aziz walked down the hill with a burdened heart. He was at the start of a dangerous journey, and he knew it. There did not seem to be an easy way out. He could not return to the SJTU or Harvest House while his mind was so unclear. That would not be honouring his profession and his patients.

He found he was walking towards St Joseph's Chapel. He had met Father O'Neill once at an inter-faith conference and respected him. They had jointly spoken of the need for a multi-faith centre at St Joseph's. While over half of the patients at St Joseph's identified themselves as Christian, an increasing number were Muslim or Hindu, with a smaller Jewish percentage.

He found himself thinking of Luqman the Wise, who said to his son, "O my son: Let your speech be good and your face be smiling; you will be more loved by the people than those who give them provisions."

Although a slave, Luqman said, "Lowering my gaze, watching my tongue, eating what is lawful, keeping my chastity, undertaking my promises, fulfilling my commitments, being hospitable to guests, respecting my neighbours, and discarding what does not concern me. All these made me the one you are looking at." Luqman became a slave but bore his bondage with grace. Even though he was from another country.

Abdul wanted psychiatry to work with human pain, to be the Esperanto that religion had failed to be, but nothing could be that Esperanto. Conservatives and Labour, Republicans and Democrats, CBT and psychoanalysis, and worst of all the split in each person, an internal civil war. What a flawed species we were. Such hope and love and such wounds and darkness. May the blessings and peace of Allah be on the Prophet. He sat on the rusty bench outside of the church. He was religious in his own way and worked with colleagues of all beliefs. However, in this moment, it was his own roots that needed nourishment in his own way.

In the name of Allah, the all-merciful and compassionate.

CHAPTER 50

Monday, December 31st 2012, New Year's Eve, 12:30pm, Brixton

Lew Masters's residence

Lew Masters slammed the rickety door of his rented flat. Greyish white paint flakes fell onto the stained entrance hall lino. He didn't care if the ugly cow next door was bothered by the sound. He had to hear her vomiting up after each meal and then her wheezy cistern. He needed to move. He was not going to be hung out to dry at Cell Block H, living hand to mouth while the toffs carried on regardless.

In his line of work, jobs were easy to come by. He could walk a new job the very next day if he wanted; one that didn't ask him to perform dodgy psychological manipulation. He could keep that separate like others did. Then he would have job security or even be promoted. Working a double life was exhausting. There was always the threat of blackmail from the toffs and betrayal from the lowlifes like Edna. A job without that would be different. They had dissed him. All of them. The toffs and his so-called boss of a pseudo-Master. What had happened?

His Master had sold his services and become a pimp leader for this so-called Society. He wondered what had happened. The shitty irony of it all was that Sarah Ransome had been better to him than all the rest. She had asked him to organise a New Year's Eve party for Harvest

House, and he would and a proper one. And look after Rose. And Tracey. They were not his enemies.

He picked up his Alistair Crowley. The page it opened at was very apt:

I doubt if there is any class which is not detestable to some other class ... It's right, what's worse; every class, as a class, is almost sure to have more defects than qualities. As soon as you put men together, they somehow sink, cooperatively, below the level of the worst of individuals composing it ...

Bloody Society. He picked up a glass half-filled with red wine and smashed it against the dirty peeling wall. He uttered a deep despairing scream, oblivious to the banging on his wall by the adjoining flat. And then he picked the largest piece of glass and cut his arm. The red wine stained the walls like blood, and a trickle of blood snaked down his arm.

"Save that for tomorrow," he thought, feeling his chest slowly rising and falling with his breath.

Tearing his clothes off, kicking his shoes away, he walked naked and erect into his small bedroom and closed the thick black curtains. If any fucker saw him from the street, that was their luck. He was tired. His bedroom needed to be his private temple. He needed to sleep before the evening shift. A New Year's Eve party, and then he would fucking make some New Year Resolutions. Lighting the tall black candles, he relaxed for the first time. *Pactum Satanum.*

Fucking hell! Fucking Professor Chris Frank. Fucking Lord Glendale, and fuck Ian Anderson especially. Gorillas. He would show who was a gorilla. Lust was holy but their sexuality was tainted. What they were doing was on another level altogether. Master! His Master was a slave and did not deserve him. Why were they calling on Him as if He were their lackey?.

His hate was a flame inside him. Baphomet. Azazel. Lucifer. They were his purity. Why had his Master lent him out to the abominations of the Society? Science. Genetics. Military. Secret Service. Keeping unwanted bloodline bastards split for their so-called higher purposes.

His penis rose up under the black sheet; now he was the one with the Honourable Member. He would keep the notes and record the messages.

155

The law of Thelema is "Do what thou wilt shall be the whole of the Law."

By following the Society, he was being a heretic. His so-called Master was leading him astray. He had not gone through all he had gone through to be betrayed by Ian Anderson.

CHAPTER 51

Monday, December 31st 2012,
New Year's Eve, 1pm

From: Penny@fightingstigma.com
To: Sarahransome@harvesthouse.com

1pm

Dear Sarah,

Hope you are settled in your new post, even though I hate you for going! It's a rotten prospect trying to celebrate the New Year without you. I didn't feel like partying tonight. Steve has messed things up for all of us.

Please take care. I know you go toffee-nosed about my sources, but your Glendale links could be shitty. Did you know Glendale's brother in America—a Harold Fitz something – is another so-called philanthropist accused of abusing children at the place he set up? Neat, huh—you create your own fresh meat supply and get socially rewarded. My source is concerned about that marble palace on your doorstep and what its funding is really for. Where there's muck, there's brass. Wishing you a safe new year, and I'm still at the Pinot Grigio—about to go to sleep after having a telly fest through the night (pathetic, heh!), and you are probably working. Steve is a bastard!

Love,

Penny

From: Sarahrant@gmail.com
To: Penny@fightingstigma.com

1:30pm

Dear Penny,

Love you, but it is more than my job's worth to receive an email like that at my work email address. Please only email me privately. Anything in a formal email can be read by anyone. Steve is a bastard, and I miss you badly. Let's talk tomorrow when you have had some sleep.

Miss you badly

Will delete this now

Sarah

CHAPTER 52

Monday, December 31st 2012

Leandra's blog

Before you ignore me as a programmed irrelevance, I am aware I am one personality, sharing a body with others called Lee and little Lara, Sandra 1 and Sandra 2, and who knows how many more. I can be shut down at any moment. Yes. We are all terminal, but I can be terminated earlier. While I can still say my alphabet, say O for Orpheus.

You heard it here. This is brought at great risk, and this blog might cease after I write it. I may cease to exist after I write it. One man in his turn plays many parts, as the Bard said, but he did not know about DID parts. I could be terminated, murdered with no corpse visible and Sandra, my so-called host, would just carry on unaware. Better than an honour killing in another country. Here we have part-sacrifice. Lost in inner space. Pay great attention as you might not find this again. Beware of SS. Help Lara. She is within me and she is the one, the child part, who experiences nearly all the pain.

When Orpheus discovered the body of his wife Eurydice, overcome with grief, his music made the gods weep. He was like Danny Delta. Even the God of the underworld, Hades, agreed to allow Eurydice to return with him from the dark underworld to the bright earth, so long as he walked in front and did not look back

159

at her. This was unheard of. There is no resurrection outside of gods. He turned to look back at her, as you all know, and lost her forever. Sad, isn't it?

But that is not the whole story. If it were, it would be a universal tale of love and loss. "Don't look back" instead of "When you come back." But it was more than that.

Some said she could be an apparition—like a hologram, a golem, a delusion, an illusion, punishment for not dying for love or accepting loss and mortality as a human should. Wanting power over the dead is for alleged necrophiliacs like Savile and for those with gaping holes where their hearts should be.

I think Ovid had the answer. The Roman poet, Ovid, said that as a result of his loss Orpheus went off women. He sexually abstained from intimacies with women too. He became the first of the Thracian people to transfer his "love" to young boys. He was the first gifted paedophile and not the last. I address that point to Danny too. He wanted to enjoy the brief springtime, and early flowering of boys before they became adults. In other words he became frozen in time before his adult love for a woman came, another denial of loss. He was not a brave homosexual.

Feeling sexually spurned and rejected by Orpheus, women, followers of Dionysus, threw sticks and stones at him, but his music saved him. All were spellbound by him, even inanimate rocks. Enraged, the women tore him to pieces during the frenzy of their Bacchic dance. Another excuse for a crime. Or perhaps the women were goaded by the gods, programmed, possessed.

The Taj Mahal was commissioned by Shah Jehan in 1631, to be built in memory of his wife Mumtaz Mahal, who died giving birth to their 14th child. All who see it think of love and loss. That was where Princess Diana sat alone and poignant to signify the breakdown of her marriage.

You may see clues there or you may wonder why I mention this. You see, it is said that a billionaire, secreted away in secret services, codenamed Orpheus, richer than Croesus, is top dog of the living gods. With friends in the CIA, The White House, and the British Parliament. Some call the group around him Illuminati; some call it Society, or just the project.

After the loss of his secret mistress and baby in childbirth, he is said to have financed a virtual immortality project. The Orpheus Project. This could keep loved ones alive, including your good self, by copying them and implanting them into younger bloodline descendants. Unlike cryotherapy and all the other ideas of meeting in heaven, Nirvana, where there is no proof, this "installed" DID ensures success.

It is only one step further than "ordinary" DID. Just read your science books about it. To do this means torturing your nearest and dearest, or some of them, to make them nicely fragmented. Then you have to carry on hurting them to keep them that way—like a Somalian clitorectomy of the soul, or a Chinese foot binding of the brain. And this way, one space, the best space inside them, could be given

160

to the implant, the apparition. The implant doesn't know they are an implant or apparition but has the words, implanted history, and memories of their real outside person, whom they could see as a mother, father, lover, or twin. Or creator. Think of that. Frankenstein's monster. That is where false memories come from!

Or rather, the memories are true, but identity is built on a terrible lie, someone else's life. You see these implanted personalities once you know how to recognise them. They are apparitions trained to be ready to die for love and face being brought back or not at the last moment. And they don't know they are a lie. They love and live in the same world as their Creators, and they breathe. One up on a sexbot! The scientists paid so richly for this research had many other uses for it. Countries queued up. Indeed, the wish for a Manchurian candidate remains strong.

So we have the bloodline fanatics following their own holy grail of 13 bloodlines since time began. And the military, the politicians, the big bankers, and researchers are all fighting it out together for a secret assassin. Oh, and Luciferians and pseudo-Satanists. Oh yes. Just think of the pleasure of these pseudo-gods. From their torture chair, they form a new brain—one part a catholic priest, one a pagan, one a Satanist, one a Luciferian, one a witch, one a Hindu, one a Jew. Who wins? They feel above it all up on the iCloud.

What a merry mixture and all in the Den or the Glen, if you understand me.

So instead of the top dogs, we also have the mongrels—diet bloodlines, bloodlines lite! Let's fragment a low-functioning bloodline link not to keep a loved one alive but to have your hands up the Madonna's skirt, in the King's heart, and the Queen's diadem.

Me? I have been a sum of all my parts. I was a programmed male Master in the body of a programmed enslaved female who didn't know she was a female slave and a male slave who didn't know they harboured a Master. All the switches between personalities—as immaculate as a Swiss clock—were alive in me. A baby, a boy or a girl, or a man or a woman. An animal. A bird. A fish. All part of the celestial trick jigsaw. A brothel on two legs. Consenting paedophilia. Part of an apparition, a sex slave, an assassin, a murderer. Just five at the moment. Check who was with Danny Delta three months ago! Poor good bad Danny. He didn't know he was a slave and a master too. And the sweetness of a red Rose without thorns. Help her. There is a red Rose with an inside Master and some of the real Creators/Masters think having sex with an inside Master is the holy grail, those pseudo-gods looking for a religion to justify their abuse. Help Rose. I met her once. She regularly came to America. Don't ask how I know these things. Sometimes I hear more than I am expected to, and sometimes bits of amnesia go before they come back stronger.

And then there is poor little Mattie sent to the UK. Who might be my daughter, son, brother, or sister. Things get rather fucked up here. And there is a D and a Z.

Z is the end of the alphabet. The Omega. Pronounced Zed or Zee. Think of it as a swarm of angry bees, or a drill.

This is a bottle sent out to cyberspace. It is in the lap of the gods who will find it. Friend or foe. Beware SS (Sandra's Searches)—the initials are not an accident. Don't blame her. She knows nothing. She was made.

They spent millions making us all but one tweak too much and Pygmalion is back to square one.

And aren't they clever? The world's mental health professionals can't even understand ordinary DID yet, DID as a brilliant defence. If they can't get that, how will they ever get to mind control and installed dissociation?

Who killed Danny Delta? Someone did. And I send this at a cost you will never know.

LIVE is the back-to-front of EVIL.

Fear of death is the secret of Orpheus—or why do they keep taking me to the brink and back. And Lara. They can only create us through cruelty. An almost-death for each new part. You can't make an omelette without breaking eggs, they say. Why do people keep needing to break eggs? Sandra is spared all the memories of pain because the rest of us take it, especially the child, Lara. The inside world is no different from the outside—it is the child who suffers most. Illuminati, New World Order, Satanism, and all the rest of their myriad mystical claptraps may be a true system for some, but for most it is just a cheap cover.

Leandra

When you come back
When you come back
Where the water meets itself
Where my hands frame the eye
Where the stars go to die
Speak the truth and never lie
Broken into myriad pieces
Each separate part
A life releases
In this celestial Helter skelter
Am I Omega am I Delta?
Fight the heavy hand of fate

It is never too late,
To illuminate.

CHAPTER 53

Monday, December 31st 2012,
New Year's Eve, 1:30pm,
The Lord Glendale Centre

Equipa Unit

Dr Simon Green's Senior Registrar and chief admirer, Charmaine Landesman, was perplexed. With highly skilled consultant psychiatrists, surgeons, psychotherapists, and psychologists on-site at the Lord Glendale, why were they asking colleagues at the SJTU to be involved with Mattie? Didn't the poor child have enough people staring into every orifice and protuberance, and constantly checking their blood counts and hormones?

Mattie's bruises looked vicious, and his bones could be seen through his malnourished skin. His female body pierced him like a sword. Charmaine understood even before Mattie whispered to her. Almost every case they dealt with involved trauma. There was the trauma of feeling alive in the wrong body, being scapegoated, and being bullied for not looking or behaving like the assigned sex. It was awful. Living in a binary world. And then there were the victims of severe abuse who needed to step out of the hurt, reviled body into a safer one. She cared about them most of all. She wanted them to be beautiful butterflies coming out of a toxic cocoon with her help.

She knew all about that. It used to be her.

Charles Landesman was a little boy she still wept over. She had kept just three photographs—not that there were many others to choose from. In the first, he is six, wearing a little sailor suit and sitting on a stony deserted beach with desperate eyes. In the second, he has an arm around Pickle, the family's poodle. The third shows him sitting uncomfortably on his grandfather's lap, the magic snake, as his grandfather called it, rearing its head against his bum. Couldn't they see? It was so obvious. That was all she kept of him.

Three photographs at six and two decades of pain before Dr Green found her, saved her. Study was her only refuge, with scholarships taking her away from home on a magic carpet. There was medicine at UCLA where she "passed" as a female and passed academically cum laude. Passing, passing. Legal name change. Transitioning. Transitioning. Moving to get away from her history, little Charlie's past. America to Cambridge. All the words she had to hear. But how many years it had taken to hear Dr Green say, "treatment of gender dysphoria does not involve trying to correct the patient's gender identity but to help the patient."

Sex reassignment therapy: what an insult. She had always been Charmaine—just the first three letters shared. Cha-cha-cha. A dance, a cup of tea. But she had done it, done it, thanks to Dr Green. He had repaired her in Cambridge. He had made her outside match what she had always been inside. And then he had invited her. *Her*. To apply for a post at his unit. Equipa was like nowhere in the world. To have the best surgical links available, voice training, clothes, walking, and makeup lessons. This was unheard of outside of secret millionaires in Thailand. To have all this here in the UK and for her to be part of it!

But Mattie. Dear brave Mattie. She really understood him. His true male self came out consciously at 6, just as Charmaine did. So why was Dr Green bringing in the SJTU? Weren't they good enough? Was it Professor Frank's idea? A worry about diagnosing DID? Not that she had anything against them. Indeed, she had skimmed through a paper by Dr Stuart in the *British Journal of Psychiatry* on "Gender and Dissociation." But he had now urgently asked her to invite them again. Indeed, he had emphasised that after his round of New Year's Eve parties, he and his wife Betsy would be flying to their holiday home in Martha's Vineyard first thing. He said he would ring to check from there even though most of the SJTU would be closed.

164

Never mind. She didn't want Mattie to have to wait a day longer than was necessary, so perhaps it was all for the best. "Charmaine, I know you will give this your speediest professional attention," he had emphasised, his strong American accent having an extra force behind it. What was so special about this? Mattie Harrison was no different to the hundreds of children and young adults desperate to be seen. Or was there an issue about the supposed parents? There was some hint of an illegal kind of transatlantic adoption. But there were always issues of capacity, age, developmental need, and history. A new body was not just for Christmas, he had said once.

They had smiled at each other. He had seen the photo of little Charlie in a sailor suit on a beach. That was why she had chosen a surname with "Land" in it and "man" in honour of little Charlie.

She would phone the SJTU. There was a site directory.

CHAPTER 54

Monday, December 31st 2012, New Year's Eve, 2pm, Knightsbridge

Lord Glendale's townhouse

Lord Glendale left nothing to chance. His purpose-built Knightsbridge townhouse had a panic room and his windows were bulletproof. Small cameras from outside and inside the house discreetly fed images night and day to his two shifts of security guards. His study housed a door hidden in its panelled wooden walls, which led to a private office and beyond that to secure storage. The Prime Minister himself had joked his security was better than No 10—it had to be.

Project Orpheus had more potential and international meaning than whatever came from No 10. And once they had placed Ian there, there would be even more potential … if he did not mess up.

Lady Rose was a possible mistake that he had no power to stop happening. Errors could happen; showing off leads to mistakes. People with a learning disability of that level lost inhibition when dissociation was installed. It just could not be guaranteed to work properly. Poor Rose. She did not deserve that. Ian's mad belief that bloodline could bypass disability was a mistake. Poor Lily. This was not good for her either, and happy as he was to sacrifice others for his plans, she occupied a rare warm place in his heart. It was not his choice to follow her bloodline when there was a blot on it anyway, and there were others allocated to support Imogen and be Godparents to baby Toby. That was one of the best chances for the future of an aristocratic bloodline. And there were plenty of easier lower-class anonymous bloodlines to access, as well as Discards.

Wellbrook was an idiot to leave his wife and an idiot to start again at this age. But it was his 400-year bloodline with its royal links that had excited the Society. Wellbrook didn't understand his genetic importance. But others in his family and friendship circle did. And they had found poor dowdy little Imogen, provided her with a job, and placed her in his path. She had the benefit of keeping her eyes closed. She could not believe Wellbrook had chosen her and saw it as her life's mission to do right by him.

Wellbrook—another one like Anderson—couldn't keep it zipped. The Society had taken care of all his lovers, not just a new wife. His bloodline could not stay secure in Rose. And they had succeeded. Toby. A part of the future. Something different to the feeder units of the already dispossessed and discredited. They were the foot soldiers.

How different Wellbrook was from him. No lovers were ever invited to Lord Glendale's home. "A man's home is his castle," he enjoyed saying while mentioning that Holfren Castle in the Peak District, one of his many properties, was a place he liked taking lovers to. As well as his longstanding suites in carefully chosen hotels. But Toby. That was different.

The launch of the Lady Rose Independence Unit was supposed to be on January 5th. She was a good PR person, Keira Denny, and he did not want to clip her wings. But safety came first, and if there was any danger of publicity about Ian and Danny it would have to be cancelled. Or it could just miss her out. Modesty.

Keira could say Lady Rose was so proud that her parents had endowed the unit in her name, but she would be living there, and it was her home, so she would rather not say anything. Or she could just cut a ribbon. It would depend on what state she was in. Or could they brazen it out? Just a seamless psychosis? The trauma of her past rape was replayed on close friends because it was safe to … Look. She showed no fear of Ian Anderson, and that was because Masters was so efficient. He kept Little Rose under. All of these issues were possible.

But, on the official level, he needed to find out what was happening with the assessment report. Professor Frank was a wimp, a disappointment. Head over heels with Lady Lily, like nearly all of them. It was not worth pressuring him though, as his memory research was a useful distraction.

Diagnosis? She could be schizophrenic and have Down's Syndrome and stay in Harvest House but not then be upgraded into an Independence Unit... for fuck's sake! PTSD? Gender dysphoria? Capacity? This problem might get so big it had to just be left, and Ian would need to be supported. Or could they get rid of Ian? Oh, how he would love to do that!

He would give Lily a ring. She was a calm, sensible woman who understood the political problem even though she knew nothing of the rest.

CHAPTER 55

Monday, December 31st 2012,
New Year's Eve, 1:35pm

From: Sarahransome@harvesthouse.com
To: Dr.a.aziz@sjtu.com; Prof.c.frank@glendale.com
Cc: Faithwalker@harvesthouse.com; Lewmasters@harvesthouse.com

1:35pm

Dear Professor Frank, Dr Aziz, and colleagues,

RR returned from her meeting with you both in a calm regulated state. There was no sign of the serious agitation that she was in previously. However, to my concern she made allegations about 1 and 2. (You will know whom these numbers refer to). As she has now stated these allegations consistently with both fearful affect and with regulated affect, I am bound by my ethical code to report this. In enabling RR to feel properly heard, I must also report that she herself requested a police interview. I am aware of the extra complexities around this and am therefore reporting to you to ascertain the next steps. Is there a Vulnerable Victim Coordinator that I should contact or is that something you will do? I am here until 6pm today and can be reached on my extension number or by email.

Sarah Ransome

Day Manager

From: Prof.c.frank@glendale.com
To: Dr.a.aziz@sjtu.com; Sarahransome@harvesthouse.com
Cc: Faithwalker@.harvesthouse.com; Lewmasters@harvesthouse.com

1:45pm

STRICTLY CONFIDENTIAL

Dear Ms Ransome,

Thank you for your thoughtful email. It is indeed a complex confidential situation, and I am relieved we are all aware of its unusualness. Dr Aziz and I had intended one further meeting, but I think we might benefit from the final assessment being undertaken by someone outside the Glendale who will not be so close to the people concerned. Dr Aziz and I will then discuss the relevant police link.

Yours sincerely,

Professor C. Frank
MB BS PhD MD FRCPsych
Medical Director
The Lord Glendale Foundation and Centre

From: Dr.a.aziz@sjtu.com
To: Prof.c.frank@glendale.com; sarahransome@harvesthouse.com
Cc: Faithwalker@harvesthouse.com; Lewmasters@harvesthouse.com

1:50pm

Specialist Assessment

STRICTLY CONFIDENTIAL

Dear Professor Frank, Mrs Ransome, and colleagues,

Given the fact that a link to safeguarding now has to be made and that the allegations are so politically sensitive, I wonder if an independent assessment could be provided by Professor Hamilton here at St Joseph's University Forensic Unit. He is a regular expert witness to the High Court and highly regarded in legal circles. This would be less far for our patient to travel.

I also think, Professor Frank, that perhaps a call needs to be made to the Glendale's lawyers apprising them of all this before the police appointment is made. The allegation is made against a significant public figure in a way that will have unknown consequences.

Yours sincerely,

Dr Abdul Aziz
MBBS BSc Hons FRCPsych
Consultant Psychiatrist, SJTU and Harvest House

From: Prof.c.frank@glendale.com
To: Dr.a.aziz@sjtu.com

2:15 pm

STRICTLY CONFIDENTIAL

Dear Abdul,

This is to personally thank you and apologise for my behaviour. As you rightly said, I have had a complex conflict of interest with Lady L being a close personal friend and my inevitable social contact with Lord G, Sir P, and IA as a result of my post.

As you helpfully suggested, I phoned Professor Hamilton immediately, who understood the seriousness of it all and will see R at 4pm and write a report immediately. It will be couriered to the Crick and Beaufort Trust solicitors. They will also advise whether we go to local safeguarding or higher levels at the Met in terms of the nature of the allegations.

I would be grateful if you printed this to keep for legal purposes but not keep it on your computer. I assure you I have regained my clinical thinking on this and will consider my role most carefully. In the meantime, I will follow your clinical lead on any treatment need so that my own personal bias is not involved.

Thank you,

Christopher

For the attention of
Messrs Crick de Beaufort Solicitors
Lord Glendale Trust Lawyers
Professor C. Frank
Dr A. Aziz

Strictly Confidential

The report is sent separately under the password provided. Please note it was carried out within two hours of the request because of its seriousness. Names have been sent separately; password protected. A courier is also delivering a hard copy.

DH.

....

Report from St Joseph's University Forensic Unit

To Leonard Crick and George de Beaufort Partners
Crick and de Beaufort LLP

6pm

Specialist Assessment

I interviewed Ms X for the purpose of this report at my consulting room in St Joseph's University Hospital Forensic Unit on December 31st at 3pm. This was undertaken at the urgent telephone request of Professor Frank, Medical Director of the Lord Glendale Centre and Dr Abdul Aziz, Consultant Psychiatrist at the St Joseph's Trauma Unit (SJTU). I agreed with them about the seriousness and urgency of the situation and the need for an independent expert and offered her an appointment at 2pm on receipt of their calls today. Although I am full-time at the Forensic Unit, I have had a long-term interest in and involvement with adults with an intellectual disability.

Ms X did not wish to attend until her art class was over and Ms Ransome, the Harvest House Day Manager, and I agreed that it was important her wishes were accepted, given she had already had an interview that day, this had come without notice, and she enjoyed art.

Before seeing her, from 2pm–4pm, I read through her file, which refers to corroborated emotional abuse in childhood while at a mainstream school and a rape by a minicab driver while in secondary school.

I have also read a psychiatric report from her assessors at the Lord Glendale by Professor Chris Frank and Dr Abdul Aziz. I also received extracts from a tape recording of the interview conducted today and full contemporaneous file notes from: [redacted]

Ms Sarah Ransome, Day Manager at the Harvest House; Mr Lew Masters, Night Manager at Harvest House; Brenda Harris, Nurse, Harvest House; Tracey O'Bridey, Health Assistant, Harvest House; and a telephone call with her mother at 5.30pm.

I was therefore fully aware of the allegations she has made against A and B.

X is the only child of C and D. Her parents are both in good health with no problematic mental health history in either family, although there is clearly continuing tension for C over her parents' divorce and her father E's subsequent remarriage. Indeed, he has only just become a father again to a baby boy, F, who will inherit his estate and title as is customary in such families.

D is also a significant figure in local and national politics.

This case is therefore fraught with confidentiality difficulties.

Background:

X was born on January 5th 1991 in London after an uneventful pregnancy. She weighed 7lb at birth and had an easy delivery. Down's Syndrome was picked up immediately. She has had an ordinary developmental trajectory despite her Down's Syndrome. She fits within a mild to moderate level of disability in terms of her functioning, and within that she did well during her statutory education at West Infant Junior School, West Senior, and the day college she attended from Harvest House, where she now resides. She entered Harvest House at 18, and on her 21st birthday in just under a week is due to enter a purpose-built Independence Unit which bears her name.

Despite a proven history of bullying in junior school and a rape in her early teens, she did not seek, or her family and school did not seek, psychiatric or psychotherapeutic support.

This does not discount the possibility of emotional problems, merely that they did not come to the attention of statutory services.

However, since a trip to Vegas on October 31st and then again from November 21st, she has been showing emotional disturbance to a level

173

that has impacted on her residential placement and the experienced staff there. This culminated in a serious outburst on Christmas Day and Boxing Day.

She has consistently informed staff there and the previous assessors that a family visit with her parents to Las Vegas three months ago is the source of her distress. She stated that she was taken to a concert of B's on October 31st, and the abuse followed after this. B is a famous American singer who was recently found dead of a suspected drug overdose. She alleges that A took her inside the house at an after-concert party at B's house, while her mother wanted to swim in the host's heated outdoor swimming pool. Inside the house, she was taken to a room where B was waiting, and both men anally raped her. She had left her mother to go inside as she was frightened of water.

Her mother, whom I telephoned as a matter of courtesy, at 5.30pm, has corroborated her daughter's account. All of it, bar the abuse.

This shows that X's basic sense of fact is consistent. This of course does not mean that her allegations of abuse are correct but that there is no reason to consider, because of her disability, that her account can be discounted.

In other words, around the incident in question, which C says was October 31st, Ms X did indeed go to a concert in Las Vegas with the people mentioned. She did indeed go to B's after-concert party at his house and went into a private room with A and B while her mother was swimming, as she has had a phobia about water since the age of 6. No explanation has been found for her fear of water.

From past contacts with her teachers or family members, there is nothing to suggest that she has ever been known to be untruthful or to confuse fact with fiction. Indeed, the police found her testimony about bullying and rape unusually accurate.

There will be a query as to her credibility as a witness in terms of her condition from A's solicitors once A is approached by police, if he is. However, apart from a vulnerability to agree with any last question put before them, children and adults with Down's Syndrome alone are not less likely to give a truthful account unless there are other psychiatric co-morbidities.

I have not detected any in this case. However, this does not preclude a seamless psychosis when presented with possible traumatic triggers. A post-traumatic stress disorder is also possible, although in this interview there was no sign of it.

Indeed, I also gained the sense from my interview with her that she would cope adequately with the pressures of court and police, given the new rulings over how vulnerable witnesses are to be dealt with in court. I do not consider such procedures would cause her undue anxiety, confusion, or distress. However, such comments come as a result of her clinical presentation today. Were she to present in the way others have described, then there might be a different conclusion.

However, I need to add one significant note of caution. Although she submitted to an internal examination following the proven rape in her teens, the experience had such a traumatic impact on her that I do not feel she would be able to manage it again.

Professor D. Hamilton
MA MB BS PhD FRCPsych

....

CHAPTER 56

Monday, December 31st 2012, New Year's Eve, 8:30pm, Westminster Square

The Redcliffe residence

It was New Year's Eve and Lady Lily faced her dressing room mirror. The smell of lilies hanging in the air around her. The fragrance of lilies for all seasons. Maria kept them in her indoor containers and garden. How strange to stay so linked to a smell. Perhaps the only compliment her mother, Priscilla, had given her: "I called you Lily because you had the fragrance of lilies."

But another year of emptiness awaited her. No grandmotherhood to thaw her, no spark to return to her and Peter ... 21 years of erosion since Rose. Oh, they had earned more money: Peter was a wise investor and his political career had grown from strength to strength with her hard work and the guidance of friends like Glendale. But all could be ruined. Rose: her ruin.

She opened her pots of cream like a chemist. Dabs and fills and eye creams, and massages. There were so many different colours and brushes of different sizes. This also was her work.

Everything could be destroyed; 21 years of building up contacts, smiling at fetes and openings, pretending to be interested. All ruined. With Ian likely to be the next Prime Minister and accused by her mad daughter, how would he respond? What would happen? And Peter's colleagues? The pleasure that Ian had been brought down and smeared by the blameless Minister of Health's daughter? A flood of Fionas and all the rest of the media hyenas. It was not bearable.

A knock on the door and Peter entered. "How beautiful you are," he said in awe.

That was something that did not change quickly. She looked after herself. She could take comfort in that. She wore her favourite Dolce & Gabbana ruched stretched silk dress.

"Your emeralds?" he suggested in his semi-appeasing way. She hated that. His taste was impeccable, and she relied on it, but a question mark seemed to have entered his soul since Rose's birth.

Until Rose, he had been so confident with her, unlike the men and women shocked into silence. He would have opened her jewellery box and taken them out himself. Or bought her something new from Asprey.

"Yes," she agreed with an appreciative smile. How well her mother had brought her up.

"Anything I can do to help?"

She turned to face him. "Will Ian be there?"

"Possibly. I am not sure if his American trip was for a week or less."

"But Glendale will be there."

"Yes. Are you worried about our Rose?"

Ours ... how she wished Rose was just his.

"Yes. Even though I know Ian couldn't have—she is clearly remembering something that happened ... that happened before ... and I don't know if Ian can understand things like this ... whether it will change your relationship."

Sir Peter twisted a fine golden curl behind her ear. He was so easy to please.

"So long as he has not harmed my daughter, there will be no problem."

Oh—the foolish man. He was not even thinking of how Ian would regard him.

"Will you tell him?" She asked innocently.

"No, of course not. The police have to do their job." He turned to the door—"five minutes, darling."

She stood still and then turned to face herself in the mirror. Slowly she placed an exquisite emerald earring in each ear. Two green frozen tears.

CHAPTER 57

Monday, December 31st 2012, New Year's Eve, USA

Major D's office

Danny Delta alive: his voice singing just as he always had. Music was immortality. But Danny wasn't coming back. There was the estuary meeting the sea, the sand, the beach house beauty, but not for him. The Society had spent thousands on his voice, his clothes, and his record cover. Stefan Solag had worked for hours on it: his best commission. That had left Ian and him with money to spare.

But there was no replica of Danny installed in another multiple. No true replacement for him to mourn with. Thank heavens he still had his Lee inside Sandra, although Lee was stuck at an adolescent stage and would never be like Danny. Thanks to his programming abilities and investment, he had been allowed to sneak Lee in because one male teenager did not upset the applecart of personalities. An adolescent was seen as less risk than a functioning adult. What a reward! That was something. Orpheus understood this. Only Orpheus with his billions had the power to choose this. Imagine, the way Sandra was as near perfect as possible; they were getting closer to the ideal prototype. If he had the billions, he could have installed Danny into a younger multiple, and his loss would have been halved. That would have been as good as real.

Z had laughed and agreed, and commented that synthetic breasts were now preferred to real ones. Reality could be changed.

With Sandra being their top prototype to date and an equal part of their political planning, she knew this aspect of his life even if she did not approve. He wished she had been made a tad more tolerant of non-binary sexualities, but that would have risked her relationship with Prince Carl-Zygmunt and broken her amnesic walls with her other parts, Lee, Lara, and Leandra. What an irony—she was an equal part of their planning and understood multiplicity in others but not in herself. She could not be made generous or open to all others, or it would contaminate her sole mission. And obviously, Lee understood him. He was lucky. The money from Orpheus was advancing all their aims—immortality installations being the staging post through which the military and scientific aims could also advance. And the biggest backers could have a mixture of aims and were somehow linked to the sacred bloodlines. These bloodlines were seen as more precious than gold, than nationhood. An Olympic flame to go from generation to generation regardless of social class. Z had impressed that on him, and Z was a scientist.

Prince Carl-Zygmunt was with Sandra now. Their useful HRH addition—even though Neuplatzstan had no place or territory. He himself could have been with her—or rather with Lee via her—but he felt Orpheus was weakest in the UK at the moment due to the Rose situation. If Prince Carl-Zygmunt was emotionally restored by Sandra that would improve his resources, and Sandra would also be stronger from the contact with him.

Pygmalion had it made, Orpheus had once joked. A rare moment of humour in such a depressed man. Well, he had helped to make Sandra, with the help of Dr Green, Z, and his CIA allies. She was one of the best, even though he didn't really go for women.

Sandra's Searches was a brilliant idea and her own. People applauded a robot that could paint. Sandra was light years beyond this. Nothing could stop her success. She combined sex kitten and strategic planning. Lara could not stop the success of Sandra; Lara rarely appeared, and Sandra's parents could be guaranteed to send her back if she stayed too long.

Leandra was more of a worry. She had linked up with Cassandra, a possible Society failure, and the reads from her *Message in a Bottle* internet blog had grown considerably. There was a serious failure in the way she had grown that he would have to attend to. This was her first mention of Z—Zed or Zee. Could she get any closer? Z would be his Omega.

179

Mattie was also a loose end, and he needed to keep watch over baby Toby. He would try a remote tweak on Leandra with a phone call after checking with Z. It was possible she had been terminated inside. Unlike Ian, he did not enjoy using gorillas.

If Orpheus needed Sandra to be stronger, it would have to happen, even if it meant Lee disappeared. His Lee. The one he loved most outside of Danny. Even though Lee was a throw-in, an extra just for him. Made for him. Orpheus had waited a long time, watching the implants and the installations. Soon it would be ready for him.

CHAPTER 58

Monday, December 31st 2012, New Year's Eve, USA

When HRH Prince Carl-Zygmunt arrived, Sandra greeted him with a careful intensity. She wore a high-necked dark-blue silk dress. The beta sex programme was inside- implicit and not crudely on display.

"What is wrong, my prince? You are suffering. Come in and rest."

Her voice was soft but deep.

A burden inside Carl-Zygmunt lifted and left him. This was what he had come for.

She led him to the large blue velvet sofa. "Sit, my prince, and I will bring your whisky."

It was Barrel Bourbon whisky—his favourite—specially stocked.

She sat by him and stroked his head. "Poor prince. It is hard for you with Ian being a stupid pig, and you and Glendale holding it."

Yes. she knew everything he needed for her to help him. She removed his shoes and knelt on the floor, massaging his tired feet.

"Don't worry. If that retard Rose accuses Ian, Sarah's Searches will focus on Harvest House or the SJTU or our little Lew. Whoever disturbs Orpheus, Major D, and my prince is my sworn enemy. Whatever is needed to keep my prince safe and happy." A shudder of relief passed through his body. This was one of the geniuses of Orpheus. The beauty of the Society.

Her hands moved higher. "Prince Carl-Zygmunt and Sandra. We are intertwined forever."

CHAPTER 59

Monday, December 31st 2012, New Year's Eve, USA

The Rt Hon Ian Anderson was angry. Orpheus had told him to fly home to the UK. Did they think he was a carrier pigeon to cross the big pond whenever someone wanted him to? The phone call had come while he was happily engaged with the young waiter he had his eye on. The boy's doe eyes were filled with tears as he pulled his trousers up and raced out. He didn't know he had been gifted by an Honourable Member.

Amusing himself in-house was less energy than takeaway and less risky when abroad. The Society could tip or clear up any mess. He would have ignored the call, but it was a seven-ringer.

Apparently Rose was blabbing to all and sundry about him and Danny. As if he would fuck her ever! It was only the Master in her he related to, the Master with the bloodline powers, and the host body was too retarded for the programming to stay. What a sham Master. If the Master operated properly, there would be no awareness of the event, let alone blabbing. Perhaps he should use Lew again. Destabilise her on a roundabout. Spin her so that Good Rose, Bad Rose, Lady Rose, and Little Rose alternated so quickly no one would listen to anything they said. Remind the man he was only needed as a gorilla. Not that he underestimated the power of gorillas—he was one himself, after all, at times. But it was the programme

183

tweaking that excited him. If he had been handed the task of Rose, it would have ended differently, even if she had to go. She was expendable even though she was bloodline. Even bloodlines could have clots!

What was the sympathy that Glendale and HRH had for Rose? Why? Her own mother didn't have any. If they were to abort her now, Lily might even be relieved. It should have happened 21 years ago. But Lady Rose was bloodline, and that was why she was spared even though the Society, outside of him, had lost interest in her. She was shoddy goods. She didn't work, and broken programmes should be discarded.

So they were worried about a scandal and press and all of that? Rubbish. Fiona could do a nice interview in *The Mercury*. He was the close family friend, deeply saddened that Rose, who was like a god-daughter to him, could have such a disturbed twist in her mind. It must be the impact of change and her birthday and memories of the rape ... no one would give it any credence, especially as her own mother, Lady Lily, would be so shocked and on his side. Lily. Now she was a different matter.

He was not scared and did not need to be back in the country. Perhaps he should phone her. Yes. And then fly back to London to assure her he was not troubled. What a political diamond she was! More concerned for that dull Peter's ambitions than for her daughter.

Stefan wasn't with him. He had not invited him, and Stefan would still be in a sulk. He knew Lily was hoping for a big wedding and advancing the political cause of gay rights, but he was not so sure. Of either. The country wasn't ready and he liked having his space to experiment. Equipa. There was much to occupy him.

Perhaps he should go home to the UK after all. Glendale's brother was being pursued by the media, so he couldn't go there. He hadn't even been allowed to phone him, "just in case." Poor Harold. So obviously a second son and not the heir, and so much more his type than the straitlaced brother, Oliver. No wonder he had endowed that children's home. His own personal larder. He had helped himself too much from that larder, and now it was closed.

Orpheus—the man and not the project—wouldn't deign to see him in person and nor would Z or Major D, the outward tough-guy but inside softy, who was grieving for Danny. You couldn't get too close. He ought to know that. You never knew who would be taken out.

He suddenly felt an unusual pang at the thought of Stefan missing him. *When You Come Back* and its harp music suddenly flooded his mind. Could he make the Redcliffe New Year's Eve party?

CHAPTER 60

Monday, December 31st 2012, New Year's Eve, 8:30pm, Knightsbridge

The Green residence

Dr Simon Green was thoroughly enjoying the New Year's Eve party. It was one of three black tie events he and his wife Betsy, resplendent in red velvet, were popping in on. They would be back in their own luxurious apartment by midnight, raising a toast to each other.

Their Art Deco mantelpiece had been covered with invitations to the most prestigious New Year's Eve events, both public and private. Not bad for the small son rejected by his tall powerful father. "Half man" was just one of the words his father lobbed at him until a scholarship to Cambridge allowed him to leave the USA. Four years later, a research and teaching post at UCLA gave him further freedom. He hadn't seen his father since.

Simon and his wife Betsy had sat for hours discussing which party/ parties they should attend. That was one of the pleasures of their marriage—the prestige involved in his work, their joint work.

As newly made Director of Equipa, he was sought out by trans people all over the world and their hardworking organisations, and their desperate partners and families. He was also loved by the literati, glitterati, and Twitterati for fulfilling their liberationist ideologies. And then of course there were the politicians and aristocrats with their hidden trans people and their hidden agendas, and there were the military and secret services. Some of these were more likely to come to his private company, Tiresias.

Tiresias had just two staff, both of whom were directors, himself and Betsy, who also acted as his personal assistant. This had been established to aid the rich and the international aristocracy who were LGBT QIPA, as well as other individuals who moved him.

He agreed to become Director of Equipa—an obvious choice—on the condition Tiresias could continue. This was agreed. Moreover, it suited Lord Glendale and others to feed certain hush-hush clients to Tiresias despite the excellent security at the Lord Glendale.

There was one agenda he was very intrigued by. There was allegedly an American billionaire—codenamed Z—who was very rich, and politically and scientifically highly connected. He was a friend of Major D, and Lord Glendale had pointed this out to him in a confidential meeting over a decade ago. The more non-binary identities were welcomed and accepted within DID internationally, the stronger the need to cover up their identities.

Dissociative identity disorder, the new term for multiple personality disorder, had a fascinating role here, as he and Major D knew only too well. Mattie Harrison, a new referral, could be a research link here. There were some transatlantic problems over parents and foster-parents, but that could be smoothed out.

From his CIA experience and scientific contacts, Major D had long seen the possibilities of this work of installed dissociation for national and international security. These were follow-ons of MK-Ultra, Monarch, and Operation Paperclip. Extra unrestricted fund subsidies came to the Equipa and Tiresias from companies linked to them both.

Tiresias was a name that had come to him immediately. A blind or blinded male prophet of Apollo with the gift of prophecy was turned into a woman for seven years...the perfect patron for transsexuality. He could also give help after his death from the underworld.

The Americans had not only liked the name of his project and the Equipa, they had even liked his surname and told him his name was his fortune—Green. It linked in people's minds with the real or phantom Dr Green, who apparently installed kabbalah programming for Mengele. So at least his father had given him one useful thing as nothing else useful had come from him. To have Major D, a crew-cut muscular giant of a man, treat him with such respect had healed something profound. To have, through that, the meeting with Z, was even more important.

Being flown to meet him in Washington as well as in the UK, he had been given the history of the research and development of chemical, biological, and radiological materials capable of employment in clandestine operations to control human behaviour. Creating dissociation was one of them.

These programmes consisted of myriad subprojects contracted out to various universities, research foundations, and similar institutions. At least 80 institutions and 145 private researchers participated. Because the agency had funded MK-Ultra indirectly, many of the participating individuals were unaware that they were dealing with the agency. This research, while controversial, offered a chance for international progress less damaging to human life than mass warfare. A successful Manchurian candidate could kill a dictator effortlessly, and no one would be the wiser as to who they were. This would save thousands of soldiers' lives in normal warfare.

As he understood it, Project MK-Ultra was first brought to public attention in 1975 by the Church Committee, but CIA Director Richard Helms had ordered their destruction in 1973. In 1977, more documents were found, there was a further Senate hearing, and in 2001 some remaining information was declassified.

He had a password. He could contact Z day and night, any day. Any research money he needed. Any research subjects he needed. Anything he wanted, they would give him. And they wanted so little in exchange. He had security clearance, and so did Betsy. He made it clear she shared all information with him.

They had never wanted children. It was an effortless decision. In return they had the freedom to develop their interests to a level neither would have imagined.

Despite the schoolboy thrill he still felt at being in such rich and powerful company, and tonight that would be Lady Lily and Sir Peter Redcliffe, Lord Glendale, and others, he could not wait for midnight. To be alone with Betsy and toast their shared life.

He was short and thin and, as Betsy had said to her friends on meeting him, "he doesn't look anything like a prince charming, but he is one." Charmaine and countless others knew that was true.

CHAPTER 61

Monday, December 31st 2012, New Year's Eve, 11pm, South Kensington

Deirdre Hislop's residence

Deirdre Hislop was sitting by her computer in her small immaculate study. There were no personal emails yet, and there were no work ones. Adverts for winter cruises, winter sales, summer holidays, and furniture had passed by her spam filter.

Through her window, she could see lights from the houses opposite. There were fireworks, a constant stream of visitors ringing bells on different doors, and people on balconies talking loudly and holding their glasses of champagne.

In one hour she would send her traditional "Happy New Year" messages to all the staff at the SJTU and linked colleagues. She had already added Sarah Ransome, the new Day Manager at Harvest House to her list. Dr Stuart would still be in Quebec or in transit back.

He would be filled and renewed with the joys of baby Jamie. She had already bought a Babygro! And a tiny soft tartan hat! Irresistible. The thought of Dr Stuart and Moira as grandparents filled her with pleasure; even though she wished James and Martine lived in the UK, Moira would want to travel to Quebec regularly, and how would that be?

Jon Levine, she guessed, would be having a drink with his mother and watching television. She wished him success in finding a partner this year. Elouise and Dan would be having a family party filled with sleeping or not sleeping children. She smiled. She felt like an invisible honorary grandmother watching over her brood at a distance.

Abdul, Mina and their children, and Amma and Abba would be singing together and drinking lassi.

And Carmen, what would she be doing? Smiling at her drunken husband or cleaning up?

But wasn't that all a distraction?

Here she was, the last of her line, on the eve of a new year. What did she want for her? Not the unit! Her! An hour to go. She owed it to herself to come up with something different. Her parents, bless them, had loved New Year's Resolutions and wishes. They would all sit down with their Parker pens and Quink—nothing so vulgar as a biro for such a purpose—and have half an hour to write down resolutions on their best thickest paper. The smell of the Quink.

Then they would all be read and discussed. Her father would wish for world peace and resolve to give up smoking, which he never did. Her mother wished for an end to homelessness and resolved to be punctual and orderly, which she never was. And she had wished for help for people who suffered, and that was her job now, and she didn't smoke, and she was punctual and orderly.

Deirdre Hislop, she remarked to herself, with great surprise and pleasure, you are a trinity! She smiled to herself! And then she went for her small bottle of champagne and pressed "Send" on her waiting-to-be-sent emails.

As she opened the bottle, relishing the pop and rush of bubbles, she gaily decided she would open one of the boxes of chocolates she had been given.

CHAPTER 62

Monday, December 31st 2012, New Year's Eve, 11:30pm, Balham

Sarah Ransome's residence

Sarah Ransome sat in front of her television with a glass of champagne and a bowl of crisps. She had meant to cook herself a wonderful dinner. Indeed, she had even written down the ingredients. But finally she could not do it and popped an M&S dish into her microwave. She hadn't even checked what it was. How she would like to be the sort of single woman who cooked herself a special occasion meal for one. A wonderful roast duck with plum sauce and Chinese vegetables and rice followed by ginger ice cream.

Her dinner party cooking had always been for Steve and their friends, so trying to do it or thinking of trying to do it made the absence of him even stronger. In fact, it had been mainly for his friends. He had not really liked Penny, Frances, or her colleagues. And she had been such a snob preferring his ambitious lecturer friends to her ground-down world-weary social work lot. Look how they had all swiftly disappeared: rats off a sinking ship.

No. Not fair on herself. Penny had never been ground-down; she would be in the midst of a party right now, but she would send her a brief message. She had not appreciated her enough. A good friend did not suddenly disappear after 20 years. And what about Frances? A New Year's Resolution, she decided, holding up her champagne glass. Get over it, stupid woman! Jettison anything to do with him. Be brave and bright and beautiful. Be grateful to Cell Block H and call Penny and Frances.

Three alerts on her iPhone. A "Happy New Year" from Penny, Frances, and that nice woman Deirdre at the SJTU. And a message from Faith that the New Year's Eve party she had suggested for H was working and Lew had really done well. Her heart lifted. Work was her solo area and had never been linked to Steve, and they had never lived in London. This was going to be a better year.

CHAPTER 63

Monday, December 31st 2012,
New Year's Eve, 11:30pm, Westminster

Sir Peter stood by the side of the bar, welcoming a moment to himself amidst the crowds. His mother would not disturb him. Her eyes always went to the kingmakers and she did not consider him so relevant! The ballroom was a glittering collage of velvet, silk, and crystal glasses. Lily was darting in and out of groups like a sparkling butterfly. He watched her alighting on one group, bringing them to life and then moving on to the next.

She could recognise incipient boredom or see where someone had to move elsewhere; when ex-partners suddenly saw each other, or political rivalries reared their heads. She had always had this capacity, but without the shared happiness, qualities that were once loved could now be viewed differently. At that moment, she was pointing out one of Stefan Solag's vast photographic landscapes to Professor Chris Frank—another of her prodigies. They were all in love with her.

He did not mind. Her genius was not just for him, his career, or out of love for him or their shared hopes. It was her; it was what she did; it was who she was. She was the firstborn daughter whose birth broke Lord Wellbrook's heart. He wanted a son and heir. Not a daughter—however beautiful. So, her birth broke her mother's heart too. But whereas Wellbrook ignored her, her mother pushed her and hot-housed her. She had to be the best son and daughter, brilliant at everything. No wonder she felt sorry for Ian. They were both like second sons. Except Lily had brains and diplomacy. There was Lady Priscilla, his mother-in-law, stiff and upright, talking to Oliver Glendale. He was the only man who could thaw a small smile from her honed face. There was his own mother approaching them: another ice queen.

Suddenly, Lily was smiling in front of him, the cat offering the mouse it had caught. In tow was a small thin rather ugly man with a large rather bland beaming wife in red velvet. Ah yes. The famous Dr Green and his wife Betsy. "Simon and Betsy, darling," said Lily in that seductive voice by which she named people without showing he might have forgotten. She somehow emphasised names as if polishing a precious gift. He used to be in awe of it. No—not a cat—somehow she now appeared like a trained puppy doing tricks. He was tired of having people served up—for what?

"Ah, Simon and Betsy—I have been wanting to congratulate you on the Equipa. It is a truly international model." He went into a parliamentary role effortlessly. He was like a robot.

They both beamed at him like lottery winners, and Lily gave him her patronising congratulatory smile … you did right, stupid husband; you did not spoil my hard work.

"Thank you, Sir Peter. It has been a wonderful party," said the small man, with an American accent, turning to his wife. "Betsy—I think we have to leave now." Betsy smiled warmly back at her husband, and Lily and Peter for a moment felt like wallflowers. Goodness. The Greens wanted to be together, alone.

"Only half an hour to the New Year," smiled Lily seductively, but the Greens were already saying goodbye and leaving. Lily and Peter looked at each other, really looked and saw the pain in each other's lives. And then the moment passed. Glendale was there with an arm around them both. "How do you both do it? You never disappoint."

A sudden extra wave of noise reached them. HRH and Ian made their way unsteadily through the crowds of people to the bar. A genuine smile transformed Lily's face. "You came back," she smiled.

"Courtesy of a private jet from our American friends," laughed CZ. Ian nodded. "We had to see you."

A vicious punch on his shoulder turned him around with alacrity. Stefan was facing him, half-pleased and half furious.

"And you!" he added; taking him by surprise, he kissed him roughly on the lips, and Lily gave a little cheer. This was the first public kiss.

CHAPTER 64

Monday, December 31st 2012,
New Year's Eve, 11:30pm,
Harvest House

The evening so far was an unrivalled success. 11.30pm and no critical incidents. Tracey O'Bridey and Lew Masters were at the centre of activities in the large dayroom. The television was on silently, unusually in the background, awaiting the chimes of Big Ben.

Residents who did not want to go to bed were having their first New Year's Eve party for years. It had been Sarah Ransome's suggestion, and to her surprise Lew had taken it on board and had instructed Tracey, as well as enlisting Brenda's help. Brenda's grownup children were at their own parties, and her husband did not care for such events. The overtime was more helpful to them at this moment than seeing out the New Year or having a party. Lew had got permission for the event, and a cleaner and kitchen assistant from the Glendale had been allocated. Lew had even been praised for "increasing the move to normalisation."

He had pushed the refectory tables to the side with help from John and Dykes. He decided it was appropriate to do that in his white vest T-shirt, and Tracey looked at his muscular arms with admiration. She also witnessed the happy blush on John's face when Lew told him what big muscles he had. When Lew turned away, John proudly showed off his arm muscles to Dykes. Faith had popped in unexpectedly at that moment, on her way back from a friend's party, and could not quite believe this was the same Lew. "Honestly," she texted Maureen, "you wouldn't believe it—he was really empowering John and Dykes." She hesitated a moment and then copied it to Sarah with a Happy New Year message.

"This is party, Faith, like mummy and daddy have. Good Lady Rose," beamed Rose, approaching her with a big hug.

"This is a proper party," agreed Faith.

"Shame mummy and daddy miss it."

"Happy New Year, Faith," smiled Brenda. "You couldn't keep away!"

"Faith wanted see Lady Rose," beamed Rose.

"That's right!" agreed Faith.

Lew Masters approached them, and Faith congratulated him, receiving a "Happy New Year" with no innuendo. How could she have got him so wrong? What had happened? And that sexualised Barbi/Bambi meets Goth, Tracey, was smiling nervously but happily.

Faith moved on to speak to Tim, who had the task of filling two remaining bowls with peanuts and crisps. The jelly and trifle had been cleared away. *The Twelve Days of Christmas* was playing on the old grey loudspeakers. Suddenly all was quiet.

"Listen," said Lew. He turned the television up and everyone listened to the 12 chimes of Big Ben.

"Happy New Year!" he shouted, and everyone called back, even Tim, pausing in his rocking. Lew stood up on a chair so everyone could see him. "Dance time," shouted Lew. "On your feet, happy campers."

Tracey laughed. There was an unusual sense of energy and pleasure in the room.

"Come on, Lady Rose. Good, good, good Lady Rose," he called. "You can help everyone because you know how to dance."

Rose was sitting next to Sinita, a glass of orange squash in her hand. She smiled warmly back at him. "Good Lady Rose here, Master."

He asked if Rose or anyone knew what song they had to sing now it was midnight and New Year's Eve. It had a dance to go with it too. Brenda beamed warmly as Rose called out *Auld Lang Syne* and held her arms out to start the dance.

"Alright Master Masters—hello Faith. Come on, Sinita. Good Lady Rose teach you dance."

They moved to the centre of the floor, holding Serby the bear between them and started dancing and giggling. A young man from the long-stay male ward followed their movements around and around, chasing their ghosts with his eyes. Two elderly women followed suit. Another stood still and curtseyed. Jon and Dykes were skipping around the room and high-fiving each other. Tim stood rocking. The room had filled.

Tracey felt strangely affected. These retards, sorry, learning difficulties people, were enjoying it. She was helping them have a nice time. And she was earning. A pittance true. But it was her money. The raves didn't have quite the same charge as money in her hands. As Lew had told her, money was power. Money would get her away from Reg. Lew had said she did not use her own power properly. She was living with a sleazebag for the sake of an address instead of getting her own place. He said with her looks she could get loads more dough. Sarah was also leaving her leaflets about courses.

She kept a wary distance from Rosie but was otherwise finding the rest of the work easier. Curiously, Rosie also avoided her.

She joined in; John and Dykes clearly knew the dance steps and pulled her hands to join them. And so did Brenda, Tracey, and Faith. Slowly everyone joined a larger and larger circle. And at the centre of it all, singing loudly, singing with all his heart, Lew Masters was the true and honourable Lord of the Dance.

Not the gorilla. But a true Master. No fear or split from Rose, no flinching around the men. And now he knew his true power. The God in himself.

And above him blinking silently on the ceiling was the small camera.

CHAPTER 65

Monday, December 31st 2012, New Year's Eve

Message in a Bottle: Cassandra's blog

This is from me on New Year's Eve somewhere in cyberspace.

In response to questions from the new Twitty Twitterati and to the Facebookers who don't read proper books or dare to communicate face to face:

Cassandra resisted the advances of the God Apollo, so he punished her by giving her the gift of prophecy but not making it believed. So here I am, not for the rubberneckers but for those who really want to know the truth.

Poor Danny Delta. He was a Monarch slave, as was/is Leandra and I, and countless others. His surname is the first clue. Delta. An assassin. This is not my fantasy. Read the Greenbaum speech by Dr Corydon Hammond. Whom was Danny supposed to kill? Himself? A part? Or was he killed for telling too much in his song? Of course, he was split. Let me tell you more.

TRIGGER ALERT: This article contains disturbing elements and might trigger Monarch survivors.

You can get DID from lack of parental care and relentless abuse and that is one kind. The most usual. And most professionals can't even get their heads around that. So think how easy it is to hide a crime against humanity when you tweak it a stage further and deliberately create it! And that you can even have real congressional findings revealing this, and no one in the good US of A or in the UK turns a hair or makes a documentary. So hello post-truthers, alternative fact-mongers! Cassandra is used to not being believed but having her facts visible and made invisible in plain sight is another matter.

So—there are at least two other kinds of DID to the ordinary, and they aim to split you deliberately. The two I know both have origins in MK-Ultra and Western torture. They may have different kinds of torture in other parts of the world. Probably do. Humans are pretty similar wherever they are and in whatever century. The Egyptian Book of the Dead included some of the basic tools for this.

MK-Ultra and Monarch. Torturing others is as old as time and as old as people, but in our time in the West the key "Godfather" is Joseph Mengele, the "Angel of Death," known especially for his experiments on concentration camp prisoners in the Second World War, especially his experiments on twins and Mind Kontrolle (hence MK). Yes, post-truthers, this is all real. Check it.

Sources say either he or his protégée in this work was also known as Dr Green. Hence the importance of the name Dr Green (see the Equipa Centre), who often appears in a mind-controlled slave. Sometimes the surname is genuine. I don't go in for conspiracy theory. But inside every slave is a Dr Green, and sometimes outside too. And people are sometimes recruited because of their names. These groups like making the symbolic literal, so their victims are seen as autistic or schizophrenic when they take words seriously.

At the end of the Second World War, the CIA under Operation Paperclip recruited Nazi doctors and scientists to whom they gave immunity from prosecution in exchange for an experimental result. Mengele's research was the core of MK-ULTRA. An unofficial part of which then developed into Monarch.

Project MK-ULTRA, so I have researched, ran from the early 1950s to the late 1960s, formally, using American and Canadian citizens as its subjects. Project MK-ULTRA involved drugs, sensory deprivation, isolation, verbal and physical abuse, and torture. It aimed to change the mind, and one part of it aimed to create "Manchurian candidates," programmed to perform various acts such as assassinations and other covert missions. Children were used too.

MK-ULTRA was brought to light by various commissions in the 1970s, including the Rockefeller Commission of 1975. Look it up! Although it is claimed that the CIA stopped such experiments after these commissions. I can tell you they simply went "underground" and Monarch Programming became the classified and secret successor of MK-ULTRA, and of course the doctors and scientists and military who had been part of these programmes continued to develop them privately, sometimes in their own families, outside the aegis of government, sometimes at the request of the uber-wealthy.

Like the billionaire called Orpheus whom Leandra tells us about in "Message in a Bottle." And know we are not connected, although I feel we are soul-sisters. Perhaps we are both messages in bottles.

The three things money cannot buy are love, mental health, and immortality. And when you hurt people, you get lonelier and have needs which will lead to madness if they are not answered. Forget Russian mail-order brides. With Monarch you have people made for someone. Monarch slaves like Danny and Leandra and me are used by the world elite in fields such as the military, politics, sex slavery, and the entertainment industry. But also for companionship. A sex-bot with brains and a heart. Watch out for the signs.

So there are many other private developments all over the world.

In deliberately creating dissociative identity disorder through drugs, electroshock, and other torture, Monarch also added ritual abuse of a Satanist or Luciferian kind to make the amnesia stronger. Some believed in it and some just used it, but the impact on the victim was the same—terrifying. As all belief systems were instilled in me with torture I now stay away from all of them.

Monarch mind control is named after the Monarch butterfly, which learns where it was born and passes on this knowledge via genetics to its offspring from generation to generation. That applies to other species too, but somehow mind controllers settled for this. This programme is based on the New World Order (yes—that again and it is real or rather it is real to those who made me!) and Nazi goals to create a Master race in part through genetics. This was Mengele's hot topic. So parents are found who can pass on the correct genetic knowledge to those victims selected for the Monarch mind control programme. They are not needed after that. Only their genes matter. The ability to dissociate is a major requirement, and it is, they think, most readily found in children like me who come from families with multiple generations of abuse. Out of many come many.

These groups, religious, atheist, political, or non-political, want an army of Manchurian candidates, tens of thousands of mental robots who will do prostitution, do movies, smuggle narcotics, engage in international arms dealing and smuggling, fight, assassinate dictators, assassinate resisters ... and so on.

And they make two groups of us. There are the Bloodliners who are destined to survive and have power in some states of mind and those who can dissociate easily genetically but are not bloodline and are Discards; they can be killed off if they find out too much ... like Danny.

199

Whether Bloodliner or Discard, the purpose of your torture is to instil the following:

ALPHA. Regarded as "general" or regular programming within the base control personality; accomplished through deliberately subdividing the victim's personality.

BETA. Referred to as "sexual" or "sex-kitten" programming, training is provided from the earliest age to become accomplished in all forms of sexuality. The greatest joy is to successfully arouse another.

GAMMA. Another form of system protection is through "deception" programming, which elicits misinformation, disinformation, and misdirection. This level causes problems with police evidence, discrediting the "main" person as a viable witness.

DELTA. This is the key part of Manchurian candidate research. The Delta is a programmed assassin developed for elite forces. Subjects are devoid of fear; very systematic in carrying out their assignment. Self-destruct or suicide instructions are layered in at this level.

THETA means "psychic" programming. This is a development of training that was automatic in multi-generational Satanist families anxious to show the genetic benefits of the bloodline. It is the true story behind the censored story of the men who stare at goats.

OMEGA. A "self-destruct" suicide form of programming. This programme is generally activated when the victim/survivor begins therapy or interrogation and too much memory is being recovered.

These are put in by carefully rotated torture that is kept in place by ongoing "ordinary" abuse.

Are you still there Facebookers and post-truth rubberneckers, and the Twitterati and texters? Is any of this familiar to you?

Take that in and then you will know I am speaking out of the bowels of big business, big pharma ... and I am still alive to help you, but I don't know for how much longer. Even a Bloodliner comes to the internal end of the line sometimes and meets the Freedom Train the Discards find. And of course, in the end, we all die.

Watch The Glendales. Watch the news for Danny. Watch Dr Green. Watch Equipa, watch Harold Fitz-Hugh West in Washington. You heard it here first. Mattie?

CHAPTER 66

Tuesday, January 1st 2013,
New Year's Day, 9am

Metropolitan Police: letter to those concerned

From: Messrs Crick de Beaufort Solicitors: Lord Glendale Trust Lawyers
To: Professor C. Frank, Medical Director
Dr A. Aziz, Consultant, St Joseph's University Hospital
Mrs S. Ransome, Harvest House Day Manager
Mr L. Masters, Night Manager, Harvest House
DC Morag Lennon, Westbridge Vulnerable Victim Coordinator

Strictly Confidential

We have read the confidential report from Professor Hamilton and the attachments. Therefore, we agree with the clinicians that a safeguarding link should be made.

The hospital is in the constituency of Westbridge SW21 and is under the area of the Metropolitan police. The local Vulnerable Victim Coordinator, DC Morag Lennon, has been informed and has all the paperwork.

From my phone call to her I can state that there will be a highly confidential CRIS (Crime Report Information System) report, which understands all the relative sensitivities. The CRIS record is initially an allegation only, but after investigation and supervision the correct classification is given to the record. Where the occurrence of a crime depends on the outcome of forensic tests; a CRIS record is created not as a crime but as a crime incident. This is suited to the high sensitivity of this subject.

We understand DC Morag Lennon will make contact with a Gold Group.

I *include below some information provided by the MPS (Metropolitan Police Service).*

> A Gold Group is a meeting designed to add value to the police response to an internal or external incident, crime or other matter. This involves bringing together appropriately skilled and qualified internal or external stakeholders who can advise, guide, or otherwise support the management of an effective response to the identified incident, crime, or other matter.
>
> The purpose of any Gold Group should be to ensure the effectiveness of the ongoing police response and, if confidence issues exist for the victim/ victim's family and/or the community, to resolve or prevent the escalation of their impact.
>
> The Gold Group should be run by an ACPO lead (Commander or above) or, if locally on Borough, a member of the Senior Leadership Team, normally Superintendent or above.
>
> The Gold Group could be comprised of various stakeholders and professionals from other interested agencies.
>
> There would be a range of ranks and officers who would perform a relevant or interested role, and there may also be IAG members (Independent Advisory Groups).
>
> There is no fixed recommendation around the number of meetings held. It would depend entirely on the nature of the incident and potential areas of vulnerability, learning and whether this would be dealt with long-term.
>
> It may be that only one Gold Group is required or several.

This is a highly confidential matter, and we remind those who receive this email that their contracts are absolutely clear on the crucial importance of confidentiality.

Yours sincerely,

Leonard Crick

Senior Partner

CHAPTER 67

Tuesday, January 1st 2013,
New Year's Day, 9am

Text messages

Leonard Crick to Lord Glendale

9:10am. Urgent meeting needed.

Lord Glendale to Leonard Crick

9.30am?

Lord Glendale to Ian Anderson and Prince Carl-Zygmunt

Urgent telephone meeting needed.

Ian Anderson to Major D

Ring when awake.

Major D to Z

Bell me when free.

....

Keira Denny to Lord Glendale, Lady Lily, Sir Peter, Sarah Ransome, Dr Abdul Aziz

Happy New Year. This is Keira Denny. I am so excited we are getting closer to the Lady Rose launch day. Thank you for permitting me to speak to you. Please let me know when we can meet or talk on the phone.

....

Dr Abdul Aziz to Dr Gawain Stuart

Are you free for an emergency talk?

Dr Stuart to Dr Aziz

Come now!

....

From: Franny@hotmail.co.uk
To: Sarahrant@gmail.com

Happy New Year! Sorry if what I have sent worries you, but I take some of it seriously and it looks quite close to you. I haven't sent you all of it.

Love

Frances

Forwarded:

....

This is from me on New Year's Eve somewhere in cyberspace.

In response to questions from the Twitty Twitterati and Facebookers who don't read proper books or dare to communicate face to face:

Cassandra resisted the advances of the God Apollo, so he punished her by giving her the gift of prophecy but not making it believed. So here I am, not for the rubberneckers but for those who really want to know the truth.

Poor Danny Delta. He was a Monarch slave, as was/is Leandra and I and countless others. His surname is the first clue. Delta. An assassin. This is not my fantasy. Read The Greenbaum speech by Dr Corydon Hammond. Whom was he supposed to kill? Himself? A part? Or was he killed for telling too much in his song.? Of course, he was split. Let me tell you more.

TRIGGER ALERT: This article contains disturbing elements and might trigger Monarch survivors.

....

The email went on for several pages.

CHAPTER 68

Tuesday, January 1st 2013, New Year's Day, 9:15am, The SJTU

D r Aziz entered the keycode for the SJTU rather than ring and have to talk to Deirdre. It felt insensitive after Christmas, and he knew how happy she would be to be back and how she would welcome everyone as they returned. He would talk to her on the way out or catch her at the staff meeting. Right now, he needed to talk to Gawain. He walked quickly and quietly along the corridor, guiltily relieved to see none of the secretaries were back yet and that Deirdre was facing the back wall of her little glass cubicle.

There was a knock on the door and the familiar boom of "Hello," but was it his imagination or did Gawain's voice sound weaker? Had the birth of his grandson and the flight emotionally tired him? He did not wish to burden him further.

But Gawain, the same bear as always, this time with a bright tartan scarf around a dark green sweater, struggled out of his seat and enveloped Abdul in a big hug. Abdul felt a tension in his body relax despite the whiff of cigarette smoke. He always worried about Dr Stuart's health.

Without words they both moved to the sofas.

"Happy New Year, Gawain," said Abdul wholeheartedly. He reached inside his case for a small parcel, bought and elegantly gift wrapped in tartan wrapping paper by Mina, and handed it over. "For Jamie," he smiled.

"And Happy New Year to you and yours, but right now I guess we have far more pressing matters, and I have been kept up to date—so over to you," said Gawain briskly.

"I will leave my concerns about the Glendale for another time," began Abdul cautiously. "But there are many. My main concerns are for Lady Rose and Professor Frank. Lady Rose has dissociative features and PTSD but has capacity, emotional intelligence, and a real beauty about her. I am sure she would engage well in attachment-based psychotherapy. The problem is she makes an absolutely clear disclosure consistently and wishes to speak to the police. What she has to say has such appalling psychological, political, and media consequences that I would feel very concerned for any therapist working with her. Professor Frank loves Lady Lily and is a close friend of hers. He knows Rose as a family friend and behaves warmly to her but cannot bear a diagnosis involving safeguarding needs. I had perhaps the most difficult clinical moment in my life, having to gently help Professor Frank realise there was no choice. He was a man in the utmost personal and professional turmoil. Indeed, at one point he left suddenly and I had to carry on. He sent me a very moving and personal thank you note. There are so many ethical issues here that I fear for anyone involved. Working with patients, however difficult, is always easier than when a colleague starts sinking. However, the impact of a forensic examination was so traumatic for Lady Rose that I am not sure she would be ready to face that again."

He paused.

Gawain stayed silent.

Abdul took a deep breath. "The worst moment was when Frank left the room in a state, and she asked if I was worried that I was in trouble. She then added … and I don't think I will ever forget it—it is imprinted on me … 'You think Professor is big man and you are little, but he is friend Chris. He will come back. Glendale bigger than him and bad man Ian Anderson and Danny Delta, but Chris is friend.'"

Abdul's shoulders relaxed and a deep sigh went through them. "When he came back, she said he must have phoned her mother and he admitted it. He blushed. She—Lady Rose knew. She understood."

There was another companionable silence. "In the first meeting, there was a moment when she used the word 'Master' and I asked if she was

207

talking about Lew Masters and she spoke in an angry male voice and threw her mug of chocolate onto the floor violently. It passed quickly, and she said Good Rose and Good Lady Rose were back. I think, in a certain altered state, she thinks she is a Master, whatever that means to her. There was also something complex in Tracey O'Bridey's interview. She said Mr Masters had told her to knock three times and call Rose by her name to get her out of a flashback. I don't know if he has an awareness of hypnotic injunctions or could be an abuser. But I hear he was wonderful on New Year's Eve, and she shows no fear of him."

Another pause.

"Anything else?" asked Gawain seriously.

"Yes. Outside of the abuse, everything she says has been confirmed by both parents. She has not lied before or had delusional fantasies. She was very clear on her bullying as a child and her rape as a teenager. If what she says is correct and/or if the media get hold of this, the opening of the Lady Rose Unit will be a disaster, and we have a conflict of interest over our local MP...and the Minister of Health."

He took a deep breath. "I feel better. Sorry. I really missed you, Dr Stuart."

"Of course you did! You are calling me doctor instead of Gawain, so you really needed to see me."

Both men laughed.

CHAPTER 69

Tuesday, January 1st 2012,
New Year's Day, 9:30am, The SJTU

Deirdre Hislop put the phone down thoughtfully. A rather pushy Senior Registrar from the Equipa—a Dr Landesman who insisted on being called Charmaine—wondered if they had actioned the referral of Mattie yet. Dr Green was insistent that their collaboration would make all the difference and set a new standard for non-binary work.

She had gently reminded Charmaine that they were still a skeleton staff for the next few days, but she had the letter and Dr Stuart would be able to consider it tomorrow.

Charmaine behaved as if the most major life disappointment had been inflicted. Her exuberant voice became so soft and slow over this delay of just a day that Deirdre found herself longing to offer something speedier. However, they had long learned at the SJTU that desperation needed to be answered with a gentle receptive pause. Why would there be such desperation when they had only just received the referral, the day before, and in the Christmas period?

Her previous doubts about the referral remained. Why would an international specialist transgender centre want their opinion? Equipa, she was sure, must have child, adolescent, and adult psychotherapists. They said so on their brochure, so it could not just be about Mattie's age.

Was there conflict in the family about her? Was there something litigious? Was it the DID or who her abusers were? It did not feel right, and she had learned to trust that aspect of her judgement.

She printed her note for the file and emailed it to Dr Stuart, Elouise, and Jon. She would be glad when Mary and Amanda returned to take on the telephone and filing tasks.

Poor Abdul. She had seen him quietly make his way to Dr Stuart's room hoping she would not see him and intercept him. She had, of course, heard and recognised his footsteps but diplomatically turned her back as he passed. She understood that would ease his mind. She had read all the correspondence and filed it under a new confidential passcode. What a complex situation. It was only a couple of times in a year that Abdul did not have the mental space to say hello, and both times were when he needed Dr Stuart's help. He so took on the cares of the world and his parents, and it was clear how he had taken on Professor Frank's predicament as well as Rose's. She had every hope Dr Stuart would help him, and at 11am Elouise and Jon would be back.

Making herself a cup of tea, she had a little break in front of her computer and smiled as she looked at the New Year messages she had received. "As you sow, so shall you reap," her parents had said and that meant the good things too.

She had received a particularly nice email from the new Day Manager at Harvest House, Sarah Ransome, who said they should meet for coffee.

CHAPTER 70

Tuesday, January 1st 2013,
New Year's Day, USA

Major D's superior was highly amused. A rare experience. So the lowly Lew Masters was a better programmer and operator than his seedy so-called Master from a low-level coven and Ian Anderson. That was one for the books. Bloodline was bloodline, but it did not mean greater intelligence or social class, and nor did being a Society operative determine intelligence. Cheers to the military man! Afghanistan had clearly made Lew, despite the blows it had inflicted. He had been a military man too. That was quite a result for the Orpheus Project that he could keep Rose stable in her main state and for a New Year's Eve party. Very impressive and important—and especially as she was bloodline. The others, who would move into her house with her, were just collateral damage. A little bit of Satanist ritual, especially carried out by someone who believed in it, had the desired effect—it was like a B movie.

With Lew on his payroll, the launch of the Lady Rose Unit could be flawless, and Ian spared. HRH was much easier to deal with than Ian—the pompous rough oaf. Why did Glendale sympathise with him? Did Oliver think Ian was like his brother? But really, Glendale and HRH sending him to America and letting him mess with hotel employees was damned bad manners on both accounts. Sending the bad egg off to the colonies! But it was useful having an HRH even from a non-existent former minor principality! Neuplatzstan! He would update Orpheus and The Society.

As for Lew, he needed respect more than payroll. He would deal with this himself.

Someone needed to deal with Cassandra and find out where she was and who she was. As for Leandra, that was more difficult. Sandra was perfection and any change to her could impact on Leandra and vice versa. He had to admire Leandra. She had got a lot right too. They would just have to ride the Wild West of cyberspace. Meanwhile, Sarah's Searches would be all ready if Rose blabbed. And were needed for the WAM conference.

Now that HRH was refreshed by Sandra, and his presence had strengthened her, it was a possible time for Major D to see Lee. Sandra was the goose that laid the golden egg and should not be stretched too much. Lee would have one of his small windows in which he could emerge. He would then evaluate what to do about Leandra and Lara. This was more important than Orpheus but linked in crucial economic ways.

He agreed with Glendale and HRH that Frank would just have to be left to it. His memory work was a useful distraction, and it was not clear how he would emerge from this. Therapy would be a problem, but they had successfully dealt with that in the USA and could import the same attack techniques. Sandra would love Sarah's Searches to get its teeth into that. That could wait. Right now, it was Lew. He had saved the day. A little piece of work with Lew, and then he would sleep.

CHAPTER 71

Tuesday, January 1st 2013, New Year's Day, USA

Lara

Me by myself
Lara.
Bad child
Kill her
Cut her
Once there was a mother a mother
A beautiful, beautiful Lady mother
A smile in eye
magic mirror of sparkle
A warm hand
lilies
Smell of lilies wafting around room
Like smoke curls
Your fault bad girl
Stupid ugly Bad girl
You did it
You made her go away
Is she dead?

Did they kill her?

So come and die me

Master with hand in my brain

Electricity

Turn me off

Mattie

Dead me

Lee

Why hasn't he come? Come back! When you come back. What happened to Danny? I thought Master would be here. He would be here. He promised New Year. Keeping me warm. Spooning behind me, cock of the walk. My man. My Major jigsaw piece. Not supposed to say his name. Could be trouble. Fills me up, Makes me whole. Chemsex. Hard to sleep without him. Hard to live without him. It's that child Lara who keeps him away with her crying. If she doesn't stop, I will lose it. Lose him. Shut up child. I can't help you. You know it doesn't work like that. If she doesn't stop, I won't be able to stop—will give her something else to cry for if she doesn't shut up. When you come back.

Leandra

So here I am—finally got out. Others in the way before. And still alive. You can't tell. It is always a surprise. A relief and a pain equally. Just one more blog tonight and maybe an email to Cassandra. Sandra is always stronger after spending time with Prince Carl-Zygmunt and Major D. They top her up, and she tops them up so fine with their Disney rubbish. "Someday, my prince will come." I ask you! Her trivial rubbish. Makes me puke. It always takes me longer to break through when they have visited.

Lee misses Major and Lara misses mum. If she is mum. Mum is a moveable feast or breast in this world. Another of their tricks. Twin people to other parts or to parts of strangers so they can't get it together and always miss someone. That way they are always craving. I'd like to top them all! For all they knew, Lara's beautiful mother was a Disney princess seen once in Disneyland. Have a hug and a photo and that's it. Mother is gone. Or it could be any friend where poor Lara has been

214

tricked, or it could be her real mother. And I have no one and miss no one except myself and will never get myself back.

So clever, you can't help admiring them. Sandra Leandra. Who would guess it? Super Barbi and the Beast. Class nerd and prom queen—the new Siamese twins. This is the real Monarch of the Glen. Major D—Tom put your trousers on...all the unzipped souls. She herself could not reach Sandra. My God, she had tried for years. She had got her password and could read her emails, but there were concrete walls around her. She could not help her. Herself.

Sandra

Ah! Awake again! So happy. Her prince had come, and he loved her and needed her. She was made for him. Everything she said and did was perfection. And Sandra 2 was with her—she could feel the beautiful sharpness and strength in her even though she didn't fully understand where it came from. She would be attending the WAM conference full of the-rapists. And writing it up. Her pen was her dagger. That was her job. Her blog could be all ready to go. And then she would wait for instructions about the Glendale. She started singing. Forget that traitor Lara hurting her parents with her arsehole the-rapists.

> When you come back
> When you come back
> Where the water meets itself
> Where my hands frame the eye
> Where the stars go to die
> Speak the truth and never lie
> Broken into myriad pieces
> Each separate part
> A life releases
> In this celestial Helter skelter
> Am I Omega am I Delta?
> Fight the heavy hand of fate
>
> It is never too late,
> To illuminate.

CHAPTER 72

Tuesday, January 1st 2013, New Year's Day, 10:15am, Raynes Park, SW20

Mattie was sitting on the kerb by the street. He was looking at his face in a pool of flashing water. He did not know where he was. Cars passed by. Was he supposed to remember a number? A colour? Or was it a letter? He was so tired. Mat tea. Red for fire engine. White for ambulance. Blue, blue, beautiful blue for the police car. Po Lease Car. Green. No. Hurt. Once there was a cat. The cat sat on the mat. Mat Tea. Sand Ra Lean Dra

Charmaine. Shah Main. Char Mane. Nice lady. Don't hurt her.

His face, as he lifted it to the words of the siren, was blue as a bruise, blue as someone's eyes. Eye. The police light is his sun. It will always shine on him and spin around. 999. Three numbers upside down. Ding, dong bell. And he smiled, knowing the blue would take him home.

CHAPTER 73

Tuesday, January 1st 2013, New Year's Day, 10:30am

Text messages

Lord Glendale to HRH and Ian Anderson

Seven rings.
All is well.
PR fine.
R fine.
Launch fine.
Leave LM alone.
Repeat leave LM alone.
Problems all sorted.

CHAPTER 74

Tuesday, January 1st 2013,
New Year's Day, 10:40am, The SJTU

A t 10.35am, Deirdre placed cups on the tray in readiness for the staff meeting. Coffee, green tea, and chamomile. She added some shortbread biscuits in honour of baby Jamie and one of the boxes of chocolates still untouched.

She filled the large kettle and plugged it in.

Remarkably, there had been no crisis over Christmas this year. No suicide or sectioning. She had her confidential file on Lady Rose ready to discuss and the concerning referral letter for Mattie. This had become more complicated by the minute with a desperate pressurised call from Dr Landesman that Mattie had been found sitting on the kerb on Joseph Street at a particularly busy junction with bruising to his face and eyes.

Nearly all visitors to the SJTU faced domestic and/or external violence and were suicidal. Why would the Equipa find this so shocking? Children and teenagers with such identity issues had rarely had a happy life. But sitting on the kerb nearby was hardly like standing on a bridge over the Thames, or the 12th floor of a tower block. Was Dr Landesman over-involved? But she had clearly been pressured by her boss Dr Green. It didn't make sense.

The phone ringing was almost a relief.

"Is that Deirdre Hislop—Ms Hislop?" asked a pleasant female voice.

After the tense sounds of Charmaine Landesman, this voice relaxed her immediately. "Yes, it is. Can I help you?"

"Happy New Year. This is Sarah Ransome from Harvest House. Your New Year message really meant a lot to me and, as I emailed, I wonder if you get any coffee break later today where you could visit me at Harvest House? As a newcomer here..."

"I'd be delighted Mrs..."

"Please call me Sarah," interjected Sarah.

"One of our OTs has installed her own Nespresso here, so we can give you a really nice cup."

"Excellent. We only have a kettle here!" smiled Deirdre, "and please call me Deirdre."

"Exactly, Deirdre! Pop over any moment you get between 3–4pm," said Sarah.

"I look forward to that." With a smile on her face, she returned to the tray.

The kettle was boiling; she could hear excited voices at the door from Elouise and Jon.

CHAPTER 75

Tuesday, January 1st 2013, New Year's Day, 11am, Brixton

Lew Masters's residence

The phone.

Fucking hell! Why couldn't they leave him alone?

If it was that bastard Anderson.

He needed energy for night duty. Did they think he was a robot? Seven rings. Damn. He would have to wake up. He caught it after the first ring of the second call.

"Masters!" said a pleased deep voice with an American drawl.

Holy shit! This was the big one. Higher than Major D.

"Sorry to wake you when you are on night duty."

Lew relaxed. He was clearly not in trouble and the geezers at the top were better than what he usually had to deal with. "It's alright," said Lew truthfully. "Is there a problem?"

"Well, there was, but you seem to have solved it," laughed the man. "It seems to me that you have the skills we don't usually expect outside of our specialist programmers."

An unusual warmth spread through Lew. A compliment was rare in his life. "Is this about R?" he asked.

"Yes. I wanted to personally congratulate you on the successful New Year's Eve," said Z.

"Thanks to you, it is also possible that the launch of the new unit is viable."

"I appreciate that, sir," said Lew, all tiredness gone.

"Well, we appreciate you: the Society appreciates you," he paused. "I have a proposition for you."

"Yes?" asked Lew, unable to keep the excitement out of his voice. He wanted to stay cool and non-committal, but he was now sitting upright in bed, watching the shards of light coming through the sides of his black curtains.

"This is the deal. You keep on doing what you know how to do with R, keeping her stable for the launch. I don't have to tell you how important that is. No one else has got the skills needed for doing that."

There was a pause. No bullshit here. This guy knew the score. He knew Lew's true potential. This was his big chance. He better not blow it. "Understood, sir."

"Okay. We fly you out here for R&R, and when I say R&R, I mean it. And you teach our programmers how you have managed it so well, especially with a disability, and we in return will give you further specialist training should you be interested in different work with us."

There was a tense pause. This was proper appreciation and recognition but no filthy lucre—yet. But this man would: he was on the money.

"Additionally—and this is the last point,"—there was a heavy emphasis on the word "last."

"We give you an immediate transfer bonus of 10,000 dollars and an immediate option on a two-bedroom flat in Ashmere Grove ready to move into and rent-free for two years with an option for longer if you are still working with us."

Lew leapt out of bed and punched his fist against the wall. "Freedom!" he shouted. "Yippee!"

There was a dry laugh at the end of the phone. It covered the thump on the wall from next door. "I take it that is a 'yes', Mr Masters?"

"Yes, sir!"

"The money transfer will take place immediately, and I will email the agent the final details. They have your name and address, and being one of the most prestigious roads in Brixton they are glad to have a national health person. The flat is yours from today, with no questions asked as to how you live. The paperwork is in your name with deposit and two years already paid."

"So, you knew I would agree," he said weakly.

"My dear Masters—your greater programming skill has been a genuine surprise to all of us! But realising a man living in a decaying flat in Brixton with difficult neighbours might like a newly upgraded private flat on the best road in the area is hardly rocket science!"

He and Masters both laughed together.

"I would like to visit and—er—have more training." He paused. He owed it to himself, to the God in him. "There is just one person…"

"You need have no further dealings with that oaf IA."

Lew Masters sat back on his bed. "Of course you know," he said reflectively,

"You, better than anyone, know what is or isn't rocket science."

Both men laughed.

"And enjoy your new girlfriend," Zed added.

There was a pause. "You really do know everything."

"That we need…I need hardly add that confidentiality is crucial for the Society and what you have achieved and how you have achieved it is for my ears only. Understood?"

"Yes, sir!"

"Sir is fine. I recognise a good military man when I meet one! But I will let you know I can also be called Z. Zed or Zee. The last letter of the alphabet. Everything stops with me. But you knew that anyway."

"Yes, sir," said Lew proudly.

"You are not a gorilla, Masters, although there are times a gorilla is more important than anyone. There are many ways a man with gifts like yours can find a place in the Society. And many places. Now we can both sleep. To the Society."

"To the Society."

CHAPTER 76

Tuesday, January 1st 2013, New Year's Day, 11am, Westbridge Police Station

DC Morag Lennon sipped her black coffee and sighed. She didn't enjoy a CRIS at the best of times and especially right now, especially one like this. Superintendent Mark Hewson had been on the news only yesterday, drawing the line between properly responding to allegations and being sceptical on the one hand or believing everything on the other. Not that it made any difference. The boys (or girls) in blue were attacked for whatever they did or did not do.

Working with vulnerable victims was her passion, but it had never involved this kind of allegation before. Based at Westbridge Police Station she had enjoyed plenty of involvement with St Joseph's Hospital, now the Lord Glendale Centre.

Harvest House, Cell Block H, had been at the centre of allegations for years, but nothing had stuck despite all her attempts. She had done a joint training with an OT there—Faith something—good woman. But despite the clear signs of trauma, no disclosure was forthcoming.

Lady Rose had never come to her attention before other than wondering what extra trauma her disability might have caused both to her and her family. Upper-class families and middle-class families could sometimes have a harder time with a disabled child than other groups. Money could buy extra care but did not remove the guilt and worry.

223

There had been a query about the night manager—Masters—before. There had been reports of sexist language and behaviour, but nothing that would stick.

Lady Rose's disclosures were not about hospital staff or residents. They had been about the Deputy Prime Minister and, as her father was a constituency MP and Minister of Health, how local police dealt with it would have a political and professional impact.

Having national as well as local constituency responsibilities meant Sir Peter Redcliffe was very hardworking, but she was not aware of any previous conflict of interest. However, what could be a worse conflict of interest for a local MP than to have his daughter allege abuse from a Deputy Prime Minister? Only if it was the Prime Minister himself or the Head of the Opposition.

She had already collected the basic facts, which were very simple and easy to substantiate. The Danny Delta concert did take place on October 31st in Vegas. Danny Delta was a friend of Ian Anderson and the Redcliffes. There was no accounting for taste. Danny Delta had rented the Grand Desert Villa, a nine-bedroom luxury villa with nine ensuite wet rooms and dressing rooms. It had vast entertainment space, basement cinema, a gym, and a huge outdoor heated swimming pool.

The careful reports of the psychiatric interview showed that Lady Rose correctly remembered where the pool was, the door that led to a small snug on the right, and the large doors that led to the entertainment space. Even though she had been frightened of water (and that might be worth checking) since an incident at the age of 6, it had not affected her coherence in describing where her mother was. Indeed, Lady Lily and Lady Rose were clearly describing the same place and time.

Everyone agreed that Lady Rose's previous allegations of bullying in primary school and rape by a minicab driver at 14 were correct. Indeed, the Judge commended her for her accurate recall. There were no signs of any mental health condition affecting the nature of her disclosure. However, the impact of the medical investigation had been too traumatic for Lady Rose and might not be possible again,

The problem was that her mother was adamant that while her daughter was truthful, there was no possibility that she was correct about Ian Anderson. He was a close friend. This could destroy his life and the allegation must remain confidential. Lord Glendale, the philanthropist who funded the Glendale Centre, had also stepped in. The family and closest friends saw this disclosure as a moment of madness due to past trauma somehow being activated because of Lady Rose's impending move to a new Independence Unit that had been established in her name.

That was possible, but then again family and friends always swore blindly that their own were innocent. They never saw it. Sometimes they were innocent, sometimes not, but family views like this did not or should not sway evidence.

But where the victim had Down's Syndrome, and the accused was a man of power and influence and the family were his friends? And there was a major press launch happening in a week or so? It was a nightmare.

At least Superintendent Hewson was a fair-minded man; he would keep his mind clear and honourable, and she would get to work on the meeting.

CHAPTER 77

Tuesday, January 1st 2013,
New Year's Day, 11am,
The Lord Glendale Centre

Keira Denny spun delightedly round in her chair. Lord Glendale had been the first to ring her back. He was really excited by her initial plans and congratulated her on them. There was a green light for the launch. Lord Glendale himself was available to speak and had promised, on behalf of Lady Lily, that she too would speak. It was not yet clear if Sir Peter would speak. The family were considering if that was too much.

Keira had been full of ideas. A mother–daughter separation and independence feature in a quality paper would be excellent. An interview with Lady Lily would guarantee coverage in fashion and women's magazines. "Woman's Hour" might be interested in Lady Lily speaking about how to help her daughter grow up when she was more dependent than average because of her Down's Syndrome. The social service correspondents might be interested in the lack of facilities for young people with disabilities, and the business sections might be interested in the mixed model of private and public funding. And, of course, the local paper ought to be interested in such prestigious local news. *The Westgate News* and *The Chronicle*, the key locals, would devote several pages, although Mark Dyer had not replied yet.

226

After sending her reminder messages out, she faxed Lord Glendale her list of ideas. He had never asked her to do this, but it had always paid off in terms of his confidence in her, which had given her more confidence in her actions.

But the real issue, the more complicated issue, was whether Lady Rose herself would speak or be interviewed. Lord Glendale had been rather ambiguous on this matter, unlike his usual forthright self.

"Leave that with me, Keira," he had said. "Her family and staff don't want to put more pressure on her when leaving Harvest House is a big issue for her. Can we leave that until later?"

"Of course," she had replied. Her mother had not been happy with it. "You are patronising her! You all are! Just because she has a disability. She is still a person. This tastes like that 'does he take sugar?' business."

Her father was even more adamant. "Don't be a pawn for the fat cats! A family gets rid of their kid by paying for a posh place and gets good publicity too."

Keira was torn.

"Don't forget the bullying in primary school," her sister added.

Keira made herself a coffee. She had found her compromise. Sinita's mother might give an interview. What about a mother with a young adult daughter at the Equipa Centre? Then different parts of the Centre could all get a boost from the publicity.

Perhaps instead, she could just meet Lady Rose and have something ready, just in case.

CHAPTER 78

Tuesday, January 1st 2013, New Year's Day, 11am, The STJU

Staff meeting

Elouise and Jon had arrived at the same time to the SJTU and noisily entered the narrow hallway.

"Happy New Year, Deirdre!" laughed Elouise, enveloping the approaching Deirdre in a warm hug. "And thank you for my New Year message. Your message is part of my New Year celebration," she added, walking into the admin room, closely followed by Jon.

Deirdre quickly turned the kettle on again.

"And Happy New Year and thanks for your message from me too," echoed Jon, kissing her on each cheek. "My mother insisted I bring you this." He produced an attractive cardboard cake box. His mother, Sylvie, provided almond cakes or apple strudel for the core team after each of his holiday visits home. Embarrassed though he had been at bringing the cake, he was moved by the genuine pleasure on Deirdre's face.

"Please give me her email Jon. This is so kind. I love her cooking and I feel really bad that I have never thanked her directly."

Jon nodded, embarrassed, his last interchange with his mother fresh in his mind. "Honestly mum, do you really want to keep embarrassing

me! It's like taking something to the teacher at Christmas as if I was 10."
Sylvie had looked slightly crestfallen, but then her face lit up.

"Chanukah and Christmas! If your Deirdre doesn't look pleased, then I will stop immediately."

He would take it to his analyst but had another week to wait.

"Can I help you with the tray, Deirdre?" he asked.

"Please," she replied—reaching to pour the kettle.

"Abdul is already there with Dr Stuart. Oh, and Jamie and Martine have a healthy baby boy!"

"Wonderful and the end of their lazy nights," laughed Elouise, holding the door open for Jon.

"So, he squeezed that flight in with just a few days. I hope he is not pushing himself too hard," worried Jon, picking up the tray.

"Stop worrying Jon. New Year resolution."

Jon grinned.

"You are such a multi-tasker Deirdre!" added Elouise. "You can come and sort my brood out anytime!"

When they reached Dr Stuart's room the door was already open.

"Come on in," boomed Gawain standing behind a smiling Abdul.

While the group exchanged hugs and greetings Abdul gracefully approached Deirdre. "Happy New Year, dear Deirdre. You will have realised I needed to..."

"Debrief with Dr Stuart?" interjected Deirdre warmly. "Of course I did and glad you had that time."

Abdul enfolded her in a big hug. "You are a real brick, Deirdre. I don't know what we would do without you," he said softly, bringing a blush of pleasure to her face.

This was her happiest New Year.

As they settled into their usual seats Dr Stuart brandished a bottle of champagne and four plastic beakers. "To the best core team I have had the pleasure of working with, to the New Year and to all our patients."

CHAPTER 79

Tuesday, January 1st 2013, New Year's Day, 11am, Westminster Square

The Redcliffe residence

Lady Lily was asleep. Very quietly, Sir Peter stepped out of their large bed. He could not face speaking to her about the party or anything right now. It all felt a sham. Of course, it had been a success and the scroungers stayed until after breakfast. It had just been too much; they had used to count parties like this as successes, but now it felt empty.

Walking quietly along the already cleaned corridors, Sir Peter reached his retreat and hung a "Do not disturb" on his study door. The house was in recess for another week, so he still had time for preparation. He had to manage his constituency, as well as his Ministerial post, and he always used the main part of his Christmas break to catch up. Since Lily had not treated Christmas as a family occasion since Rose's birth, this was inevitable. They had both accepted Christmas as a sterile work time with one glittering ball, one lunch with both mothers, and a few necessary small dinners. Now the ball and Christmas were over; everything could be put away.

Their artificial Christmas tree, decorated in green and gold this year, was an interior designer's dream. In another week Maria would store it and the baubles away for another year, unless Lily chose a different colour scheme.

When Rose was 6 years old, almost 7, he took her out to buy a tree. She was so excited. After they got home she sat on his knee, pointing to the pictures in the Christmas book he had bought her. "Lady," she said, pointing to the Christmas angel.

"Yes," he replied.

"Lady angel. Beautiful lady, like mummy," he explained.

"Lady mummy," she replied.

"Would you like to choose a lady angel for the tree?"

Rose looked around the room excitedly. Then she looked sad. "No lady."

"In the shop," laughed Peter.

"Rose and daddy shop. Angel."

How bright she was! How lovely! Why couldn't Lily see that? They had friends with 3-year-olds who did not chat so happily. And such beautiful blue eyes and golden hair she had, just like her mother.

He took her out to Harrods that year to choose the Christmas angel. She pointed to the most beautiful one, a porcelain angel with magnificent blue eyes, golden blonde hair, and a glittering blue dress, just like her.

"Like Rose," he smiled and kissed her head.

"No papa! Like mummy. Beautiful Lady mummy angel. Ugly Rose. Dirty mongol."

He thought his heart would break and he scooped her up in his arms, but she wasn't sad. He could not bear it. Who had used such language with her? Who had dared? He had no words. His beautiful child of 6. Already taking in her difference in this devastating pragmatic way.

In the taxi, they sat in silence, Rose happily holding her golden angel for the tree. When they got home, he lifted her in his arms so she could fix the angel on the top.

"Rose chose the beautiful angel on top of the tree. A lovely lady like Rose will be," he said.

Maria came in at that moment and stood quietly smiling at the tender moment.

"Rose ugly. Stupid dirty girl," said Rose angrily in a discordant deep voice.

With surprising force, she threw the angel onto the floor where it splintered.

Shocked, Sir Peter lowered her to the ground. He had not seen Lily walk in.

Rose burst into loud tears. Scrabbling on the floor to pick up the porcelain pieces, she rushed to her mother. "Sorry beautiful Lady mother. Beautiful angel. Bad dirty mongol Rose. Good Rose back."

Lily, his Lily, just ignored their child and beckoned to Maria to take her away, as if she was rubbish, something broken and damaged that should be taken away.

She looked at him with a raised eyebrow, the damaged sperm, the one who loved their damaged daughter, and then slowly left the room.

He had not bought a Christmas tree since.

Six years old and what she had already suffered. His love could not heal her. It was her beautiful mother's love that she wanted, and she would never get it. He could never make his wife love her; he loved his wife, and he loved his daughter. Twenty-one years. Twenty-one years with two broken parents, and a mother who closed the door to her heart.

There was something else at 6 too, the reason why he needed to be undisturbed.

Lily had been approached by Ian, or the other way round. Whichever way it was, they had recognised each other. It wasn't sexual. It was obvious Ian was gay from the start. The daughter, who was supposed to be a son, unwanted by her own father, and the envious man who was not born an aristocrat.

Goodness! He poured himself a whisky, despite the early hour. He had never realised so sharply before. Lily treated Rose the same appalling way her father treated her. Look at the damage they had caused. He had to tell her.

Some six months earlier, in the heat of a summer Sunday, Ian had invited them all to some impromptu lunch event. "Rose must come. She is 6, isn't she? She will love the swimming pools. They've got slides and all sorts of fun for children."

He was not free, but to his surprise Lily had agreed, even though she usually never went anywhere with Rose. Why had she gone?

He was home when they returned, aware of a tension he had carried all day. Rose was silent, a frozen damaged doll. Lily was an ice-cold robot. She handed Rose to Maria and left the room. "What's the matter Rosie?" Maria asked gently looking with concern at Sir Peter.

Rose's face suddenly darkened, and a deep ugly sound came out of her mouth. "Not Rose. Stupid mongol girl. Ian did magic snake in water. Dirty Rose."

Maria and Sir Peter looked at each other with shock. But as he picked her up in his arms she burst into tears and cried, "Sorry, Papa. Good Rose back."

Lily would never speak about it. Maria was loyal to her mistress first and foremost, refusing to encourage any comment from him. From that day on Rose avoided all swimming pools.

He did phone Ian and thank him for entertaining Lily and Rose. Hoping he would hear something.

"She is so genetically like her mother," said Ian, a strangely incomprehensible comment to Peter.

The issue was that he and Lily were running on empty. She would hate her daughter for the rest of her life, and his love would not be the antidote. He would stay in parliament for the foreseeable future and for what? A loveless retirement? He could not do it.

What had happened to Rose? Had she really been—he could hardly bear considering it—raped at 6 and at 21 by his wife's close friend? The reports spoke of dissociation and trauma. Was that where that deep voice had come from? A flashback? Ian had a deep voice, plummy in that nouveau toff way—as his father used to say.

For a moment he wanted to kill Ian. That pompous jowly face. Could he have hurt his daughter? Called her a mongol? He felt the cold force of him. His Rose, his baby. She deserved to have a voice.

Today, when she woke, he and Lily would speak.

CHAPTER 80

Tuesday, January 1st 2013, 11:15am, The SJTU

After the greetings, and the unusual dip of champagne to toast baby Jamie, the senior management group settled down to business.

"And goodness, it was only a week," laughed Elouise, "You'd think it was a month the way we carry on!"

"And what a week," said Gawain.

"I'll just collect the beakers and put the bottle in the fridge—we don't want another surprise Professor Frank visit," said Jon.

Seriousness took over.

"Okay." said Gawain, "Welcome back! First, I want to thank you all for your extraordinary attendance a week ago. I cannot tell you the difference it makes. And Deirdre, thanks for keeping cover over this period. It is not expected ..."

"Or allowed by elf and safety," added Elouise.

"But it allows us to start the new year in a focused way."

Deirdre beamed with a spot of colour on each cheek and lowered her head.

Elouise noticed and felt touched. Deirdre was such a formidable, almost rigid woman and so unquestioningly loyal.

"And a thank you to Abdul, who has had the assessment from hell in this period."

Abdul nodded appreciatively.

"But at the Glendale! Describe it!" Eloise pleaded. "Please!"

"Goodness," said Gawain. "I am a puritan. I had an update from Abdul earlier and never even asked."

"I think it is highly relevant," smiled Jon. "Especially as we are hearing about the external meaning of the place."

There was a pause.

"Briefly then," said Abdul seriously, "because I really did not feel comfortable there. It was like a top-secret military centre combined with a luxury airport lounge and a five-star hotel: thick blue carpets and glass, ponds with koi fish, security like the House of Commons, glass walls that open and close at the touch of a button, lifts that are rooms, money and efficiency and secrecy and efficient unsmiling Stepford wife secretaries." His voice had become unusually louder, and there was a tense silence in the room.

"So," said Gawain, "linked or not linked, with that disconcerting image in our minds, I will ask Deirdre to start with an unusual referral." Here he paused and looked humorously at Abdul. "From the Glendale, or should I say the Stepford Wives Centre, and then I will update you all on Lady Rose."

Abdul laughed and his shoulders relaxed. Deirdre handed everyone a copy of her correspondence with Dr Charmaine Landesman, including the phone contact.

"Please hand it back at the end of the meeting for me to shred," she said. "As you all know, Dr Stuart has made several friendly overtures to different units at the Glendale with either no acknowledgement or an official reply form with initials and no full name. Abdul's description of his visit fits the lack of emotional connection we have experienced."

She looked protectively at Abdul.

"Now, I don't know if you know this, Elouise, because it was such a traumatising assessment for you, but suddenly we have Professor Chris Frank, Medical Director of the Glendale, and Dr Simon Green, Director of the Equipa, making a joint child referral. As you can see, Mattie is 12 and transgender, but there is no background history given. We don't know if he/she is DID. Mattie was suddenly removed from their parents or adoptive parents in a terrible state, mute, underweight, and covered in welts. The Senior Registrar, Dr Charmaine Landesman, is so concerned for him that after a referral arrived, on very expensive paper, on New Year's Eve, when no clinical staff would be expected to be here—she rang first thing this morning asking why we hadn't responded.

I had to work quite hard to keep her calm. And then again, just before this meeting, she rang to say Mattie had been found sitting on the kerb on St Joseph Street with bruising to his face. As opposed to seeing him running off and being vulnerable to attack, either as borderline or involved in a traumatic re-enactment, in Dr Landesman's view this was highly dangerous behaviour. Given that trans patients have often gone through so much trauma, why is this case being so emphasised? Where is the pressure coming from?

And to repeat, unlike any usual referral no adequate background details or clinical history have been provided. Apparently, the child speaks with an American accent."

Deirdre put her file down and looked around.

Mattie. That sad face.

Elouise looked shocked. "I have not seen a child in such a terrible state outside of war. I did not know what sex. But that little body was a famine area and a torture area. I wouldn't have thought they were in a state to manage medication."

There was silence.

"Why have they referred to us?" Asked Deirdre.

"She's not a cousin of Lady Rose, is she?" asked Elouise, breaking the tension with a laugh.

"Humour helps us understand," said Gawain seriously. "It makes me think there is a connection between the two cases, even if it is just about DID. But it is not obvious and of course we have your internet sources we can come to later, Elouise. And thank you for keeping me informed. I have also been keeping an internet file myself."

Abdul looked at Gawain intently. "It could be a fear of the diagnosis and/or a controversial disclosure hiding in it."

"Jon?" asked Gawain

"I smell danger," said Jon,

"Okay. Then listen to the update on Rose and see what thoughts occur."

Deirdre collected the notes on Mattie and handed out an update on LRR.

236

"Before starting," said Abdul. "I need to emphasise that this is obviously highly confidential and concerns an influential colleague as well as a patient. Perhaps these features also link it to the Equipa referral, where a new colleague is also behaving unusually. Gawain has already been updated. I will try and be as brief as possible. Lady Rose has a mild intellectual disability but a remarkable emotional capacity and emotional intelligence. She definitely has the capacity to make a disclosure and go through a legal process.

She has been consistent in the details she has provided. There is no clinical reason to dispute her capacity to provide testimony outside of a serious dissociative disorder. By this I mean that if, for example, Rose is dissociative and had sex in one state and in another mental state did not accept it, and clarity of her disclosure could only work if she was properly understood. Of course, in a trance state, whether post-traumatic or DID, her clarity could also be affected.

DC Morag Henny, our local Vulnerable Victim Coordinator, is organising a CRIS report which is what happens when there are complex confidentialities."

"And titled families," added Elouise pointedly.

"Yes. And more than titled when her father is our local MP and Minister of Health. So then, what are the problems? The Lady Rose Independence Unit will be having a major media launch in a week, and if Rose is not stable she could name her alleged abusers to the press. Who weighs up the clinical importance of her right to speak versus security? How will that impact on her security here and any treatment for her? How would we protect her treatment team?"

There was a gasp from Elouise and Jon as the implications sank in.

"I never even thought of that," said Elouise. "The idea of writing up session notes with that kind of intrusion is really hard."

"Would it be on a very brief need-to-know basis?" asked Deirdre.

"Yes. And no names but a number code," said Gawain.

"Yes," continued Abdul. "This is inside and outside, and too close to home. Professor Frank, who has various rights over us and this unit, is deeply over-involved with Lady Lily and cannot bear any problem Rose causes her. He left the assessment to phone Lady Lily during the interview; something Rose was deeply aware of. Indeed, perhaps even more worryingly, he initially wanted to deny her capacity to make a disclosure. Totally confidentially—I consider the strain of this case led

237

to unethical behaviour and a near breakdown. He is a man on the edge. I have worked on this with him and can leave it for the moment."

There was a tense silence.

"There is a complex clinical issue. She either has internalised the voice of an abuser, or she has a dissociative identity disorder, in which the thoughtful 'Good' Lady Rose is one personality state, the Master is another, and a frightened Little Rose is the third. If the latter, which I am inclined to endorse, it would also come from a disorganised attachment, as almost all cases of DID do.

However, being clear and public about this diagnosis could be dangerous to Rose. There could be a furore over the diagnosis, a furore over some amateur detective work by those who accept the diagnosis, and a whole range of responses along the spectrum. And harm to her parents if newspapers pick up on the knowledge that this comes from abuse and a disorganised attachment."

"Poor woman," said Elouise. "Lady Lily got a shock at having a child with a disability, and her upper-class background did not help her with it, then she gets punished again with this diagnosis." She paused and looked at Gawain.

"And this is where I need to bring in the outside," said Gawain. "Because having researched the emails you sent, Elouise, I carried on researching on the internet. I consider there is something real here we have to face. Cassandra's blog is validated, at least the main part is, by congressional records and I have brought Professor Colin Ross's book *Bluebird* for you to dip into, which provides the actual congressional records. Cassandra and Leandra seem to me to be two women, or personality states, who have gone through hell. That does not mean everything they say is true. However, some things they know from lived experience deserve to be listened to. We have huge social amnesia over "scientific" and psychological research and actions during the war and post-war.

What there is no validation over is that there is a nefarious link between Ian Anderson, Lord Glendale, Danny Delta, and Rose—oh and Dr Green. We know they all know each other, and we know there was a Dr Green alleged to be linked to Mengele. It is clear some of these groups use names in a deliberate way to pass on messages. It could be disinformation or there could be a real link, and we have to hope the police will not be frightened as it is they who need to investigate and not us. It could also be dangerous for Rose if there is any particular reason why someone wants her fragmented. There could also be an attempt

238

to minimise her capacity to give evidence if she has a controversial diagnosis."

He paused.

"I agree," said Elouise. "Of course, it is dangerous in cyberspace," she added, "but we disregard information at our own peril. Some of it is likely to be real. We need to bear it in mind when thinking of Mattie or looking back on Child A."

"Adam," said Gawain softly. "We need to be able to say the name."

There was a moment of silence.

Looking at her iPhone, Deirdre added that she had just received an email from Sarah Ransome. Someone had written to Sarah yesterday, and she had just forwarded it to her.

> *Please take care. I know you go toffee-nosed about my sources, but your Glendale links could be shitty. Did you know Glendale had a brother in America? His name was Harold Fitz or something ... who is yet another so-called philanthropist accused of abusing children at the place he set up? Neat, huh? You create your own fresh meat supply and get socially rewarded.*

"Ouch!" Jon said. "I didn't know you knew Sarah, Deirdre," said Abdul. "I find her a really thoughtful new addition to HH. She has transformed things in just a few days."

"Only just," Deirdre smiled with a secret delight.

"That was a useful subject segue," said Gawain thoughtfully, "because we have to add Harvest House and our role there, as well as the Lady Rose and Abdul's role there into the mixture."

"Yes," added Deirdre. "Apologies if I am stepping out of line, I am not the clinician here, but I think we should spare Abdul undertaking the Mattie assessment or being Rose's therapist because of that." She embarrassedly lowered her head.

"Wow!" Elouise said, clapping her hands.

"What a politician you are!" applauded Jon. "I had not thought of that."

Abdul smiled warmly and appreciatively. "Thank you."

"Yes," added Gawain, "please always gift us with what you are thinking, Deirdre. I wondered about Jon assessing Mattie and Elouise being on standby for Rose. My countertransference is that Mattie will end up with a similar presenting problem to Rose, and the Equipa will find this hard to deal with."

"They are not equipped for it," joked Elouise.

"Exactly!" smiled Gawain.

"How soon for an appointment Dr Stuart?" asked Deirdre wryly. "My clinical intuition doesn't extend that far."

They all laughed.

"Jon? When would you be willing to see Mattie?"

"Thursday, but here—not at the Equipa. And only on condition a full history is sent."

"Got that, Deirdre?"

"Definitely, Dr Stuart."

"A thought I didn't want to forget," said Elouise slowly. "Just so it is noted. I was thinking about Child A...Adam...The concert was Halloween and she showed disturbed behaviour on the solstice, November 21st."

There was a moment's silence.

"This is reminding all of us of your ritual abuse case, Elouise. All the solstices affected them, and the full moons."

"Yes. I had supervision from Dr Judith Kestle in America, remember. She will be speaking at a major conference in Washington on Wednesday, which means our lovely media will be ready to pounce again."

Mattie—a child in such pain. Adam. The clear blue eyes of Lady Rose.

CHAPTER 81

Tuesday, January 1st 2013, New Year's Day, 2pm, Brixton

Lew Masters's residence

Lew had not been able to go back to sleep. A state of euphoria had taken him over. The power in him had been seen and recognised by someone he could trust and admire. Even his flashbacks felt muted, calmed. He had been recognised as a soldier. His life was changing. He could feel it: every part of his body felt energised and open. Goodbye to this ugly dustbin and the dirty cow next door, and the noise and filth. The flashing lights that went on all night, the drunks, spit and vomit on the pavement.

He had packed already. He knew from his army days how to travel light. Everything essential that he wanted was neatly folded or rolled up into the one huge black leather case and his antique black leather Gladstone bag. Travel light, travel smart; don't be underestimated.

He kicked the walls as he dressed in a white shirt and a new smart suit bought to keep Sarah Ransome happy. He savoured the return thumps from his next-door neighbour. They were like broomstick thumps from an old witch he would never have to hear again! He was moving away from all of this.

He looked at his large suitcase bulging under its leather straps, just as his muscles bulged through his smart shirtsleeves. Here was his life in two cases. The temple of his home and the temple of his body.

He had decided to go by taxi, which meant he could take everything at once. He never had to return except for picking up his bike. Luckily it was not parked outside but round the corner. No one to say goodbye to.

He did not want to be on his motorbike with all his leather clobber to get his new keys. The initial discomfort of shirt and tie had worn off, and he had enjoyed the new respect he had earned.

He trusted Z. Somehow he knew the place would be right. He could just go to the posh estate agents and be given the keys, and Z, or rather one of his minions, would tidy everything up and redirect his mail. Glasters and Merrimack dealt with the prime sales and rentals. This would be a £2000 per month kind of place, not like the £600 per month he was used to.

A hoot came from outside: the taxi was there. Goodbye to the rickety door and the grey-white flaky paint. Goodbye to the smelly kebab shop. Goodbye to neighbour noises next door. A slam, a huge slam, of the front door. Out into the taxi went his heavy black leather case, and off they went to the Gladstone.

The taxi drove off quickly onto the wider streets, the cleaner streets. Even the air was different. At Glasters and Merrimack, he knew there was a parking space, and he could leave the taxi waiting there. No time to be mean today. He laughed. No rent to pay for two years!

"Wait for me here," he ordered the cabbie as he pulled up in front of the entrance.

"As long as it takes, mate," said the driver affably, "so long as I am paid."

The agency was spacious and expensive. Bright red tub chairs and matching carpets, with green plants adorning the walls. The smell of money was heavy in the air. He knew that smell: filthy lovely lucre.

Walking in, trying to hide his nerves, he was surprised when a smartly dressed older man approached him. "Mr Masters? We were expecting you! Erm—Lord Glendale said we would see you shortly. Delighted to meet you. I am Steve Glasters. A partner here."

Lew suppressed a grin. The big man had anticipated his timing and had already passed it on.

"Ashmere Grove is our most sought-after road in this area, as I am sure you know, and we are particularly delighted with the renovation at Lucia House."

Oh, the big man had really done it for him—even the name! Lucia–light–Lucifer. The last letter of the alphabet.

"I just need your signature on the lease in these places and your Trust has already paid two years' rental in full in advance. We are delighted to have a senior health service professional in Lucia House. All the paperwork and character references have been processed, but obviously it depends on your liking the property. I am ready to take you there now."

"I like it," said Lew. "I will take it."

Steve Glasters looked taken aback. "Your trust clearly researched it well," he said.

"Yes," said Lew. He just wanted to be there. Alone.

"You are clearly a man of quick action."

"I will come back when I am unpacked with any questions," Lew offered.

"I am on night duty tonight, so on a tight schedule."

"Ah. I understand," said Glasters with relief. "Thank you, Mr Masters. If there is any missing paperwork, we can give it to you when you return. Here are two sets of keys. You can leave one set with us if you require us to help with letting builders in or anything."

"No thank you," he said. "I mainly work nights, so my sleep is during the day and it really matters! These are the only keys?"

"The keys to individual rooms and the window and garden keys are in the house. These are the only external ones, and brand-new since the refurbishment. Our clients like their own privacy at this end of the market."

Lew nodded.

Mr Glasters handed him the keys. "Enjoy Lucia House," he emphasised. "Here is a leaflet for you about it with all our numbers on it if there is any problem day or night."

"Thank you," said Lew. He took the leaflet and the elegant bunch of keys with their leather Glasters and Merrimack fob gently and shook hands. Such restraint. He wanted to grab them and fly.

Outside, the taxi awaited him. "All settled, mate?" asked the driver, folding up his Daily Mirror and starting the ignition.

"Yes, thanks. Lucia House, Ashmere Grove."

"Big change of scenery, mate. You are really going up in the world."

"Yes," said Lew. Yes! Yes! Yes!

243

CHAPTER 82

Tuesday, January 1st 2013,
New Year's Day, 3pm,
The Lord Glendale Centre

Unusually Lord Glendale was in his office at his Centre. Major D had made his instructions about Lew and In Anderson explicit. Lord Glendale had understood his reasoning perfectly. Ian was a liability as well as being non-bloodline, and it was only his political potential that continued to hold weight with the Society over future collaboration. Lew deserved his promotion, however obvious and narcissistic his name and his language. However, there would be a mess.

No, that was not the problem. It was the compound impact of all the spotlights on the Glendale at the same time. His stupid brother, another one like Ian, Danny's post-mortem, Rose's volatility, the CRIS business with the Vulnerable Victim Coordinator, Morag Lennon, the launch of the Lady Rose Unit, Professor Frank's weak spot, Mattie, Dr Green, Keira Denny, and Lily. Then there was Cassandra and Leandra. And outside of that were the complex interlinked issues of the USA, Russia, and Europe, not to mention the future plans of the Society.

He had contacted all his troops, contained their fears and looked confident. He had to trust that, however events unfolded, he was adequately informed, and the checks and balances would keep the Society safe.

He laughed. This was his forte, his Machiavellian streak. His pleasure in the game of life. Yes, there was the immortality of the selfish gene, but for him it was also far more simple than that. Project Orpheus combined the interests of all groups and was awash with dollars, but the military aim was the one to save lives. Everything else was collateral damage.

His father was emotionally destroyed by war. He described a maelstrom of body parts exploding all around, arms and legs, brains, hearts…his whole platoon. Destroyed. No wonder he was vicious to his two sons. Did Harold get the worst of it? The second son? Certainly, he was seen as the softer of the two and father wanted to destroy the softness in them. Not that Lady Olivia was soft. It was not just the impact of the Second World War. Vietnam had also damaged the men in her family.

No wonder the Manchurian candidate had become the new gospel, so much safer than a nuclear race. Just one person, carefully brainwashed, could assassinate the dictator, and no blood would be lost beyond one person. People who condemned the research as unethical didn't have to face the sights his father saw. What was the problem with his brother and a few disposable boys against losing the finest of the fine? For each rape, think of a platoon of the finest young men, all unscathed. That was a small price to pay. Forget the religions and pseudo-religions, it was the military who needed this. Robot armies were not the future, but programmed soldiers could well be.

CHAPTER 83

Tuesday, January 1st 2013, New Year's Day, 3pm, The SJTU

"You look very smart today Deirdre," said Elouise, checking messages in the admin cubbyhole.

She had caught Deirdre unusually applying an extra coat of her discreet lipstick in her tiny office. Deirdre seemed to have an extra sparkle about her today.

"I am off to have coffee with Sarah Ransome at Harvest House, and I want to leave a good impression," smiled Deirdre awkwardly, caught a little off balance.

"Oh, that could be really good for us with everything that's going on," said Elouise enthusiastically.

"Elouise, apologies if this is intrusive but are you and Dan really okay with the idea of providing therapy for Rose, if that is seen as the next step? It is quite an undertaking, and no one would blame you for saying no. Please give yourself and Dan time to think about it." Deirdre felt happier being on home ground.

"Thanks, mum," smiled Elouise, giving Deirdre a hug. "Now look after you and have a nice cup of coffee."

Deirdre lowered her head, suddenly shy, and reached for her jacket.

"Oh wow! That's gorgeous, Deirdre," said Elouise admiringly. "Isn't that Burberry? You have such classy, elegant clothes. I think with all this Glendale stuff I need to smarten up."

Deirdre smiled more easily. She was comfortable with her work clothes. "What was it Abdul said? Stepford wives! We need to help the Glendale by staying ourselves."

Reaching for her handbag, she stood up to go. "I'll report back!" She strode off, feeling like a queen of the catwalk.

CHAPTER 84

Tuesday, January 1st 2013,
New Year's Day, 3pm, Harvest House

Sarah put the phone down thoughtfully. Morag Lennon had been extremely helpful, but the planned CRIS meeting was still of concern. There were only five days until the launch of the Lady Rose Unit, and it still had not been settled whether Lady Rose herself could speak publicly at it or not. Keira Denny, the energetic young PR woman, was being understandably pushy. It was a complicated position for them all to be in and, as she had honestly told her, everything about the new unit remained unclear.

Indeed, it was still not completely certain whether Sinita, John, and Dykes were going to move with her, and there were Sinita's parents to consider. The confusion over the exact staffing of the new unit was also still looming.

Was there going to be a formal division of work between the hospital part of the service with its male and female ward and the small Independence Unit, or was her post going to straddle both? Luckily, after the success of the party there was an air of pleasure in Harvest House and Lady Rose had been unrecognisable. Gone was the clinging and panic, and in its place was a charming capable young woman. Sinita, John, and Dykes had all clearly benefited from the change of mood too.

She knew Dr Aziz would be the psychiatrist, which was a great comfort, but the final positioning of occupational therapy was still unclear. This was not the right way to start the new year; she would telephone Lord Glendale himself, if necessary, as well as the kind Professor Frank.

A ring on the doorbell and she realised with pleasure that it would be Ms Hislop, Deirdre, from the SJTU. Finding out how linked services worked might help her understand the situation better, and gaining a new colleague or friend could make an emotional difference.

Deirdre stood on the doorstep feeling slightly nervous. The entrance was dated and faded in a rather similar way to the SJTU, but visitors to the SJTU, an outpatient facility, knew they would meet a staff member when they rang the bell. Harvest House, however, was residential. Might the learning disabled residents, no, what was the correct language now? People with intellectual disabilities? Might they open the door—or even Lady Rose?

Although Harvest House was, like the SJTU, a shared runt of the Glendale site and the nearest neighbour, it was also new to her. Was she wearing the wrong sort of clothes? Too smart? Was it a jeans-and-apron kind of place? Oh goodness—this kind of worry was what the residents must pick up on all the time. And she sounded like the awful Edna!

The door opened and an attractive middle-aged woman with a beaming smile held out her hand. "Deirdre? I am Sarah. Welcome."

CHAPTER 85

Tuesday, January 1st 2013,
New Year's Day, 3pm,
The Lord Glendale Centre

Professor Frank was watching the koi fish; how serene they were! They moved so slowly and gracefully in their liquid territory. Here was he with the most beautiful surroundings he could dream of, carrying out his work, and he had not yet calmed himself.

Although he had an aversion to "deep" psychotherapeutic treatment, he was a solid enough researcher to know that this was linked to a fear, as well as his concern at lack of adequate research. What he was facing now could not be answered by the methods that usually aided him. The staff gym at the Glendale had a clever concealed running track that went around the whole building, but physical workouts could not reach this, nor could yoga.

He walked back to his desk and pressed the illuminated "Do not disturb" button, which none of his assistants would override and sat heavily on his chair.

"Face it, Frank!" he exclaimed to himself. A sound that was a mixture of a laugh and a cry came out of his mouth. It was a woman he had been deeply attracted to but never asked out. They were both star students and were about to take a scholarship paper. She had high-fived him and he said, "Face it, Frank!" and she said, "if you can only talk about yourself in the third person, you will never succeed in the way you want."

There was the wound; his younger sister, her husband, and children, lived in Australia and had made no contact with him since their mother died ten years ago, blaming him for all the grief she had gone through. Their father had died in a car accident when they were four, leaving the family with untold debts.

One of those rainy days, with his mother too depressed to take them out of their tiny flat, he and Linda would fight like caged animals. The words "I'll send you away!" had branded him. She denied it later and there were hugs and tears, but the words stayed with him. On his seventh birthday, together with other presents, his mother proudly showed him an elegant grey blazer, with dark-blue edging, white shirt and dark-blue tie, and short trousers. "It's for St Cuthbert's! Your Uncle Edward is paying for you to have a proper education, a year of pre-prep and then prep."

He had screamed and cried, but he was taken off in a car in his smart new uniform by his uncle, and had instantly died inside. He was dead for seven years until he was returned, and the grey uniform disappeared. No one ever spoke of it. These days it was called boarding school syndrome. They had been seven terrible years with no proper memories, except for the bullying and tears.

When his mother found lumps in her lymph nodes 15 years ago, at only 60, he and Linda took her away to a Swiss spa hotel to help her immune system. Here his life changed yet again. They sat looking out at Lake Lucerne through the huge windows and he asked, "Why did you send me away at 7?"

His mother and sister looked at him blankly. "Away? Away with the fairies? What are you talking about?"

"The pre-prep and then prep boarding school Uncle Edward paid for with the grey blazer and cap edged with blue braid and little grey trousers—after my seventh birthday." Again, they both looked blankly at him.

"I would never send you away," said his mother emphatically. "After your father died, the two of you were all I had. You were a dayboy at St Eldred's from seven. Unless it was from your boarding school fantasies, I don't know where a grey blazer comes from. You loved them when you were ten."

Linda looked at him intently. "Physician heal thyself," she said. "Seems to me that you felt rejected by dad because he died and shoved that onto mum but now is not the time for your rubbish when we are here to strengthen mum."

251

"That's right," said his mother. "With a tiny guard and passengers and even a tub of miniature flowers for the platform."

"Yes," agreed Linda enthusiastically, "I loved that."

Now it was Chris who looked blank. He had no memory of this. He felt annihilated. His whole sense of his life was threatened. He could not leave it alone. He could feel and smell the grey blazer. Her words "I'll send you away" had hurt him so deeply for so many years.

His sister had glowered at him, and there was no more discussion. His mother, his poor mother, had declined rapidly after that and although she accepted his apology, something broke in their tiny threesome that could not be repaired.

He became obsessed with memory research to try and understand how he could have gotten something so wrong. He promised her he would find the answer, and she smiled weakly at him. "Too late," said Linda, who disappeared to Australia after their mother's death and barely spoke to him at the funeral.

Lily reminded him of his mother. Something about her coldness as well as her beauty. Here she was, facing agony because her daughter had false memories and at 7, a similar age to himself. Lily told him everything, and although Harvest House did not have the details, he knew about the swimming pool incident at 6 with Ian.

A deep sigh rippled through him, and he felt he contact with the feelings that had been inaccessible before. He would be able to sleep tonight. But somewhere inside him a small boy in a grey blazer sobbed silently. He held a piece of blue braid and curled up and died.

He pressed cancel on the "Do not disturb."

CHAPTER 86

Tuesday, January 1st 2013, New Year's Day, 3.30pm, The Lord Glendale Centre

"Dr Aziz on the phone for you, Professor Frank," said his assistant.

Chris Frank took a deep breath. How kind of the man! It was alright. He was alright. He had sorted it. "Put him through."

"Good afternoon, Professor Frank. I hope I am not disturbing you," came Abdul's gentle voice.

"Face it, Frank!" he ordered himself.

"Are you free now?" he asked with intense urgency. "Can you come here now?"

"On my way," said Abdul.

Professor Frank sobbed into his handkerchief and then left a message for his secretary. "Dr Aziz is coming to see me about an emergency. We are not to be disturbed."

Frank lay his head on his arms and sobbed.

Dr Aziz walked quickly to the Glendale. He was deeply concerned for Professor Frank. The man was clearly tortured and something about the Lady Rose case had broken through his formidable defences. He would provide a confidential consultation, but he could not be the man's therapist. He had experienced this before with CBT and other short-term treatment colleagues. People thought that when it came to their own emotional problems, it could all be done with friendship.

He went through the security process without a pause and would have found his way solo to Professor Frank's office suite even without the "steward" who accompanied him.

Once at the suite, the assistant pointed to the way in. "Professor Frank is expecting you, Dr Aziz," said the assistant.

"Aziz," said Professor Frank, holding out his hand.

"Frank," replied Dr Aziz, shaking it.

"How are you? I was concerned."

Professor Frank pointed to the sofa and placed a hot chocolate on the coffee table. "To be honest. I need your advice."

"Over the conflict of interest between your personal and professional role regarding Lady Rose!"

"Yes."

Face it, Frank! Face it!

"Do you find our professional career choices are linked to damage Dr Aziz?"

"Of course," said Dr Aziz gently. "We are all vulnerable flawed beings, and our career choices show our hopes and our fears. If I had not witnessed and been horrified by the Muslim–Hindu riots, I would never have entered psychiatry. For years, if I did not succeed in bringing peace to warring families or teams, I felt I was watching a riot all over again."

There was a long silence.

"Yes," said Frank. "That is where I am. That is where it is. I knew you understood. There is something at the heart of my career choice that is still raw and I did not know it and it is replicated by the Lady Rose situation."

"So, this is a gift you have been given, Frank: the chance to repair something that was hidden, that took you by surprise and needs attention."

"A gift?" asked Frank. "It doesn't feel like a gift."

"No. Of course not. But understanding how it happens and where it comes from will strengthen you in everything else you do. If you felt you could tell me any more about it, I might be able to suggest someone suitable..."

Chris Frank sat bolt upright on his chair. "This is confidential. Totally confidential," said Frank slowly.

254

"Of course," said Abdul.

"I have … had a false memory of being sent to boarding school from 7, until I was 14, just after my father died. I raised it with my mother and sister 15 years ago when my mother was dying of cancer. She said it never happened and my insistence made her feel more ill. Here with Lily, I am seeing Rose like myself, the child who makes the parent die through a false memory."

"And was it?" asked Abdul gently.

"Was it what?"

"An incorrect memory."

Professor Frank stared incredulously. He felt his heartbeat growing faster. "What are you saying?"

"I am saying this is why police are needed for us professionals. You thought you went to boarding school, and because your sister and mother changed their mind, you tried to change yours. You do not have proof … but you might have been right. Lady Rose, she may or may not have been hurt in the way she says. Only the police can work it out, if even they can …"

"So, if you were me … what would you do?"

"I would want to do right for that little child. I would want to check out schools with that uniform and check archives. And if I got conclusive proof that I was wrong, I would want to understand that little child, who had already lost his father, and was scared of losing his mother."

"Thank you, Dr Aziz. I think I will manage better now."

"I think you will too. But you don't have to … and if you feel that what you need is more, I can recommend someone."

"Dr Aziz, I cannot thank you enough. When I first met you at the SJTU, I felt a link when you told me about your life in India. Do you know, I have never even considered this before."

"Then you have your work cut out, Professor Frank! But please remember, it does not matter if that little boy was right or wrong. He matters: He is a child, and we must be interested."

He stood up and handed a card.

"This has my private mobile number."

Professor Frank stood up.

"Thank you."

CHAPTER 87

Tuesday, January 1st 2013,
New Year's Day, 5pm, Ashmere Grove

Lew Masters's new residence

Lew Masters walked, or rather swaggered, around his new domain. All tiredness had gone. He could be awake for a hundred black suns with a charge like this. He was electric. The flat settled about him like a silken cloak, rippling in his wake. His whole life had changed.

In two hours, his faithful Gladstone and big black case were emptied. His existing clothes, one suit, five vests and pants, five pairs of black socks, four shirts, eight t-shirts, and three sweaters, lay dwarfed in the wide wardrobes and chests of drawers. His two pairs of boots, two pairs of trainers, one pair of sandals, and one pair of smart black casuals nested in a shoe closet and his motorbike clothes had a wardrobe to themselves.

The bathrooms were filled with towels, flannels, and soaps, even a fluffy dressing gown. Fresh Egyptian cotton sheets on the spare bed and black satin sheets on his bed. Oh, the big man knew him alright! The old life could be washed away from him.

The wide shelf under the vast mirror was his altar. His tall candles stood proudly there. A hidden safe held his *Book of Shadows*, his Alistair Crowley, upside-down cross and pentagram.

In a black lockable box inside his wardrobe went his official papers, birth certificate, A levels, health care certificates, and driving licence. There was also his discharge note from the army, after he was wounded by a sniper and deemed unfit for further action. He rubbed his arms. No one would guess he had been wounded now. He was sure he was top brass.

And that was it; that was all he had to show for his life.

The fridge here showed more of a history than him: it was full. His favourite beer and wine was there. He wished his Ma could see him now—wherever she was. She rarely knew what planet she was on, let alone register that she had a child. A neighbour had seen him wandering around the street half-starved, so he was put into care. All that time, he was more worried for her than himself. Now look at him: caring for poor, unwell women.

All this for using his brain—what a reward!

He would go into Harvest House early to see Sarah Ransome. As he could not sleep anyway, he could find out how Lady Rose was today. He knew how to keep her safe. There was the potential pleasure of Tracey too, especially now he had a pad like this. She was so innocent despite appearances…

CHAPTER 88

Tuesday, January 1st 2013, New Year's Day, 3:45pm, Harvest House

Deirdre walked back from Harvest House with a spring in her step. It was a dull day and Harvest House shared the same arid unofficial car park as the SJTU. However, she had never gone out to visit someone in another unit socially in the centre.

Faith and Maureen, the OTs, had come over once or twice for Dr Stuart or Abdul, but it would be really nice to see them on their own territory and enjoy that gourmet coffee, as well as Nurse Brenda. Perhaps she would buy that coffee machine for the admin room! That would give Mary and Amanda a surprise when they returned.

The big surprise was the cleanliness. She had heard about the smell and the difficult combination of old institutionalised facilities and the attempts to make the rooms more dignified. The staff sleepover room had been particularly notorious for its poor state, and yet there was HH, clearly outdated but also clean and bright.

She was particularly pleased to have met Lady Rose, a young woman with the most remarkable eyes and hair. She liked the way Sarah had introduced them so naturally.

Once they were in Sarah's office, they both chatted away as if they had known each other for years. Deirdre was able to see that Professor Frank was kind at heart and that a CRIS meeting was being prepared.

Sarah was concerned she could not prepare Rose for the forthcoming launch without knowing what that group would decide. If Rose was involved with any further police link before the launch, would it relax her, or bring her more anxiety? If it got to the press, how would it damage her life in the new unit?

Deirdre really understood this and without mentioning the confidential SJTU meeting was able to tease out some of the issues. She was also able to help Sarah understand the confusing lines of authority, line management, and supervision between social services, health, the university, and the Glendale, as well as clarifying the resources of the SJTU.

The two women were so compatible that Deirdre, after her second coffee, was impressed enough to hesitantly mention the information she had found on the internet about Ian Anderson and Lord Glendale. To her pleasure Sarah had then immediately taken it further and told her about her close friends, Penny and Frances, from her old workplace, who had also emailed her the same information. Both women were careful to stress the uncertain probity of the information.

It was Deirdre who realised that 45 minutes had gone, and she had better get back to the SJTU. However, she had invited Sarah to come over once the CRIS decisions were made.

CHAPTER 89

Tuesday, January 1st 2013,
New Year's Day, 4pm

Answer machine messages

Deirdre Hislop to Charmaine Landesman

> We are pleased to let you know that a Consultant Psychotherapist, Jon
> Levine is able to meet your patient MH in his office at the SJTU at 10am
> Thursday, January 3rd. Please send a full history by tomorrow 4pm latest.
> ...

Professor Frank to St Cuthbert's Prep School

> Do you maintain records of pre-prep pupils in the 1970s? This is a matter
> of urgency.
> ...

Professor Frank to St Eldred's Prep School

> Do you maintain records of pre-prep pupils in the 1970s? This is a matter
> of urgency.
> ...

Keira Denny to Lady Lily

Dear Lady Lily—I am very excited about the forthcoming launch and would like to check out your views on some of the exciting plans I have over your speech.

CHAPTER 90

Tuesday, January 1st 2013,
New Year's Day

CNN Breaking News

When you come back
When you come back
Where the water meets itself
Where my hands frame the eye
Where the stars go to die
Speak the truth and never lie
Broken into myriad pieces
Each separate part
A life releases
In this celestial Helter Skelter
Am I Omega am I Delta?
Fight the heavy hand of fate

It is never too late,
To illuminate.

As the world plays Danny Delta's last song, which went platinum in record time, there has been concerning news that the cause of death was a massive drug overdose.

Like Michael Jackson, it appears the death was caused by an overdose of fentanyl, a synthetic opiate that is more potent than morphine and is a powerful painkiller. He also had traces of midazolam, diazepam, lidocaine, and ephedrine in his body.

"This raises more questions than it answers," said a close friend, Frankie Futura. "How did they get there? Did he jump or was he pushed?"

His brother Byron Santiago could not be reached.

CHAPTER 91

Tuesday, January 1st 2013,
New Year's Day

Sandra's searches website

So here we go folks! Tomorrow, Wednesday, January 2nd, is the annual conference of WAM. Those good people who care about abused children in Washington. Yes, Washington, the political home of our great country, will host this gathering to make sure that the A-word gets proper attention.

In our God-fearing country, it is not A for America or even A for Apple anymore, but A for Abuse and frankly I am getting fed up with it.

Aren't you? I am not talking here about those poor abused kids we fail to help, the real victims.

I am talking about false accounts of abuse, especially organised abuse and fantasy ritual VIP abuse. This is where gullible or sick therapists or THE-RAPISTS as I call them, destroy families. I should know. I was one of them. My poor family was. Read my web page.

Speak later.

Sandra Harrison

Text messages

Major D to HRH Carl-Zygmunt, Z, and Sandra

Excellent piece of work by Sandra's Searches.

HRH Prince Carl-Zygmunt to Sandra

Your prince is so proud of you.

Z to Major D, Lord Glendale, HRH Prince Carl-Zygmunt, and the Rt Hon Ian Anderson

All is well. Wishing you all a successful and Happy New Year in this interesting time. Wanting you all to know we will remember not to turn back but to go forward with confidence.

CHAPTER 92

Tuesday, January 1st 2013,
New Year's Day, 4pm, Gloucestershire

Ian Anderson's residence

Ian was scowling; he was already regretting his public kiss with Stefan. He had escaped to his sculpture studio in the grounds of his Gloucestershire home. Stefan would not disturb him here. As a photographer, Stefan would never intrude on another artist's space. But he had not stopped pushing, all through the rest of the party, and the rather dangerous drive down; he wanted a civil partnership or a marriage.
That was too much too fast, and Stefan was not his erotic ambrosia. He was something else...something too fragile to speak about...

They had met on Brighton seafront when he was taking a break from the party conference. Stefan had an outdoor exhibition on the Beachfront. They recognised something in each other at first sight nearly a decade ago, and had been together ever since. Stefan was loyal and discreet, but his utter fidelity was somehow exhausting and frightening.

Prowling around the large space like a caged animal, still high on champagne and lack of sleep, he paused for one moment to focus on his favourite—and only—wooden sculpture.

He had found a large piece of driftwood at Chesapeake Bay on a particular holiday in America, one he would never forget. It was a holiday that was the opposite of Stefan's—it cried out for a special carving. What a time he and Harold had experienced in Washington, endowing his feeder school with an Honourable Member. Forget the rituals or the Thai beach houses. This was the ultimate nectar of the gods...

"Create like a God, command like a King, work like a slave"— Brancusi.

Those were the words on the driftwood. He straightened himself.

Calligraphy had been an earlier passion and here, in this one piece that he would never sell, he could combine woodcarving, calligraphy, and painting. His studio. His space. His muse.

He would only work as a slave for himself now. Never for anyone else again, unless, like the country, they benefited through him. His benefit was the country's. He would be a slave to his own star: his understanding of finance and strategy would serve the UK, but he was not a slave to the country. Not even a slave to the Society. Whatever their punishments would be for dissent. Even as a non-Bloodliner, he was still the elite.

His mother had been a cleaner and he never heard the last of it at his exclusive secondary school when his brilliance got him a scholarship. Those golden boys who went on winter holidays in the snow and came back with a tan, who went to Biarritz, Montego Bay, and smelled the Clacton day trips on him.

"He's a bit dusty," said the House Captain, the golden boy Ambrose Fitch, languidly, in that particular upper-class drawl. They had been holding him over the filled toilet bowl.

"He needs polishing," agreed the future Lord Tamiz, pushing his head down into the toilet water.

"Just a little more elbow grease needed," added Ambrose, pushing him half out of the top floor classroom window and pulling the window down to keep him there.

How these insults pricked away at him. Burned him.

Together with the beatings and daily ritual humiliations.

Towel stolen in the showers.

Books removed.

Dead things in his bed.

Each of these moments burnished and polished.

His mother ignored it all. "You are the one with the brains," she said, "They are just jealous. Keep your head down and shine. You will end up knighted."

267

Keep your head down...she didn't know what that meant.

His father, a shop assistant for life, just kept away, not quite understanding how he had produced a son like this.

How he had longed for that golden boy, the Hon Ambrose—his secret ambrosia—with his lazy walk, how a master of the universe would walk...the way his gold hair just curled around his ears. How his teenage dreams were filled with violent acts, sexual acts towards him!

How Ambrose would beg for mercy or long for him. The fantasies were interchangeable. Ambrose would beg for mercy, but it was too late and he would slowly torture him to death, keeping him alive as long as possible. Until the memory of his sneer died and died.

If he was kind, he would not kill him, and they would come together in a seismic orgasm. Ambrose would be his sex slave. His tanned golden-brown arms were padlocked. His dreams had not changed for decades. More shameful now, more shameful than his preteen dreams of Ambrose: approaching him with longing, besotted with him, forsaking his sidekicks for him.

How he hated that young boy Ian—that puppy with his pleading eyes—how he wanted to kick him, kill him.

Don't go there! Not right now! "That way madness lies." Deep breath and he straightened himself.

The only good thing about the New Year's Eve party was his friendship with Lily. If he could ever have been with a woman, as opposed to training them, it would be her. The golden New World Order princess: hair like Ambrose, small pert bum like Ambrose, and small breasts that did not intrude. She knew him too, recognised him, knew what he had gone through. Just like Harold did. Funny that. The second son of a Lord, the firstborn unwanted daughter of a Lord and a proletarian. All three feeling something similar. True friends and fellow sufferers. He had only met her because the Society wanted him to access Rose and Lily's husband.

Stefan was no Ambrose born with a silver spoon in his mouth. He was like him, from humble shameful origins. It was his skill in photography and his brains that propelled him upwards from his poor family.

The party was a disparate ill-disciplined group he did not need but could manage. Parliament was effortless after public school. He was almost on top of the tree there. "Deputy" was no insult in the UK. The country needed him.

A weight suddenly left him as he realised a decision had been made. He would be Prime Minister. Poor James was deteriorating and would not last another year. He could win, would win, an election. But not with Stefan at his side; that was the answer.

They could take it further after he became Prime Minister, after the first term when he had shown his worth. He would tell Stefan now.

Stefan would wait.

"When you come back."

He gave a little spin to his Lazy Susan table, turning round his latest sculpture. Pentheus. The man of sorrows. Torn apart by women in a possessed fury, including his mother. Pentheus was made to look just like the Hon Ambrose, so exquisite and with such a downfall coming.

Sadly, it was not the real Ambrose; he had run to fat and ruin. Alcohol had addled him, and he had sunk his family fortune. No need to give that one his comeuppance! After all, Ambrose got salt in the wound every day from every newspaper report about the Deputy Prime Minister; every television appearance, all of which showed how polished Ian Edwards was, how cleaned up, how brave of a poor working-class lad to go to a posh school…And if Ambrose ever dared to write a *Daily Mercury* type story: "When the Prime Minister was my fag" or

"How I shoved the Prime Minister's head in the toilet and flushed it"…then he would get him for sexual abuse and boarding school syndrome. Sweet.

And Lord Tamiz was dead. A car crash at 30, in India. Arranged by the Society as an early bonus. Good. He had read about that in the nationals, hidden under Foreign news; he had been a man of no national importance. In a better mood, he locked the door, carefully glancing with pride at the clean concrete floor. He had his mother's genuine interest in how to run a tidy ship and his studio was also his thank you to her: they were the true bloodline, but red, not blue.

CHAPTER 93

Tuesday, January 1st 2013,
New Year's Day, 4.15pm

From: Bursar@steldreds.com
To: Prof.c.frank@glendale.com

Dear Professor Frank,

Thank you for your email. I am pleased to say that as a school with a proud history going back two hundred years we do indeed keep records of our pupils.

You will appreciate, I am sure, our confidentiality policy which means that we require a copy of your birth certificate and proof of current residence or work before we can release such information to you.

Yours sincerely

Anthony J. Reddit
Bursar

From: Bursar@stcuthberts.com
To: Prof.c.frank@glendale.com

4:30pm

Dear Professor Frank,

Thank you for your enquiry. Our office is closed until Friday, January 4th.

Best wishes

The Bursar

From: Lewis&Cromwell@LC.com
To: Prof.c.frank@glendale.com

4:40pm

Dear Professor Frank,

Thank you for your enquiry about your late Uncle Edward Chapell's payment towards your school fees.

In the absence of any living relatives of the late Mr Chapell outside of yourself and your sister, my partners and I see no problem in researching this information for you.

We do keep our files 50 years after business is concluded, but it will take administrative time to locate and copy the relevant information. There may be a small administrative photocopying charge or you may feel like visiting us.

Yours sincerely

Frederick Lewis
Partner

CHAPTER 94

Tuesday, January 1st 2013, New Year's Day, 5pm, Westminster Square

The Redcliffe residence

The last cleaners had left, supervised by Maria. The last crumbs of cake, the last bottles of champagne, the wax from the aromatic candles, round tables from the ballroom, the glasses, the table linen, the flower arrangement, and spent fireworks from the lawn were all removed. The glittering space relaxed back into its own skin. All was quiet. As if even the imprint of all the voices and crowds, the silks and satins had been hoovered out of the air.

An overwhelming smell of lilies, and silence.

Lily was still lying on the cold splendour of the marital bed, on top of the silk sheets and white brocade cover. A long ivory silk peignoir, like a fallen statue.

She and Peter must have been sleeping almost in segregated shifts since the last guests left after breakfast. Each time she woke, he was not there; wherever she was, he wasn't. Was this significant? Something different seemed to have happened to him. He was spending more and more time in his study. Next year, it should stop at 3am, she thought. Everyone was ageing.

They did not have to cater for breakfast too ... *if there was a next year.*

Where did that voice come from?

She lay there, feeling the distance between them. There had been no discussion between them. No congratulations from him on her matchmaking, her personal and political successes, hosting the first public kiss of Ian and Stefan, hiding Sir Robert's wife from his new mistress, aiding a disagreement between the Whip and the new lady MP.

Even her mother had managed to say her dress was "not uncomely," and Peter's mother had said, "the champagne was better than last year." But there were no compliments from Peter for the menu she had chosen, the pairing of champagne. They used to enjoy that. How happy he was last night; she appreciated him and his art so much. How happy with his public kiss from Ian.

Goodness! More of a kiss than she had received, she realised. Peter's toast to her had been too faint-hearted and the lapdog way he gazed at her adoringly had gone. She neither had the confident man she used to have before Rose, nor the lapdog. What was happening? Ian appreciated what she had achieved, and so did Oliver; but not Peter.

The image of Dr Green, that ugly little Simon, and his odd wife Betsy flashed in her face. The way they smiled at each other, how they couldn't wait to get home alone for midnight just to be together.

She and Peter used to be like that. Before Rose and before they all fell down with Down's ... or rather before Rose did. A lifetime of postnatal depression. Hello Woman's Hour! *Vogue*! *Westbridge Weekly*. I am suffering from postnatal depression that has lasted 21 years!

A knock on the door jolted her and Peter walked in, still wrapped in his burgundy dressing gown.

She would have commented that his unusual knock on the door could have woken her up, but a look at his pale drawn face silenced her.

Was he going to confess to an affair? Bankruptcy?

"Are you up to talking?" he asked tersely.

"About last night?" she questioned, playing for time.

"No."

"Oh."

He sat on the side of the bed and smiled faintly at her. "Sorry darling, it was the success it always is. You have a genius for that, as we know, the matching, the introducing, the food, the wine, the clothes. But no, that isn't what has disturbed my sleep."

She reached for a lace shawl at the side of the bed and gracefully wrapped herself in it. Usually he would have hugged her by now.

"We need a conversation about what you cannot speak about."

A pause.

"Rose…Our daughter."

There was silence.

There it was.

She froze.

Usually he would apologise if she looked upset, but something was different.

"When Rose was 6…"

She looked up, shocked. She thought he was going to talk about the birth.

"When Rose was 6, Ian invited you and Rose over to a wonderful place with a swimming pool."

"Yes," she replied blandly, equanimity restored, wondering why he had gone there.

"She never wanted to go near water again after that."

"Yes," agreed Lily.

"And?"

There was silence.

"Do you remember what she said about that day?"

Another silence

"It was 15 years ago, Peter!"

"I am asking, do you remember?"

A pause.

"She wanted me to bring her Disney princess swimsuit and she was so excited to be there. She takes personal invitations very seriously. You don't notice it, Peter, but very few of our friends really wanted us to visit with Rose. Ian and Oliver were the only two really, and of course Maria. But we pay her."

Peter was watching her, clearly moved. This was better!

"When I took her to see Ian or Oliver, I felt myself. I was so happy taking her, although sad you could not come too. It was early in my friendship with Ian, our friendship with Ian. It felt so good on that sunny day. Everyone takes from us wanting your political clout and my hospitality, and Ian was giving something. I was there as Lily, and not the mother of a mongol, a mongrel."

All connection broken, Peter leapt out of bed and smashed his fist against the wall.

Lily huddled in shock. "What are you doing, Peter? Stop it."

274

Facing her with blazing eyes and barely able to speak, he stood still until his breathing calmed.

"Lily called herself a mongol when I took her shopping for a Christmas tree at 6. I could not understand where such a word had come from. I never thought it could have come from you." He walked to the door. "I can't continue this conversation yet. Rose said … no … I can't … And I am sick of the smell of lilies everywhere. It is like a mausoleum."

Out he went and slammed the door.

It felt like the whole room was shaking. The bed, the chandelier, the paintings in their gilt frames. But it took time for Lady Lily to realise it was her. Something had broken between them, had died, and they would never be the same.

CHAPTER 95

Tuesday, January 1st 2013,
New Year's Day, 5pm, Ashmere Grove

Lew Masters's residence

Out of the shower, Lew looked at himself in the mirror. Thanks to the automatic demisting device, there was no mist, and Lew felt himself becoming, growing. A rebirth.

Cream on his face, his body: his temple. Muscles rippling. Towels and underfloor heating. A coffee while drying.

Like a surgeon, he called for each item of clothes—vest, T-shirt, sweater, pants, trousers, socks, trainers—and handed them to himself reverentially. The smart trousers, shirt, tie, and shoes went into a clothes bag to be fitted to his motorbike.

Everything felt different.

Washed, dried and dressed: his motorbike leathers came last like another skin.

He took the lift down to the ground floor just to enjoy its existence. No sign of any neighbours, and the street was quiet before he roared away, leaving the tranquillity in his dust.

CHAPTER 96

Tuesday, January 1st 2013, New Year's Day, 5pm, Harvest House

"Last piece of work for today before I go," smiled Sarah.

"We work hard, friend Sarah," said Rose.

"Serby working too," said Sinita, making one of his paws wave at the architect.

Jon and Dykes nodded seriously.

John McRae, the architect, had spread out the plans on Sarah's large table. Facing him were Rose, Sinita, John, and Dykes. Both grinning, Sarah and Faith placed a tub of Lego figures and furniture in the large square marked "community room."

"Okay," said John.

"I know you have visited your new home nearly every day, and you have watched us rebuilding it and making it right for you. All the bedrooms, as you know, are on the top floor. All the bedrooms have their own toilet and bathroom, just like you have now in Harvest House."

"But now," said Faith, "we want to see if you can recognise where your new rooms are on the architect's plans. Where do you live? Let us start with you Rose, as this building has got your name on it. Which is your room, Rose?"

"Rose lives in Lady Rose House," said John

"So she won't forget where she lives," laughed Dykes.

"That's a really good point," laughed Sarah.

"I never thought of that. What would John House sound like?"

"Going to the John," leered Sinita.

"Dirty John," mocked Rose in a deep low voice.

"Rude," shouted Dykes, his small frame tensing.

"Rude, rude," echoed Sinita.

John smashed his fist on the table, knocking the Lego over, and Dykes began to cry.

McRae stepped back, uncertain what to do, but before Sarah or Faith could speak they were interrupted.

"It's cool! It's cool. It's cool," repeated a calm authoritative voice, holding his hand up for a high five.

They all looked with relief as Lew Masters approached, in a smart shirt, trousers, and tie.

"Good Lady Rose here, Master Masters. Sorry John. Sorry Dykes. Bad Rose gone. Dirty Rose, not Dirty John."

"Good Rose! Good, good, good," smiled Lew, "good afternoon, Mrs Ransome, Faith. McRae. Hope you got my message. I was going to try and come early just to ensure smooth running in this last period before the move."

"Well, thank heavens you did, Lew. And please call me Sarah. I wanted to thank you so much for the party's success."

"And me too," said Faith, "credit where credit is due! I told Sarah and Maureen!"

"Thank you," said Lew formally and rather awkwardly.

"Good party, Mr Masters," said John.

"Serby danced," said Sinita.

"Because of you!" emphasised Lew. "Without you he could not dance."

"Because of me!" said Sinita, startled and smiling.

"Clever Sinita."

"Clever Sinita! Nice John," said Rose.

"Nice, John," agreed Dykes.

"My name is John too!" said McRae, relaxing and moving back to the table.

"Nice John 1 and nice John 2," said Rose.

The whole table settled, and John picked up the Lego pieces.

"John 1 picking up Lego," said Lew, coming forward and sitting by McRae.

"High five Mr Masters. I am number 1," said John happily.

"So," said Sarah, "we were getting everyone to see where their new bedroom would be on John's plans here. Faith and I thought we could use Lego to stand for people so they could put a Lego person in the bedroom they will have."

"And now is the time for everyone to choose the colour paint they want."

"Pink, pink to make the boys wink," grinned Sinita sticking her tongue out.

"What is a wink?" asked Faith.

"Like a twitch," said John, "like Tim has."

"Well, tomorrow, Wednesday," said Faith, "when Sarah and I are back, we will decide on the colour charts because John's decorators are painting the rooms tomorrow afternoon."

John McRae stood up to fold his chair.

"Sarah! Apologies if I am intruding," said Lew, "but since I am here early, if you wanted me to complete the exercise you and Faith were doing with the Lego, I could do it—unless that is for tomorrow and John needs his plans. Your call."

Faith and Sarah looked at each other.

"John—is that a spare copy we could keep until tomorrow?"

"John 1 or 2?" asked Dykes with a grin.

"I am number 1," laughed John.

"Well. I am John 2," said McRae, "and I have a copy, so this is for you."

"Good," smiled Lew.

"Good Lady Rose," said Rose.

"Yes," agreed Lew.

"Well, thank you, Lew, thank you so much," said Sarah picking up her bag and coat.

"Bye, Lew," said Faith, picking up hers.

"Bye," he replied, "can we complete this task in your office, Sarah, rather than move it?"

"Yes," she agreed, looking around, "everything is locked up."

And out she went with Faith.

"What has happened to that man?" asked Faith.

"How can he go from Trump to Obama in one day?"

They both laughed.

"I don't want to question it," said Sarah.

279

"I can actually leave with a clear conscience today."

"And on time!" grinned Faith.

"In fact I feel really bad about all the negatives I said about Lew. Look at the way he facilitated all of them!"

"Change is always possible, but it doesn't mean what you said wasn't right for them!"

"Bye Tim," called Faith as they saw him rocking by the door.

A careworn but smiling Brenda appeared.

"Have a good evening. Tim—come and do some drawing with me."

Tim slowly stopped rocking like a machine winding down. A smile appeared on his face. "Bye Faith, bye Mrs Ransome."

"Bye!" called Sarah.

"How would you like a celebratory drink down St Joseph's Rise, The Green Arrow?" asked Faith, turning to Sarah on an impulse.

There was a momentary pause.

"I would love to," said Sarah. Two invitations in one day! That moment had been the first thought about Steve too! Things were looking up!

CHAPTER 97

Tuesday, January 1st 2013, New Year's Day, 5:30pm, Westminster Square

The Redcliffe residence

Still wrapped in a white lace shawl, Lady Lily sat on the ruins of her marital bed. The pain of her father's marriage to poor plain Imogen had faded. Even the birth of the baby son and heir, but she had never expected anything like this from Peter. Even her mother had warmed slightly to him, saying he was not a bolter and was malleable. She wanted to phone her but knew she would get no sympathy. Lady Priscilla was sharp and clear, but there was nothing soft about her.

Whatever tears she may have shed when Lord Wellbrook left her were private, silent ones. His photographs were removed from the albums, his clothes and books thrown out, and she carried on with her charities and Lily. She neither sought solace nor showed pain. All her emotions were Botoxed: she had a stiff upper face. Peter's mother was no different. The two elderly mothers, Priscilla and Marjorie, were so similar. Such stoics ...

Ian? No, dear friend as he was, he might worry too much about a scandal. If Rose repeated her magic snake delusions, it might still hit the press and stick to him. He would be in Gloucester with Stefan, and she couldn't disturb Stefan. He would be hoping for marriage and happiness, and would be frightened at a wobble like this.

Oh goodness! What a gap…all those besotted men…Chris, Paul, Robert, Welwyn…they were too weak as it was when it came to her.

Tears suddenly came to her eyes. She did not really have anyone; no father and an ice-queen mother and mother-in-law. No sister, no real daughter. She paid for Maria and this was too private.

Oliver, Lord Glendale. He would understand all of it. She phoned speedily before she could change her mind. To her relief Glendale answered immediately.

"I saw it was you—my champagne Lily, what a sparkler! I wouldn't have picked up for anyone else, my hostess with the mostest! Too much champagne—Dom Perignon of the most exquisite year! 2006? And how it went with your wonderful new menu! And don't think I didn't notice how you helped Stefan and acknowledged the Greens. What a woman!"

Lily's whole body relaxed. Oliver was a father who would always love and appreciate her. He said everything she had wanted Peter to say.

There was a pause.

"Lily, love! Here I am telling you what was on my mind when you must have rung me for a reason. What is it? Peter annoying you? Ian? Do I need to prod them for you?"

A strangled sob.

"Lily! Do you want me to come over?"

A deep breath.

"Just speaking to you, Oliver, I feel better. There. You are my tonic, and I am your champagne."

"Well, that is certainly less expensive for you," he grinned. His tone grew serious. "What's happened? Rose? Toby?"

How well he understood her. She took a deep breath.

"Peter and I just had a big argument, and I don't know if we can repair it."

"Rose?"

"Of course."

"Ian?"

"A bit. Peter. He was preoccupied with when Rose was 6, shortly after Ian and I became friends, and Ian invited us all over to visit him in this lovely place with two swimming pools. Peter wasn't free, but Rose and I went. It was a sunny day. At some point Rose said Ian had a magic

282

snake in the water, and Rose has had a water phobia since then, but that wasn't the problem. Peter has worried about the ambiguous meanings of the word "snake"—you men, what show-offs—especially after her mad comments about Danny, and there were all sorts of blow-up toys and animals in the water, but they were all small."

"And?"

"The big thing...the really big thing was I said how nice it was to have a friend invite me over with Rose where I felt like myself, and not just the mother of..."

"A Down's child?" asked Oliver gently.

"But I didn't say that," admitted Lily embarrassedly.

There was a pause.

"I said 'mongol', and Peter exploded."

Silence

"And?"

"He went back to his study—and told me he didn't like the smell of lilies." A burst of stifled sobs.

"My poor girl. I am coming over now."

CHAPTER 98

Tuesday, January 1st 2013,
New Year's Day, 5:30pm,
Harvest House

Brenda popped her head around the corner into Sarah's room. "A cup of tea or coffee, Mr Masters, Mr McRae? Don't work too hard, Mr Masters."

Lew smiled approvingly. He could get used to this respect. How strange! Coming in early was doing right by Major D, Zed, and the Society's aims as well as doing right by Sarah and Harvest House. Hell! He was even calling her Sarah! If he didn't watch it, he would be managing a hospital next.

"Thank you, Brenda. Black coffee please, and I am Lew."

Brenda smiled warmly as if she had been given a present.

"Ooo…ooo," mocked Sinita.

"And builder's tea for me," said Jon McRae.

"What about me? I am John 1!" said John.

"Go for it, John 1," said Lew smiling at Brenda.

"Do you want to help me bring the drinks?" she asked, looking at the four residents.

"I get tray," said Lady Rose.

"That's really good practice for your new home," approved Brenda.

Lady Rose smiled graciously as she went out to get the tray. "Good Lady Rose here, Master Masters."

"Very good, Lady Rose," agreed Lew watching her carefully.

"Very, very, very, good."

"Serby help with drinks," said Sinita, following quickly behind.

"So, now you know where you and Dykes are going to be," said John McRae, tentatively.

"Next-door neighbours, John 2," said John proudly.

"Right next door, so you can knock on the wall to say hello even before you get out of bed."

"Knock knock. Who's there?" asked Dykes

"John 1!" shouted John laughing.

"Don't know how you keep everyone calm," said Jon McRae quietly to Lew as Brenda, Rose, and Sinita returned with the drinks.

Lew smiled. "Strange how we choose the work we do," he said.

Rose and Sinita handed everyone their mugs.

"More good practice for your new home," said Brenda. "I know everyone has been telling you that. On the other hand, we need the men helping next time as it was Rose and Sinita this time."

John looked upset. "Don't like the kettle."

"You can do the jug of water, John 1," said Lew, "as that needs muscles."

Dykes smiled happily. "John 1 has got muscles. Strong man."

There was a nervous knock on the door, and Tracey's head peeped round the corner. "So this is where you are, Mr Masters," she said, walking in hesitantly after seeing Lady Rose.

With Mr Masters' permission she had not checked on the patients after they went to their rooms that evening. The memory of that transformation was still engraved in her mind despite the success of the party last night.

"Like in *The Omen*," she had said to Reg, her disgusting "landlord," her disgust for him cleverly covered by her description of Rose. Rose was a shock; he wasn't. He was her normal, her rent, her address. That price was starting to feel more expensive each day.

She would talk to Mr Masters—Lew. Ask his advice about a new place. He was hot. Look at the muscles on him!

"Like *The Omen*?" Reg had reflected. "And a posh mongol too!" It had even delayed his need to be sucked off.

"Come in, Tracey," said Lew with a wink. "You dressing up or down?" She giggled like a young teenager.

"A bit like you, Lew," she said daringly. She was wearing trousers and a tight black sweater instead of her usual short skirt. She had felt

285

awkward and naked on first walking in, but having been recognised she now felt comfortable.

"You Lew!" rhymed Sinita.

"Lulu," added Dykes.

"We're going to the zoo, zoo, zoo," sang Rose.

There was a burst of laughter, and then Lew raised his hand to signal a pause.

"High five, everyone." Said Lew, "Let's leave Sarah's office now. Thank you, David, for the plans. Good work everyone. Brenda will take you back to the dayroom. See you in the office, Tracey. You might as well bring that spare cuppa with you."

CHAPTER 99

Tuesday, January 1st 2013, New Year's Day, 6pm, Westbridge Police Station

Superintendent Mark Hewson was shocked. He was an urbane man, liked by politicians as well as the bobby on the beat; it took a lot to shock him. He had an eye on becoming a future Commissioner of the Metropolitan Police, the formal title of Britain's top cop. Although the Met was based in London, it carried various national charges, including anti-terrorism and protection of the royal family. The post was answerable to the Home Secretary as well as appointed by the Queen so even-mindedness and strategic thinking were crucial. Chief Superintendent and Deputy Commissioner ranks were still above him and he had to tread very carefully.

There had been a curious call from the philanthropist and highly political peer, Lord Glendale, on behalf of Lady Lily, who was apparently in the room with him, asking him to say that the call was to be confidential and shouldn't get back to her husband, the Minister of Health. Hints given that complex Anglo-American research was at risk came from the CIA using an unlisted American number. Underlying this was the possible indiscriminate disclosure of abuse by a woman with Down's Syndrome naming the Deputy Prime Minister as the perpetrator—her mother's best friend.

The CRIS meeting was already set up for tomorrow, so this was an attempt to bend his ear beforehand, a helpful contextualising at best or prejudicial at worst. He would have to be very careful. Luckily, DC Morag Lennon was a sensible sort who was up to date on vulnerable victims. He was of course generally up to date but had little experience of witnesses or offenders with Down's Syndrome, other than the difficulty of being believed on the one hand and the tendency to repeat the last sentence said.

He felt he had successfully thanked the callers in a neutral but warm way, assured them he understood the sensitivity, and said when the CRIS meeting was.

CHAPTER 100

Tuesday, January 1st 2013, New Year's Day, USA

Z was satisfied. Lew was even better than he expected. He had completely stabilised Lady R and the other subjects, gained the respect of old and new staff alike, and evaluated and perfected his own stabilising techniques, which some of his people could learn from. The top installers were one thing, but this level of "lower" work was the one most short of skills. Lew's use of the triple hypnotic injunction as positive reinforcement, bypassing fear responses was particularly effective.

He was loyal too.

It did not matter if Sir Peter allowed press access to his daughter. With Lew there it would be safe, and if there was any breakthrough of other personalities she would be whisked away. The CRIS could be a trigger, but it should be easy and pragmatic to agree to no interviewing of her until after the new unit was open. Major D had tackled that call to Hewson well. Glendale could always be relied on too. He was on his way to deal with Lady Lily right now.

"Project Orpheus" was the most important project since the 1940s. The funding from Orpheus himself and the link with Glendale meant there was a greater chance of the bloodlines being replicated. If they were happy, the scientists could proceed. A UK hiccup could not be allowed to delay it.

Z. He liked it. The final letter of the alphabet. The small number he spoke to directly knew him as Zed or Zee (UK or USA). Or, as he would like to say to Ian, "Call me zzzzzzz and think of a swarm of angry bees or a drill."

CHAPTER 101

Tuesday, January 1st 2013, New Year's Day, 7pm, Westminster Square

The Redcliffe residence

Sir Peter had left the flat without a word. This had never happened before. She could hear his courteous but clipped voice inform Maria he would be dining out this evening; loudly enough for her to overhear. Even with an abyss taking hold of them, he gave this courtesy.

Peter had always been so safe she never even thought of him as an anchor; now she was adrift. She had managed to wash and dress but stayed in her bedroom, frightened of Maria seeing her like this.

A separation? Divorce? Like her mother, was she going to be the "former" wife of …? The single dinner guest, the object of pity and curiosity.

Oliver would be here soon. She would see him in her study. Walking as languidly as she could, she hoped to get to her study without being seen by Maria, but as always, Maria was with her in just a few steps.

"Oh Maria!" she said in a steady voice, "this whole launch is so exhausting! Lord Glendale will be here in a few minutes to discuss it. Could you bring us some smoked salmon canapés and any other leftovers? You know his favourite champagne, the Dom Perignon 2006. We still have some specially saved for him. In my study, please!"

Nodding graciously, it took all her energy to slowly walk along the corridor to her study instead of running and screaming. She could feel Maria's sympathetic and confused eyes burn into her back.

CHAPTER 102

Tuesday, January 1st 2013,
New Year's Day

From: Stockleys@stockleylaw.com
To: Laconicolawyers@justice.com; SandraSearches@Sandra.com;
Prof.c.frank@glendale.com; PA-lovingpa@alienation.com;
Fiona@dailymercury.com

ALERT—WAM Conference: Wednesday 1am

The Washington Association for Maltreated Children is meeting tomorrow for a major conference on ritual abuse at Union House. Around 250 members are expected. Dr Judy Kestle will be evaluating the evidence against the West House, a major Washington Children's Home. It had been endowed by Anglo-American philanthropist Harold Fitz-Hugh West, whose late mother, Lady Olivia Glendale, is buried at Arlington Ceremony. His older brother Lord Glendale is a major philanthropist in the UK. Some of the survivors, now adults, will be testifying.

In other words, the leprosy we have seen spreading over the Western World in the form of false accusations and broken families will spread unless we all link together.

Support for Harold! Wrestle the Kestle!

From: Prof.c.frank@glendale.com
To: Stockleys@stockleylaw.com
Cc: Scepticsolicitor@justice.com; SandrasSearches@sandra.com;
PA-lovingpa@alienation.com; Fiona@dailymercury.com

Automatic response

Professor Frank regrets he is not able to be part of this correspondence.
Please delete him from this correspondence.

....

Sandra's searches website

Well, I said I would write more about WAM and I keep my promises.

So WAM is holding its major conference in Washington, the political capital of our country. Good for them. Yes. Really.

I don't want faceless public health officials who don't understand how the personal is the political and how abuse destroys mental and physical health. We fail to hear that at our own cost.

Abuse kills worse than cancer. I will repeat that. Abuse kills worse than cancer.

Yes. This is Sandra speaking. Sandra who had terrible images of abuse drip-fed into her mind by damaged therapists.

Yes. You see, I know how awful abuse is because the images fed into my mind broke me down and nearly destroyed my family. And for genuine victims, it is even worse.

So don't ruin the day by backing WAM.

Wam bam, no thank you mam!

Especially when an honourable philanthropist like Harold Fitz-Hugh West is being attacked yet again. Is there no end to it? The poor man endows West House, a Washington Unit for disturbed orphan boys. He doesn't have to. But for that patriotic piece of work, he is smeared.

All we have is our good name and when we are smeared we lose our identity. His older brother, Lord Glendale, lives in the UK, where he is also a famous philanthropist. They come from a proud Anglo-American family—their mother, Lady Olivia, is buried in Arlington, for goodness sake. And their father was a Vietnam hero. Lady Olivia is a blueblood American descended from the Rockefeller line.

We care about human rights here. We care about justice. We are the greatest democracy in the world. When a man has been investigated and cleared, he is innocent. Right? Because otherwise we are back in the McCarthy days.

So WAM—we need you to help our abused children but don't bring in a rehash of the old red-devil-under-the-bed satanic monster West gobbling the raw meat boys at West House.

Thank you for listening.

You know who I am. The woman was nearly destroyed by her the-rapists.

Sandra Harrison

CHAPTER 103

Tuesday, January 1st 2013,
New Year's Day

CNN Breaking News

While investigations continue into the death of platinum singer and musician Danny Delta, we bring you explosive new information. Byron Santos, the reclusive younger brother of superstar Danny Delta, has said in a potentially libellous video on YouTube, "My brother would not have destroyed himself. He was not on this cocktail of shit. Someone has given it to him. Ask the Oval Office. Ask the President. And if I disappear or go mad or die it is not by my hand. That's all I have to say."

This echoes the words of Danny's closest friend Frankie Futura. There is no response as yet from police investigating the circumstances of his death. Record sales of When You Come Back have continued. It is still unclear whether Danny Delta left a will.

CHAPTER 104

Wednesday, January 2nd 2013, 7am, UK

Daily Mercury

When You Come Back
By specialist reporter Fiona Roberts

The haunting music and words of Danny Delta went platinum in record time in the USA within hours of the megastar's death on December 28th and sales are rising in the UK.

However, disturbing questions still remain.

None of them will be answered by the incendiary response of his brother, the reclusive songwriter Byron Santos who has just released a sensational and potentially libellous YouTube video.

We think our readers deserve to know the full story, as hysteria on social media builds up, and conspiracy theories are becoming such a danger to innocent people's reputations, let alone the security of democracy itself.

"My brother would not have destroyed himself. He was not on this cocktail of shit. Someone has given it to him. Ask the Oval Office. Ask the President. If I disappear, go mad, or die, it is not by my hand. That's all I have to say."

The video went viral on social media with conspiracy theorists and trolls out in force. Byron Santos has been unavailable for any questioning and has made it clear that he has nothing further to say.

At the same time, we have ugly clouds of suspicion crossing the pond as our most generous philanthropist, billionaire Lord Glendale, was at his last sell-out concert and after-concert party on October 31st together with the Deputy Prime Minister, the Rt Hon Ian Anderson, and the Minister of Health and his family, Sir Peter, Lady Lily Redcliffe, and Lady Rose Redcliffe.

Lady Rose, who will be 21 on Saturday, will be moving into a special Independence Unit bearing her name at St Joseph's University Hospital.

Lord Glendale, whose Trust has endowed the Glendale Centre and Equipa Centre on the St Joseph's University Hospital site, has the misfortune of having a younger playboy brother, who has long been the centre of other rumours. Harold Fitz-Hugh West established and endowed West House, Washington's largest Children's Unit for orphans with behavioural disturbances. Rumours which have not been proven in court linked him with allegations of abuse.

Do you have any stories about this? Write to Fiona@themercury.com

....

Text message

Glendale to HRH Prince Carl-Zygmunt and Ian Anderson

What on earth is Fiona up to? I thought she was tame. Asking for more stories is asking for trouble for us.

....

From: Markdyer@dailychronicle.com
To: Keiradenny@glendale.com
Bcc: Fiona@dailymercury.com

8:30am

To Keira

I will indeed be coming to the launch of the Lady Rose Independence Unit. Thank you for the invite.

From: Keiradenny@glendale.com
To: Lordglendale@glendale.com

8.40am

Your opinion on my plans is urgently sought as I am now being besieged with media interest over the Lady Rose launch following the *Daily Mercury* doing their usual, and it is, of course, all focused on Danny Delta and your brother. Can we meet in person today as some issues are too delicate for the phone?

CHAPTER 105

Wednesday, January 2nd 2013, 8:40am, Harvest House

Lew Masters came out of the staff bathroom in his motorbike gear. There was no need to wait until Sarah, Faith, and Maureen arrived to show how well he was cooperating. The gorilla's advice had been good after all. His stock had never been so high. Besides, he wanted to return to his flat, to savour it, touch it, go round slowly … oh so slowly, looking at it all and becoming it. How he had worked, and this had just fallen into his lap.

"Do what thou wilt shall be the whole of the law," said Crowley and how he had longed to follow it. What a laugh he had been as a Crowleyite! He had followed everyone else's will, and sucked it in, but never actualised anything deep and true.

How could a new year create change so quickly? All those years of reinventions. He had thought he might pimp Tracey, get her more money than that wanker Reg or he could bring her in to the coven as sexual candy.

Tracey was in the office making huge dark lines under her eyes with her kohl crayon. She still looked barely legal, poor kid. She grinned when she saw him, embarrassedly putting her makeup bag away.

"Cool! From a stiff's suit to leathers!" He laughed. "And who else is wearing the trousers today?"

Tracey nodded happily. They had joked that night about their slowly changing clothes.

"Easier for riding, Mrs Ransome will agree."

She had also found the night shift surprisingly easier, and warmer, wearing trousers instead of her skirt.

"Would the little lady like to ride my steed?" he asked. He asked seriously and felt vulnerable and awkward. Luckily, she did not appear to notice.

"Which one?" she giggled and then blushed. Fuck this! She didn't do blushes. "Or you could ride mine," she said.

"What a power couple," he laughed, "his and hers bikes."

There was a moment's pause.

O'Bridey, heads you ride mine or tails I ride yours. It is for coffee at my new pad. Just to show you how the un-*reg*-istered live."

"He might get cross," said O'Bridey, worriedly. "Because he usually waits to see me when I first get back."

"I bet he does! Bet he is just bursting. Well, you could phone him to say your boss needs you to put in a little overtime because of plans for the new unit. Your conscience can manage that, I think." Lew watched her looking worriedly at the floor. He knew that expression from when cult fodder were asked to talk about a Master to test their loyalty. He didn't need that. He would look at his flat himself. She could wait. Another day.

"I'm off without a Trace then," he laughed merrily, showing nothing had been serious. "Hope you've got enough breath for Reg! What a job. Don't blow it." Without a further look backwards, he walked out, high-fiving Sinita on the way.

The door closed followed by the sound of his machine roaring into life.

Tracey ran back into the staff toilet. Holding a piece of toilet paper tight against her mouth she gave way to violent sobs. "Fucking stupid cow," she said to herself. "Stupid, stupid cow." She kicked the door with her pointed black boots.

Back to Reg and his stink and her being his skivvy and sex worker just to have an address, just to carry on. She heard too late the footsteps coming into the room.

"You alright in there?" came Sarah's warm concerned voice. "I've just come in and Sinita said you were upset."

Unlocking the door without a pause for thought, she found herself rushing into a warm motherly embrace.

"It's okay," said Sarah. "It is going to be okay. Let's get you a cup of tea, plenty of time. I am 15 minutes early." Putting an arm around her, she led her towards her office.

Sinita, standing outside the toilet door, looked at them, worried.

"It is OK, Sinita. Tracey got some bad news, but we are going to share it together and then she will feel better."

"Want Serby?" asked Sinita, thrusting the grubby bear towards Tracey.

"No thanks, Sinita, but that is very kind."

"Serby is going to move to a new place," said Sinita. "Tracey, move to a new place. Will be nicer."

Sarah carried on walking, but Tracey stopped in amazement and wiped her eyes. "You are so cool, Sinita, and you are right. I have got bad news; I have to move. But it is good news because my old place is shit. Oops. Sorry, Mrs Ransome."

Sarah smiled calmly. "Well done, Sinita, for guessing what was upsetting Tracey. You have done half my job for me."

"Clever Sinita. Move from shit place, Tracey. Will tell Rose," said Sinita happily as she turned away from them.

"How did she know? She knew. She really knew," said Tracey.

They walked into Sarah's room and she sat for a moment watching as Sarah took her coat off and moved towards the kettle.

"Sorry Mrs Ransome. Can I make you a drink? I feel better now."

"Well, thank you Tracey. Black coffee please, and whatever you would like. I haven't learned how to use Faith's fancy machine, so it is just the Gold Blend for me please. Was last night alright?"

"Yes, Mrs Ransome. It was all the excitement about the new unit and where they would live, and Mr Masters was just so clever at helping them all with it." Her voice trailed off.

Sarah could sense her longing and conflict.

"Lousy digs?" asked Sarah.

"Mm."

"Having to do unwanted extras?"

Tracey looked up, shocked.

"You are not going to sack me."

"Tracey—that's the third time you have said that. You remind me a bit of me when I was your age."

"You? You?" said Tracey horrified. "I can't possibly … You are all classy."

302

"Tracey, you needed an address to do the course, right?"

"Yes!"

"And a man came with the address, right?"

"Right."

"Bingo!"

"Bingo? You?"

"Yes."

"And you have told me that?"

"I have."

"Why?"

"Because I can see you will be good at this, Tracey. You will finish your course and then the next level and then a degree, and then you will have a job like mine. And once upon a time, a woman sat me down and told me this just like I am telling you, and it changed things just at the right time. Now, I think the building that provides rooms for the nurses has got a couple of spare rooms waiting for the next intake. Brenda told me. It would only be temporary, but how would you like a temporary place to give you time to look around and find somewhere."

Tracey looked at her, her mouth hanging open in surprise. "Oh yes, Miss, Mrs Ransome. I can't thank you enough."

"You call me 'Miss' as if I was your teacher, and I am not Mrs Ransome anymore because my husband left me. Don't get taken in by appearances, Tracey. Sinita knew what was going on better than me. Lew Masters knew how to manage difficult issues here when he did not look as if he would."

Tracey sighed, and a bright smile spread through her body. "OK, Sarah!" she said with a strong voice. "I will go back for my clothes. It is not hard. I have only got one case."

"You do that, Tracey, and I will ring the nursing home."

Tracey sprung up with a burst of energy.

"Much better clothes for riding your bike, Tracey! And it might make it safer for when you go to your digs as well. But if you need help getting your clothes, Lew won't be asleep yet, and I think he would be glad to help. I don't want to be sexist but there are some tasks he might do better than me."

CHAPTER 106

Tuesday, January 1st 2013, 9am, The Lord Glendale Centre

Professor Frank's office

Professor Frank had been in his office early. He was not going to the CRIS meeting later but wanted all his notes in order. Dr Aziz would update him. But his mind was filled with the results of his personal memory research. His mind was reeling from the information he had in his hands. He had held his A-level results, his university acceptance letter, and his degrees. All had changed his life. But nothing like this.

From: bursar@steldreds.com
To: Prof.c.frank@glendale.com

8:30am

Dear Professor Frank,

Thank you for the speed of your email informing us of the courier delivery with your birth certificate, copy of your passport, and distinguished CV. I am pleased to say that as a school with a proud history going back two hundred years we do indeed keep records of our pupils.

I am, however, in the strange position of having to report that there is no record of a boy with your name and parentage actually attending the school at all despite there being contact.

However, what I think might explain the confusion is that we possess a letter, which is scanned and attached and will be sent to you in hard copy, which is from your mother and which thanks us for the interview and offer of a place, but states your uncle had funded a place elsewhere at St Cuthbert's as a boarder and, as her husband had died, she felt following your uncle's advice about how to do best for a fatherless boy was most in keeping with the situation.

I hope this answers your query and do please get back to me if you have any questions. I have to say, after reading your CV that I felt very disappointed we could not boast of you as an old boy.

Yours sincerely

Anthony J. Reddit
Bursar

Professor Frank held his head in his hands and found he was weeping uncontrollably. Pressing the "Do not disturb," he cried as he could not remember crying before.

So Aziz was right.

Why had he automatically doubted that little boy, the little boy who had stroked the braid on the cap and twisted the loose thread at the bottom edge of the blazer?

The little boy who knew the name St Cuthbert's and St Eldred's so well and knew the difference between them.

The little boy in the man who put his ill mother's and his sister's memory first.

The memory man who had spent all these years apologising for his terrible mistake, which he had never made. The memory man who had lost all those years. He could not remember a single classmate or teacher. His sister who had gone to the other side of the world to get away from a lie.

From: Bursar@stcuthberts.com
To: Prof.c.frank@glendale.com

9:15am

Dear Professor Frank,

Thank you for your enquiry. Our office is closed until Friday, January 4th.

Best wishes

The Bursar

From: Lewis&Cromwell@LC.com
To: Prof.c.frank@glendale.com

9:30am

Dear Professor Frank,

Thank you for your further enquiry about your late Uncle Edward Chapell's payment towards your school fees following your forwarded email from St Eldred's.

We thank you for your cheque to enable us to expedite this work, and the dates and confirmation from St Eldred's school you provided will definitely aid us in tracking down the information. I will be back to you as soon as we have an update.

Best wishes

Frederick Lewis
Senior partner

From: Cfrank@Gmail.com
To: Linda@lindahouse.com **(DRAFT)**

Dear Linda,

Please read this. It is the last thing I will ever ask. If you do not reply, I will not contact you again. You might want Larry and your children to sit with you. As a scientist, I hope you realise I would not be making contact on such a matter frivolously. We lost our father as close siblings, and issues around this subject meant I also lost my mother in her last days and you, your husband, and my only nephew and niece.

You will recall only too well the conversation when I said: I was sent away after my seventh birthday to be a boarder at St Cuthbert's—the pre-prep and prep boarding school Uncle Edward paid for with the grey blazer and cap edged with blue braid, along with the grey trousers.

You and mother looked blankly at me. "I would never send you away," mother said emphatically, "after your father died, the two of you were all I had. You were a day boy at St Eldred's from 7."

Well, now I have definitive proof from St Eldred's that I was never a day boy there. Mother had taken me for an interview, and they offered me a place, but then mother wrote to say Uncle Edward was paying for me to be a boarder at St Cuthbert's.

I am currently awaiting more documentation from the lawyers.

Chris

CHAPTER 107

Wednesday, January 2nd 2013, 9am

From: Dr.e.redine@sjtu.com
To: Dr.g.stuart@sjtu.com; Jonlevine@sjtu.com; Dr.a.aziz@sjtu.com;
Deirdrehislop@sjtu.com

> 9am
> Emergency meeting
>
> Dear all,
>
> With the CRIS meeting now happening and more rubbish in *The Mercury*, there are worrying clinical issues if I am to take Lady R on, and I would appreciate a discussion today. Forewarned is forearmed, and we might find ourselves pushed by Keira Denny into statements we have not discussed.

From: Deirdrehislop@sjtu.com
To: Dr.e.redine@sjtu.com; Dr.g.stuart@sjtu.com; Jonlevine@sjtu.com;
Dr.a.aziz@sjtu.com

9am
Emergency meeting

Dear all,

Lunchtime Emergency Team meeting at 12:15am. Dr Stuart's room.
Sandwiches provided.

CHAPTER 108

Wednesday, January 2nd 2013, 9:45am, The Lord Glendale Centre

As she made her way to Lord Glendale's suite, Keira was embarrassed to realise she was feeling like a schoolgirl. The uncertainty she struggled with was whether this schoolgirl was about to be praised or punished. She had needed to acquaint her boss with the toxic concoctions of the *Daily Mercury*. It was irrelevant whatever response she got and there was no way she could have anticipated it.

She had a slight worry she might be out of her depth. She shined at national PR for good causes. She had not dealt with this kind of controversy. A "fat cat" problem, as her father put it. Should she suggest top PR backup, or would that be an abdication of authority? Would he suggest it?

She was also aware of her excitement at being involved in such a high-level issue, even though she did not like herself for feeling excited.

What was an easier experience to admit was the thrill of being ushered by one of Lord G's aides through an unfamiliar passage to a lift to a corridor to the large antechamber on the outside of the private Arlington Suite on the top floor—protected like a precious jewel. She had only been invited there a couple of times.

Glendale's rectangular antechamber doubled as a highly confidential conference suite for top security research and had the familiar glass panels that could open out, creating further rooms. It had the same dark-blue carpet and modular seating and the yellow motif as the rest of the complex, but was there was no hustle and bustle here; it was quiet and calm.

"Please wait here, Ms Kenny," said the steward, pointing to the higher-backed luxurious modular seating nearest to the door of the Arlington Suite. "I am sure Lord Glendale will send for you soon."

He walked away from her to speak on his walkie-talkie, announcing her arrival, and disappeared into the lift.

She looked around: a deserted airport, an evacuated luxury hotel reception; all enveloped in an unfathomable hush. It must have cost millions.

Suddenly, a glamorous blonde-haired woman in a blue suit came almost invisibly through a panel. "Please come through, Ms Denny. His Lordship is expecting you."

Walking through the panel into a security area where her bag and jacket were checked (as if that hadn't already happened downstairs), she was then ushered through into the Arlington Suite.

Here the glass was replaced by wood panelling stretching down the gracious corridors with their gleaming wooden floors. There were chandeliers and oil paintings of American Presidents and British Prime Ministers accompanying her on her journey.

"His Lordship is expecting you," said one of the ubiquitous air stewardess assistants.

Lord Glendale's room had floor-to-ceiling windows that looked out onto the manicured gardens and elegant drive down the hill to St Joseph Street. As he had told her on her first visit, he had modelled the room on the Treaty Room of the Oval Office with a splendid copy of the desk doubling as a table. There was a great mirror over the mantelpiece, copied at great expense. A Steinway grand piano and beautiful panels of olive green velvet on wooden poles standing out against the off-white walls. There was even an electrified Victorian crystal gasolier.

This was the nearest she would ever get to the White House, and there were hints the President himself had visited, or even stayed here. She did not know if there was any residential accommodation.

Lord Glendale was sitting behind his famous desk. He was a handsome man in his prime with thick salt-and-pepper hair, a Californian tan, and sparkling grey eyes. There was a tray on the table and a smell of fresh coffee. There was also a bowl of jellybeans and another of nuts. She would be terrified of breaking the china!

"Keira," he said warmly, standing up and pointing to a comfortable chair facing the desk. "Would you like coffee, water, or juice? I can offer pomegranate."

"Pomegranate," she accepted gratefully. That would remove the fear of dropping the china!

He reached for a wood-covered filing cabinet on the right of the mantelpiece that doubled as a fridge, and brought out a glass and a small jug of juice. Did the White House have that too?

Nervously she stood up and approached the desk to pour herself a glass. At least she was wearing a trouser suit and flat shoes and didn't have to worry about her legs, skirt, or shoes.

Why was she feeling like such a female child? Why was she giving such power to this man in the room? A man who had just received a public blow too, and had a tricky brother. Her job was to protect him and the Glendale, as a professional—not to expect parenting!

"Lord Glendale, thank you for seeing me so quickly. I have various ideas and thoughts but obviously needed to check out how you were feeling after such nastiness and whether you had ideas of what I could do to help."

Glendale beamed at her, the desk appearing smaller and the distance between them easier. "You are showing me my good taste in appointing you, Keira. Please call me Glendale. In company my title needs to be used, it is quite useful, but I have got used to Glendale as if it was a first name because I don't like the name Oliver as everyone thinks of Oliver Twist."

Keira laughed. "I could use that, sir ... I mean, Glendale!" Lord Oliver Glendale does not like his first name as people think of Oliver Twist, who asked for more, when he always gives more.

"Say that could be useful!" he agreed.

"And how do you feel sharing a name with a film star."

Keira grinned. "I'm afraid I was named after Keir Hardie."

He raised an eyebrow quizzically. "I will keep an eye on your politics then."

And then his face grew serious. "Tell me your response first."

Keira had thought about this carefully. "Fiona Roberts likes to write pieces that keep all her options open. She writes within a millimetre of libel for each option she raises. This is why people like *The Mercury*. The news is no different than any other halfway paper. It is the nastiness people enjoy. But this also means that they know it's all rubbish.

I really don't think it is worth your or the Glendale's dignity to respond to such unpleasantness other than to benefit from the free publicity being given to the unit.

The real question in my mind is the live press conference on Sunday. If Lady Rose is able to be present, it would silence the press wanting to talk about your brother or Danny Delta, as that would obviously be exploiting someone with a disability. If Lady Lily and Lady Rose both presented together, that would be even more useful—taking it away from Sir Peter's position. Then it is about a mother and daughter, and your presence is also minimised. Sinita's mother is happy to speak and is a real salt-of-the-earth woman who has gone through hell and knows that made her daughter's life harder too. I don't want her talking about abuse as that will bring up the taxi driver, etc. Also, Sarah Ransome is a really lovely woman who will include the Lady Rose Independence Unit under her management remit. She was a real whistleblowing powerhouse at her last place. Having her speak is symbolically saying brave whistleblowers approve of the unit."

Glendale was listening with the deepest concentration.

She suddenly realised she had gotten carried away with her ideas and stopped.

"Sorry, sir, I mean Glendale. I got carried away there."

There was silence.

She felt nervous.

To her surprise, he clapped his hands. "Keira Hardie, I really don't think you know how sensational you are. Leave Lady Lily and Lady Rose to me. I totally back up your ideas. Ask your Sarah to speak and make sure you include the whistleblowing in your introduction." He stood up.

The interview was over. "Thank you. That was stellar advice."

Turning around to face the Presidents and Prime Ministers, she sailed out of the room. Keira Hardie: she liked it.

CHAPTER 109

Wednesday, January 2nd 2013, 10:30am, Westbridge Police Station

Themeeting had gone better than expected, thought Superintendent Hewson. Morag Lennon had gathered the reports with equanimity and due diligence. There were more lawyers than expected and significant political tension. The *Daily Mercury* had stirred things up again in their usual way and this had led to a private message from the Prime Minister's office, despite the reported unwellness of James Dalkeith, concerning Ian Anderson and Lord Glendale.

However, there had been a clear consensus.

There was no safeguarding issue over Lady Rose at the moment. Her family and Harvest House were able to ensure she did not see Ian Anderson and get triggered again and Dr Aziz would ensure she received treatment at the SJTU. It was not appropriate for her to receive this at the Glendale, despite Lady Lily's strong wish for this, as Professor Frank had a clear conflict of interest. Additionally, however unfair, focus on Lord Glendale's link with Danny Delta and the rumours around his brother would bring extra publicity over the issues of her receiving treatment at the Glendale, or could be seen as an exercise in depriving her of independent treatment.

Professor Frank was not at the meeting, and Dr Aziz brought a message from him stating that his presence could be a conflict of interest at this point. This had considerably aided the meeting. Dr Aziz was clearly used to high-level diplomacy and set a tone that aided the discussion.

There were now witness statements from the October 31st poolside party thanks to the help of Interpol. It was clear that all of Lady Rose's descriptions were correct and could be validated except for the allegation of abuse. It could not be ruled out, in terms of the other facts provided, that there was evidence that both Danny Delta and Ian Anderson were not in the outside pool or around it at the time Lady Rose said she was inside with them. It was also clear that none of the witnesses could vouch for anything Rose had said and done when she was not visible at the poolside.

Morag was convinced Lady Rose was a credible witness and had an excellent memory. Her past statements were accurate, and she had a proven history of providing accurate evidence. However, there was clinical evidence that when stressed she could sound very different and have a very different perspective on what was happening.

The evidence from Tracey O'Bridey and Lew Masters was particularly compelling and useful here as it was also contemporaneously noted and signed. It showed that Lady Rose could enter another state of mind when she thought she was male and spoke differently and violently about hurting herself. This raised the possibility that she had self-injured when triggered by the sight of the outdoor pool—she had had a water phobia since the age of 6, and the self-injury was experienced by her as if it was from an external person, Ian Anderson.

This was a controversial clinical area—dissociative identity disorder—and it would not be helpful for the police to be embroiled in this when the experts themselves all disagreed. That was why it had been agreed to hold a further CRIS in a couple of months after she had begun treatment at the SJTU. This would allow her to make the transition to her new unit without the added stress of further interviews.

Ian Anderson posed a complex issue as he knew all about Lady Rose's allegations because her mother and father were close friends of his—more the mother than the father, who appeared to be less sure. He had also notified the Whip's office and appeared to be very forgiving and sad for Lady Rose herself and her mother. It was not a love affair with the mother, as Anderson was known to be gay. Morag would also have a meeting with Lady Rose to let her know she had been taken seriously and the police had lots of work to do and so did she, moving and starting therapy, but they would meet up again. All in all, so far, considering how it could have been, there could not have been a better outcome. Dr Aziz would update Professor Frank, and supportive therapy to aid the move would be undertaken by the SJTU.

CHAPTER 110

Wednesday, January 2nd 2013, 11am, The SJTU

eirdre had arranged a 3pm coffee break meeting with Sarah in her "office." She had initially worried whether seeing Sarah there would be any breach of confidentiality but realised she could turn the sound off on her telephone. Even though she instinctively trusted Sarah, she could not allow patient messages to be overheard by a non-SJTU professional.

Once she had sorted that out, her anxiety moved to her "cubicle." In the previous central and smaller premises, she had nevertheless had a proper room. A former converted broom cupboard with no window, it nevertheless had room for a small desk and chair with wraparound shelving. No. There hadn't been room to meet with anyone there. Memory did strange things.

Unlike Sarah, she did not have a proper room to talk to someone in. The soundproofing was inadequate, and it was, of course, all within view. She was about to unusually voice a complaint that, as Operations Director, she did not have a proper room when, patting her French pleat and reshaping her elegant scarf, she realised she felt shy. They were both women of a similar kind, and on their own. She liked Sarah and it was rare for her to want to make a friendship.

At least Amanda was back, full of energy too. The piles of letters, opened and divided into preliminary piles, bills, referrals, and reports were now on her desk, and she had already checked the phone messages, filed them separately, and started on the main filing.

Her children didn't start back at school for another two days, but her mother-in-law was babysitting, and, as she confided to Deirdre, she was only too delighted to be back in adult company.

"Christmas was wonderful, but now they are glued to their tablets again and getting irritable. How has everyone been? Did you miss me?"

Unusually, Deirdre had been confused about when the rest of the admin team would be back. This whole Lady Rose/Glendale/Equipa conundrum had affected her more than she liked to think. She had thought carefully about how she would update Amanda about the confidential new information and what were the essential need-to-know bones of it.

"I'm afraid we have some unpleasant media interest in poor Lady Rose moving into her new home just because her family had been to a concert of that Danny Delta in October. If you get any reporters calling, be polite, take their names, and say you will get the Operations Director to call them back."

"Oh, I really like that *When You Come Back* song. Poor Lady Rose. You'd think they had more important things to feast their nosiness on."

And that was that. She was just so sensible—a really good choice. Deirdre was now freed from her refreshment-making role. Amanda had checked the green tea, ginger, chamomile, and black coffee (Gold blend) supplies. Deirdre had also added casually that at 3pm the new Day Manager of Harvest House would be popping in.

"Oh, that will be good to put a face to the name!" said Amanda approvingly.

"I don't know anyone from there. Oh no, that's not right. I met Maureen, an OT from there. Really nice. But that's it, and the Glendale people don't talk to anyone."

"Well," said Deirdre. "I am pleased to say Dr Aziz has made contact with Professor Chris Frank, the Glendale Director; we have been contacted by a charming PR Director from there called Keira Denny (who will help if we get persecuted by the press) and Dr Charmaine Landesman from the Equipa whose referral Jon will see on Thursday."

"Why does everything exciting happen when I am away," laughed Amanda, and off she went to get the tea ready. "And thank you for my lovely card and New Year email."

CHAPTER 111

Wednesday, January 2nd 2013, 11am, Westminster

L ord Glendale had wasted no time after his productive meeting with Keira Denny. What a brain she had! He had immediately contacted Priscilla and Marjorie for an emergency meeting, having primed them with an evening call on Tuesday after his visit to poor Lily.

They were all united. Lily had got to take responsibility for her feelings about Rose, whether through therapy or other means, however much she did not want to! Losing Peter would destroy them both, and his political ambitions. Without Lily, Peter could be a jobbing constituency MP, but that was it. It was Lily's strategic thinking that led to all his major posts and links.

Without Peter, Lily would be another beautiful single top-drawer woman devoting herself to charity.

Priscilla and Marjorie both understood the seriousness of the invitation, cancelled other arrangements, and what's more had already spoken together and made steps to intervene in yesterday's upset. They shared the same background and understood the necessary code of behaviour.

Marjorie had been shocked at her son's passionate response to Lily's language lapse. It was understandable to express anger and loss through language in order to manage. Her daughter-in-law had not shouted or said this publicly. She was trying to explain; that was all.

Peter did appear to have listened and returned home at 11pm last night. However, he stayed in his study. Marjorie had even texted Lily to update her. She had grudgingly accepted Lily's place in her son's heart, but the threat of losing her was another matter. Lily was her daughter-in-law: her son's wife. An impeccable political hostess, if nothing else!

Meanwhile, in a cold Victorian manner, Priscilla had impressed on Lily her duty to her husband. Greet him warmly. Be apologetic, and be kind to Rose even if it killed her. Oliver had pointed out that Lily turning her back on Rose was like Lord Wellbrook turning his back on his daughter. That had really affected her. She had wanted to think her resilient approach to his loss had meant Lily was not affected. Of course, she was and so was her mother.

The coffee meeting now was to relay Keira's excellent advice. It fitted in seamlessly with how they had operated. Marjorie would suggest to her son that to make up for her incapacity to love Rose in any easy way, it should be down to Lily to do the media work for the new unit and not Peter; he had done enough. Priscilla would exhort her daughter to make amends to Peter by arranging a visit to see her daughter solo: a pilgrimage.

The Times and *The Guardian* would be given exclusive access to family photographs of Lily and Rose (not at the age of 6), and no further information would go to Fiona. The way she had tried to solicit further information made her unsafe, and that was the end of her benefits. Major D would investigate her piece.

CHAPTER 112

Wednesday, January 2nd 2013, 11:45am, The Lord Glendale Centre

Professor Frank's office

From: Lewis&Cromwell@LC.com
To: Prof.c.frank@glendale.com

11:45am

Dear Professor Frank,

Thanks to your scanned letter from St Eldred's providing names and dates and your couriered cheque, which allowed immediate separate resourcing for your query, we have been able to access the relevant documentation for you, which is attached.

As you will see, your late uncle, Edward Chappell, paid for your education as a boarder at St Cuthbert's from the age of 7 to 14, after which you gained a scholarship to a local day school. With no child of his own and with a strong sense of duty to his widowed sister, your mother, and with you being her only son, he clearly felt this would help ensure your future. The school had a special pre-prep boarding year for 7-year-olds in difficult circumstances before the main entries at 8 years.

Please forgive my personal presumptuousness, but having read your distinguished CV I feel your uncle would have been deeply gratified at the success you have made of your life.

This is the only remaining documentation concerning your family's link to Mr Chappell. His bequests have long since been settled, and you and your sister are, I believe, the only living relatives.

With best wishes for your future and to your sole sibling, Linda.

Frederick Lewis
Senior Partner
Lewis & Cromwell

The password for these attachments will be sent one minute after this email.

Unusually, for a man who filtered any need almost at its source, he found himself phoning Dr Aziz. With a bit of luck, after the CRIS meeting, he might still be walking to the SJTU and free to speak.

Aziz answered immediately. "Was the little boy correct?"

"Yes."

A pause.

"I have an email from the lawyers and the school. From 7 to 14, I was a boarder."

"And for this, you lost your mother and sister and perhaps other relationships."

"Yes. And chose this career."

"We all choose our careers from damage and repair. And your work has been of integrity. Somehow you knew deeply how damaging a traumatic re-editing of the truth could be."

There was a pause.

"Yes. That is true. So that is not wasted."

"No. Truth and honest work is never wasted. And now you know that little boy was brave and correct, even though he would still have mattered if he hadn't been."

"Thank you, Aziz. My life has changed again. Strange. When I met you, in Delhi, I was struggling deeply with my memory research and the meaning of it. The way I was treated there by you, and your mentor, helped me."

"I am glad. When I said India was an old country, I meant it. These so-called memory wars are not wars between truth-tellers and liars. It is a struggle to face trauma. And you have faced it. I am sorry. I…"

"You have your SJTU meeting now. I have taken your timetable into my memory! I am so glad you were free right now. Thank you for your update. It was clearly a good CRIS meeting."

"And I am glad too. It is not that often we can tell a 6-year-old boy that the grownups could not face something but he could."

"Goodbye, Dr Aziz."

"Goodbye, Professor Frank."

Face it. He had faced it. He, Christopher, 7 years old. He faced it. Now he would see if his sister could, and if she could not, that would be a problem for her and her family. He could not do more.

And this time it would not be a draft:

From: Cfrank@gmail.com
To: Linda@lindahouse.com

Dear Linda,

Please read this. It is the last thing I will ever ask. If you do not reply, I will not contact you ever again. You might want Larry and your children to sit with you. As a scientist I hope you realise that I would not frivolously make contact on such a matter. We lost our father as close young siblings and issues around this subject meant I also lost my mother in her last days and you, your husband and my only nephew and niece.

I attach two legal documents for you. One is from our Uncle Edward's lawyer confirming, with the invoices, that he paid my fees for St Cuthbert's *Boarding* School from the ages of 7 to 14 when I won a scholarship. St Cuthbert's had a special pre-prep boarding year for seven-year-olds in special circumstances. Age 8 was usually the youngest for boarding.

The second is from St Eldred's, confirming I was NEVER a dayboy there.

Mother had taken me for an interview, and they offered me a place, but then mother wrote to them to say Uncle Edward was paying for me to be a boarder at St Cuthbert's.

Please forgive me for the word in capital letters, that is if you are still reading this email. I think, as a mother yourself, you would understand what it might mean for a 7-year-old to be in boarding school, let alone for a 7-year-old to have his sister and mother deny it, when it was year after year.

You were only 4 when I was first at boarding school, and I do not expect you to have any memory of that. However, since I was there for years you would have had a working memory but clearly lost it in loyalty to your mother. As you will know, my whole research is on the traumatic base of such distortions.

A little boy without a father and without a mother and sister for most of the year.

Christopher

Without going over it, he pressed "Send." Now he felt filled with rage, which was as unusual for him as feeling tearful. He wanted to fly out to visit her, scream at her in front of his remaining estranged family— "Your mother is a liar. She denied my trauma. She closed her eyes to it. She did not want to see it. All she wanted was to mother herself."

He sighed. So that was what it was like. To be the victim and be accused. To have everyone agree it was his fault his mother had died young full of the pain of her son's false memory. When that poor little boy, that little boy of only 7, had to face everything on his own. How he had turned away friendships and relationships, burdened with the inability to trust after such abandonments. Once there was a woman. She turned to him gently and asked him why he said, "Face it, Frank!" Where was she? A research grant at Harvard? Married with grownup children?

Frances…Frances Earnest. How they had laughed at each other's names. When they first met at university, her flatmate, Sonia, had said: "Frances Frank or how about Dr Earnest Frank. That is just too much! The importance of being Earnest."

Frankly, he had lost everything. Face it, Frank.

CHAPTER 113

Wednesday, January 2nd 2013, 12pm, Westminster Square

The Redcliffe residence

Lily sat huddled at her desk facing her computer, chastened after calls from both her mother and mother-in-law and Maria asking if Peter would be joining her for lunch or not.

He had not asked for a divorce, but neither had he shown any sense of tenderness to her. His face had the same drawn ransacked look of a man who had only just realised his whole life was a lie. On top of this, there was Oliver, and he and Ian had all agreed on what she had to do.

She had no choice; she would have to act on it. She was going to have to be the best actress in the world because there was no way she was going to have any therapy, and there was no way she felt any differently for Rose. If anything, she hated her more. If Rose had been normal, there would never have been an upset like this.

If Rose had been normal, there would have been mother and daughter shopping expeditions, playdates, school open days, end-of-year dances and plays, seaside holidays, laughter. Happy family photos, not set-piece historical photographs of Rose with the royals, as if there was a desperate need to prove the highest in the land accepted her.

Wheeling a pram and enjoying all the "coos" and "ahs" from neighbours and friends instead of the sudden looks of pity and confusion. Talking to "normal school" mothers instead of all the disability circuits.

Twenty-one years of wasted life. How she wished she had had an amnio and an abortion, but Peter would not countenance it and the gang of two, PM (Priscilla and Marjorie, mother and mother-in-law) considered it could be bad for his career. Who would have thought his career could destroy her like this? Who had cared about her choice?

She took out her thickest cartridge paper. This was a letter that had to be written and placed in an envelope on his desk. Email was not safe for such a letter.

Dearest Peter,

This upset between us has taken a long time to become explicit and perhaps it is inevitable that it is just before our only child, Rose, attains the year we always saw as majority, 21. Not 18. Key to the door. And we have built for her the house and the door.

Perhaps only now can we both look at how our lives have changed, for good or ill, over the last 21 years.

The first thing I have to say you will not like. But I cannot write honestly to you without saying it. And we owe the truth to each other ever since we first fell in love and swore to be faithful and swore to be truthful. I keep my promises. And I still love you.

From my teenage years, I had always intended to have amniocentesis once I found my prince charming and got married. I am not proud that I wanted that. I wish I had been the kind of maternal girl who would fall in love with whomever I carried in my body. But you know I was not. You know I was made in the image of both of our mothers, expected to be beautiful and sparkling, a political asset, a great hostess, a fashion plate ... You know how my mother hot-housed me.

I considered I would only manage to have one child. It was with great fear and love I agreed to your wish for two children. I did not know if my body could take it. Yes. I ride and go to the gym, ski and swim, and do all the things women like me are meant to do to keep their bodies beautiful. The irony is that my body was made to be as perfect as possible to be the right wife for you but not to be the best body for a mother. I did not tell you how I was scared my skin would stretch and burst with something growing inside me each day.

I felt there was a parasite within despite the smiling false face I put on. You were so loving and considerate when I was sick, even holding my hair off my neck when I vomited. I will never forget that. I could tell you about being nauseous because that happened to women. But I could not tell you about my terrors, of holding a vampire inside me who was sucking me dry.

I was a failure.

I knew I would be a candidate for postnatal depression. My mother had it. Not surprising. Having a daughter instead of a son for the great Lord Wellbrook with his unbroken ancestral lineage of sons for four hundred years. And I know baby me would have picked that up. And that was all before Rose was born.

I was made for you—the you that I first met and loved. A kind loving blue-blood who needed a similar wife. I was not made to be the mother of your child.

As the baby of a mother who would have gone in for designer genes had they existed then, of course I would want an amnio. But the mothers disagreed and so did you. Not good for a potential Minister of Health, a rising constituency MP who cared about health matters, to have a wife linked to any controversy about amnios and abortion.

How I drank! Do you remember an evening when you were surprised your whisky bottle was nearly empty? When we went past the amnio day, I knew I would be helpless and broken if anything was wrong with the baby, a cleft palate, an extra finger. Not the baby's fault. Mine.

But the way I could have just about managed, having an amnio and an abortion and trying again a few years later—that was taken away from me.

When Rose was born, I received my punishment. I was off my father's family tree and she was off mine. No chance of an ordinary grandmother's future. No chance of reversing it, sending her back inside. She was there.

And what's more, like a savage joke from God, she looked just like me, distorted. The same eyes I would have loved in a normal daughter. The same hair. But not on a pristine model. On a damaged one. Had she looked like you, it might have been more bearable.

I tried to hide my collapse under rules and organisation. Just like my mother after father left. Because Rose felt like a bereavement too. So, I closed my heart and carried on. Twenty-one years of hiding from you, dear Peter. How did it happen?

Did you know how ugly I felt inside that I had a baby I could not love the way even the most common ugly woman could? Did you know her eyes and golden hair mocked me each day as if to say, "You think you are beautiful, but you are the most ugly kind of woman who exists—a woman who cannot love her baby properly."

328

Perhaps looking at her, I looked at her with the eyes with which my father looked at me, "look at that disgusting blue-eyed golden-haired female! Is it for this that I married my cold controlling wife? Is it for this that I risked my four hundred years of male descent?"

Perhaps neither of us knew how damaged I was. A boarding school upper-class train wreck.

I tried. I tried in ways you will never know. I fought for her speech therapy when her voice could not be understood. And I got her the best. I fought for her heart check-ups. I went out with her to friends and family, soaking in the "does she take sugar," the pity, the triumph, the aggression.

And when Ian ... yes, we need to come to this. When we met Ian, even though he was from the "other side," we recognised each other. He was the common boy mocked at public school by the upper crust, who still had the potential to rise, and I was the upper crust mocked and unwanted for not being a boy. He was a friend, a true friend of a kind I hadn't had.

We both know the way men are drawn to me, not women. Even poor Chris Frank. I hate watching them blush, flush, and lose everything attractive about themselves because they do not know a beautiful woman. A freak.

Ian was, and is, different. He sees me as a kind of twin.

So when he invited us out in that sunny spontaneous way, I was so happy. I cannot tell you how rare it is to receive an equal invitation that includes Rose. Rose was happy because I was. The swimming pool was filled with plastic floats of every kind, sea serpents, tortoises, an elephant, boats: it was a child's paradise. There was an inside pool that had a tunnel that took you outside and a gentle wave machine. Rose was in her Disney swimsuit. I did not feel like the mother of a child with a disability. I felt like me. Me. A mother with her daughter. Really rare for me to feel like that. It gave me hope for Rose, and for us, that I could feel some pleasure out with her.

Yes. I used the "M" word. That is the environment I feel and face every day I went out with her. Do you think she has not heard that word? People have the words they were brought up with: retard, mongol, Down's, learning difficulty, handicapped. She will know it, because she is clever, and she does pick things up.

I am sorry. It hurt you deeply. I did not want that. I wanted you to know how rare that day was.

Rose was laughing and splashing with Ian and other people there, and I said how much I would love to do a real circuit, get some real swimming in, and Ian said, "then go ahead, Lily. We are alright here, aren't we, Rose?" Rose giggled and nodded, and so I did a swim all around the pool. I trusted her with him.

When I came back, he was holding her and she looked worried. "Afraid she didn't like her mummy not being here," he said. I turned to Rose to take her in my arms.

"Mummy's back now," I said. She did not come into my arms. Usually, she wants to be there even when I don't, but not this time.

"Out of the water ... Out of the water," she shouted. Other people were looking around. "Out we go then, Rose," I said and mouthed a sorry to Ian. She carried on crying noisily with everyone watching. I put her on the side of the pool as I climbed and held her hand as we walked back to the changing room. Every step I could feel peoples' stares and some of their unsaid thoughts.

"That's poor Lady Redcliffe. She's got a Down's daughter. All that money and beauty, but it doesn't stop her from having a daughter like that. I thought they were supposed to be happy all the time. Makes me glad I have my son."

All the way to the changing rooms with each cry of hers taking away that tiny new moment of joy I had felt. Can you imagine that? Would my new friend ever invite us again? When I dried her, she looked at me really intently and said, "didn't like Ian's magic snake in water. In bum."

Well, she is at the age to be aware of the differences between boys and girls and men and women, and there were all these blow-up toys in the children's end of the pool. I could see how she missed me and was alone with a man who was not her father (although there were lots of people in the pool all the time). She had a sexual awareness she could not make sense of.

I forgot about it and became inured to her not being willing to go in the water with me even though that spoiled an activity she and I could have enjoyed together. I think the October concert with Ian and me there at the time reminded her of this. She has now put her sexual worries and excitement from the minicab driver into these two memories.

I do not ignore abuse, nor would friendship stop me from recognising a paedophile. However, I was there on both those occasions and understood the context in which she behaved like this. You loved her from the start. You loved me and you could see me in her as well as her in her. Don't you see? You always loved me better than I could love me.

Now she is 21: our baby, our only child. She is going into a beautiful home that I will be happy to visit. I suggest I visit her before the weekend and have a significant discussion with her and that she and I are part of the launch with you sitting watching us.

I cannot make up for 21 years. I cannot be false, but I can do my best. Let me know if that is enough for you. If it is not, I will understand. You aren't like my father. You have stayed.

With my love,

Lily

She found that tears were slowly falling down her face. She signed the letter, folding it carefully. It was her best Velke Losigny handmade paper and envelopes. He would know that: her man, her partner.

Walking down the corridor, she knocked on his study door out of courtesy but knew it was empty. Walking inside, she placed her envelope at the centre of his tidy desk. The photographs of Rose with the Queen and Prince Philip, with James, the Prime Minister with Ian and her.

What amazing historical people her daughter Rose would have known. Her secret normal daughter.

She had written. She had done her best. She would give it a little time and then speak to that pushy Keira and Sarah Ransome. Chris had been surprisingly silent. Perhaps she was losing everyone—her lapdogs, her mongrels...perhaps there was nothing left.

She found herself humming Danny's last song:

When You Come Back. What a talent! What a voice! And one of the few truly memorable days of her life since Rose's birth. And both of them were contaminated by her thorny Rose. People would pay thousands for an after-concert party. And how she swam in that beautiful pool free of everything. Letting go of everything. A Hockney pool.

CHAPTER 114

Wednesday, January 2nd 2013, 12:15pm, The SJTU

E veryone was sitting in their usual seats in Dr Stuart's room when Amanda made her way in with the tray.

"Happy New Year," she smiled at all.

"We missed you, Amanda," said Gawain warmly.

"It is just cupboard love! Just because I'm coming back with the sandwiches," joked Amanda. As everyone reached for their mugs, she nipped back to the office for the sandwiches; all put in a large carrier bag for easy carrying together with serviettes. It was good to be back again. "Mainly egg mayo," she warned, "and a few turkey salads too."

"Thank you, Amanda," said Deirdre, handing out agendas to the team.

Gawain looked around attentively. "Okay. As you can see, we have a packed emergency agenda. Deirdre has put the CRIS meeting at the top because, although it has only just happened, it affects all the other items. Abdul—can you start us off?"

Abdul looked around seriously. "I am pleased to say there has been appropriate and sensitive action concerning Lady Rose. Supt Hewson chaired excellently. Basically, as Lady Rose is safe at Harvest House and will not see Ian Anderson there or in the new unit, there is currently no safeguarding problem. Morag Lennon—our very good Vulnerable Victim Coordinator—showed that everything Rose has ever said has been correct, and all facts pertinent to this case can easily be proved except the abuse. The problem is that because, while in a dissociative state, she threatened herself in a male voice, there could be doubt on her testimony. Given she is moving, and this is a major transition, there is agreement for supportive therapy here at the SJTU. There will be a further meeting of the Crime Report Incident System will follow in a few months. Morag will speak to Rose and let her know they are taking the allegations seriously. It means her move to the Lady Rose will not be overshadowed by ugly publicity."

"Thank you, Abdul, and well done for the way you have managed Professor Frank."

"Yes. He has had a very complex conflict of interest. I was the right person in the right place for him. I cannot say more, but I respect the man."

"Apologies for butting in, but is it me who is going to have to see her with the Deputy Prime Minister watching over me and the Minister of Health?" asked Elouise.

Deirdre leant forward in great concern. "This is really important. There is going to be a concerning pressure on whoever sees Lady Rose."

There was a pause.

"I'm sorry," said Jon. "I don't feel up to it. It's not like I have children like Elouise. I just feel frightened to be honest."

There was another pause.

"I really took to her," said Abdul. "We had a good connection. She is witty and rather beautiful in a strange kind of way, but..."

"You are the supervisor for the Lady Rose," interjected Deirdre.

"Yes."

There was another pause.

Gawain took a sip of his coffee.

"I could take on the group supervision," he offered.

"I am happy to offer any individual supervision," said Elouise, "and I really wanted to take this on, but to have a friend sending me all the stuff about Glendale and Ian Anderson. This is just too much. I feel I'd end up in the Tower of London." She paused. "I need to remind you that the American consultant I went to for my ritual abuse DID case, Dr Judith Kestle, will be speaking at the WAM conference in Washington, and I don't feel up to the publicity that could come my way."

"And I feel I'd be struck off the analytic training," added Jon.

"Okay," said Gawain. "We've sorted it. We are the key resource for anyone we see, so we need to be sure we are as resourced as possible at the start. Thanks for being so clear, Elouise and Jon. How do we clear our decision with Supt Hewson and Professor Frank?"

"I can deal with that," said Abdul.

"Now you are doing too much, Abdul," said Deirdre with concern.

"Yes," agreed Gawain. "I will contact Superintendent Hewson, DC Morag Lennon, and Professor Frank, saying that because of the seriousness of the situation we considered it most appropriate for our senior consultant psychiatrist and therapist to undertake the supportive work as he met her at the assessment, and they took to each other. This will be easier for her at such a charged time. This means other staff will have to take on Dr Aziz's role, and we will liaise with Sarah Ransome over what might suit Harvest House and Lady Rose best."

"I am seeing Sarah at 3pm today so perhaps I can take that chore off you, Dr Stuart."

"Thank you, Deirdre. How useful for us that you have made a link."

Deirdre looked down at her notebook to hide her pleasure. "So apart from the list of new assessments, which can wait, the other key emergency item on the agenda is the referral of Mattie Harrison," she added.

"Has the full background report come yet?" asked Jon.

"No."

"Okay. Deirdre, can you remind them I want background details?"

"Yes, straight after this meeting."

"Okay," said Gawain. "And there is the issue of Keira Denny, who does the PR for the site."

"Not very successfully with *The Mercury*," laughed Elouise.

"No. But no one can stop that rubbish!" said Gawain, "However, she is a really bright woman with great integrity and she is going to get a Lady Lily and Lady Rose scoop. She will keep the emphasis on mothers and daughters and avoid all that American melodrama mind control abuse malarkey."

There was a pause.

"She is also going to interview Sarah Ransome and might want some backup from us."

"Meeting over," said Gawain. On that note, people started picking up their mugs to carry them out just as Amanda came in with an empty tray to take over.

"I have missed you, smiled Deirdre. As she walked down to her "cubicle," somehow she did not think of it as an office today; she found Elouise following her in.

"Have you got a moment, Deirdre?" she asked earnestly.

Deirdre beckoned her onto the chair facing the desk, so at least her face would not be seen in the outer office. "The Lady Rose case?" she asked gently.

"Yes. How did you know?"

"Well, I had asked you to think very carefully about taking on such a case with young children, and I am delighted you decided not to."

"Really? I feel such a pathetic coward. Coming out all strong about it and then chickening out with the American connection and everything."

"You are putting your family first," emphasised Deirdre. "And besides, Abdul is the right person for this task politically," she added.

There was a knock on the door, with Jon miming he would like to join them. Deirdre opened the door and brought in a folding chair. This cubicle really was too small.

"Lady Rose?" he asked. They nodded. "I just needed to come in and apologise for not taking it on, but I can't face it, and that is partly because I know my supervisor won't."

Deirdre gently repeated that Abdul was the best choice for all kinds of political reasons, and he also wanted to.

"Okay. I am now off to lecture the medical students for the afternoon. Thank you, Deirdre. And mum—Sylvie—was really pleased you liked her cake."

Ah! His therapy room was free this afternoon. That was the answer. She would meet Sarah there.

"Thank you, Deirdre," added Elouise, getting up. "I don't know what we would do without you." She followed Jon out, and Deirdre sat in a happy daze.

She had rewarding work and a home she really loved; Amanda had already loaded the dishwasher and was noting telephone messages. Her hand unconsciously touched her French pleat.

Coming out of the cubicle, she smiled at Amanda and told her she would be meeting Sarah in Jon's therapy room and to put that down in the room bookings. The anonymous therapy rooms that did not double as staff offices felt too shabby. She also asked her to ring Dr Landesman to remind her about the full case history of Mattie Harrison.

"I have already phoned," said Amanda cheerfully.

"So glad you are back," said Deirdre.

CHAPTER 115

Wednesday, January 2nd 2013, 1pm

From: LadyLily@Redcliffe.com
To: Prof.c.frank@glendale.com

    1pm

    Dear Chris,

    Hope all is well with you.

    Lily

From: LadyLily@Redcliffe.com
To: Keiradenny@glendale.com
Bcc: Lordglendale@glendale.com; Priscilla@rivendale.com;
MarjorieR@armthorpe.com

    1pm

    Dear Keira,

    Thank you for your thoughtful message. I would indeed be will-
ing to be involved and appreciate your thinking on the safest way

to do it. It is hard when the personal is also the political, as you so insightfully said.

As asked, I am sending you some detailed thoughts as background notes for you, and you may quote anything here you find helpful.

I have been very cautious over the media due to fear it would be seen as deliberate political scheming by an MP's wife. And when Peter became Minister of Health, it became even more important for his privacy and Rose's that we avoided extra publicity. There could be delight at the thought of Rose's existence from parents whose children shared the same diagnosis, but fear from parents whose children had another disability! There could also be those pleased that a privileged white middle-class couple with such apparent power did not succeed in raising a child without a disability. And those who thought it was something you could catch from getting near to someone—like the measles. Whatever we did carried personal and professional consequences, both positive and negative.

We chose to make some things public. It was not the mother and daughter outings, buying clothes, going to family parties; not the photographs with HM, the Queen or MPs.

The fact that the negatives in her life, her awful experiences were, after enormously fraught discussion, made briefly public, was very complex. Rose herself told us about the bullying, and we were proud of her for her courage in speaking up. It was Rose who said, "Speak and tell. It is bad to hurt people" and it is Rose who at 14 shared her broken heart with us. She told us she had been raped by a minicab driver whom her school had often used. She insisted on telling the police and when he was found guilty in court, she was so proud of herself. She knew how rare it is for a rapist to be convicted and so she was proud as a young woman with a disability; she had succeeded in gaining justice. The Judge himself commended her for her courage at only 14. Rose and us (and I will check with Rose today if I am allowed to give you this to print) all wanted this public to encourage other girls to come forward.

Rose achieving the age of 21 and moving into a bespoke new home to aid her independence, alongside three of her friends from Harvest House, is different to all of this. It is being allowed the key to the door, instead of being the dependent adult at home who never truly grows up. This has been helped by the bank of mum and dad, and the Glendale and St Joseph's but for the adults living there, it will be their true home.

337

I will speak to Sarah Ransome this afternoon and see if I can visit my daughter this afternoon.

With best wishes,

Lily Redcliffe

From: LadyLily@Redcliffe.com
To: Sarahransome@harvesthouse.com
Bcc: Lordglendale@glendale.com; Priscilla@rivendale.com;
MarjorieR@armthorpe.com; Prof.c.frank@glendale.com

1:15pm

Dear Sarah,

How kind of you to have kept me properly informed of all the complex issues surrounding my brave daughter's experiences.

With the major event of her birthday and the opening of the unit on Sunday, I wonder if it would be OK if I popped in this afternoon for a casual chat with Rose, if she is free and willing and if nothing else is arranged? Maybe I could even see her in her new home (even if it is not quite ready).

I could come at 4pm.

Best wishes,
Lily

From: Keiradenny@glendale.com
To: LadyLily@Redcliffe.com
Cc: Sarahransome@harvesthouse.com; Lordglendale@glendale.com

1:20pm

Dear Lily,

Thank you so much for your powerful and moving response. This really includes everything we want to cover, and it is a journalist's dream to have this level of quotable resource. I will, of course, await permission for anything involving Rose.

In the meantime, Woman's Hour has requested an interview, as have *the Guardian*, the *Sunday Times* and the *Mirror*.

I will liaise with your PA over suitable times.

Thank you so much.

Your help will make such a difference to the meaning of the Lady Rose Redcliffe Independence Unit.

Keira

From: Sarahransome@harvesthouse.com
To:LadyLily@Redcliffe.com
Cc: Lordglendale@glendale.com

1:25pm

Dear Lady Lily,

How kind of you to respond to my email in this way.

Rose said she will be thrilled to see you at 4pm at her new home. She is allowing me to be present if that is okay with you.

Please be aware that there will be work going on in the building for the opening of the unit.

With great anticipation,

Sarah

From: Sarahransome@harvesthouse.com
To: Deirdrehislop@harvesthouse.com
Cc: Dr.a.aziz@cjtu.com; Faithwalker@harvesthouse.com;
Maureenbrady@harvesthouse.com

1:35pm

Dear colleagues,

As this is unusual and affects all of us, regarding the launch this Saturday, I felt it was appropriate to let you all know that Lady Lily is visiting her daughter at 4pm at the new house, in preparation. Rose is delighted and has asked me to come too. She has also asked me to invite her new friend

Abdul. I said I would pass this message on and leave it to you to formulate your response!

Best wishes,
Sarah

P.S. I am meeting Deirdre at 3pm at the SJTU if there are, by any chance, any comments or thoughts?

From: Lordglendale@glendale.com
To: Priscilla@rivendale.com
Cc: MarjorieR@armthorpe.com

1:45pm

Well done P&M. What a team! Please support her.

Oliver

From: Priscilla@rivendale.com
To: LadyLily@redcliffe.com

Dear Lily,

I wish to commend your actions at this hard time.

Mother

From: MarjorieR@armthorpe.com
To: LadyLily@radcliffe.com

Lily

Peter is an idiot. He will come round. Don't crumble. You are needed.

Marjorie

CHAPTER 116

Wednesday, January 2nd 2013, USA

WAM conference

Dr Judith Kestle was exhausted, but there was nothing new there. She had been exhausted for the last 30 years. She had been given the early morning spot; all the sooner to get controversy over with.

The Community Collective Hall in Union House was a good space, enough to seat 300 people. More importantly, it charged very little to social justice organisations. The yearly meeting always tried to provide low-cost entrance fees for survivors and the unemployed.

Although they had a fair sprinkling of mainstream professionals, most of the audience were the voluntary sector and survivors. Judith had been specifically invited to discuss the situation about the West House and its so-called philanthropic founder Harold Fitz-Hugh West.

A child psychoanalyst working privately, her life had turned upside down 30 years ago when, by coincidence, she took on two separate children for treatment who had both been previously placed in West House.

A had only been 8 and B was 10. They both had the similar kind of dysfunctional backgrounds she was used to. Both showed angry explosive behaviour at times, alternating with high levels of anxiety and flashbacks. The level of trauma in each had been overwhelming and she had required further supervision from her training institute.

Worryingly, both boys were making similar disclosures of organised abuse, naming different House fathers, teachers, and Harold Fitz-Hugh West himself. Both said he had shouted, "Go West young man!" when beating them or penetrating them anally.

Ethically, she had to consult safeguarding and police and they flagged up major concerns. The medical investigation had revealed anal scarring and concerning burn marks in both boys, which did not appear to be caused by self-injury. However, the moment the police became involved further problems emerged.

The parents of Boy A and the foster-parents of Boy B, who had previously complained about their boys being taken to West House, had been deeply grateful to Dr Kestle for her work with them. However, they were suddenly funded by sympathisers from false memory groups and stating that Harold was a saint and Dr Kestle was a dangerous, unregulated, delusional woman creating these problems.

The medical reports somehow "disappeared" from the police station, her supervisor became "ill," and a series of complaints were sent to her Psychoanalytic Society and the APA. Both had become more risk-averse and appeared to have lost their theoretical understanding of shooting the messenger. This had wasted a year of her life. More worryingly, much more worryingly, both traumatised children were suddenly removed from therapy ... in the same week. This had left her with great concern for them all these years, let alone all the other possible victims of West House.

She was perfectly aware that arrests could not be made based on hearsay, and the McCarthyist danger would be that if those men were arrested, just on her account, so could good people. As she stated in her books and lectures, she was also aware that the entirety of human relationships were based on accepting hearsay! You listened to someone, and they listened to you, and overall they told the truth.

When it came to organised and VIP abuse, something different happened. Everything was suddenly "alleged." Professionals had transformed "neutrality" into scepticism, and disbelief.

"In the midst of all this, Ahmed, who was Boy A, as the courts named him, turned up again years later, able to show only too clearly what had happened since. He was not speaking today at the conference, thank goodness. His life had been threatened enough.

The juvenile facility, suicide attempts, robbery with violence, and terrible nightmares and flashbacks had all been part of his life. However, somehow in the last couple of years while sleeping rough he had met a girl called Judith, and moved into her squat. He had started to turn his life around. He had phoned first to check she was the same Dr Kestle he had seen as a child, and then came for a one-off meeting, with his Judith beside him.

She would never forget it. Twenty-three years old and the burnished brown of his face had already faded under his dirty grey hood and exhausted eyes. He was so thin, as was his girlfriend, Judith, a tiny waif with long dyed black hair, eyes fixed in terror on her.

He told her what he had not been able to say to her before because his parents were paid off to remove him from therapy. He had witnessed the murder of another boy, who had been raped alongside him.

This boy was called Yakshit and was half Indian and half American. This other man, who was English—and liked being called the Honourable Member—couldn't keep his hands off Yakshit. He kept calling him things, because of his name. He went at him and was still at him when W had finished doing him. Then Yakshit went all limp. He was done in. With a British accent, this man had just laughed and laughed and called the dead boy "Tamiz," saying he was dead meat. He kept kicking him; even W looked shocked. This Honourable Member looked weird and stoned. West just pulled the body away from him, told him to go, and told Ahmed that he would be done in if he said a word.

It seemed almost straight away, but couldn't have been, that he was returned to his parents and social worker with a long psychiatric letter saying why he was too bad for West House. No time was allowed for any goodbyes. He could not see any other boy. He saw Yakshit's naked bloody body pulled along the floor like dead meat and then he was shoved away; thrown back to the mad parents who had forced him there in the first place.

Someone had got him into therapy and Dr Kestle really made a difference, even the old man noticed, and then somehow they had lots of money and everything changed and his parents told him it was her, Dr Kestle, who made him mad and wouldn't let him see her again.

He had seen a programme on television with a picture of W and it included a photo of the English man, Anderson. He called himself the Honourable Member, and they had to call him and his cock that too.

"I am telling you," he had said, "not to be crude or disrespectful, but in case it helped police. I'm not going to do anymore about it. I have had enough. But I will sign and date a statement for you that I permit you to use with my original name." Then, with his frightened partner clutching his arm, he speedily left, hood peaked over his face, half covering it. He said he would not give her his new name or address in case it put her at risk. He had phoned her from a public box in a different city to leave no link.

Two men she did not know, who had been children at West House, were speaking after the interval. It was them she worried about most now. They had not been advertised on the programme to try and protect them from publicity, but who knows how much they understood the risk they were taking.

There were a few cold or hostile faces in the audience amidst the cheering, and she worried for Brendan, Douglas, and dear Ahmed. Their faces had the same worn-out, transparent look that was all too familiar to her.

The conference application form asked for people's organisations, but it was easy to slip people through who belonged to various groups and could simply choose or fake a neutral one.

There was no Sandra down on the attendance list, only "Sandra's Searches," but that Sandra could easily be a DID programmed multiple with one state primed to be a "retractor." This was a relatively new tactic of the high-level perpetrator groups and so far had fooled some of the public—aided of course by toxic papers like the Daily Mercury.

Oh, and here it came; someone from Parental Alienation, who obviously had not put that name down on the registration form. She could hear her voice, almost with a will of its own, go through the standard reply.

"To be wrongly accused is to be abused and that is awful. Luckily this is not even estimated as high as 2 per cent. However, it would help all countries if wrongly accused adults went to trauma therapists for help instead of getting caught up in … blah blah blah."

Then came the usual applause and it was over. Thank goodness. Now please let Brendan and Douglas manage all those ground-down faces in the audience.

She could see the bright sparkling faces of the multiples, who thought they had gotten away from their abusers. Some of these were professionals in the field … what a field. She could see the faces of the hopeful professionals who still thought they could "save" someone; the police who thought their investigations would be allowed; the tiny number of decent investigative journalists. What good colleagues had supported her, what good organisations, but she had long passed the age of thinking anything new would happen. The poor children. Would any of the allegations be followed through when it was VIP alleged perpetrators?

She stayed in her seat while people around her stirred for the coffee break. A personal cloud of misery hung over her. She did not feel like being questioned further; she had nothing new to say. The cults were right: eat or be eaten; kill or be killed. What substantial changes had happened in the last 30 years? Yes, there were more articulate survivors and survivor sites, and a few more courageous professionals. But was anything really any different? She would stay to hear the men and leave at lunchtime.

CHAPTER 117

Wednesday, January 2nd 2013, 2:30pm, The SJTU

Sarah Ransome walked towards the SJTU with a sense of hope and pleasure. She had only been in the post for just over a week and already there were positive changes. The most difficult staff member, Lew, had made a dramatic turnaround, changing the whole atmosphere of Harvest House. The new "home" was almost ready. Her relationship with the residents of Harvest House had already developed and she had the beginnings of possible friendships with Faith Walker and now Deidre. She had dealt with her own authority adequately with both the Glendale, and Lady Lily, and the SJTU and, what's more, the number of times she had even thought of Steve today had dramatically diminished.

A visit to the SJTU to meet Deirdre again and then to the Lady Rose Independence Unit to meet with Lady Lily. She was getting to know her new environment, and after only a week. Harvest House was clean, that toxic Edna was working properly, and somehow she had found a temporary bed for Tracey in the nursing home.

She did not want to go further at this moment in understanding why Tracey reminded her of herself, or why she evoked such a strong maternal feeling. She would save that for later. Maybe she would even get some therapy for herself. Right now she was happy, in a way she had not been for months.

The SJTU was clearly made at the same time as Harvest House, the architecture having the same rather dismal institutional style, although, when done up, it could easily fetch a fortune. The number pad for staff to key in the entrance code sat rather awkwardly on the door like a brooch pinned wrongly to a blouse with the bell for visitors on the right of it. She pressed with her right hand, shyly holding a bag of Danish pastries in the other.

Deirdre had been unsure whether to wait in the cubicle in order to hear when Sarah arrived or wait in Jon's therapy room and have Amanda bring her. In the end, she decided to be in her cubicle as the kettle was there.

"That's your visitor," called Amanda, amidst the filing. "Want me to answer?"

"No, that's fine!" A self-conscious pat of her still too tight French plait and she went to open the door. Sarah beamed warmly at her and held up her bag of pastries.

"A little something with our coffee."

"That's so kind," said Deirdre taking the bag.

"We don't go beyond chocolate digestives here." She pointed to the glass door and invited Sarah into the admin room. "Welcome to our palace where we get the coffee. That little cubicle is my domain, and this is Amanda, our senior administrative assistant. Amanda, this is Sarah Ransome."

Amanda looked up from her desk with a warm smile. "Well done over your new job," she smiled.

"Thank you," replied Sarah. "This is a really bright large space. We have a large social area and the sleepover room and night staff office is a good size, but I can't get more than three people in the room with me in my office."

The kettle had already boiled, and Deirdre put the mugs and plates on a tray, taking out the Danish pastries with great care and pleasure and arranging them elegantly on a plate.

"You are making me jealous," called Amanda.

Deirdre grinned. "Follow me," she said, "we are meeting in Jon Levene's therapy room as he is out teaching this afternoon." She looked at the range of patient art down the old corridors and wondered how

347

institutional it looked to Sarah. At least Jon had made his room pleasant. The square room with its wooden floor and brown walls was brightened by a patterned red rug and modern art paintings. He had brought in a 1930s lampstand which fitted perfectly and had both a beige Ikea day bed and two-seater sofa, desk with swivel chair and coffee table. It was immaculate. Due to the room shortage, staff rooms and therapy rooms had to double up, so nothing could be left on the desk.

"Now this is like Faith and Maureen's office," nodded Sarah appreciatively. "Therapy rooms of whatever kind have a similarity about them."

"You mean Ikea?" asked Deirdre.

They laughed.

"Please do take a pastry," began Sarah just as Deirdre offered her the plate.

They laughed again.

"I think we can see we are both used to being the carer," said Sarah wryly, taking a pastry. "My husband left me six months ago and my job has always been about looking after other people."

"And I am the last of my line and have always been on my own; this unit feels like my extended family," offered Deirdre, also picking one up. "They all come into my cubicle when they are worried about something like Lady Rose."

"And although it has only been just over a week, I have already found a safe bed for a young, exploited staff member."

"Here's to a good new year for care for carers," said Deirdre, lifting her mug like a wine glass.

"Skol!" said Sarah.

They both relaxed into a companionable pause

"I have one piece of official business for you," said Deirdre, dabbing her mouth with a tissue.

Sarah looked up with interest.

"Following your helpful email about Lady Rose, we discussed who would take on the therapeutic task. Confidentially, we first thought our senior female consultant therapist Elouise Redine would be the right match, but after considering the complex politics and the attachments she has already made we all thought it would be good for Dr Aziz to take on the role."

"Oh, I am so pleased," said Sarah happily, "and relieved given I am seeing Lady Lily and Rose at 4pm. That is if I am allowed to pass it on. It would really relieve Rose."

"That's what Dr Aziz thought, and he said I could tell you to pass on that he would come to the launch. As this is a particular kind of supportive therapy, he did not feel that would be a boundary breach."

"Absolutely, it is aiding her in her real world where she really needs the support. It upsets me when therapists go so po-faced about their boundaries without thinking of its meaning."

CHAPTER 118

Wednesday, January 2nd 2013, 3pm, Ashmere Grove

Lew Masters's residence

Lew woke up in great spirits and looked around slowly. Lucia House, Ashmere Grove. He was just beginning to trust that his flat was real and not a dream. It was still there. What a start to the new year. This was just the beginning. Alpha and Omega, A–Z. The whole success of the launch depended on him and the reputation of that dishonourable bastard Ian Anderson as well as Glendale. Tracey had surprised him; just an hour after he had left work, she had phoned him nervously. She wasn't a kid who liked to ask for help. Even though she was 4 years over, she looked barely legal, but liked to think of herself as a tough street kid.

She had told him all about Reg, the seedy bastard, and she was frightened of picking up her tiny case of belongings. Sarah Ransome, his new conquest, had suggested he would be the knight in shining armour or rather the play-dirty tough-guy who could menace Reg without turning a hair and get his tarnished little lady out. Ransome had even found a temporary bed in a nursing hostel for her.

So, he had said goodbye to his palace, gone back to Harvest House and picked up his runny mascara'd eye candy. He could feel her heart beating through the back of his leather jacket and knew she had the hots for him, as well as being frightened.

She lived in the basement of a seedy dilapidated terraced house just 20 minutes from the hospital. He had guessed her home would be like that. The tiny front garden was overflowing with unemptied bins and old furniture, mangy old cats were walking around, and there were peeling windows and a cracked door. He walked down the steep uneven stairs first. The smell from the bins was ugly. One night of luxury and his nose was different! Ringing the dirty white doorbell, he was not surprised to see the unkempt man who answered the door, a grey towel around his flabby waist. The leering smile turned to anger as well as fear when he saw Lew there.

"Is this Reg?" he asked Tracey loudly, while she stayed on the pavement looking down.

"I ain't touched her," said Reg, suddenly frightened.

"That's good, isn't it," said Lew ominously. "Because that would really make me angry."

Tracey walked down slowly, hiding behind Lew.

"Okay. Go pack. Quick as a flash. I will keep an eye on this old paedo while you do it."

Tracey darted through the door, squeezing herself as tiny as possible to not touch Reg.

"Fucking little prickteasers. You give them a roof over their heads, and instead of thanks, they go and bring the heavy mob." Reg's shoulders sagged and he walked in dispiritedly to the bedroom that could be seen through the door. Dirty clothes on the floor, cigarette ends, empty beer bottles. Poor kid, to have been here.

Reg sat on the bed, with Lew standing alert inside the entrance, no words passing between them. Tracey emerged with a bright pink suitcase, a teenage princess's leftover Christmas prezzie, nearly tripping in her hurry to get out of the front door.

"No fucking goodbye then," said Reg, sitting depressed on his bed.

"She will blow you a kiss if you are lucky," called Lew.

Carrying her bag, he leapt up the stairs to pavement level, fastened her case to his bike, handed her a helmet and they sped off.

Without any thinking, following the God in himself, he drove straight back to Ashmere Grove. He wanted to take her and clean her. He wanted her to feel what he had on changing his dirty environment.

He had washed the dirt off him, and the vomit of next door and her broom-handle banging. He wanted to pass his good luck on, and be one of the good guys: Lucifer-the-Light-Bearer.

Her face when they got off his bike. Her eyes. She could not believe it. Just like him. "This is my pad," he said, the first person he could say it to.

"You're having me on, aren't you?" she said. She looked at him worriedly. "You are not squatting in a rich pad, are you? I can't get into any trouble if I want to stay at college and keep my job."

He said nothing, savouring it. Just walked to the door. His door. Let her see his stairs, his lift. "We'll put your case in the lift with you," he smiled.

She walked in, Alice in Wonderland, her eyes round as saucers as he took the stairs and met her at the top. She stood there looking. "How can you live here?" she asked.

"How could you live with Reg?" he asked. "I had a change of luck. Someone who believes in me," he added. "Now. Let's get you a drink in the kitchen, and then I will show you to the spare bedroom with its own wet room."

"Wet room?" she asked, worried. "You are not one of those golden shower pervs?" she asked worriedly.

He laughed. He had his own Eliza Doolittle. This was better than a programmed multiple! "It means that the whole room is like a shower cubicle."

"Blimey."

He walked along to show her his room, the spare room, the kitchen, the lounge.

Her "oohs" and "aahs" were like nectar to him.

"For me? Just for me to wash in? To sleep in? Not with you. Just me?"

It was his own Goldilocks and the three bears, but with the Big Bear letting Goldilocks have the run of the place. He would never forget this moment, not till hell froze over. Yes, he could hear little snores; she was still there asleep. He would leave her sleeping, and get in his own shower, his own rainforest. He would wash and dress, get some food ready, and then drive her to HH.

352

CHAPTER 119

Wednesday, January 2nd 2013, USA

Major D looked at his computer in horror.

In the background, Danny's last song, *When You Come Back*, was playing loudly. His emails to Lee seemed to have been returned by Sandra. Sandra was amnesic to Lee. How was she doing this? How had this happened? The tweaking had gone wrong unless it was a computer malfunction. Keeping Sandra this strong was fair enough, and she was needed for the project.

But Lee... Lee was enough splits away from Sandra and other personalities to usually have his own time, and Sandra did not interfere or even know of his existence. She saw Lara as an outside person, and just thinking of the name Leandra made her sick. The amnesia held beautifully. Lee was even further away. But Leandra too was silenced.

He stared at his phone. Glendale did not have the skill, nor did Anderson. Could HRH have done anything to Sandra on his last visit? Unwittingly, or by following someone else's suggestions? There were strict rules to keep the amnesia between strong enough states.

Something had gone very wrong.

Just then, a ping signalled the arrival of a new email.

From: Sandra2@aol.com
To: DMajor@music.com

Major inconvenience. Sandra's Searches. Nothing else.

How clever she was. With a pun, Major, she had cleverly been ambiguous. He had been inconvenienced and he was a Major! She had shown him that no one else could really communicate at all, and it was not personally deliberate, but because of this sodding WAM meeting which was using all her energy.

He had never approved of the use of Harold and West House. Pissing in your own tent with your own nameplate outside. For that moment of greed or laziness, the project was in danger. The Lord Glendale Foundation carried Oliver's name, but it was a vast enterprise: children, adults, LGBT, forensic, different units, the SJTU, completely independent staff… it would never be linked.

He had told Z of the need for Sandra's Searches to deal with WAM. Nothing new would come from WAM. It would all be over soon, and then he would be with Lee.

When you come back
When you come back
Where the water meets itself
Where my hands frame the eye
Where the stars go to die
Speak the truth and never lie
Broken into myriad pieces
Each separate part
A life releases
In this celestial Helter Skelter
Am I Omega am I Delta?
Fight the heavy hand of fate

It is never too late,
To illuminate.

CHAPTER 120

Wednesday, January 2nd 2013, 4pm, The Lady Rose Independence Unit

A t 4pm precisely, her chauffeur held out his right arm so Lady Lily could alight from her car outside the Lady Rose Redcliffe Independence Unit. There was a vestigial tarmac road from St Joseph's Rise (that still ignored the SJTU and HH), and the former warehouse looked its distinguished upgraded best. There was no full sign yet as there was still deliberation as to whether the house should be called Lady Rose House, Lady Rose Independence Unit or Lady Rose Redcliffe Independence Unit. As her high heel elegantly landed on the tarmac, Lady Lily thought for a moment that maybe it was safer to not have a surname. If Peter divorced her, which name would Rose keep? The thought suddenly shook her. She checked her iPhone; still no response from him, although Maria told her he had popped home between engagements and had taken her letter. There was no point keeping things from Maria; she always eventually found out.

To her relief there was no beaming crowd waiting on the doorstep. At least she could ring the doorbell privately before the vampire took her. Sarah Ransome answered the door, a thoughtful attractive woman in her late forties. No fake camaraderie or obsequiousness. She felt a twinge of relief.

"Lady Lily, welcome into your own bequest. I feel a bit like an intruder answering the door. However...your daughter thought you might like to meet in the lounge."

Lily had seen the plans from that John McRae and the different updates on the work, but she was pleasantly surprised by the tastefulness of the surroundings, and the smell. It was not a chore to visit this building.

Sarah knocked on the lounge door and when Lady Rose called, "come in," she opened it and was welcomed into the room by her daughter. The lounge was elegant and practical, with white walls and an engineered wooden floor covered with a multicoloured velvet rug. There were two large sofas, four armchairs, as well as little matching coffee tables and a large television. There were no paintings on the wall yet and a pleasing smell of fresh paint and new flooring. Wearing a smart new navy-blue dress from the Westbridge M&S, Lady Rose was sitting on a blue velvet sofa. With her right hand she pointed to a dark green armchair with velvet bluebirds on the pillow.

"A seat for you, beautiful Lady mother," she said. Sarah watched Lady Lily wince at the word "mother," and felt a pang of sadness for both mother and daughter. "What drinks can I bring in for you?" she asked. "Once Rose's house is up and running next week, she will be making the drinks for her guests, but for today I can do it."

"In lady mother's house, someone else to make a drink," said Rose emphatically.

Lily found herself laughing unexpectedly. "She has got you there, Sarah!" she laughed.

"She has," agreed Sarah. "I never thought I would have to admit that upper-class residents might get a bad deal!"

Both women laughed.

"Lady mother agreed with good Lady Rose," smiled Rose. "...coffee for good Rose, as we don't have a Nespresso, and Lady mother has green tea, which helps her be beautiful."

"Well, she is certainly beautiful," agreed Sarah, "But would you like green tea?" she asked, turning to Lady Lily.

"Actually yes. My...er...Rose knows my taste."

With a heartbeat of excitement, Sarah left the room to make the drinks. This daughter was more like her mother than either of them realised. This was certainly a more conducive environment than Harvest House.

When she came back into the room with drinks, Rose smiled at her.

"I think Lady mother likes it here better than Harvest House," she said.

"I do," agreed Lily.

"Well, so do I," smiled Sarah. "Who wouldn't prefer it here?" she continued. " It is luxurious and clean and new, and there will only be three other people here with Lady Rose, and they are all her friends. No long-stay ward. Private toilets with each room..."

"And no bad smells," said Lady Rose. "Poor Tim would like to live with good Lady Rose "But he leaves shit on the toilet floor, and that makes it smelly."

Lily wrinkled her nose.

"I am afraid Rose is right about that," agreed Sarah. "Poor Tim has not yet been able to find a way to stay clean and dry. To live here, you have to be able to."

"How have you managed it?" Lily asked Sarah. "The smell?"

"You get used to it," said Sarah.

"When you are the mother of a baby, you don't mind your baby's smell, even though you mind the smell of other babies. When you run a unit, you get used to everyone's smell... I have to say, I realised I would need to wear perfume working here."

Lady Lily burst out into loud laughter. "So, you don't like it either?"

"No one likes smelly rooms, Lady mother," responded Lady Rose. "Nice friend. Sarah wears poison perfume when she comes to work."

"That's correct, Rose!" grinned Sarah,

"What a name for a perfume."

"Poison to hide the toilet smells," giggled Lady Lily.

"Harvest House needs to be covered with poison," giggled Lady Rose.

"This is so much nicer than Harvest House, Rose. Will you show me around?" asked Lily.

"Like Maria shows daddy's friends?" asked Rose.

"No. Like when mummy and daddy show Marjorie and Priscilla a new vase or curtain," corrected Lily

"And they say nothing nice," grinned Rose.

Lily burst out laughing.

"You are quite right, Rose. They never say anything nice. Never." She turned to Sarah. "What have you been doing since you started here? She is so clever."

357

"She is so clever," agreed Sarah, "That is why this is such a wonderful 21st birthday present to have the key to such a door."

Rose was sitting thoughtfully. "Poor Lady mother," reflected Rose. "Her mother never says anything nice or father's mother."

Lily's eyes filled with tears. "Do I ever say anything nice to you, Rose or am I like my mummy?"

"You said I was a clever, beautiful mother."

"That's true," said Sarah. "And I was here as a witness, Lady Lily, when you said she had understood better than me the class issues of serving drinks, and you said she had a good memory."

Lily looked genuinely surprised. "So I did," she marvelled.

"Sometimes," said Sarah tentatively, "and I hope I am not offending either of you, Lady Rose and Lady Lily, and I am especially calling you by your titles to say this—sometimes an upper-class background, and having a title like 'Lady', can lead to families not praising each other enough."

"Praising?" asked Rose seriously.

"That means saying nice things about someone," said Lily.

There was silence.

Then Rose spoke. "So, families Priscilla and Marjorie don't say nice things to beautiful Lady mother and she doesn't say nice things to mongol daughter, but she does. She does say good things."

With a traumatised look at Sarah, Lily suddenly strode across the space and held her daughter's face in her hands. "Shall we look at your beautiful new home, lovely clever daughter?" she asked.

"With pleasure, beautiful Lady mother," agreed Rose standing up and holding her mother's arm and the two women started to walk out of the room.

Sarah found herself rushing into the downstairs toilet, to blow her nose and cry.

CHAPTER 121

Wednesday, January 2nd 2013, USA

WAM Conference

The conference was breaking for lunch. Brendan and Doug had spoken. Instead of the usual excited buzz, there was a deep silence. The two men, who had only recently met up again, were still sitting on their podiums, surrounded by concerned conference-goers. Luckily they had already given their evidence to the police, so no one could say they had contaminated their evidence by meeting each other.

Everything was different, even though everything was the same. There were many survivors and victims in the hall who had endured appalling acts of torture. The two men were no different. Yet to hear two further witnesses speak about West House was revelatory and, of course, Dr Kestle had a signed statement from a previous inmate of West House too, Boy A.

The cold and sceptical faces had revealed themselves. There was a scramble to the outside where the Wi-Fi signal was strongest; newspapers had been notified. By the afternoon, the conference would be filled with media.

Having discharged her duty and exchanged phone numbers with the two men, Dr Kestle decided to leave. She had offered a place in her car to them, but they decided to stay. She could not face what would happen; she had seen it all several times before and did not have the energy for the afternoon session too.

After the conference, there would be first the sanctification of the brave survivor and the outpouring of national guilt and the "how can people do this." Next, finding any testimony that was contradictory because trauma memory was never exactly in the way police needed it. The doubting of everything the survivor said would follow, and finally the vilification of the survivor; of anyone who helped them, whether police, social worker, or therapist.

Two little boys, Brendan and Doug, just like Ahmed and Boy B; that made four. Not to mention Yakshit. Five—five boys. All the other suffering children in the world. Little Adam in the UK, too. She had given up expecting a case like this would be adequately prosecuted. She was at the age where not only policemen looked young, but lawyers and judges too. The reality was too much for society to bear when it came to groups like this, especially when there were high-level connections. Would the UK connection manage anything more honourable? She doubted it. Police were under orders everywhere; hierarchy existed everywhere. Dr Elouise Redine, a British consultant she had once aided, had said in a paper that she had more status as an adult psychotherapist than a child one. Hierarchy everywhere, with children at the bottom, along with the animals and birds.

As she wearily stood up to leave, after her line had emptied, she lowered her head in the hope of avoiding any more communications. There was a rustle by her side, and a young, black woman, shyly holding a bunch of primroses, held them out to her. "Dr Kestle, you won't remember me. Chalondra."

Dr Kestle looked up, astonished. "Little Chalondra? We changed your name from Moron."

"Yes. I was a part of..."

"Tara," interjected a newly animated Dr Kestle.

"You remembered!" said Chalondra, with tears in her eyes.

"We stayed with the therapist you got us, and there are just two of us now, Tara and me. Tara agreed I could come to the conference because I have done counselling training but most of all, to give these flowers to you."

"Yes," said Dr Kestle softly, taking them reverently. "Winter flowers to bring light and I told you that you brought light to Tara and the others like a primrose and not to look down on yourself."

She opened her arms tentatively, and Chalondra fell into them, primroses of light and colour enveloping them. "Thank you for coming today and bringing these," said Dr Kestle. "Today you have brought winter light to me at a time when I felt very dark."

CHAPTER 122

Wednesday, January 2nd 2013

From: Stockleys@stockleylaw.com
To: Laconiclawyers@justice.com; Sandrassearches@sandra.com;
PA-lovingpa@alienation.com; Fiona@dailymercury.com

STOP PRESS

At the Washington WAM meeting two mentally ill men, Douglas and
Brendan (surnames not given), made allegations of abuse against Harold Fitz-Hugh West and the Rt Honourable Ian Anderson, the Deputy
UK Prime Minister. They followed a talk by controversial psychoanalyst
Dr Kestle, who was removed from working with two child residents
who had lived at West House over a decade ago. This was a result of the
bizarre delusional stories they told as a result of her treatment. This is like
any fantasist aided and abetted by mad therapists all over the world and
cannot be allowed. There is enough real abuse, but this kind of grotesque
action in which the reputation of honourable citizens is smeared without
the benefit of police or court is anti-democratic and unethical.

CHAPTER 123

Wednesday, January 2nd 2013, 12:30pm, London

Lord Glendale and HRH Prince Carl-Zygmunt met separately. Anderson was a fucking liability, and so was his own brother Harold. Just as he had sorted P&M and Lily had made her successful visit to the Lady Rose Unit. Peter and Lily were about to make up, another positive. Keira had been brilliant, and he felt the PR would work, but the Society could have done without this.

James Dalkeith, the Prime Minister, was clearly unable to hide his growing health problems. Close friends and supporters hoped his increasing tiredness would allow a graceful retirement before signs of Alzheimer's became apparent. Ian might be even more useful to the Society—if they could get through this.

There were just too many loose ends.

What was Fiona playing at: would she report on WAM to retaliate for not getting the Lady Lily interview?

CHAPTER 124

Wednesday, January 3rd 2013, 6pm, Balham

Sarah Ransome's residence

Sarah found herself weeping for joy when she got home. In all her years of trying to help mothers deal with the pain of their grownup daughter's disability, she had never felt so privileged as to have witnessed Lady Lily and Lady Rose.

The meeting had been better than any could have predicted and she wrote it up fully, sending copies to Professor Frank, Dr Stuart, Dr Aziz (and she told Rose Dr Aziz was coming to the launch and was going to see her each week), and Deirdre.

She had also met with Keira and given an interview about Lady Lily and Lady Rose. They had given advance permission, and she also had permission from the Trust and all concerned. Other journalists had then spoken to Lady Lily, and it was real and moving: not just a political game.

As if that wasn't enough, Lew had also brought Tracey into work, all clean and washed and well slept and looked after. The bed at the hostel was arranged and she was also able to update them on how moving the meeting with Lady Lily was.

Somehow it was all so seminal, and she had never had a day in her life like it. Yet something was missing.

At that moment the phone went.

It was Deirdre, deeply moved by her report and wondering how she was.

It was perfect timing, just before the name "Steve" even came into her mind.

"To have a moment like that once in a whole career is moving enough, let alone in your first couple of weeks," said Deirdre.

She felt she had arrived. She had been seen. Rose had been seen for the first time. And she had a new friend.

CHAPTER 125

Wednesday, January 2nd 2013, 7pm, Westminster Square

The Redcliffe residence

Lady Lily arrived home transformed. "Is Peter here?" she asked Maria. He wasn't. Never mind. She had spoken to Oliver, and that would suffice. Her daughter—her Rose. She hugged her stomach, her real stomach that had carried a real baby inside it.

She was a mother.

She spun Maria round in a waltz. Sarah—what a fine woman! She was beautiful and did not realise how she had aided the process. Sarah had also called Keira, and everything happened because she was free; Keira was free and Rose was happy to talk, and everything happened naturally.

Keira was able to get *The Times* reporter and the *Guardian*; who knows who else. All the press that was needed was done. There would be no political speeches on Saturday, no dry comments from hospital bureaucrats, or even a Glendale spokesman.

All it needed was what Rose, her daughter, had suggested. Rose herself would show people her new home.

"I want roses," she said, "everywhere. All colours, and fragrant too. Remove the lilies."

"Yes, my lady," said a bemused Maria. There was no smell of alcohol on Lady Lily; she could not understand it.

When Peter returned home, broken and mute, his wife blazed before him in a radiance he had never seen, and a fragrance of roses filled his senses.

Rose.

CHAPTER 126

Thursday, January 3rd 2013, UK

The Chronicle

Sensational interview with Lady Lily takes over front-page news.
   Society beauty, Lady Lily, breaks a 21-year silence talking about her daughter, who moves into Lady Rose House on Saturday, on the grounds of St Joseph's University Hospital.

The Guardian

Lady Lily Redcliffe and her daughter, Lady Rose, talk together for the first time about upper-class roles and how it affects attitudes to disability. Interview and photos on page 15.

The Times

Alike and unlike: how down's syndrome affects identity and bonding.

The Mirror

Two beautiful flowers, Lily and Rose.

The Daily Mercury

We told you more was coming. At the WAM conference in Washington yesterday two new alleged survivors came forward speaking of abuse by Ian Anderson, the Deputy Prime Minister and Harold Fitz-Hugh West, brother of billionaire phi-lanthropist Lord Glendale whose ...

The Critical Thinker BBC

Disability organisations have reported a surge of support since the sensational interviews with Lady Rose Redcliffe and her mother, Lady Lily.

MENCAP have issued a statement thanking Lady Lily for her honesty.

CNN Breaking News

The UK has been overwhelmed by positive disability news. Only the Paralympics has produced as much positive press. And all because of two upper-class titled women, Lady Rose Redcliffe and her mother, Lady Lily.

BBC News

Sarah Ransome, Day Manager of Harvest House, was party to one of the most moving events in her life when ...

Woman and Health

See our stunning photographs of two society beauties.

All around the world, and throughout the day, the photographs Keira had organised shone out from television and newspapers. Lily's voice and Rose's voice were speaking from YouTube, from the radio, from the news.

Taking over from news of the British Prime Minister's increasing ill-ness and the two abuse survivors who spoke at the WAM conference.

CHAPTER 127

Thursday, January 3rd 2012, Knightsbridge

Glendale sipped his coffee while watching the news on his giant screen. Next to his coffee was a filled champagne glass. Days like this were rare.

He ordered bouquets of roses to be sent to Lady Lily, Lady Rose, Sarah Ransome, P&M, and Keira Hardie (as he now called her).

He also sent, via other anonymous sources, five-figure donations to the main mental health charities for war veterans, as well as the disability charities in honour of Lady Rose. It should not have happened to her.

A message came to him from Z, copied to Major D, Lord Glendale, Orpheus, HRH Prince Carl-Zygmunt, Ian Anderson, and Lew Masters

We step forward again.

....

And at Harvest House, Little Rose was sobbing in Brenda's arms.

"Lady mother. Where is Lady mother?"

"Good Little Rose. Good Little Rose. Good Little Rose," said Lew.

"She will come soon."
"Not dirty? Not bad?" asked Rose
"Clean, good, clean," said Tracey.
"Hold Serby," said Sinita.

CHAPTER 128

Thursday, January 3rd 2013, UK

BBC News

James Dalkeith has decided to take retirement after a long period of illness. MPs on both sides of the House gave him a standing ovation. A review of his contribution will follow shortly. Meanwhile, the Right Honourable Ian Anderson will be seeking an audience with Her Majesty the Queen. Although Deputy Prime Minister, this does not mean he will automatically be the next leader. There is no constitutional rule. If invited to temporarily become Prime Minister, this will only be until a later election is called. If accepted, he will become the 14th Prime Minister to serve HM Queen Elizabeth II since her coronation in 1952. Wartime Prime Minister Winston Churchill was already in the post when the Queen was crowned following her father's death.

The Daily Mercury

Working-class scholarship boy in line for top job.

The Sunday Times

Grammar School boy.

CHAPTER 129

Thursday, January 3rd 2013, 9am, Harvest House

D r Aziz, updated late last night by a joyfully incoherent Sarah, and this morning by a thoughtful Deirdre, decided to stop by Harvest House on his way to the SJTU.

He wanted to personally thank Rose for the invitation to her new home celebration, and to let her know he would be seeing her each week.

She was sitting holding Sinita's hand, and cuddling Serby.

"Is like this, nice friend Abdul—very simple—Ian Anderson put willie in bum. So did Danny Delta in Vegas after his concert. That was because he got the sweets from Ian. Danny Delta bad but inside Danny is nice friend Daniel. But Lady mummy can't listen as Ian is her friend and she doesn't want me to tell. Ian is big man, and I am mongol. Beautiful Lady mother said she loved Rose. Little Rose happier, and good Lady Rose and Little Rose friends."

CHAPTER 130

Thursday, January 3rd 2013, 2pm, The SJTU

Gawain was seated at his computer, a troubled frown on his face. If Rose was correct, then the country's new Prime Minister was a paedophile and possibly even worse. If the Cassandras and Leandras of the internet were even partly right, then the core of the Glendale Foundation could be rooted in corruption and his own unit in danger of collusion.

WAM, Adam, Mattie Harrison, Sandra's Searches, Leandra, Cassandra, Harold Fitz-Hugh West, Lord Glendale, Ian Anderson, who else? Lew Masters, Master: How far might it go if true? Would they ever find out?

His precious unit, with its fine staff, was a small ship against the huge international storm waves. Give him the strength to do right.

Reaching into his desk drawer, he took out a photo of baby Jamie. His grandson. His line. The world could not be made right in time for baby Jamie. All he could do was his best. Jon Levene had brought him a moving precept from the Jewish Torah. He and Abdul had both pondered over it.

"It is not for you to complete the task, but neither may you desist from it."

He sighed, stood up and stretched, and the frown slowly left his face. He pressed the intercom.

"Whenever you are free, Deirdre?"

AFTERWORD

Thursday, January 3rd 2013, 8pm
Transatlantic phone call

Elouise: Dr Kestle. Thank you for speaking to me. I wanted to talk to you after seeing the news about WAM. How are you?

Dr Judith Kestle: Older and weaker, but I'm still here. How are you, love? And with your little ones at the same time as all of this.

Elouise: Not so little now. But you always warned me about treating a child the same age as mine.

Dr Judith Kestle: Yes. We cannot dissociate as professionals in the same way when the patient is the age of our child or children.

Elouise: There is a child I saw on Christmas Day who has haunted me. Mattie. Just saying the letter M feels disembodied. Transatlantic suspicious adoption. Trans and possibly through DID.

Dr Judith Kestle: And you felt you recognised something of the American organised RA/DID set up?

Elouise:	Yes. And even more so due the complex high-level connections that are becoming clear over here. But every time it looks like there is adequate proof and understanding will follow...
Dr Judith Kestle:	...the whole case falls apart; the clinician is attacked and before you know what has happened ten years have passed!.
Elouise:	(laughing and crying) Yes. The big ones get away even when you, and the police, think the case is so clear.
Dr Judith Kestle:	And of course I am aware of the connection your hospital has with Lord Glendale and therefore the possibility of a connection with what his brother has done for years. Hence the link to me.
Elouise:	Yes. The good people connect up just as the dangerous ones do! You always know a call from me is never casual.
Dr Judith Kestle:	But remember, even when at your most despairing, this is only an extension of the usual. The richest and the most celebrated get away with things all over the world.
Elouise:	Yes. Reminds me of one of Dan's mother's songs from the 1960s—"It's the rich wot get the pleasure and the poor wot gets the blame!"
Dr Judith Kestle:	But bringing extra hope to a dead-eyed child is more important. Do you know, I was sunk in despair at the WAM conference, but then an adult I knew as a child came to bring me a primrose, remembering what I had said to her all that time ago. It seems to me your heart is responding to an SOS from this Mattie, and that's why you have rung. Even though Mattie is the same age as your children. There are wars we cannot win. But prioritise, and this child is within sight of you.
Elouise:	There is a Senior Registrar, Charmaine, very, very committed. So maybe we can divide the work.
Dr Judith Kestle:	And there you are...

Thursday, January 3rd 2013, 9pm
Transatlantic phone call

Lord Glendale: Orpheus has survived again

Major D: But Danny did not.

Lord Glendale: Did he do it, or was he pushed?

Major D: The poor bastard was a Delta

Lord Glendale: And why did he hurt R? It seems so unlike him. He never wanted to hurt anyone.

Major D: Z thinks the Bloodliners slowly got to him. Ian especially. If Ian had not been at the concert, then Danny would still be here. And Rose would not have been hurt, and we would not have to cotton wool Lew.

Lord Glendale: I wish we did not have to deal with Ian.

Major D: So do I. But he doesn't fit our termination guidelines, and the Orpheus lot want him for political links.

Lord Glendale: All the fine soldiers who died, all the courage of our soldiers lost in war, and yet he survives.

Thursday, January 3rd 2013, 10pm
Transatlantic phone call

Prince Carl-Zygmunt: I miss you Sandra. You are a part of me. You were made for me.

Sandra: You are my Prince. Come back soon.

Friday, January 4th 2013, 8:30am
Phone call

Deirdre Hislop: Morning Sarah. What a way to start the New Year. Are you free for dinner tonight at mine?

Sarah: What a wonderful idea. Couldn't think of anything nicer. I don't even have to pretend to consult my diary. You know there is nothing in it!

(Both laugh)

Friday, January 4th 2013, 6pm, London
Text messages

Lew to Tracey

Coming on a date with me tonight Trace?

Tracey to Lew

You mean a date? You taking me out?

Lew to Tracy

What do you think it means? Of course. And not just out, but a real slap-up eat-as-much-as-you-like out.

Saturday, January 6th 2013
The Saturday Post

A flowery hello. Those beautiful flowers, Lily and Rose, are taking a healthy holiday. Sir Peter Redcliffe, Minister for Health, has apologised to his constituency for his first break in years. "We need to celebrate Lady Rose moving into her own Independence Unit and have family time together first."

Monday, January 8th 2013
The Times

Professor Christopher Frank has gone on a three-month sabbatical to visit relatives in Australia. He says that while there, he will be undertaking some research on memory with leading American memory researcher Professor Jennifer Freyd. Dr Simon Green will be Acting Director in his absence.

Monday, January 8th 2013
Message in a Bottle: Cassandra's blog

*Choppy waters across the pond. Glendale, Mattie. Carl-Zygmunt.
Ian Anderson Prime Minister?*

Just remember it is a simple ragbag of 5. One for each finger on one hand.
1) the billionaires wanting immortality, install your copy
2) the proud soldiers wanting to protect their men,
3) the jaded perves wanting a brothel on two legs,

378

4) the Bloodliners, and
5) the lonely wanting someone made for them.

Monday, January 8th 2013, 6pm
Text message

Chris Frank to Abdul Aziz

Thank you.

Monday, January 8th
Email

Mattie Harrison to Cassandra's website

Help.

When you come back
When you come back
Where the water meets itself
Where my hands frame the eye
Where the stars go to die
Speak the truth and never lie
Broken into myriad pieces
Each separate part
A life releases
In this celestial Helter Skelter
Am I Omega, am I Delta?
Fight the heavy hand of fate

It is never too late,
To illuminate.

CHARACTERS IN ORDER OF APPEARANCE

Deirdre Hislop, Operations Director, SJTU

Sir Peter Redcliffe, MP, Minister of Health

Mary and **Amanda**, Administrative Assistants, SJTU

Dr Gawain Stuart, Group Analyst and Psychiatrist, Director, SJTU

Lady Rose Redcliffe, daughter of Sir Peter Redcliffe and Lady Lily

The Right Honourable Ian Anderson, Deputy Prime Minister

Dr Abdul Aziz, Consultant Psychiatrist and Psychotherapist, SJTU (married to Mina with children Alisha and Alesha)

Lord Glendale Centre, A magnificent new Centre endowed by Lord Glendale, including the Equipa LGBT Centre and Memory Research

Dr Elouise Redine, Consultant Psychotherapist, SJTU (wife of Dan, mother of Latoya, Denzel, and Tyrone)

Mattie Harrison, traumatised child aged 12

Jon Levine, Consultant Psychotherapist at the SJTU and Trainee Psychoanalyst

Jonas, Caretaker, SJTU

Mo, Junior Caretaker

Professor Chris Frank, Director of the Lord Glendale Centre

Lady Lily Redcliffe, Wife of Sir Peter and mother of Lady Rose

Maria, Housekeeper to the Redcliffes

Lord Oliver Glendale, Billionaire philanthropist

Mona Lasky, Part-time Carer for Lady Rose

Lady Priscilla, Mother of Lady Lily

Lady Margorie, Mother of Sir Peter

Lord Wellbrook, Lily's father

Imogen, 2nd Wife of Lord Wellbrook (and mother of baby Toby)

Stefan Solag, Lover of Ian Anderson and photographer

Dr Simon Green, The Equipa Unit

Sarah Ransome, Day Manager of Harvest House

Faith, Senior OT, Harvest House

Maureen, Junior OT, Harvest House

Carmen, Cleaner, wife of Mo

Lew Masters, Nurse and Night Manager, Harvest House

Edna, Cleaner at Harvest House

Tom, **John Finch**, **Dykes**, and **Sinita**, Residents of Harvest House

Brenda Harris, Nurse, Harvest House

Tracey O'Bridey, Agency Care Assistant Harvest House

Moira Stuart, Wife of Dr Stuart, Scottish dancing teacher (mother of James)

Harold Fitz-Hugh West, Brother of Lord Glendale

HRH Prince Carl-Zygmunt of Neuplatzstan

Sandra Harrison, Mind-controlled link for Prince Carl-Zygmunt and Major D

Leandra, **Lara**, and **Lee**, Sandra's other personalities

Z/Zee/Zed the American link to the Orpheus Project and superior of Major D

Mark Dyer, Reporter for *The Chronicle*

Fiona Roberts, Reporter for the *Daily Mercury*

Major D, American link to the Orpheus Project

Danny Delta, Rockstar loved by Major D

Sylvie, Mother of Jon Levine

Pam, Old friend of Elouise

Penny and **Frances**, Old friends of Sarah Ransome

Dr Charmaine Landesman, Senior Registrar to Dr Green

Keira Denny, PR, The Glendale Foundation

Professor Hamilton, Consultant Psychiatrist

Betsy Green, Wife of Dr Simon Green and his assistant

Messrs Crick de Beaufort Lawyers, Trust Solicitors

DC Morag Lennon, Vulnerable Victim Coordinator

Superintendent Mark Hewson

Frankie Futura, Friend of Danny Delta

Byron Santiago, Brother of Danny Delta

Ambrose Fitch, Head boy of Ian Anderson's school

Lord Tamiz, a pupil of Ian's school

Anthony Reddit, Bursar, St Eldred's

John McRae, Architect, Lady Rose Independence Unit

Reginald, boyfriend of Tracey

Dr Judith Kestle, American Abuse Pioneer

Stockleys, Laconic Lawyers, Loving Pa, pro false-memory groups

Brendan, Douglas, Ahmed, Boy B, Yakshit, American child victims

Chalondra, Former patient of Dr Kestle

Q & A TO AID READING GROUPS

Why did you write this book?

Those of us who have been working in the field of child abuse since the 1970's have seen the way survivors and victims are not listened to when their experiences are extreme and unusual. This has especially applied to those alleging torture from organised abuse. Regardless of all the serious books and papers on this subject the subject remains taboo, especially when it involves allegations of VIP abuse and victims with mental health problems. I said to my husband that when I retired from practise that I would write a novel about it and after I retired he asked, "well, when are you going to write it?"

What happens when a health service team receive an allegation of VIP abuse? How do they deal with it? I hoped a fictional exploration would aid such questions.

Are the St Joseph's trauma team and other practitioners in the novel based on clinicians and administrators you know?

The qualities of people I have had the privilege to work with—integrity, truthfulness in the face of pressure, loyalty, kindness—are all there in the exemplary health service teams I created! But the people those qualities inhabit come from my imagination. As a child, adolescent, and adult psychotherapist/psychoanalyst my own knowledge of procedures and process could also be applied to the fictional characters.

Why do you have a heroine with Down's syndrome?

My maternal grandmother had a mild intellectual disability, and my paternal grandmother was illiterate. My father was a pioneer in disability education and nearly all my working life has been with children and adults with a disability, over 80% of whom had been abused. I was shocked at the extra courage needed to make an allegation and to have it listened to. Jon Stokes and I at the Tavistock Clinic in the 80s had used the term emotional intelligence long before it was coined elsewhere to show that intellectual disability did not wipe out emotional capacity for understanding. Lady Rose, one of my key heroines, understands her mother and her predicament to a startling level. Despite the dissociation she experiences her emotions and truth cannot be destroyed.

Why is significant action centred on upper class and aristocratic backgrounds?

In my 1992 book *Mental Handicap and the Human Condition* I spoke of the anguish of upper-class boys sent off to boarding school at 8. This was before boarding school syndrome was named. I wanted the emotional problems in government and the lack of adequate mental health support to be linked to the early separation problems of so many upper-class MPs. Most health service therapists and psychologists are middle class. The lack of understanding of upper class and aristocratic trauma, including the pain of daughters and second sons, holds us all back. I also wanted to underline the fact that abuse exists in all layers of society.

Is it science fiction or can dissociative parts really be installed?

Colin Ross's book *BlueBird* is one of the best books on this subject which uses congressional material to show the reality of installed dissociation. Post Second World War, with the advent of the Cold War, there was an increase in experimentation to try and create a Manchurian candidate.

Unlike 'ordinary' dissociative identity disorder, which is an unconscious brilliant creative defence, installed or implanted dissociation is deliberately created. It requires, like all DID, a background of early trauma and disorganised attachment, but then adds deliberate conditioning and torture to install obedient parts who identify with their experimenters.

Does the Orpheus Project exist?

The Orpheus Project comes from my imagination and represents my psychological attempt to make sense of the motivation of some of these rings. Orpheus desperately used his gift of song to make the Gods feel pity for his loss of Eurydice. He was allowed to bring her back from the dead if he did not look back. He looked back and lost her. I consider the unbearableness of mortality is a key issue behind the need to control the life of another to the extent of wanting to create a 'hubot', a human who is like a robot. Providing a life 'copy' of yourself in another body is a way of trying to gain immortality. In a way, it is a step beyond sex-bots.

Are retractors, victims who then change their minds, all Dissociative?

No. People can change their mind for all kinds of reasons without being dissociative. However, because of the lack of understanding of this level of installed dissociation, police and courts are missing out on some vital evidence in people who dissociate.

It looks as if you provide a clear moral compass at the start with a depiction of a 'low level' abuser but then have him change for the best.

Forensic therapists are very aware of the tragic trigger points and emotional identifications that can lead to acts of violence. What is amazing is the number of victims/survivors who do not pass on their pain to others. Change is possible for many of those who initially pass on their trauma but then take responsibility for altering.

You have a deputy prime minister, a prince, and a rockstar as abusers: are the characters in the novel based on real people?

Health service staff have had to deal with the problem of allegations against politicians, royalty, celebrities, and leading figures, whether correct or incorrect. All too often there is a complex split response in which survivors are only listened to after their alleged abuser has died—Jimmy Savile, Cyril Smith MP, Epstein or are savagely attacked for naming those who have not been proven guilty.

What happened to those victims and professionals who had evidence of the wrongdoing of the above-named but were not listened to? I wanted my fictional figures to be ways of exploring the impact of such difficult situations. At the white flowers campaign meeting held in the house of a commons, where I had the privilege of speaking, I met survivors who informed me they never thought they would dare to enter the building or even vote again because of abuse by parliamentarians.

Carl Beech was one of several citizens who named the late Edward Heath, former Prime Minister, as an abuser. He was found to be a fantasist. He received a savage custodial sentence longer than murder. To be wrongly accused is to be abused and to be in the public eye and wrongly named is devastating. But what is the message sent with such a sentence? What is the message sent with the vilification of Tom Watson MP for acknowledging abuse allegations that reached parliament? And where is the questioning as to why Carl Beech should appropriate the accounts of others?

As one fearful survivor commented, "they always told me I would never be believed because my abusers went all the way up to Westminster. When Tom Watson MP spoke, I felt I could vote, and visit parliament. I started to feel braver. But if he and Operation Middleton are attacked for doing the right thing—what would happen to me? My abusers were right."

If Edward Heath was wrongly named, are you resurrecting a damaging allegation by having a top politician guilty of such crimes?

Around the world abuse knows no class or hierarchy boundaries. Tragically it is part of life in all areas of work. The hard-won gift of a democracy is that however long we keep our eyes closed in the end we are free to open them. I hope this book provides discussion for health service teams to enable them to think of procedures if such cases came their way.

Your 'top' people in Orpheus get away with it. Does that lessen the moral authority of the ending?

After half a century of being aware of abuse I have seen how rarely justice is done. What mattered to me most in the ending was that a mother and daughter were able to come together, and a psychiatric team remained honourable.

Freud wrote over a century ago that the best prognosis for trauma was if your mother supported you and abuse was by a stranger. Although our heroine has suffered more than that she is deeply loved by her father, has a good team around her and now has her mother's love. Attachment is the precious ingredient that leads to the biggest personal and social change. Attachment and bearing witness.

The powerful nearly always get away with it temporarily but seeing change and hope grow in a former victim who becomes a survivor is deeply profound.

Will there be a sequel?

I hope so. Mattie is very much in my mind, and I want to show the process of change and the hurdles the team including Charmaine and Elouise will face. I also want to know what will happen to Lew, Sarah, and Deirdre.